The Unfinished Art
of Theater

performance works

SERIES EDITORS
Patrick Anderson and
Nicholas Ridout

This series publishes books in theater and performance studies, focused in particular on the material conditions in which performance acts are staged, and to which performance itself might contribute. We define "performance" in the broadest sense, including traditional theatrical productions and performance art, but also cultural ritual, political demonstration, social practice, and other forms of interpersonal, social, and political interaction which may fruitfully be understood in terms of performance.

The Unfinished Art of Theater

Avant-Garde Intellectuals in Mexico and Brazil

✦

Sarah J. Townsend

NORTHWESTERN UNIVERSITY PRESS

EVANSTON, ILLINOIS

Northwestern University Press
www.nupress.northwestern.edu

Copyright © 2018 by Northwestern University Press.
Published 2018. All rights reserved.

Printed in the United States of America

10 9 8 7 6 5 4 3 2 1

ISBN 978-0-8101-3740-0 (paper)
ISBN 978-0-8101-3741-7 (cloth)
ISBN 978-0-8101-3742-4 (e-book)

Cataloging-in-Publication Data are available from the Library of Congress.

CONTENTS

ACKNOWLEDGMENTS

The very ethos of the avant-garde as it is commonly construed hinges on the idea of a total break—an act of creativity that incurs no debts and is not bound by any retrospective need. In this book I have done my best to unravel that idea, and I am happy to acknowledge that my own debts are many.

The Unfinished Art of Theater began as a dissertation written at New York University. The first nod, then, goes to my dissertation director, Diana Taylor, and to Martin Harries, Mary Louise Pratt, and Jill Lane for their many insights and advice, and also for knowing when to hold back and let me figure things out on my own.

No one else knows and understands this project as well as Kahlil Chaar Pérez. Kahlil has seen it all from the beginning and has helped give it shape by talking through ideas with me, giving pointed feedback on the manuscript, and occasionally telling me: Sarah, it's time to take a break and have a drink. In addition to being the truest of friends, he is always my first reader.

Several other people read parts of the manuscript. Jonathan Eburne, Tom Beebee, Ignacio Sánchez Prado, Jonathan Abel, and Martin Harries were all generous with their time and helped make it a better book. Anna Indych-López was a fantastic workshop respondent to a draft of one article that was also a chapter-in-the-making, and I received valuable feedback on one of my chapters when it was workshopped by the faculty and grad student fellows at Berkeley's Townsend Center for the Humanities during my time as a Mellon Postdoctoral Fellow in 2010–2011. A third chapter was workshopped at the Tepoztlán Institute for the Transnational History of the Americas in Summer 2014, and the conversations I had with fellow participants at the São Paulo Symposium at the University of Chicago in May 2013 were notably helpful. At various points Manuel Cuellar, Deborah Caplow, Eduardo Contreras Soto, and Heloísa Pontes all shared key references and/or tips on unpublished archival materials that found their way into the book. The two anonymous readers for the press offered suggestions that improved the final version immensely; series editor Nicholas Ridout took a keen eye to the next-to-last draft, and it has been a pleasure to work with such a professional crew at Northwestern University Press, including Gianna Mosser, Nathan MacBrien, Maggie Grossman, copyeditor Christi Stanforth, and indexer Steven Moore.

Harder to quantify but in some ways even more important were the many informal conversations with colleagues and friends that helped shape my thinking about this project, or just my thinking in general. For their wise words and comradeship, I am grateful to Sarah Wolf, Michael C. Cohen, Martin Harries, Marcial Godoy-Anativia, Lena Burgos-Lafuente, Licia Fiol-Matta, Pilar Rau, Pablo Assumpção Costa, Fred Riccardi, Pedro Meira Monteiro, Peter Reed, Ivonne del Valle, Daniel Nemser, Manuel Cuellar, Rielle Navitski, Abeyamí Ortega, Emilio Sauri, Ericka Beckman, Sarah Thomas, Aiala Levy, Juan Pablo Lupi, Amber Workman, and Kaitlin McNally Murphy. Special thanks to Sarah Wolf and Pilar Rau for welcoming me into their apartments in New York during research trips, and to Abeyamí Ortega for hosting me in Mexico City.

State College (where I have spent the last five years) can be a challenging place for a person who winds up there alone, and so I was lucky to arrive at Penn State with a good cohort of new colleagues. Judith Sierra-Rivera, Hoda El Shakry, Shaoling Ma, Marco Martínez, and Justin Clark are responsible for some great memories during those first two years. More recent arrivals whose conversation and friendship I value are Matt Tierney, Anita Starosta, Tracy Rutler, Christian Haines, Magalí Armillas-Tiseyra, Courtney Morris, Bruno Jean-François, and Julie Kleinman. A warm thanks to my Latin Americanist colleagues in the Department of Spanish, Italian, and Portuguese—John Ochoa, Julia Cuervo-Hewitt, Judith Sierra-Rivera, and Krista Brune—as well as to Matthew Marr, Mary Barnard, Maria Truglio, and my department head Giuli Dussias, who went to great lengths to support my research. Class sessions and conversations with grad students also sharpened my thoughts on various points, and I especially enjoyed my chats with Fernando Fonseca Pacheco and Alex Fyfe at Saint's Café.

This book was written with the support of a Mellon Postdoctoral Fellowship in the Humanities at the University of California, Berkeley and an American Council of Learned Societies New Faculty Fellowship at the University of California, Santa Barbara. It draws on my research at a number of different libraries and archives. In Brazil, these include the Arquivo Público do Estado de São Paulo, the Instituto de Estudos Brasileiros at the Universidade de São Paulo, the Arquivo Edgard Leuenroth and the Centro de Documentação Cultural Alexandre Eulálio (both at the Universidade Estadual de Campinas), the Biblioteca Nacional do Brasil, and the Museu da Imagem e do Som–Rio de Janeiro. In Mexico, most of my work was at the Archivo Histórico de la Secretaría de Educación Pública, the Biblioteca de las Artes del Centro Nacional de las Artes, and the Centro Nacional de Investigación, Documentación e Información de Artes Plásticas. The staff at each of these places was helpful, but special mention must be made of Roberto Pérez Aguilar at the Archivo Histórico de la Secretaría de Educación Pública and Elisabete Marin Ribas at the Instituto de Estudos Brasileiros. João Malatian at the Theatro Municipal de São Paulo shared several beautiful images of the theater, and Elisabeth di Cavalcanti Veiga graciously gave me permission to reproduce a woodcut image by her father Emiliano di Cavalcanti. In the United States, I depended on the assistance of librarians and staff members at the New York Public Library as well as libraries at Harvard University, the University of Texas–Austin, and Southern Illinois University in Carbondale. A slightly abridged version of chapter 3 appeared in the journal *Cultural Critique*, and part of a much earlier version of chapter 6 appeared in *Modernism/Modernity*.

Last but certainly not least are people who have played the part of family, whether that is their official designation or not. In Santa Barbara, Pablo Frasconi and Fredda Spirka will always have my gratitude. In Los Angeles, Murray remains in my heart. In Lodi, the Hux Vineyard crew led by Barb Hucksteadt, Tom Hucksteadt, and Tom Townsend has kept me in good spirits over the years (in more ways than one). Thanks as well to Tom for the many road trips, and for his occasional inquiries as to what was new among the intelligentsia. Rachel Townsend and Nick Van Veldhuizen have given me a couch to crash on in the Bay Area more times than I can count, and some of my favorite memories from the past few years are of spending time with them, and with Finnley and Devlin.

I dedicate this book to Steve and Sandy Townsend, each of whom in very different ways gave me the best education a kid could hope for, and whose love and support I have never once had a reason to doubt. I also realize that I was very lucky to have had access to the formal education and professional opportunities that I did; given the defunding of universities and declining labor conditions in academia, it is far from certain I would be so fortunate if I were starting out today. In addition to my parents, then, I want to give a nod to all the would-be authors whose own books, for reasons not of their own making, remain unfinished.

The Unfinished Art
of Theater

Introduction

✦

The Uneven Stage of the Avant-Gardes

At a certain point in *O banquete* (The Banquet), a collection of pseudo-Platonic dialogues by the Brazilian writer and musicologist Mário de Andrade (1893–1945), the character most closely identified with the author turns to theater to exemplify the social role modern art should play. Janjão is a composer who integrates folkloric melodies into pieces with titles such as "Antifascist Scherzo" and "Symphony of Labor." In a conversation with a young writer, however, he argues that theater is the art "most suited to the intentionality of struggle" because it is an "open" form that allows for "the stain, the sketch, allusion, debate, advice, an invitation." Contrasting it with sculpture, which creates fixed objects of art (or at least this is how they appear), he hints at something that many an artist and theatergoer has experienced in the flesh: because it unfolds over time, and because its realization requires a material stage as well as the presence of a collective audience, the "art" of theater is more difficult to disentangle from the process of its production and its sociopolitical and economic stakes. To put it in the lingo of avant-garde and modernist studies, theatrical "autonomy" is especially precarious and fraught, but this is also what gives it a very particular power. For this reason, along with design, Janjão classifies theater as an *arte do inacabado*—an "art of the unfinished."[1]

Mário de Andrade had a little experience with theater: during the 1920s and 1930s he had drafted (or started to draft) a number of pieces, and as the director of São Paulo's Department of Culture he oversaw programming at an opera house where he and other members of the *modernista* avant-garde had made their collective debut at the Week of Modern Art in 1922. Yet like the other works I discuss in this book, his own theater remains unfinished in a sense very different from the one his fictional character would later describe. One of his pieces, which he labeled a "profane oratorio," is both a spoof on Brazil's foundational act of independence and an allegorical rendition of the Week of Modern Art, though with a cast of 550,000 singers and five thousand musicians it seems deliberately impossible to perform. A few years later, he started to collaborate with novice composers on a project to create a truly "national" opera by drawing together musical traditions from all the races and regions of Brazil; but while the music was performed, Mário's would-be libretti were archived in the form of outlines and preliminary drafts. Even the handful of plays by avant-garde writers that made it to publication during this era failed to find a stage: in 1933, Mário's fellow modernista Oswald de Andrade (no relation) penned an audacious anti-imperialist pageant for a small theater in a club frequented by leftist artists, activists, and working-class immigrants, but the stage was forced to shut down during the performance of another experimental piece with a mostly black cast. Almost forty years later, during a commemoration of the Week of Modern Art, the critic Décio de Almeida Prado wistfully noted that while others were celebrating the birth of Brazil's modern literature, music, and art, he and other theater folks could "hardly help but feel a little on the margins, as if excluded from the party."[2]

In certain respects the situation is very different in Mexico, the other geographical pole of *The Unfinished Art of Theater*. In the wake of the Mexican Revolution (1910–1920), the founding director of the Secretariat of Public Education José Vasconcelos led an unprecedented expansion of the cultural apparatus, including mass literacy campaigns and the construction of schools, libraries, and his own pet project: a "theater-stadium" where some sixty thousand onlookers and auditors gathered to witness thousands of performers sing, dance the *jarabe tapatío*, and form gigantic human pyramids. But Vasconcelos first envisioned such spectacles in the context of a never-performed (and unperformable?) play, and in his speech at the stadium's inauguration he stressed that what spectators were about to see and hear was only an *ensayo*—an "essay," but also a "rehearsal," or a performance still in development and incomplete. *Ensayos* were everywhere in Mexico during the 1920s: the term was also used to describe the short skits performed by the indigenous subjects of artist-ethnographers who joined with members of the *estridentista* avant-garde to form a theater group inspired by a Russian cabaret-style revue. The Murciélago (or Bat) made its much-hyped debut for an envoy of U.S. businessmen and then quickly folded its wings; a decade later, however, it was cited as an inspiration for the new National Dance School, which planned to premiere its style of "choreographic theater" with a pantomime ballet featuring Troka the Powerful, a figure who represented the medium of radio but was (most likely) meant to be embodied as a puppet. The pantomime (most likely) never happened, and now Troka is remembered as the host of a children's radio program. Still, the specter of his puppet double occasionally returns, as do remnants of other fragmentary, "failed" experiments involved in the expansion and (re)creation of the cultural infrastructure in Mexico.

The years between the two world wars loom large in genealogies of modern culture. In both Mexico and Brazil avant-garde artists formed part of an expanding network of circulation, collaboration, and conflict with their counterparts in other parts of the world: Diego Rivera was commissioned to paint murals in San Francisco and Flint, but he also drafted a manifesto with Leon Trotsky and André Breton right in Mexico City, and although Oswald de Andrade spent plenty of time in Paris, he also argued over futurism and fought fascists with the immigrants and itinerant intellectuals who were arriving in São Paulo from Italy, Germany, and elsewhere. But despite the internationalist outlook of the avant-garde, most of the figures who traverse the pages of this book also played a prominent role in shaping the new cultural institutions and repertoires of national identity that arose in the context of major geopolitical shifts and a rearticulation of the global economy. One of my claims is that the emergence of a "modern Mexican" and "Brazilian" culture is bound to both the legacy of particular avant-garde intellectuals and to the *idea* of the avant-garde—an idea that implies a performative break with the past. Yet Prado's lament about being left out of the festivities, like Vasconcelos's depiction of the stadium spectacle as a work in progress, suggests that avant-garde theater can also be a reminder of what remains tied to the past. If, as Victor Turner insisted, the verb "to perform" has its roots in the Old French *parfournir* ("to complete" or "to carry out thoroughly"), both the unstaged pieces of Brazilian *modernismo* and the would-have-been performances of Mexico in the era of the avant-gardes seem to be evidence of an unfinished or uneven historical transition.[3]

The Unfinished Art of Theater pulls back on the futuristic impulse endemic to the avant-garde by exploring how theater became a key site for reconfiguring the role of the aesthetic in two countries on the semi-periphery of capitalism from around 1917 to 1934. This book argues that precisely because of its historic weakness as a "representative" institution—because the bourgeois stage had not (yet) coalesced—theater was at the forefront of struggles to redefine the relationship between art and social change at a moment marked by the (re)consolidation of the modern state and the emergence of a class of intellectuals identified as belonging to an international avant-garde. Drawing on archives in Mexico City, São Paulo, Rio de Janeiro, and locations across the United States, it reveals the significance of little-known genres and texts that belie the rhetoric of rupture typically associated with the avant-garde: ethnographic operas with ties to the recording industry, populist puppet plays, children's radio programs about the wonders of technology, a philosophical drama, and a never-performed "spectacle" written for a theater shut down by the police. In doing so it also opens up the study of Mexican and Brazilian culture, remapping their geopolitical coordinates and bringing avant-garde intellectuals from these two countries into dialogue with other theorists of the peripheral and passé. To borrow a phrase from the Russian revolutionary (and critic of the avant-garde) Leon Trotsky, this book stakes a claim for the "privilege of historic backwardness" by showing how these "unfinished" works can illuminate the ways in which the very *category* of avant-garde art is bound up in the experience of dependency, delay, and the uneven development of capitalism.[4]

The unfinished aspects of these pieces and projects frequently register as a symptom of lack, a sign of weak sovereignty and the precarity of art. But they can also, and often simultaneously, signify an excess or potentiality that bleeds beyond the bounds of existing disciplines and trajectories of development. In the following six chapters I approach the unfinished as a site of social conflicts, ideological contradictions, material limitations, and affective obstacles. At the same time, I also foreground it as a means of unraveling the reification of art and ideas, of working against deterministic views of history and elaborating a relational understanding of art—not only in its intersections with politics and economics but also anthropology, musicology, philosophy, new and old media technologies, and other cultural practices that vanguard artists helped (re)define. Ideas about the avant-garde and its "agency" (to use a fraught word) are genealogically entangled with a certain paradigm of theater and performance that privileges presence, embodiment, and immediacy. What I seek to do instead is to think through the materiality of theater and to account for what Hal Foster calls the "deferred temporality of artistic signification," or the way its effects play out in and over time, in the back and forth between present and past.[5] This unfinished dimension is especially evident in Mexico and Brazil during the interwar era for reasons that ultimately have to do with these countries' integral but subordinate role in the world system at a moment of crisis and change. Yet what is more obvious on the (semi)periphery can also illuminate dynamics that in the center are harder to see. After all, the annals of the European avant-garde are also littered with pieces that were never (or never successfully) staged and projects that fell short or simply fell through, whether for lack of money, the limitations of technology, political repression or fear, conflicting visions among collaborators, the tug of "outmoded" institutional structures on the senses, or because experimenting with certain kinds of bodies was easier on the page than onstage. This is all to say that even as I piece together six very specific stories grounded in archival evidence and a close attention to diverse types of texts (along with some theoretical speculation), I also seek to model a more general methodology of reading, watching, and listening for what is unfinished.

Avant-Garde Autonomy and Its Dependencies

In September 1922, Brazil hosted an international exposition in Rio de Janeiro to commemorate the centenary of its independence from Portugal. The Mexican government sent a military delegation in addition to musicians, painters, and writers and joined France, the United States, and dozens of other nations in constructing a pavilion to display its commercial, artistic, and anthropological wares. In an arresting account of Mexico's showing, the historian Mauricio Tenorio-Trillo dwells on the role of José Vasconcelos, the quixotic figure around whom the first chapter of this book revolves.[6] Less than two years earlier Vasconcelos had taken on the task of creating the Secretariat of Public Education with the stated aim of making education available to all—no mean feat in a country where the already low literacy rates had fallen during the decade-long revolution, and where multiple indigenous groups spoke multiple languages other than Spanish. Much of the communication and transportation infrastructure had been damaged or destroyed, rebellions and assassinations were still daily news, and the U.S. government was withholding recognition of the new regime as the president wavered on whether to expropriate the properties of U.S. citizens and oil companies. Brazil, on the other hand, still had eight years to go before the Revolution of 1930, an expeditious, top-down affair that would bring the eventual dictator Getúlio Vargas to power. Yet already at this stage there were signs of instability: anarchist-led strikes and an uprising in 1918 had put the elite on edge, the coffee economy was ever more volatile, and two months earlier young army officers in Rio had taken up arms against the Republic and demanded democratic reforms. None of this, however, dampened the enthusiasm of Vasconcelos. In the travelogue he published three years later, he describes Brazil as a land of progress and potential—even as he speculates that the authorities took measures to keep black and poor people out of his sight. Prior to the exposition he had visited São Paulo, which he hails as the most significant industrial center in Latin America, an idyllic city where all of the workers are happy and everyone knows how to read.[7] And even though the Amazon was not on his itinerary, the prologue to his book insists that one day all of the world's peoples will converge there to form a "cosmic race" and found the techno-aesthetic utopia he dubs Universópolis.[8]

Tenorio-Trillo reads this as evidence of a "south-south kind of fascination," a case of mutual admiration and intrigue between the two giants of Latin America.[9] Judging from the press, he suggests, some Brazilians were equally in awe of Vasconcelos's ambitious educational program, and his speech at the dedication of a statue of the Aztec warrior Cuauhtemoc on the anniversary of Mexico's own independence on September 16 was applauded for its eloquence. At the crux of Tenorio-Trillo's ironic narrative, however, is an encounter that never occurred. Back in Mexico, Vasconcelos was fostering the emergence of what would become one of the world's most iconic avant-gardes: though not exactly an avant-garde artist himself, he sparked much of its organizational momentum and some key ideas, as when he sent Diego Rivera and others to Italy to study fresco techniques and then commissioned them to cover the walls of government buildings with murals. Among the Latin American avant-gardes of this era, the only other movement that rivals the Mexican *vanguardias* in terms of its prominence within studies of "global modernisms" (to use a current term) was the one gaining momentum in Brazil at the time of his visit. Yet Vasconcelos says nothing in his travelogue of having heard about the Week of Modern Art that had taken place in São Paulo only a few months earlier, and if any of the Brazilian modernistas attended one of his public lectures in Rio or São Paulo, it apparently failed to leave much of a mark.[10]

Direct dialogues between the avant-gardes of Mexico and Brazil were not especially common, and although such connections occasionally turn up, they are not central to this book. The (relatively minor) differences between Spanish and Portuguese may have contributed to their lack of exchange, but a more compelling explanation is that the circuits of culture, commodities, and immigration (as well as structures such as the Communist Party) worked to orient writers and artists from both countries toward Europe and the United States. Counterintuitively, the fact that Mexico City and São Paulo were becoming cultural capitals in their own right probably also acted as a disincentive to more regular communication. Still, there are reasons for drawing these two vanguards into proximity.[11] Although they share an Iberian heritage, Mexico and Brazil arose out of divergent histories of colonization and state formation: Mexico City, built on top of the Aztec capital of Tenochtitlán, was the administrative center of New Spain prior to its hard-won independence in 1821, but Brazil took shape as a more loosely integrated colony of Portugal, and in an odd inversion Rio de Janeiro became the seat of the realm when the Portuguese court fled from Napoleon's invading army and decamped there for thirteen years. For much of the nineteenth century Mexico was torn by civil wars, foreign invasions, and the loss of half of its territory to the United States, until in 1876 Porfirio Díaz established a de facto dictatorship that would claim credit for the "pacification" and "modernization" of Mexico. In contrast, Brazil became an empire after its easy break from the mother country, and only in 1889—the year after it became the last country in the hemisphere to abolish slavery—was a republic with a weak federal government formed. Throughout the twentieth century both countries would continue to play a "dependent" role in the world economy, yet they were also regional powers and could be said to belong to what Immanuel Wallerstein designates as the semi-periphery.[12]

By the beginning of the twentieth century Mexico and Brazil had small but growing concentrations of light industry and were avid consumers (as well as early producers) of the new entertainment media of film and phonograph recordings. Yet partly for these reasons they were places where the unevenness and contradictions of capitalist development were especially apparent. Both were still predominantly rural and starkly divided by disparities of region, race, and class; access to schooling and literacy rates were notably low; and their economies hinged on the export of primary commodities such as minerals and henequen (Mexico) or rubber and coffee (Brazil), which in many cases was directly controlled by external investors and in almost every case relied on foreign financing and foreign-built infrastructure (i.e., railroads and telegraph lines). In Brazil, where the export boom inflated the fortunes of the landowning oligarchy, Roberto Schwarz has noted that the dissonance between the liberal ideology of this era and the "backward" social relations it helped to sustain generated an uneasy and shameful sense among intellectuals that "modern" ideas were "out of place" in Brazil.[13] Of course, he acknowledges, ideas such as individual autonomy, the universality of law, and "disinterested" culture failed to accord with reality in Europe too, but they were more obviously askew and felt embarrassingly "inauthentic" in a country where slavery had only recently ended and relations of patronage formed the basis of social bonds. Yet in an insight that informs my own interpretation of modernismo, Schwarz argues that this affective experience of incongruity itself gave rise to a "Brazilian" national identity.

This was Latin America's "Export Age," a period when the region became increasingly integrated into global market relations, primarily through the export of raw materials and the import of manufactured goods. Although this setup had already been shaken by World War I, the fallout from the stock market crash on Wall Street in October 1929 precipitated a more profound shift in which the state assumed a more central role in the economy and extended its reach into new dimensions of social life.[14] In this book I situate the avant-gardes of Mexico and Brazil in this transition—a period of struggles over economic realignments, but also changes in the dynamics of sovereignty and a transformation of the fields of culture and knowledge. Giovanni Arrighi describes the entire interwar era as a time of "systemic chaos": although Britain had long been losing ground, its hegemony finally came to an end as the disintegration of free-trade imperialism coincided with the Russian Revolution, the rise of Germany, and a worldwide wave of popular rebellion.[15] Ultimately, this capitalist crisis became the occasion for a restructuring and expansion of the world economy in which the United States secured its supremacy; curiously, though, it was at this very time that artists in many parts of Europe and Latin America laid claim to the category of the cultural avant-garde, which only among later generations of artists would gain purchase in the United States.[16]

Exactly how all of these moving pieces connect is far from straightforward, and even some "theories" of the avant-garde that foreground its relation to capital take a surprisingly narrow view. Take, for example, the oft-cited argument of Peter Bürger. Bürger, who privileges Dada as the most radical and paradigmatic movement, defines the avant-garde as the "self-criticism of art in bourgeois society": rather than simply attacking outdated styles or forms, it sought to destroy art as an *institution* by undermining its so-called autonomy, or detachment from the "praxis of life." Only with the late nineteenth-century doctrine of aestheticism, or "art for art's sake," did this impulse toward autonomy come to full fruition, and only after that was it possible for "art" to be grasped as a concept and social construct.[17] According to Bürger, the avant-garde took aim at the apparatus involved in the production and distribution of art (including academies and museums), and also at the ideas underpinning its sacred status (or what Walter Benjamin would dub its "aura"), as when Marcel Duchamp lampooned the notion of individual creativity by signing his name to a mass-produced urinal.

This might be a plausible explanation of what Duchamp and certain other individuals set out to do, but it is less than satisfying as a general "theory" of the avant-garde. As Hal Foster has noted, Bürger takes the avant-garde's own rhetoric of rupture at face value—one symptom of which is his hostility toward the neo-avant-gardes, whom he accuses of institutionalizing the earlier, "historical" avant-garde and thus turning it into the "art" it despised. In Foster's words, Bürger "projects the historical avant-garde as an *absolute origin* whose aesthetic transformations are fully significant and historically effective in the first instance."[18] In doing so, he overlooks the time lag involved in reception and debate, and the fact that Duchamp accrued some of his "subversive" effect as the result of retrospective interpretations. Foster goes on to point to the "residual evolutionism" (10) in Bürger's account of artistic autonomy and its cognition. But there are some additional issues that deserve mention. First, Bürger's story of the avant-garde's emergence ignores tensions, contradictions, and differences *within* and *among* the movements included in this category; and second, his evolutionary narrative of art presumes a certain kind and degree of institutional development that was far from universal, even within Europe. In other words, he ignores the multiplicity and *unevenness* of the avant-garde—in part because he fails to factor in its geographical spread.

In Mexico and Brazil, too, the art-for-art's-sake injunction gained ground in the late nineteenth century, as did many of the stylistic trends associated with aestheticism in Europe. And how could it have been otherwise? Both Mexico City and Rio de Janeiro had an official art academy and national conservatory where students received a classical training, usually from European instructors, and up-and-coming artists and musicians often continued their studies in Paris, Madrid, and/or Italy. In literature, Spanish American *modernismo* (not to be confused with the avant-garde movement of the same name in Brazil) cultivated a genteel, urbane style with echoes of French symbolism and Parnassian poetics and was fond of evoking exotic, often orientalist locales. But in this context, the claim to aesthetic autonomy could only be fragile and vexed. Modernistas such as the Nicaraguan poet Rubén Darío upheld the spiritual, aesthetic value of their own work as a defense against the crass commercialism of the United States, yet as Ericka Beckman observes, the luxury imports that litter the opulent interiors they evoke betray the imbalances and dependent relations of the Export Age.[19] In his work on the *desencuentros*, or "dis-encounters," of modernity in Spanish America, Julio Ramos also points out that the small size of the reading public and book market led many modernista writers (who tended to come from an emerging middle class) to work as journalists and cultivate their refined aesthetic in the mass-market venue of the daily newspaper.[20] In Brazil, which had a roughly parallel movement known as *parnasianismo*, Roberto Schwarz puts his finger on the same basic problem when he describes "disinterested" culture as an idea out of place in a country where patronage was the name of the game. In short, the institution of autonomous art that Bürger imagines as the fully formed object of the avant-garde's attack was anything but—and as a matter of consequence, the avant-garde itself is harder to define. By insisting on their own avant-garde status, the artists of Mexico and Brazil destabilized the so-called universality and autonomy of European art (at least in a certain sense), but this often went hand in hand with a push to create their own local "autonomous" institutions of art.[21]

In recent years, Bürger's paradigm has fallen out of favor, as have other such "totalizing" theories of the avant-garde. In fact, the very category of the avant-garde has acquired a dated air. In leftist politics and debate, the tide has turned away from vanguard party politics and toward anarchism and more horizontal forms of organization. At the same time, in the academic world, there is a growing move to integrate "avant-garde" movements into "global," "comparative," or even "planetary modernisms"—ever more expansive, flexible frameworks that purport to unsettle borders, allow for diversity of definitions, and diffuse the teleological thrust behind the idea of a singular avant-garde. But there are also some imposing desires, assumptions, and institutional pressures at play in this effort to decenter the study of modernism and the avant-gardes. Much of its momentum comes from scholars whose primary background is in Europe or the United States, and although this can make for new insights into old problems, limited linguistic skills and knowledge about local conditions and critical traditions tend to favor the interpretation of texts and works of art as (!) autonomous objects. Of course, so-called specialists are hardly immune to this problem, and regardless of who the critic is, the salutary push to burst the field's Eurocentric bubble often fuels exceptionalist claims and a desire to champion "marginalized" works from other regions of the world, where in fact said works are often quite canonical. In other words, in the process of going "global," the problem of art as an institution is all too often shoved to the side.

As an example, take Fernando J. Rosenberg's *The Avant-Garde and Geopolitics in Latin America* (2006), a book that shares some of my own concerns and has more than a few merits. The author's argument, illustrated with close readings of novels and travel narratives from Argentina and Brazil, is that whereas the European avant-gardes simply refigured imperialist assumptions, their Latin American counterparts "explored the limits of a national, culturalist response to crisis of the universality of civilization" by creating "narratives of space" that undermined the linear narrative of progress.[22] He describes this as a practice of "embodied universality" and endorses it as a model for approaching the cultural politics of our own age—yet for all his talk of geopolitics, he avoids any discussion of Latin American avant-gardists who espoused fascism, dismisses all examples of polemical (i.e., leftist) work as a "repression of critical consciousness," and devotes two chapters to Mário de Andrade without noting the writer's own ambivalent experiences in creating new cultural institutions under the auspices of the state. In effect, Rosenberg's readings redefine "politics" as an ethical-aesthetic category and privilege a specifically *literary* form of "cosmopolitanism." But is cultural nationalism (his main bugbear) just a bad style that can be (un)written on the page? Is it accurate to attribute a progressive function to works of literature on the sole basis of form or their *representation* of social relations? What about the materiality of art and the apparatuses on which it depends? Rosenberg's focus on space as a critical category in the study of the avant-gardes is on point. And yet solutions crafted within the closed confines of poetic or narrative space often fail to hold up when space becomes something more than metaphorical and actual bodies are involved.

In the next section I turn to the question of why theatrical works—even when they never make it onto a physical stage—tend to prove more resistant to the mode of interpretation Rosenberg and others practice. First, however, it is important to recognize that the "geopolitics" of the avant-garde were connected to the very problem of artistic autonomy that such readings ignore. In 1923, in a polemical essay published the following year in his collection *Literature and Revolution*, Trotsky observed that the most vibrant futurist movements had emerged not in "advanced" capitalist countries such as the United States or Germany but in Italy and Russia, two comparatively "backward" countries on the periphery of Europe.[23] Avant-garde art, in other words, was not a direct reflection of economic and political modernization but a response to the experience of what he refers to on other occasions as combined and uneven development. In his account of the Russian Revolution, the founder of the Red Army points out that the expansion of capitalism draws all regions of the world into a complex, self-contradictory totality, such that while the more "primitive" countries are "compelled to follow after" those regarded as more advanced, it is impossible for them to replicate the same series of cultural stages observed in places where capitalist relations of production first emerged.[24] Competition and constraints imposed by the dominant countries can foster certain aspects of their growth while hindering others, as can aspects of their own culture, and they can adapt ideas and technologies from elsewhere without having to reinvent the wheel. "The privilege of historic backwardness—and such a privilege exists—permits, or rather compels, the adoption of whatever is ready in advance of any specified date, skipping a whole series of intermediate stages" (31). As a result, development in such countries looks less like a steady progression than like a "drawing together of the different stages of the journey, a combining of separate steps, an amalgam of archaic with more contemporary forms" (32). Yet this seeming peculiarity is not actually a deviation from the norm: unevenness, Trotsky insists, is "the most general law of the historic process," the logic of which "reveals itself most sharply and complexly in the destiny of the backward countries" (32).[25]

Trotsky's recognition of heterogeneity and asymmetry as constitutive elements of the historical process offers an implicit critique of economic determinism, which condemns weaker countries to mimetically reproducing the imperial powers' past, yet his emphasis on the interdependence of all nations is also aimed against Stalin's claims about the viability of building socialism in one state. Both principles also underlie Trotsky's insistence on the *relative* autonomy of art. While he zealously defends Russian futurism against "petty realists" and sees it as a "necessary link" in the creation of a new art still to come, his understanding of revolution as a single if internally contradictory and discontinuous process also undercuts the sense of temporality and agency associated with the avant-garde.[26] The "Bohemian nihilism" of the futurists,[27] their hyperbolic disavowal of the past and call for the immediate fusion of art with "life," too hastily relinquishes the weapons afforded by (bourgeois) art, which is "always a complicated turning inside out of old forms, under the influence of new stimuli that originate outside of art."[28] Writing in the context of Lenin's declining health and his own struggle with Stalin for leadership, Trotsky too seems to hold out hope for a time when art will be more integrated into everyday praxis, but he warns against instrumentalization and argues that such a "synthesis" can't be fully realized in the here and now. Political revolutionaries, he says, know the future can't be built from scratch, and the only way to move forward is by working through the contradictions and unevenness out of which the revolution, like futurism, arose.

Little did Trotsky know that some thirteen years later he would find himself in a different semi-peripheral, (post)revolutionary country after a Mexican avant-garde artist named Diego Rivera negotiated an offer of asylum on his behalf. In exile from his own country, Trotsky would live in the house of Rivera and Frida Kahlo and survive an assassination attempt led by another avant-garde muralist—David Alfaro Siqueiros—before dying a few months later in a second attack. Today, of course, the language of backwardness both he and Schwarz employ has the same outdated air that clings to the idea of the avant-garde. Although the concept of unevenness has long played a part in modernist studies and is currently enjoying a resurgence in discussions of world literature, much of this work is marked by a strange silence surrounding the history of debates about uneven development and all the political and economic issues that were (and are) at stake; often the idea of development is deemed irrelevant when the avant-garde is subsumed into global or comparative modernisms, and unevenness is redefined as a principle at work *within* the literary or aesthetic field.[29] My own wager, however, is that rather than skirting the issue of temporality, our critical discourse needs to reckon with the contradictions and teleological trajectories that capitalism creates, which can't be unthought or undone simply by coming up with a new paradigm or loosening the definition of a word.

The Banal Equipment of the Theater

What, then, of theater?

Trotsky never singles out theater for special attention in his discussion of futurism, and it is far from certain that his approach to the art would resemble the one I develop in this book. Yet in 1925, just a year after that essay appeared, Walter Benjamin submitted his postdoctoral thesis about a set of strange, seldom-read plays—works which, in the opinion of most previous critics, had probably never been performed.

As the author himself acknowledges, the German Trauerspiel of the seventeenth century was an "eccentric" form with a penchant for ostentation and exaggeration, prone to the use of archaisms, neologisms, and morbid scenes of royal martyrdom and violence—all evidence, Benjamin said, that the Trauerspiel was an attempt to transform the medieval passion play for an era in which the law of the Church was giving way to the rule of absolute kings and queens.[30] The neoclassicists of the following century dismissed the Trauerspiel as a bungled attempt to revive Greek tragedy, and even the Romantics reserved their admiration for Shakespeare and Calderón de la Barca, whose works achieved a "suppleness of form" absent from the works of their German contemporaries (49). In Protestant England and Catholic Spain it proved possible to make masterpieces to mark the times; but in the fragmented states of Germany, still wracked by the religious wars, the authors of the Trauerspiel were unable to marshal the power of illusion to redeem the fallen kingdom of this world.

For Benjamin, however, this inability (or refusal?) to overcome their own creaturely condition is what granted these works their strange virtue. True, the German Trauerspiel was awkward and extreme; its plot was fragmented into "crudely illuminated" figures and scenes, and its puppet-like characters seemed to lack even the slightest psychological motivation. Yet to a certain degree the same could also be said of *Hamlet* or *Life Is a Dream*, as of the Baroque as a whole. The baroque style was one of ornate involutions and circumlocutions, spectacular contrasts and contradictions, and dizzying "antinomies of the allegorical," all of which were driven by the desire to escape the fate of transience and arrive at "that *one* about-turn"—the moment of salvation when the fragments form an aesthetic whole and allegory suddenly "loses everything that [is] most peculiar to it" (232). The more successful examples of baroque drama achieved this: in the lush pageants of Calderón de la Barca, a virtuosic illusion delivers the secular equivalent of a divine miracle, and all conflicts come to a close in an awe-inspiring apotheosis. The German Trauerspiel, on the other hand, refuses redemption and remains faithful to its earthly condition of immanence; it retains its peculiarity to the end, because "in the spirit of allegory it is conceived from the outset as a ruin, a fragment." Unable to overwhelm its spectators with the magic of stage machinery, it allows them to see the "banal equipment of the theater," and in doing so it not only illuminates its own mechanisms of representation but also emblematizes the conflicts and contradictions of its era (235).

Benjamin was just beginning to engage with Marxism at the time he wrote this text, and it would be a few more years before he met Bertolt Brecht, who would have a profound impact on his ideas about theater and politics. Even so, this text is notable for the way it approaches the materiality of the stage as a place from which to think through world events. Historians often refer to the seventeenth century as a "general crisis" involving not only the decline of papal authority and destructive wars but also economic volatility linked to the intensification of maritime competition and inflation caused by the influx of silver from the New World mines. Benjamin only vaguely alludes to this turmoil, and he shows no sign of recognizing this as a key moment in the global expansion of capitalism. Nor does he seem to know that the baroque found some of its most spectacular expressions in the colonial pageantry of those regions of the Americas under Iberian rule. Still, hovering in the historical backdrop of his interpretation is the emergence of the European nation-state system and a new order of international law in the wake of the Peace of Westphalia in 1648. Germany remained on the margins of all this: still just a group of principalities within the Holy Roman Empire, it would not gain the status of a sovereign nation for another 231 years. For Benjamin, however, the truth of a phenomenon was found not in the "average," but in the "remotest extremes and the apparent excesses of the process of development" (47). In its fragmentary form, the German Trauerspiel reveals the uneven temporality of secularization and state formation; it enacts the splintering of power into the realms of religion, politics, and art; and in its failure to match the feats of Calderón and Shakespeare, it registers the asymmetries and asynchronicities that arise when God's earth is divided into semi-autonomous but ultimately interdependent domains.

At one point Benjamin hints at an analogy between the Trauerspiel and expressionist theater, suggesting that his remarks on these arcane plays are also an argument about the art of his own times, which reacted against but in some respects perpetuated a discourse on theater that also shaped some of the early attempts to create a "national" theater in Mexico and Brazil. Within the German aesthetic tradition, theater was the arena where progressive intellectuals could reach beyond the small coteries of the literary elite and elevate the masses by bringing their senses and rational faculties into play. Friedrich Schiller, for example, argued for the importance of a standing national theater by evoking its capacity to create consensus, to unite spectators of different classes and regions just as it creates a bridge between each individual's reason and emotions, "uniting the noblest education of the head and heart."[31] The theater is where

> effeminate natures are steeled, savages made man, and, as the supreme triumph of nature, men of all ranks, zones, and conditions, emancipated

from the chains of conventionality and fashion, fraternize here in a
universal sympathy, forget the world, and come nearer to their heav-
enly destination. The individual shares in the general ecstasy, and his
breast has now only space for an emotion: he is a *man*. (345)

Indeed! Audience members are joined in their common condition as
spectators through a process of abstraction in which contingencies of class,
geography, and gender melt away—a process mapped onto a developmental
narrative that uses "culture" as a yardstick for distinguishing "savages" from
"men." How does an image achieve this edifying effect? What does the ideal
spectator see? Schiller cites a few exemplary plays, but plotlines and stylistic
niceties are hardly his main concern. As David Lloyd and Paul Thomas point
out in their genealogy of the convergence of theories of the state with theories of culture in Germany and Britain, the medium is the message of cultural
pedagogy. The stage functions as a "moral institution" not because of the
particular objects it places before the public's eye but by virtue of its social
form—the spatial relations, normative narratives, and logics of identification
it rehearses in a re-creational space.[32] Theater is where individuals learn to be
represented, which becomes the precondition for political participation, just
as the stage serves as a paradigm for all those other "representative" bodies
that emerged to interpellate individuals as subjects of the democratic state,
among them the parliament, the classroom, and the political rally.

Of course, theaters were also hotbeds of factious fervor in the lead-up
to the French Revolution, an event Schiller of all people had no desire to
see repeated. History's many tales of theater riots might be exaggerated and
overplayed, and they are certainly symptomatic of a common fantasy (and
fear) about the convergence of politics and art. Still, it remains true that
improvisation and onstage accidents heighten the element of contingency,
as does the possibility that spectators will fail to feel their hearts flutter with
fraternal love and might even interrupt the action or debate its significance in
a more physical manner than the mediations of print would allow. Instead of
making people forget the world, theater can make them more acutely aware
of it. Social distinctions often become more apparent when the "public"
materializes in the form of actual individuals occupying the same space (with
others left standing outside the door), and if readers of novels usually manage
to overlook the labor of the printer, theater is more apt to unsettle assumptions about what Nicholas Ridout refers to as the "work of time and the time
of work" because it involves actors performing something uncannily like
labor in the presence of audience members during *their* leisure time.[33] In her
study of national theater movements, Loren Kruger contends that the more
manifest "impurity" of theater's autonomy from the sociopolitical realm
makes it a powerful yet precarious vehicle for establishing cultural legitimation: "At once more and less than art, theatre straddles the disputed border
country between the aesthetic state and the political. . . . This constitutive

contradiction in theatrical autonomy enables the construction of theatrical nationhood as at once a cultural monument to legitimate hegemony and the site on which the excavation and perhaps the toppling of that monument might be performed."[34]

This—the toppling part—is one way of understanding what many of the European avant-gardes claimed to do. As liberal democracy strained at the seams and the abstraction of social relations was driven to new levels by imperial expansion, the intensification of finance capitalism, and the growth of new technologies of communication, the very principle of representation came under fire, and nowhere was this so evident as on the bourgeois stage. At a time when new media were blurring old boundaries and promising the possibility of reaching new audiences, theater seemed to some to be irredeemably retrograde, hindered not just by hundreds (thousands!) of years of tradition but also by two fundamental limitations: the human body and the material stage. In a text written during his time among the Tarahumara indigenous people of northern Mexico, Antonin Artaud called for a "total spectacle" that would abolish the text and physically engulf the spectator with the aim of throwing him into "magical trances."[35] Artaud's plan to resacralize theater, though equally enamored of "danger" and hostile to the dramatic text, was in other ways quite different from the brief *sintesi* of the Italian Futurists; and although the "theater of totality" envisioned by the Bauhaus school in Weimar Germany employed some of the same circus-inspired techniques as Vsevolod Meyerhold's Soviet theater and drew on a similar vocabulary, there was an immense gap between the offstage realities in which the two projects sought to intervene. Yet despite these differences, all of these artists are commonly associated with the trend toward "total theater"—an all-encompassing, synesthetic spectacle in which every genre and medium mixes and the stage disappears as art and action coincide.

This specter of total theater is one of the foils for my own approach to theater as an unfinished art. Genealogies of total theater typically trace it back to Richard Wagner's notion of the *Gesamtkunstwerk* (total work of art), which promised to supersede the decadent art of opera and abolish the distinction between social classes by recovering the vitality of the folk. Like a number of other critics, Martin Puchner stresses the importance of the Wagnerian legacy for European and Euro-American modernism *and* the avant-garde, but he also sees it as a pivot on which the distinction between these two categories turns. Whereas avant-garde artists embraced the growing theatricalism of the era, modernists such as Mallarmé, Joyce, and Stein—and even playwrights such as Beckett and Brecht—redoubled their emphasis on "literariness" and textual mediation as a defense against the seemingly unmediated mimesis of theater. Puchner teases out the disavowal and dependence at the heart of this "stage fright" by focusing on the neglected genre of the closet drama, a play seemingly meant to be read rather than performed. In some cases the text revolves around long intellectual dialogues with little action, though in others the actions are too grandiose or impossible to enact mimetically onstage (as when a character instantaneously changes sex). Although Puchner acknowledges that the antitheatricalism of some modernists was an elitist defense against the masses, he also recognizes it as a form of resistance to the codification and commodification of the physical theater, as well as to the spectacular pageantry of fascism in which avant-garde theatricalism could become caught up.[36]

But if a certain understanding of performativity grounded in immediacy is considered characteristic—even constitutive—of the avant-garde, where does this leave the "unfinished" theater of the avant-garde in Mexico and Brazil? How can it be integrated into broader narratives of avant-garde theater? Among U.S.-based scholars, one significant exception to the usual omission of theater in discussions of the *vanguardias* and Brazilian modernismo is Vicky Unruh's influential *Latin American Vanguards* (1994), which managed to put several long-ignored works on the critical radar and sparked my own interest in this area. Published at a moment when performance studies was beginning to gain greater visibility, the book draws heavily on the ideas of Richard Schechner in depicting Latin American vanguardism as a mode of "aesthetic activism."[37] Yet in her desire to validate the work of these artists according to a very particular notion of performativity and avant-garde agency—Peter Bürger is another of her main models—Unruh neglects the fact that many of the pieces she discusses weren't actually performed. Much like Fernando Rosenberg, she endows the text with an enormous degree of autonomy and agency, though in this case the move is even more paradoxical because what is at stake is *theater*. The materiality of theater, its dependence on an apparatus, and the "banal equipment of the theater" about which Benjamin wrote recede into the background as performance becomes a phenomenon that can be realized on the page.

The materiality of theater—even or especially when the apparatus isn't there—is precisely the place from which I try to rethink the avant-garde. Artists and intellectuals in Mexico and Brazil drew on many of the same ideas about theater as artists and intellectuals in Europe and the United States—hardly a surprise in light of the transoceanic and hemispheric circulation of ideas, artists, techniques, and texts. But the experimental projects of Artaud and even Marinetti (in "backward" Italy) were predicated on the existence of the stage they set out to destroy; in Mexico and Brazil, there was less pretense that theater was or had ever been a "symbolic," "representative" institution.[38] The nation-building novels of the nineteenth century could make lily-white maidens swoon over noble savages (even if only a small percentage of the country's inhabitants could read these foundational fictions), but the very prospect of enacting a similar scenario onstage inevitably brought uncomfortable realities to light: social prohibitions stood in the way of an actual indigenous man and an actual white woman kissing before an audience of respectable citizens, and even if it were allowed, bringing a noble savage from the Amazon or Chiapas (where few people from the principal cities had ever set foot) and giving him acting lessons (while also teaching him Spanish or Portuguese) was not on the table. In Mexico, efforts to create a national theater in the postindependence period were stalled by ongoing political instability, and although Brazil had more stable institutions and local companies, its elite was even more preoccupied with opera. The Gran Teatro Nacional in Mexico City and the Teatro Lírico in Rio de Janeiro did occasionally offer operas by "national" composers, but as the consummate art of the Export Age, opera acquired much of its prestige from its status as an import, and most performances were given by touring companies from Europe. In Brazil, some canonical authors from this period wrote plays, though they are seldom read or staged today, and the plethora of *revistas* (musical revues) and *comédias de costumes* (similar to a comedy of manners) were not quite regarded as "art." Both Brazil and Mexico saw turn-of-the-century attempts at theatrical realism (also rarely read today), and Spanish American *modernistas* often wrote about theater in their newspaper *crónicas* (chronicles), but if anything their antitheatricalism was even *more* marked than it was among European modernists due to the very fragility of literary autonomy.[39]

Avant-garde artists in these two countries railed against *el teatro burgués* or *o teatro burguês*, but for some it was both the symbol of an imported, imperial order *and* a spectral sign of the sovereignty their own nations had never achieved. The engagement with mass culture, so central to definitions of the avant-garde, also had a distinct inflection: although it raised the profile of more "popular" cultures and helped generate a shared sense of national identity, the very media through which images and sounds of the popular circulated were dominated by economic interests in Europe and (increasingly) the United States. To put it succinctly, there were more obvious obstacles to the effect of immediacy on which the transformative potential of total theater was imagined to hinge.

Theater and performance studies have undergone some shifts in recent years, a development I would suggest is related not only to the rise of media studies but also to changing ideas about the avant-garde. In her work on the "archive" and the "repertoire," Diana Taylor stresses that performance is a mode of knowledge transmission no less mediated than written or digital documentation.[40] There is also growing interest in what Fred Moten and Rebecca Schneider refer to as the "inter(in)animation" of the past and present, which troubles the sense of presence, immediacy, and futurity common to certain shared understandings of both performance and avant-garde action.[41] In this book I try to resist the compulsion to prove that theater in Mexico and Brazil was *just as* "avant-garde" or *just as* "performative" as in Europe. At the same time, I push back against the discourse of national or regional exceptionalism typical of so much scholarship on the avant-gardes in Mexico and Brazil. The works I consider have their own peculiarities, but even in their strangeness they share key characteristics with their metropolitan counterparts, and for a number of them, proving their own alterity isn't exactly the objective. Several are guilty of the same "sins" as the old modernism (e.g., primitivism), none manage to entirely evade the "trap" of teleology (though some give it a twist), and all fail to meet the expectations of uplifting otherness that often drive the redemptive narratives of an expanded modernist and avant-garde studies. Yet in keeping with some of the critics I cite, I insist that these examples of an unfinished art can draw out certain truths about the avant-garde as a whole.

Unfinished Business

The Unfinished Art of Theater is not meant to offer a comprehensive overview of avant-garde theater in Mexico and Brazil. Particularly in the case of Mexico, there is a dizzying array of pieces and projects that receive barely or nary a mention in this book.[42] In general I chose to sideline the slightly better-known plays and groups, which also tend to be those that correspond more closely to conventional definitions of "theater." More intriguing to me were the things I came to glean only little by little through sneaking suspicions, fortuitous finds, and a lot of legwork. This book draws on my research in a number of different archives, though the majority of my time was spent at three sites: the Archivo Histórico de la Secretaría de Educación Pública in Mexico City, which held a rather random (and sketchily catalogued) collection of materials that has since been incorporated into the Archivo General de la Nación; the meticulously organized personal archive of Mário de Andrade at the Instituto de Estudos Brasileiros in São Paulo; and the Arquivo Público do Estado de São Paulo, where I immersed myself for weeks in the records of the DEOPS, Brazil's former political police force. The process of learning how to navigate each of these archives, of trying to discern under what label or branch of the bureaucracy a specific kind of information or material might be—and whether it was even likely to exist—gave me invaluable insight into the messy reclassifications and realignments that were taking place during this period. If you go looking for a category called "theater" in the archives of these years, you are likely to find either that it isn't there, or that very little is stored in the boxes with that label. Yet theater—the word, the idea, the material traces of theater practices and projects—is everywhere else. More than any concrete document I read or saw, this shaped my sense of how an unfinished art became a site around which so many other categories and concepts were drawn.

The book is divided into two sections: the first on Mexico, the second on Brazil. Each of the two sections has three chapters that follow a roughly chronological order, though within each chapter I frequently loop back to earlier moments and look ahead to future developments that retrospectively reshaped the period on which I focus. In my view, it makes sense to read the book from start to finish, if only because the seemingly straightforward arc of the narrative serves to cast the temporal complexities of the avant-gardes into relief. That said, there are certain similarities between the analogous chapters in each section, and taking note of them can illuminate some of the oblique ways in which the two countries were linked by their mutual involvement in the global circulation of capital and culture. Rather than giving a rundown of the chapters in consecutive order, then, I prefer to take this opportunity to draw connections across the Mexico/Brazil divide while also highlighting some of the secondary motifs that recur throughout the book.

The first chapter in each section circles around the issue of origins and definitions: the prehistories and (anti)foundational acts of the avant-gardes, their debates over nomenclature, and the dynamics of disavowal on which they depend. In each case I dwell on the early 1920s, and I foreground a figure who played a pivotal role in the formation of the vanguard but was (or is) regarded in some sense as marginal—even antithetical—to its ideals. The protagonist of chapter 1 ("Rehearsals of the Tragi-Co[s]mic Race") is the aforementioned José Vasconcelos, a hard-to-classify character whose institutional innovations as founding director of the Secretariat of Public Education were arguably among the most significant factors in the early development of the Mexican avant-garde. If this connection occasionally posed problems for the artists, it has caused even more consternation among critics—particularly given that Vasconcelos's vision of *la raza cósmica* eventually became an ideology closely associated with the Institutional Revolutionary Party (often referred to by its Spanish acronym, PRI), which monopolized the presidency for seven decades starting in 1929. This chapter grapples with the tenuous distinction between "art" and "ideology" in a (post)revolutionary context, and it restores a sense of contingency to the cosmic race by shifting attention away from Vasconcelos's so-called *ensayo* (essay) *La raza cósmica* to alternative meanings of *ensayo*, which can also refer to a rehearsal or a preliminary experiment. When read through the lens of his bizarre essay-cum–closet drama *Prometeo vencedor* (Prometheus Triumphant) and the rehearsals for the inaugural mass spectacle of his giant "theater-stadium," the cosmic race appears as a more fragmentary figure for a shift in ideas and practices of sovereignty that entailed a remaking of the body and its senses.

Pugnacious and polarizing, Vasconcelos cuts a striking contrast with Mário de Andrade, the conspicuously coy poet and music teacher who makes a star turn in my account of the Week of Modern Art in chapter 4 ("Parsifal on the Periphery of Capitalism"). Like Vasconcelos, however, Mário formed part of a symbolic chain linking an emphasis on racial mixture as the basis of nationhood to a genre similarly coded as "mixed": the aura surrounding the "pope" of Brazilian modernismo (I argue) was bound up in the open secret of his not-quite-white origins and queer (a)sexuality, as was his characterization as the Brazilian Parsifal—a counterpart to the chaste, self-sacrificing knight in Wagner's opera of the same name. This chapter complicates the common depiction of the Week of Modern Art as a rupture from the past by foregrounding its setting in an opera house and showing how the participants formulated their call for the "new" in and against the "anachronistic" language of opera. I tease out the tense exchanges and veiled disputes among the proto-modernistas in a series of articles leading up to the event and speeches given on (and off) its operatic stage; then, in the last section, I reflect on the retrospective work of memorialization, focusing on Mário's own parody of the Week of Modern Art in the form of a "profane oratorio" for 550,000 singers. My discussion of the modernistas' operatic attachments and the sense of shame surrounding Mário's persona offers a queer angle on Roberto Schwarz's notion of Brazilian liberalism as an idea "out of place," giving a new inflection to his argument that modernism in Brazil arose out of (and not simply despite) the experience of backwardness and dependency.

Some of these threads carry over into the second chapters of each section, both of which explore the intersections of ethnography and art while also tracing the shared circuits of emotions and economics. Chapter 2 ("Primitivist Accumulation and *Teatro sintético*") constructs a critical genealogy of "synthetic theater," a term used by the Italian Futurists but also associated with the Chauve-Souris, a touring revue troupe founded by Soviet émigrés in Paris that gained fame for its skits about the diverse social classes of prerevolutionary Russia and its imperial peripheries. In Mexico, the idea spawned several projects, the most notable of which grew out of a collaboration between affiliates of the *estridentista* avant-garde and artist-ethnographers who started out working with indigenous communities under the direction of Manuel Gamio, the so-called father of modern anthropology in Mexico. Directly modeled on the Chauve-Souris, the Teatro del Murciélago juxtaposed short, archetypal scenes of urban and rural, indigenous life. Its objective? To create a "synthesis" of the primitive and the modern in the form of an amalgamation of music, dance, painting, and pantomime that was billed as a "toy store for the soul." My narrative reaches its climax with the group's debut in 1924—a special function for a delegation of U.S. business representatives who were in Mexico to reestablish economic ties disrupted by the revolution. Throughout the chapter I show how the push for cultural and economic integration was imagined as entailing the production of particular emotions, and I ask how the primitivist desires of the avant-garde relate to the future-oriented impulse of capitalist development and its contradictory reliance on modes of accumulation regarded as precapitalist or "primitive."

Similar issues are at stake in chapter 5 ("Phonography, Operatic Ethnography, and Other Bad Arts"), which revolves around the operatic libretti and scene summaries that Mário de Andrade drafted during the late 1920s and early 1930s. Based in part on his observations and notations of songs and dance-dramas from a trip through the Amazon and another to the Northeast, these short, comic *opera buffa* were intended to "deregionalize" the diverse performance traditions of Brazil in order to create a truly national opera—just as *teatro sintético* was meant to accumulate and synthesize the traditions of Mexico. Unlike the estridentistas, however, Mário was resistant to staging these pieces, even though the music composed by his collaborators was performed. The chapter examines his ethnographic operas in relation to his embrace of the phonograph as a means of preserving the "dying" sounds of black and indigenous Brazil, and it investigates his personal ties to the Victor Talking Machine Company, which had begun to supplement its operatic offerings with recordings of Brazilian "popular" music. Here, affects and emotions take a negative turn as I also ask how Mário's own disinterest in seeing these works staged might be connected to the refusal of work and (re)productivity exemplified by the main character of the one libretto he finished—a folktale trickster named Pedro Malazarte, whose last name translates as "bad arts"—and Macunaíma (Evil Spirit), the protagonist of his famous novel and its never-written operatic adaptation. In addition to addressing questions of labor and value, this chapter intervenes in the growing field of sound studies by adding an international dimension to the largely U.S.-based accounts of the early recording industry and the intertwined histories of sound media and race.

In fact, at several moments along the way I almost decided I was writing a book about theater and sound: from the first chapter, where I touch on Vasconcelos's notion of "auditory mysticism," readers will note that in nearly all of the projects I discuss, the "unfinished" aspect of theater has an intimate connection to the aural realm. Another place where audio technologies come to the fore is in the final chapter on Mexico, or chapter 3 ("Radio/Puppets, or The Institutionalization of a [Media] Revolution"). Here I hunt for and reassemble the archival remains of a radio/puppet who (probably) failed to make his stage debut in 1933—the same key year as the nonperformance of the play around which the final chapter on Brazil revolves. In Mexico, as in Brazil and elsewhere, politics became more polarized following the stock market crash of 1929, an event that coincided with the formation of what eventually became the PRI. This chapter considers the little-known afterlife of the estridentista avant-garde and shows how artists were at the vanguard of the Left's eventual alliance with the state under the progressive presidency of Lázaro Cárdenas. At its center is the story of Troka the Powerful, an aural automaton who hosted a radio show designed to teach children about the wonders of technology. Troka's eyes were streetlights; his nerves were telegraph wires; his muscles were cranes; his arms were radio towers. And his voice? It was the medium of radio itself. Yet the power of this aural automaton was more complex than it first appears, because it turns out he was first conceived as a marionette. In showing how Troka was born from the mutual remediations of radio and a puppet movement inspired by experiments in the Soviet Union, I make the case that an attention to the dynamics of uneven development can contribute to efforts by scholars to counter the rhetoric of media revolution and rethink the temporality of media change.

A similar rhetoric also fuels the dream of total theater, a specter I finally tackle head-on in chapter 6 ("Total Theater and Missing Pieces"). During the Tropicália counterculture movement of the 1960s, artists who claimed the legacy of modernismo drew on the discourse of total theater in conscripting Oswald de Andrade's unperformed plays from the 1930s as the missing pieces of a national avant-garde. Here, in this closing chapter, I make one last metacritical move by reading Oswald's strange and unwieldy "spectacle" *O homem e o cavalo* (Man and the Horse) against the total theater paradigm and in dialogue with Benjamin's analysis of the German Trauerspiel. Drawing on records from the archives of the political police, I reconstruct the story of the "modern artists' club" where Oswald's play might have been performed if the theater had not been shut down by the police at a moment of tension over the status of the provisional president (and future dictator) Getúlio Vargas and the rise of the fascist Integralist movement. The records of police informants and other ephemera shed light on how the club became a site where artists, anarchists, Trotskyists, Communist Party loyalists, intellectuals, working-class immigrants, and black performers all intermingled for a brief time. Its connection to this forgotten social milieu illuminates the stakes of Oswald's seemingly unstageable play—an allegorical tableau of world history starring Cleopatra, talking horses, Fu Manchu, a black man "disembodied" by a Fascist, and a Poet-Soldier who predicts Hitler's genocide of the Jews.

Mexico

Chapter 1

✦

Rehearsals of the Tragi-Co(s)mic Race

April 27, 1924, was not a good day for José Vasconcelos, the man who would go down in history as the premiere "cultural caudillo" of the Mexican Revolution.[1] With only a week to go before the inaugural ceremony of the new National Stadium, the founding director of the Secretariat of Public Education was struggling to hold his own against a barrage of negative publicity. The sixty-thousand-seat arena was supposed to be the crowning achievement of his sweeping cultural reforms—proof the Mexican people could accomplish constructive goals and the new government could deliver on its promises, even if large parts of the country had yet to be "pacified" and political assassinations were still a common affair. Instead, his pet project had been plagued by controversy from the start. First, he had tangled with the architect, who had trouble wrapping his unimaginative head around the fact that the stadium was meant to be not a mere "racetrack" but a revival of the ancient Greek open-air theaters. Then Diego Rivera had requested some modifications in the design to accommodate his plans for the interior murals, causing his diehard enemies to howl and every architect in the city to protest that painters, sculptors, and other "decorators" should stick to their area of expertise. Now Rivera was all riled up and on the verge of lambasting his critics in the press as semi-civilized vestiges of the prerevolutionary bourgeoisie. And as if all of that weren't enough, rumors were flying that Vasconcelos was either about to quit or be fired—rumors he knew were true.

All of that, and now this. Five thousand schoolgirls were assembled in the stadium, rehearsing the songs they would sing en masse while others formed improbable pyramids or danced a traditional *jarabe tapatío*. Everything seemed to be going fine, but the day was exceptionally hot and no one had thought to bring refreshments, so around high noon the children began to collapse. It was just a *mild* case of sunstroke, though try telling that to the parents watching in the stands who descended in a panic, setting off a stampede out of which several girls emerged even worse for wear. Still, none of the injuries were serious, and surely a hundred heat-frazzled schoolgirls out of five thousand wasn't such a bad tally. Alas, the daily *Excélsior* disagreed. The next day its front-page headline screamed, "More Than One Hundred Girls

Were on the Verge of Dying of Sunstroke in the National Stadium." Then a string of subheaders such as "Great Alarm in the City" led up to the article's histrionic first line: "Yesterday, over thousands of homes in our capital and outlying areas of the District, the horrifying grimace of tragedy appeared."[2] Never one to hold his fire, Vasconcelos immediately dispatched a communiqué to every classroom in the city urging students to ignore the newspaper, a commercial rag in cahoots with the bullfighting impresarios and other purveyors of dishonest entertainment who recognized the stadium as a threat to their ill-gotten gains. Yes, he conceded, the incident was unfortunate, but in fact a mere *fifty* girls had fainted, and it only demonstrated the urgent need for a "theater-stadium" where "our race" would forge its physique and create the "art of the future"—an art that would put an end to all the *ensayos*, all the rehearsals foiled by the foibles of the human, all-too-human flesh.[3]

The National Stadium was demolished in 1949 due to cracks in its foundation, and today few residents of Mexico City recall its existence. Far more often Vasconcelos is remembered for his messianic cultural "missions," which sent newly trained teachers into rural areas to spread the gospel of good hygiene and teach impoverished peasants to read the *Iliad* and the *Mahabharata*. But despite his penchant for the classics and his eventual transformation into a peevish librarian, Vasconcelos is a hard man to pin down, not least because he was instrumental in creating the conditions for the emergence of the Mexican avant-garde. Shortly after assuming office he reached out to Rivera and David Alfaro Siqueiros, still on extended sojourns in Paris and Barcelona, and offered to subsidize their studies of Renaissance fresco techniques in Italy before luring them back to Mexico with commissions to adorn the walls of government buildings. He also encouraged artists to immerse themselves in indigenous cultures (even if he drew a clear distinction between such sources of inspiration and actual "art"). Some avant-gardists mocked his spiritual rhetoric and political pretensions, especially after his self-exile and return for a failed presidential run; yet few were as focused on the future as Vasconcelos, and it is possible his grandiose plans for radio and other new media would have intersected with the technophilic dreams of the avant-garde had his time in office not been limited to a few turbulent years. Such connections, both uncanny and concrete, make his cultural politics difficult to define and undermine any easy understanding of the avant-garde as contrarian to institutional authority. The one thing on which almost all critics agree: whatever connections or stylistic similarities they might share, Vasconcelos was an ideologue, not an artist.

This distinction relies on his status as the author of a singular and very powerful idea. What now goes by the name of *La raza cósmica* was first published in 1925 as the prologue to a narrative of his diplomatic travels through South America, but the body of the book has gradually withered for lack of attention even as the preamble has usurped its name and become a discursive double for the cosmic race—an idea Antonio Cornejo Polar aptly described as "the hymnal exacerbation of some sort of *supermestizaje*," an overwrought expression of the metaphor for cultural miscegenation that remains "the most powerful and widespread conceptual device with which Latin America has interpreted itself."[4] Vasconcelos left reflections on race and aesthetics scattered across a wide array of speeches, stories, articles, government bulletins, and so on, yet the obligatory point of reference in any discussion of his creed is a text that has long since shed its identity as a preface without acquiring a well-defined form of its own. *La raza cósmica* is strident and programmatic, yet it seems too longwinded and expository to qualify as a manifesto; its allegorical bent and idealist tone make it vaguely akin to a utopia, but the narrative lacks the utopia's fictional frame. If only by default, then, it tends to get lumped in with the genre of the essay, or *ensayo*—a respectable, un-avant-garde denomination that links it to a long line of intellectual reflections on Mexican identity.

In certain respects, this is strange company for it to keep. Written in the months after its author resigned his powerful post in opposition to the incoming president, *La raza cósmica* rejects nationalism in favor of an Ibero-American alliance against Anglo imperialism and prophesies a future in which the Brazilian Amazon serves as the site of Universópolis, a technological wonderland where all of the world's races converge at the dawn of a new "aesthetic era." In Mexico, however, such prosaic details did little to prevent the cosmic race from being repurposed as the protagonist of a powerful narrative of national identity. Whether in schoolbooks or academic treatises, it came to be depicted as an a priori idea, the master plan behind Vasconcelos's foundational acts; often it was (and still is) projected onto the entire postrevolutionary period, serving as a stabilizing figure that lent coherence to the contradictions and contingencies of culture during those messy, uncertain years. Over the past several decades, as the government has abandoned the ideology of revolutionary nationalism and lost even the appearance of legitimacy, critics have called attention to the less savory aspects of Vasconcelos's career—including a flirtation with fascism in the early 1940s—and his futurist fantasy now stands accused of underwriting the developmentalist designs of the single-party state.[5] It has become obligatory to note that although the essay attacks social evolutionism and the segregationist policies of Jim Crow, its call for racial mixture is driven by a desire for racial whitening; its ostensible "universality" erases rather than embraces difference. Yet despite (or because of?) its periodic dissection, *La raza cósmica* is still lodged in the cultural canon, and its Idea remains.

But what happens when ideas take the form of figures, bodies, and actions on a virtual or physical stage? In what follows I uncouple the cosmic race from its textual twin and reexamine it in the light of Vasconcelos's little-known experiments with theater. If the essay has become a comfortable lens through which to view the cosmic race—a kind of second skin—this chapter defamiliarizes its physiognomy by tracing the genesis of this foundational idea and bringing it into play with an alternative meaning of the *ensayo* as a rehearsal or unfinished work. To begin, I show how the essay genre is often imagined as quintessentially modern in its refusal to obey distinctions among disciplines or rigid definitions of form, a quality that in Mexico (as elsewhere in Spanish America) tends to be associated with the celebration of *mestizaje*, or racial mixture. In the following section, I rewind the clock in order to trace a set of recurring concerns across a set of disparate texts that Vasconcelos wrote during the armed conflict in Mexico, including his treatise on the Greek philosopher Pythagoras, his legal defense of the revolutionary Convention of Aguascalientes, and his scathing remarks on—of all things—the essay genre. For Vasconcelos, forging a common ideology, creating a new artistic genre (or form), and birthing a new race were (almost) all one and the same. What linked them was rhythm—a phenomenon at once corporeal and abstract that suggests a certain connection between the cosmic race and recent attempts to rethink the concept of ideology in relation to affect and embodiment. Nowhere is this more evident than in his *Prometeo vencedor* (1920), a "modern tragedy" conceived (according to its author) as an essay but born into the world of print as an unperformable play. Rather than attempting to salvage this deeply strange and rarely read text from the heap of history's mistakes, I show how its apparent failures allow readers to see what would later be called the cosmic race not as an expression of identity, but as a self-reflexive (and even ironic) allegory enacted on a speculative stage. By contrast, the construction of Vasconcelos's "Theater-Stadium" and the rehearsals leading up to its debut (which bring the chapter to a close) illustrate the contradictions and constraints he and other intellectuals faced in their attempts to create a material stage on which their projections for the future could enfold.

If rehearsals imply an understanding of art as part of a process of production in which error is integral, I recast the cosmic race in such a light in order to unsettle its retrospective reification. This move also aims to put pressure on Vasconcelos's curiously ex-centric relationship to the avant-garde. Although he never claimed allegiance to the avant-garde, this is not an automatic disqualifier: the word *vanguardia* was used in an inconsistent fashion during the 1920s, and critics today routinely deny this classification to artists who collaborated with figures comfortably ensconced in the vanguard canon while bestowing it on others who rejected it at the time. A fuzzy category in any context (not unlike the essay genre?), the avant-garde is especially difficult to define in a place such as Mexico. Who or what counts as *la vanguardia* in a country where the revolution has already taken place, a country where a "revolutionary" government fosters the formation of a new class of intellectuals and artists with ties to the international "avant-garde" and conscripts them to help build the infrastructure of the state? This chapter follows a circuitous (and somewhat essayistic) course, skirting the edges of the avant-garde and dwelling on its pre- and posthistories in order to pinpoint what is at stake in excluding a figure such as Vasconcelos—to explain why he is denied the designation of "artist," and why he fails to fit into a category he did so much to create.

When Is an Essay Not an Essay?

Reflections on the essay genre almost invariably invoke Michel de Montaigne's original use of the term *essai*: a text conceived not as a finished object, but as an exploratory trial or attempt. Long derided as incomplete, improvisatory, and even degenerate, the essay has been celebrated in more recent times as an exemplary vehicle of thought, a heterodox genre that enjoys relative freedom from disciplinary injunctions and the strictures of predetermined form. In "The Essay as Form" (1959), Theodor Adorno describes it as a "hybrid" mode of writing (*ein Mischprodukt*) that registers the historical separation of science and art even as it mediates this opposition through its dogged negation of method. Tied to the transitory and ephemeral, the essay "thinks in fragments," coordinating constellations of elements rather than subordinating them to discursive logic or finite totalities. "It does not insist on something beyond mediation—and those are the historical mediations in which the whole society is sedimented—but seeks the truth content in its objects."[6] Rather than striving to transcend language, the essay engages in a mobile praxis of self-reflection on the very act of signification, which is also to say that it is more than just an apposite medium for expressing a critique of ideology: it is also a textual performance in the sense that its fluid, unfinished architecture enacts a critique of ideological form.[7]

More than a decade before Adorno penned these reflections, the Mexican writer Alfonso Reyes situated the essay genre in relation to the changes wrought by new technologies of communication. "Las nuevas artes" (The New Arts, 1944) begins with the premise that six *medios*, or media, are responsible for transmitting culture in contemporary society: schools, the press, theater, museums, radio, and film.[8] Reyes notes that the appearance of radio and film have aroused opposition from traditionalists anxious to defend the integrity of the older arts, and his objective is to counter such hostility while forestalling any threat the expansion of the "public" might pose by assimilating these mass media into the orderly realm of "art." Theater, he argues, is wrong to view film as a rival, because the cinema merely brings the true nature of its performative cousin into clearer relief, introducing a distinction between two different "artistic orders" that were once regrettably "confused"; nor should print culture fear radio, because books respond to different needs than broadcasting, which extends the benefits of learned culture to more people even as it revitalizes the lost art of oratory. Reyes even acknowledges that these new arts have provoked a series of "generic transformations" that have revolutionized the "classic contours" of literary functions outlined by Lessing in his *Laocoön*. Today, the literary field is divided into the lyric ("the purest poetry"), scientific literature, and the essay. Only in the final sentence, as a self-reflexive flourish, does he define the essay as the "centaur of genres," a site where all of these cultural forms commingle, "where there is a bit of everything and where everything fits . . . capricious child of a culture that no longer responds to the circular, closed orb of the ancients but to the open arc, the process in motion, the 'Etcetera' " (403). Once again, the essay appears as an unfettered space of intellectual freedom; and yet here it is clear that this freedom is not an effect of its exclusion from established institutions of knowledge but a corollary of its authority to regulate their proper function. Neither high nor low, the essay is a nongenre or transmedium that holds the taxonomic order in place while eluding its strictures, the necessary exception to the rule that Derrida dubbed the Law of Genre: "Genres are not to be mixed."[9]

Adorno frames his argument as a polemic against a tradition of German idealism that condemned the essay for its ontological impurity, and his claims about the critical force of its "consciousness of non-identity" presuppose its discontinuity with orthodox forms of truth. Only by turning his logic inside out is it possible to account for the essay's relation to an intellectual tradition that has enshrined "hybridity" as a first principle.[10] Throughout Spanish America, too, the essay is regarded as an idiosyncratic, liminal genre that cuts across conventional boundaries—a "centaur," in Reyes's oft-cited formulation. Yet as the countless anthologies and metacritical essays on *el ensayo hispanoamericano* suggest, this misbegotten stepchild of modern knowledge has not been outcast from the dominion of truth but is instead hailed as a "natural" forum for reflecting on the linguistic, racial, and cultural contradictions characteristic of the (post)colonial condition. Take, for example, Germán Arciniegas's "Nuestra América es un ensayo" (Our America Is an Essay, 1963), a charming and in many respects insightful text published in a journal affiliated with the Congress for Cultural Freedom, an international organization of liberal anticommunist intellectuals covertly funded by the CIA.[11] In this imaginative genealogy of the genre the author capitalizes on the essay's elasticity by gathering a long line of historic documents under its umbrella. This retrospective act of reclassification leads him back through *La raza cósmica* to Domingo Sarmiento's *Facundo* (1845) and Simón Bolívar's *Manifiesto de Cartagena* (1812) all the way to the colonial chronicle, at which point he boldly asserts that "essays have been written among us ever since the white man's first encounters with the Indian, in the sixteenth century, several years before Montaigne was born."[12] In one fell swoop, the Colombian writer lays claim to the Enlightenment by conflating the birth of this quintessentially "modern" form with Latin America's own imagined origins—an "encounter" between two racially defined extremes that confounds the "pure" categories of Eurocentric thought. The irony underlying this gesture is heralded in the title of Arciniegas's text: "Our America" *is* an essay, a trial or an attempt but also, in Spanish, a *rehearsal* for a New World, a performance perpetually deferred.[13]

This spirited defense of the ensayo challenges Europe's imperial pretensions by shifting the locus of modern truth to the "historical mediations" (Adorno) that occur on the Old World's outer edge. But its power hinges on a paradox, because it reifies antifoundationalism, and it redeems violent social contradictions as emblems of identity by racializing the very principle of mediation. Often described as a type of *mestizaje formal* or *mestizaje literario*, the essay came to be seen as exemplary of a more general interdisciplinary impulse endemic to a region where reality itself elided all rigid categories. Nowhere is this more evident than in Mexico, where mestizaje served as a master metaphor of the developmentalist state for much of the seven-decade rule of the Institutional Revolutionary Party (PRI), which began in 1929. Noting the essay's monopoly over discussions of national culture, the anthropologist Claudio Lomnitz portrays it as part of a symbolic chain linking the nation's "mixed" economy and "mestizo" population to the figure of the *pensador*, an intellectual-at-large who enjoys proximity to power (and often holds bureaucratic posts) while maintaining a critical pose. In Mexico, Lomnitz argues, these interpretive "syntheses" are *too* flexible and too closely tied to public opinion as well as the particular political conjunctures out of which they arose: although they often draw on social scientific theories, the knowledge they generate is never formalized according to a clear method or standards of empirical proof, so once it has been consumed, all it leaves behind is a symbol or stereotype that can be pressed into the service of any number of political positions. With the official shift to an embrace of "pluralism" and the rise of cultural studies in the late 1980s, the psychodramas of Mexican identity elaborated in essays such as Octavio Paz's *Labyrinth of Solitude* took a critical hit; yet the tools of textual deconstruction fail to disable their representations of national culture because their labyrinthine contradictions lead right back into the belly of the centaur where nature and culture meet.[14]

Lomnitz says nothing of *La raza cósmica* or its author, but it can be argued that they act as a limit case for the tradition he traces. Starting in 1906, Vasconcelos collaborated with Alfonso Reyes, Diego Rivera, Antonio Caso, Pedro Henríquez Ureña, and others as part of a circle known first as the Ateneo de la Juventud (Athenaeum of Youth), and later as the Ateneo de México. Touted in retrospect as the intellectual prelude to the Mexican Revolution of 1910, the Ateneo defined itself in opposition to the *científicos*, a group of businessmen and academics schooled in the doctrines of French positivism who occupied prominent positions in the government of the long-standing dictator Porfirio Díaz. Seeking alternatives to the científicos' deterministic view of society and technocratic outlook on education, the *ateneístas* steeped themselves in Schopenhauer, Nietzsche, Henri Bergson, and the ancient Greeks, embracing metaphysical inquiry and the ethical

dimension of art as part of what Horacio Legrás describes as their preference for "a philosophy of the indeterminate and an unforeseeable future [*un
devenir no previsible*]."[15] As discontent with the dictatorship's program of
modernization under the aegis of foreign capital grew, the more bellicose
among them also exalted the superior aesthetic sensibilities of Latin America
over and against the soulless conflation of culture and commerce attributed
to the United States. In doing so, they drew on a set of motifs and ideas
also associated with *modernismo*, the self-consciously cosmopolitan literary
movement that had emerged throughout the continent in the decade prior
to the Spanish-American War of 1898. But the modernistas were known as
poets and writers of *crónicas*—anecdotal accounts of literary miscellanea or
urban ephemera written for newspapers. In contrast, most of the ateneístas
would make their mark as the authors of *ensayos*, a genre whose emergence
was facilitated by the growth of the book market and increasing autonomy
of the cultural field. Freed from the exigencies of the newspaper, Julio Ramos
explains, the ateneístas staked their authority on a holistic notion of culture
and an opposition to the division of intellectual labor into distinct disciplines.
The essay, in his words, served as a paradoxical "form of metaspecialization,
a reflection on and critique of specialization."[16]

The essays of Alfonso Reyes, who spent most of the revolution and subsequent decades as an ambassador to Spain, Argentina, and Brazil, exemplify
the ateneístas' continental outlook and refusal to define their mission in
narrowly nationalistic terms.[17] Vasconcelos espoused similar ideals, yet his
involvement in the nitty-gritty business of building national institutions made
it easier to assimilate his (in)famous text as an essay of Mexican identity—
despite all the evidence that it doesn't fit. His actions while in office were
doubtless instrumental in creating an institutional space for the *pensador*,
but *La raza cósmica* was published in Barcelona, less than a year after its
author noisily resigned as head of the Secretariat of Public Education and
then ran a failed campaign for state governor of Oaxaca before going into
exile in the United States. In 1929, when he returned to run as an opposition
candidate in the presidential elections, the government used voter fraud and
violence to assure the victory of the newly formed Party of the Mexican Revolution (forerunner to the contemporary PRI); after this Vasconcelos became
even more of a persona non grata, and although he was brought back into
the fold as the director of the National Library in 1940, the first Mexican
edition of *La raza cósmica* only appeared in 1948. Finally, to hark back to
Lomnitz's insights, just how is it that a "cosmic" figure of the future can serve
as a stereotype or symbol?

Far from eschewing formalization, *La raza cósmica* draws together a
dizzying array of discourses, flexing all its rhetorical muscle in a strenuous
attempt to integrate Greek myth, experimental physics, Plato, Pythagoras,
Nietzsche, Aztec cosmology, Christianity, Mendelian evolution, Bergson, and
Buddhism. Woven through this discursive jumble is a speculative narrative of

human development that projects the "synthesis" of the world's four races: white, black, yellow, and red. In a twist on the Comtean law of three stages, Vasconcelos contends that for eons after the dawn of history, humans were stuck in the material, or warrior stage, when conflicts were decided by brute force; at present we are in the intellectual, or political stage, distinguished by the formation of nation-states under the tyrannical rule of reason and the ascendance of Anglo-Saxon imperialism, with its ideology of evolutionary racism. The ultimate objective, however, should be to arrive at a spiritual, or aesthetic stage, when all peoples will peacefully coexist "beyond good and evil, in a world of aesthetic *pathos*."[18] This apotheosis of the aesthetic will retrospectively redeem the existence of Latin America, whose superior "intuition" and long history of racial assimilation have prepared its people to become the medium for a new, "universal" race—a "synthetic type who will gather together the treasures of History, in order to give expression to the total desire of the world" (15). Yet even as he constructs this teleology, Vasconcelos also underscores its contingency: according to his vision, the new über-race will found the Amazonian city of Universópolis, which will send airplanes of educators forth to save any stragglers—though if this does *not* happen (a possibility he leaves open), the blond people of the North will found their own xenophobic dystopia and call it Anglotown.

I leave it to others to critique the racism of Vasconcelos's notion of "aesthetic eugenics" (according to which ugly people will lose the desire to reproduce, allowing black people to be "redeemed" and Indians to leap from the ancient past into the future); nor is this the place to delve into its unacknowledged debts to the Porfirian positivists, who had already begun to recuperate the mestizo as the privileged subject of Mexican history. Suffice it to say, none of the *científicos* had ever written anything quite like this. Ignacio Sánchez Prado makes a similar observation, noting that the common critique of the cosmic race as a falsification of reality misses the point, because an accurate depiction of the facts was never its aim. An example of the "utopic essay," an ephemeral genre that flourished in Mexico in the 1920s and 1930s, *La raza cósmica* had as its objective the creation of a unifying political ideal.[19] For Julio Ramos, too, Vasconcelos is pivotal because in *La raza cósmica*, "cultural authority has become ontologized, constituting the base of a new 'theory.'"[20] The essay's capacity to integrate competing discourses gave sub-stance to Vasconcelos's mestizo ideal, such that "the super-vision of culture materialized in the 'total form' of the essay came to represent the distinctive attribute of the 'cosmic,' 'Latin' race" (241). This observation lucidly points to the essay as one of modernity's points of *desencuentro*, or divergence—a fragment that, in Spanish America, has acquired the symbolic shape of a social totality defined as unfinished because of its dependent position in the global economic and political order. But Ramos overstates the ease with which culture "has become" an ontology; he too quickly passes over the pro-cess through which it was "materialized" in the form of the essay. As a result, his argument has a strangely familiar ring: *La raza cósmica* and the cosmic race are one and the same; form and content coincide. In short, the cosmic race *is* an essay.

But to play the devil's advocate: how do we know *La raza cósmica* is an essay? Nowhere in the text itself is there any explicit indication of its generic affiliations, and all early editions of the travelogue simply label it *el prólogo* (prologue). True enough, its utopic subject matter overlaps with a number of other Spanish American "essays," but as Ramos himself concedes, it is atypical in its strong theoretical thrust. Of course, generic classifications are seldom unequivocal, because genre is not an empirical quality found in a single text; it rests on readers' recognition and reactivation of stylistic conventions and common themes.[21] In Fredric Jameson's description, "genres are essentially literary institutions, or social contracts between a writer and a specific public, whose function is to specify the proper use of a particular cultural artifact."[22] But who is the "specific public" in this case? *La raza cósmica* was published on the other side of the Atlantic and is addressed to readers throughout the vast and diverse region of Latin America. Concrete data on reception is hard to come by, but it seems unsafe to assume all of its readers were familiar with the conventions of the genre. The 1920s were an era of social and artistic upheaval, a period when accepted typologies were called into question and the very notion of a "public" was under pressure from new media and the expansion of literacy. In other words, it was a time when the institutions that enable shared frameworks of interpretation were under radical and contentious reconstruction—a process in which the author himself played a prominent role. Add to this the difficulty inherent in recognizing the codes of a genre defined by its idiosyncratic nature and *lack* of formal rules.

From our own vantage point, then, *La raza cósmica* might look more or less like an essay. But what if it isn't—or isn't only, or wasn't always—that?

Who Knew Vasconcelos Had Rhythm?

This question is more mystifying than it should be given that Vasconcelos himself dedicated many pages to the question of genre and form. These early writings on aesthetics have fallen out of fashion, and his other activities during the Mexican Revolution receive almost as little attention, perhaps because of the tendency to draw a sharp distinction between the military conflict (1910–1920) and a subsequent "cultural revolution" (1920–1940)—as if questions of culture were put on pause during the armed struggle and could be abstracted from the bloodshed of war. Another possible reason for the omission are judgments of the sort made by Carlos Monsiváis in an essay from 1968, at the height of the youth counterculture movement and just months before government forces fired on protestors at the Plaza de Tlatelolco: in a tone of equal parts affection and condescension, Monsiváis insists that Vasconcelos misunderstood the revolution and concludes that his only consistent quality was his "conservatism," the fact that "he detests change because it brings him close [lo aproxima] to the masses."[23] How then to explain the fact that he was one of very few intellectuals willing to jump into the revolutionary fray, and one of even fewer who aligned themselves with its most radical leaders (at least for a time)? One of the reasons Vasconcelos is a sore spot in accounts of the avant-garde is that he muddles the binaries on which narratives of transgression depend: in a strange way, he came closer to achieving an approximation between intellect and action than many avant-garde artists in Mexico did, and their own relationship to "the masses" owed a good deal to his complex role in the revolution and its aftermath.

An early and ardent supporter of Francisco Madero, the liberal reformist whose anti-reelection drive against the dictator Porfirio Díaz sparked the initial uprisings, Vasconcelos edited the campaign newspaper and—on the multiple occasions he was forced out of the country by Díaz—lobbied U.S. officials and corporate interests on Madero's behalf.[24] Yet at the end of 1914, a year after Madero's ouster and assassination, Vasconcelos turned up for the Convention of Aguascalientes, where he supported Pancho Villa in renouncing the more conservative presidential claimant Venustiano Carranza and then accepted a post as minister of public instruction in the oppositional government backed by Villa and Emiliano Zapata. The convention (and subsequent meeting of the two military leaders in Mexico City) is typically taken as the high point of the popular revolution, but Vasconcelos's authorship of its most significant theoretical statement is routinely overlooked. Dated October 29, 1914, the document is framed as a formal legal opinion defending the sovereign authority of the convention and its refusal to recognize Carranza as the executive power. Dispensing with preambles, the opening sentence defines sovereignty as the "power of the people to govern themselves according to their own will"[25]—a simple and conventional enough statement, though it raises a series of thornier questions: Who are the people, and how is their will expressed? In the midst of revolution, when the very apparatus of the state has been called on the carpet, on what basis can an individual or collective body claim the right to rule?

Unwilling to entirely forgo the sanctity of written law, Vasconcelos initially grounds his argument in an appeal to the Constitution of 1857, which affirms the right of the people to change the form of their government through means left unspecified but typically interpreted as including armed insurrection. The constitution itself, Vasconcelos points out, allows for its own temporary suspension at times when the existing government fails to comply with the principles its magna carta enshrines. Yet as Joshua Lund and Alejandro Sánchez Lopera have observed, the young lawyer quickly runs up against the limits of the liberal democratic framework he purports to uphold.[26] Just a few pages into his text, he sets the constitution aside and

turns to another, "possibly more important" justification of the right to revolution and the legitimacy of the convention—one that exists "independently
of the laws governing us."[27] Revolutions, after all, "begin by rebellion, they
place themselves immediately outside the pale of the law, they are antilegal-
ist, and therefore sovereign and free, recognizing no other overlordship than
idealism"; liberated from all social norms and united by the very experience
of struggle, the "good and the strong meet like brothers" and form assemblies
empowered by the "double right of a superhuman inspiration and of a victorious strength" (10). To put it another way, the sovereignty of the Convention
of Aguascalientes derives from a heady combination of ideas, emotions, and
guns. Or as Vasconcelos unapologetically puts it, "Revolutionary assemblies
do not mete out the justice of the textbook, but that which is imbedded [sic]
in the heart. Our fight against the landed interests could never be solved
within the legal order." All constitutions protect the existing social order, and
it is only by exceeding such strictures that the revolution can achieve its most
important objective: the expropriation of land from the latifundistas and its
redistribution among all Mexicans willing to work it. The convention must
"draw up resolutions on this point and put them into effect immediately, so
that all the reforms thus brought about may be accomplished facts before the
legally constituted congresses of the governments succeeding the Convention
can labor against the national interests" (15).

Even among the factions joined in opposition to Carranza, the Zapatistas'
demands for radical agrarian reform were a bone of contention, and it would
be hard to find a similar document from this period that pulls so few punches.
Vasconcelos gently chides the martyred Madero and others for limiting their
goal to a transformation of the political system and failing to recognize the
priority of the revolution's economic imperative—a necessarily violent process of redistributive justice that can and only ever could occur *outside* the
limits of the law. Much as the conservative jurist Carl Schmitt would do a few
years later in Weimar Germany, Vasconcelos defines sovereignty as the power
to suspend the legal order, or to declare a state of exception; in contrast to
Schmitt, however, he refuses to grant this right to any individual leader, and
he identifies the enemy of "national interests" as the *state*. Only a revolutionary assembly such as the convention can exercise the sovereignty of a people
that exists by virtue of having cast off the shackles of government, forcibly
taken possession of the land, and "hurl[ed] themselves against everything
which has restrained the infinite longing which each soul carries within him,
haughty and victorious" (9). For all the idealism at work here, it is also a
hard-nosed acknowledgment that any subsequent legally elected government
would work against the interests of popular sovereignty: barring a revolution
on an international scale (a possibility Vasconcelos never entertains), even a
regime with the most egalitarian pretensions would have to reckon with the
threat of U.S. invasion and the exigencies of imperialist capital. Thus just
as Schmitt compares the exception to the miracle, an event impossible to

rationalize or accord with the rules of reality, Vasconcelos describes it as an almost otherworldly, mystic experience.[28]

In fact, Vasconcelos and Villa (both notoriously contentious) quickly butted heads, and the coalition between Villa and Zapata collapsed within months: exercising sovereign power at the national level seems to have held little appeal for the two regional leaders, who were probably all too aware of the contradiction Vasconcelos had signaled in his text.[29] After two more years of warfare Carranza retook the presidency, and although the Constitution of 1917 made history for its guarantee of basic "social" rights, he resisted implementing its provisions on land reform and labor. Villa was increasingly marginalized, and while Zapata and his followers carried out appropriations of land and sugar mills in Morelos (as well as an experiment in communal self-government), he was killed in an ambush in 1919. Meanwhile Vasconcelos stayed far from the fray. During five years of exile he did a stint teaching English in Peru and hopped from one U.S. city to another, watching on as his vision of the convention as a utopic resolution of revolution and governance grew ever more remote. Cut off from any direct ties to popular struggles, he made a seeming 180-degree turn toward the "aesthetic"—though a similar preoccupation with laws and their limits riddles his writings from these years.

Francisco Madero had mixed his politics with a heavy dose of spiritualism and claimed to have begun his campaign against Porfirio Díaz at the behest of the dead president Benito Juárez; Vasconcelos was skeptical of séances, but he shared his idol's esoteric inclinations as well as his interest in Indian philosophy and modern-day Theosophy, an international movement that sought to synthesize new scientific findings with Hindu and Buddhist concepts of karma, reincarnation, and a seven-stage process of "cosmic evolution."[30] The itinerant exile ran with this mystic streak in *Pitágoras: Una teoría del ritmo*, an essay—identified as such in the opening line—written in New York and published in Havana in 1916.[31] One of the most mysterious of the pre-Socratic philosophers, in part because he refused to commit his ideas to writing, Pythagoras was credited with discovering the laws of harmony and developing a theory of the universe according to which the movement of celestial bodies corresponds to mathematical equations and produces a "music of the spheres." This synthesis of music and math, along with his reputation as a revered pedagogue, made him an enticing model for turn-of-the-century artists and writers—including many Spanish American modernistas—who were resistant to the growing specialization and segmentation of knowledge and experience.[32] Pythagorean principles are also encoded in Diego Rivera's *La Creación*, commonly considered the inaugural work of the muralist movement and read as an allegory of the cosmic race. The mural was unveiled on March 20, 1923, at a ceremony presided over by Vasconcelos and marked with a speech by Manuel Maples Arce, a young poet who had started to make a name for himself as the leader of an avant-garde group known as *estridentismo* and who took the occasion to hurl insults at

defenders of impressionism before declaring the National School of Fine Arts
a "brothel of pictorial art."[33]

The earliest textual evidence of Pythagoras's teachings dates from centuries after his death, and later commentaries inevitably involve a large dose
of speculation. This suited Vasconcelos just fine, since it allowed him to offer
a novel "interpretation" of the Greek's system as governed not so much by
harmony as by the kinetic principle of rhythm. As a prelude he outlines two
distinct and opposing ways of understanding the world: one "objective, ana-
lytic, intellectual, in a word, scientific," and the other "synthetic, what has
been called intuitive but is rather the aesthetic perception of things."[34] Plato
and others after him aligned Pythagoras with the first worldview by overem-
phasizing the mathematical factor in his correlation of harmonic intervals
with numerical ratios. But the conceptual distinction between form and matter (insists Vasconcelos) was not yet established in Pythagoras's time, and
when the cult leader pointed to numbers as the essence of all things, he was
really just using the notion of the "number" as a symbol for the phenomenon
of rhythm, or a movement that was "regular" (acompasado) but at the same
time "indefinite" and irreducible to abstract formulas. In fact, this was surely
the "lost secret" of all the Greek mysteries, or esoteric schools: everything
in the universe, independent of any perceptible motions it may make, has
the capacity to vibrate in tandem with "our intimate tendencies" and "our
essence of beauty" (7). Pythagoras spoke about cosmic "harmony," but he
must have intuited that harmony and pitch are first and foremost a function
of rhythmic vibrations—a point confirmed by modern physicists such as Hermann von Helmholtz, whose landmark Die Lehre von den Tonempfindungen
(On the Sensations of Tone, 1865) proposed a theory of hearing based on
"cochlear resonance," or the hypothesis that microscopic structures in the ear
similar to the strings of a piano vibrate in accordance with the frequencies of
incoming sound.

This appeal to the findings of physiological acoustics muddies the schematic opposition between scientific and aesthetic worldviews, setting up a
tension similar to the one rippling through the author's earlier argument
about sovereignty and revolution. As Veit Erlmann has argued, Helmholtz's
neo-Kantian attempt to reconcile an empirical approach to the physics of
hearing with a transcendental epistemology was symptomatic of an ongoing crisis of rationality in which the ear became a pivotal site for wrestling
with agency and what it meant to "know." Sympathetic resonance was an
observable phenomenon (at least in its effects), yet it destabilized the distinction between subject and object fundamental to the very premise of reason.
According to Erlmann, Helmholtz's revisions to his theory over the course
of several editions of his book were related to his struggle to circumvent an
entrenched dualism between the "objective" or "physical" mechanics of sensation and the "subjective" or "psychic" element of perception—a problem
also tied to his conception of music history and an overarching theory of

knowledge. Like earlier thinkers drawn to the idea of resonance, his work pointed to the "ear as a form of embodied knowledge, as something we think with" while revealing the "deep interpenetration of fact and value, objectivity and affect, and most of all—science and music."[35]

Ever the synthesizer, Vasconcelos opts to assimilate resonance into rhythm, an equally evocative and even fuzzier concept that was in the midst of a decades-long surge in popularity. As the critic Michael Golston points out in his work on modernist poets such as Ezra Pound and W. B. Yeats, much of the fascination and anxiety surrounding rhythm had to do with its strange ability to stand as the epitome of the organic while also seeming uncannily mechanical.[36] The rhythms of the body—of circulation, the beating of the heart, and respiration—were said to work in sync with the changes of the seasons and other movements of the natural world; yet Georg Simmel warned that new technologies were altering the age-old rhythms that once formed the basis of communal life,[37] and others attempted to harness the power of rhythm, whether to cure the body of its modern ails or to optimize the exploitation of industrial labor.[38] Such concerns were often bound up in ideas about race: as Vasconcelos surely knew, the notion of rhythmic motions propelled by antagonistic forces was integral to the social evolutionism of Herbert Spencer, and Nietzsche opined that each language was distinguished by its unique tempo, which had its basis in the physiological "metabolism" of the race.[39] Émile Jaques-Dalcroze, a closer contemporary, invoked the trauma of World War I in presenting his pedagogical program of eurythmics, which trained children in carefully controlled movements and dance. For Dalcroze, differences of climate, custom, and history had fostered a distinct "rhythmic sense" in each group of people, leading him to propose the segregation of eurythmics centers by ethnicity on the grounds that the "reduction of racial temperaments to a common level would be disastrous for the intellectual level of humanity."[40] At his Hellerau Institute near Dresden, Dalcroze welcomed musicians and artists, who offered performances at a "festival theater" constructed by Adolphe Appia, the Swiss stage designer known for his mises-en-scène of Wagner.[41] Among Dalcroze's enthusiasts was Samuel Chávez, an architect who trained at the Hellerau Institute and on his return to Mexico in 1921 was encouraged to introduce "rhythmic gymnastics" into the curriculum of the public schools, where it became essential to the students' training for the festivals and mass spectacles that were a hallmark of Vasconcelos's program.[42]

Vasconcelos doesn't cite any of these ideas (though he does quote Nietzsche on music), and there is not a word about race in *Pitágoras*. His priority in this text is simply to establish that an ability to tune into good vibrations allows certain special individuals to transform not just minds or even souls, but also flesh and blood. Pythagoras may have been the leader of a secretive cult, and his rarefied ideas about the cosmos might seem distant from everyday concerns, but just as rhythm (like resonance) bridges the divide between body and mind, it can also connect inspired geniuses to the common folk, allowing philosophers today as in the past to overcome the demagogy of "those who fear the masses listening to the voice of the sincere thinker [*pensador*]." Who exactly the modern-day demagogues are is unclear, but a vague allusion to "legislative abuses" tenuously links the author's push to supersede the limits of reason and the individual subject to his earlier struggle to transcend the constraints of liberal democracy. Mystics, he suggests, are the "laborers of thought" (*los obreros del pensamiento*), and while "the collective factor in mental labor is indeterminable," it is also undeniable, if only because thought—as a form of rhythm—is "contagious." It is also intensely physical, so Pythagoras and his followers engaged in "collective exercises, music, and dances" in order to beautify their bodies and prime them for the process of "contemplation"—a woefully inadequate word given that what they were doing was nothing less than tapping into *el ritmo de lo real*, or "the rhythm of the real" (38). If the basic building blocks are atoms, which are made up of electrically charged, moving particles, then rhythm is both the substance and spirit of matter—and this in turn is proof of Henri Bergson's notion of a shared *élan vital*, or vital force immanent in all organisms.[43] In short, rhythm acts as a conduit between our consciousness and the material world, and "music teaches us the secret of art, which consists of freeing matter from the empire of necessity, and imprinting on it, in contemplation, a movement of irregular rhythm, the inverse of that which natural mechanics imposes on it" (45).

Clearly the still-incipient development of quantum mechanics is mixed up in all this, and some of it might not sound so strange today in light of the recent resurgence of vitalist ideas, including those of Bergson: although the "new" materialists (such as Jane Bennett, who writes of "vibrant matter") generally emphasize the agency of things over people while Vasconcelos does the inverse (at least here), their mutual destabilization of the boundaries of the human means that this very distinction tends to break down.[44] But a grumpier sort of materialist might feel compelled to ask: what is all this mystical business about "rhythms" and "vibrations" actually about? Golston points out that the ability of rhythm to mean almost anything and its opposite makes it the "ideal ideological cipher, since it can so easily *signify*."[45] This is a tempting explanation given the subsequent fate of Vasconcelos and his larger-than-life idea, yet it assumes there was already something there to cipher. At no point during his time in government or even long after did Vasconcelos ever retract his views on the need for a radical redistribution of resources, and considering his warning about the limitations of any postrevolutionary government, it is hardly a surprise that his relationship with the Obregón regime was always tense. Far better than any of his peers in the budding intelligentsia, and far better than a lot of his later critics, he saw the paradox in which his own identity as an intellectual was enmeshed. The revolutionary assembly had afforded a momentary solution by enabling his vision of an exceptional form of sovereignty, a law unbeholden to the unjust social system. In his text on Pythagoras he turns to the "irregular rhythm" of aesthetics as another way of imagining the exception, another way of imagining collective power, and another way of imagining the material world as capable of change. Conveniently, of course, the key to making things move is the philosopher, who "interprets the whole" and thus acts an *artista en grande*—an artist on a large scale (40).

Vasconcelos had a thing for tragedy, and his own fatal flaw was his inability to see politics in terms other than those of national sovereignty. Yet as in Greek tragedy, his *hamartia* was not simply a subjective failing but also in part the result of objective forces and constraints (i.e., "the gods"). In *El monismo estético* (1918), a series of three essays—again identified as such in the first line—some of these real-world pressures begin to surface and his ethereal argument about rhythm acquires more (literary) shape. He starts out in the introduction on a familiar note, explaining that what follows should be taken as preliminary remarks meant to "prepare the path" for a system of aesthetic metaphysics that will someday supplant dialectical reasoning with a form of cognition based on a Kantian "intuition of synthesis."[46] He also devotes several long paragraphs to his future plans for a series of essays inspired by Nietzsche's book on the birth of tragedy, which will address the topics of evil and irony, "auditory mysticism," and dance. The overriding concern in this book, however, is literary genre and form. The volume's first essay, on the "symphony as a literary form," follows the evolution of philosophical genres through time, starting with the epic poetry of the Greeks, from which the dialogue and the discourse are "born." The author soldiers on through the medieval treatise, and eventually all the way up to the very genre in which his own thoughts are expressed—at which point he suddenly emerges as his own antagonist.

Yes, it is true: the man known as the author of a famous essay *hated* the essay genre. Vasconcelos scorns it for all the same reasons its defenders are wont to cite: it is an "incomplete," "pluralist" form that "neither obeys rules nor proposes to create them," a genre "marred by mediocrity" that merely expresses personal opinions or critique without proposing to construct a system of its own (24–25). He concedes that a few exceptional essays (ahem, ahem) manage to exploit their "formal indetermination" to open up new avenues toward a "total vision," but as a rule, he says, "the essay is nothing but a transitory genre, from which it becomes necessary to liberate ourselves" (24). If it sounds like something more than stylistic niceties are at stake here, sure enough—it turns out the essay is also the favored form of "the English, empiricist, evolutionist school" whose "minor brains" lack the ability to establish "fundamental principles" (3–4). For all its humble appearances, it is an agent of oppression, a vehicle for a discourse of biological racism that consigns Latin America to the primeval past and an incomplete form that imposes the worldview of an "anti-mystic, anti-heroic, and anti-religious race of businessmen" (12). This pernicious influence is the bête noire against which the Mexican writer conceives his own system of "totalist thought, intoxicated by an infinite, mystic essence" (5). Vasconcelos extols lyric, tragedy, and the Platonic dialogues (insisting that Plato was a Pythagorean despite his claims to the contrary), yet rather than advocating a return to any of these forms, he proclaims that today's "modern mystics" are on the verge of creating an entirely new one—the "literary symphony," which will do in writing what Beethoven's Fifth (a "modern tragedy") does with music. Philosophers should act like composers and "arrange ideas like orchestral themes, developing them through endless paths and profound analogies" (39). As examples of works that have begun to hew this road, he cites Bergson's *Matter and Memory*, Nietzsche's *Thus Spoke Zarathustra*, and Ibsen's *Peer Gynt*—an unorthodox "essay on the relation of body and spirit," a philosophical parable "for all and none," and a fantastical play originally written to be read rather than performed onstage.[47]

What do these examples have in common? For one, all three are generic oddballs; second, all call into question the ability of the human form to serve as a stable medium of signification. Vasconcelos's "aesthetic monism" seeks a new mode of thought as well as a new mode of expression, a genre that subsumes all those currently existing in order to surpass the limitations of form. Yet these dual objectives also imply a third: the task of creating new bodies. "Within a profoundly biotic sense," the author proclaims, his notion of the aesthetic "reforms the law of sensation, replacing its practical sense with one that is disinterested and aesthetic" (43). Physiology. Knowledge. The work of art. Where does the connection lie? As his musical model suggests, rhythm once again provides the key. Recapping his argument from *Pitágoras*, the author states that an imperceptible "energy" lies latent in the physical world, waiting to be stimulated into action by the rhythm of consciousness. The task of his literary symphony is to make things "move in unison with the spirit"—or, extrapolating just a bit, to create a shared experience of the aesthetic that alters the vibrations of individuals' electrons and atoms, bringing all men into "biotic" accord (18). The final text in *El monismo estético*, titled "The Mystic Synthesis," is presented as a first attempt at enacting these ideas, though Vasconcelos coyly admits that his transcendence of generic conventions remains incomplete ("Perhaps this is an *ensayo* for a literary symphony"). It makes a strenuous effort to meld religions and aesthetics, to augur the existence of a "Jesus Christ Buddha" that would "exceed the human form" (100), but it never frees itself from the imperative of logical argumentation. Far from mystical, it is the most lackluster text in the book.

The language of race, the obsession with synthesis, the cosmic debris: enough of the key elements are there to surmise that the cosmic ("synthetic") race will be born not through acts of sexual miscegenation, but through a mixture of genres that sets all bodies vibrating on the same frequency. Lest we rush ahead of history, however, it is important to insist that this is not exactly "ideology." As Louis Althusser argued, "Ideology has a material existence"—it is as much a matter of institutions, apparatuses, and bodily practices as of ideas.[48] In his example of a person on the street who is hailed by a policeman ("Hey, you there!"), the interpellation of the subject takes place by means of a "one-hundred-eighty-degree physical conversion," or the *almost* automatic motion of turning to face the voice (118).[49] Martin Harries points out that Althusser highlights the theatricality of his own example, referring to it as a *"mise en scène"* and "my little theoretical theater."[50] This imaginary stage is what enables Althusser to narrativize a process he emphasizes has always already taken place *in* ideology and *outside* time, since "ideology has no history."[51] As Harries explains, "Such a translation from unthought, timeless ideology into aesthetic medium is necessary in order to recognize how ideology works: the model of the theater makes it possible to imagine in temporal sequence something that does not belong to the order of time at all."[52]

Vasconcelos, of course, was coming at things from a different angle, and not only because the voice in his scenario was that of the philosopher rather than the police. Written in exile, in the middle of a decade-long revolution when most of the state apparatuses Althusser refers to were not in place, these early writings can be seen as attempts to imagine how ideology works, in ways remarkably consonant with Althusser's observations. The Pythagorean rituals, the model of aural interpellation, the inseparability of thought from the body: even Vasconcelos's attraction to experimental physics resonates with Althusser's broader struggle to redefine the relationship between science and philosophy. And so it is perhaps no coincidence that just two years after his text on aesthetic monism, Vasconcelos too would construct his own "little theoretical theater."

Cosmic Upsets and Promethean Failures

José Vasconcelos wrote his first play sometime around 1918 while in the seaside city of San Diego, California. As he tells it in a brief foreword, he started out writing an essay on the subject of evil and irony—part of the series of projected works inspired by Nietzsche that had been announced in the introduction to *El monismo estético*. For some reason, the essay simply wasn't working. So the future cultural caudillo wrote, rewrote, and changed course several times until he came up with a "modern tragedy" about an anti-imperialist prophet who exhorts his followers to shun procreation in preparation for the advent of an "aesthetic" era. His mea culpa: "I must acknowledge that I set about doing one thing and ended up with something else."[53] This struggle with form has to do with the fact that he "deviated" a bit from the question of evil in order to put forth a tentative "doctrine" that his cohorts had previously dismissed as too *tétrico* ("gloomy," "pessimistic," or "funereal"). Once he presents his embryonic idea in this new guise, he wagers, even the skeptics will concede that it possesses "enormous possibilities of beauty" (6). Though it may fail to meet the demands of discursive thought, it is justified by its potential as an aesthetic phenomenon.

Seventy years later *Prometeo vencedor* is still waiting for its day to dawn. It is hardly a surprise that the book had few readers when it was first published in Mexico back in 1920—after all, the country's infrastructure was a mess after a decade of war, and all those libraries, schools, and journals Vasconcelos would go on to create were still just hazy ideas. But in the voluminous pages of criticism devoted to extolling, decrying, and deconstructing his legacy, this strange relic of the revolution receives little more than the occasional footnote, the odd sentence tacked onto the end of a paragraph as an afterthought that acknowledges, "Ah yes, and he also wrote that unfortunate play."[54] Indeed, even the most open-minded reader is likely to wonder how a paean to beauty and idealism could go so awry. Suffice it to say that the play's most enduring legacy is having served as the ironic inspiration for Renato Leduc's *Prometeo sifilítico*, a scabrous masterpiece of obscene antipoetry in which the Greek hero's crime against the gods is not stealing fire, but revealing the divine secrets of sexual innovation to humanity, whose carnal knowledge has failed to progress from the dark ages of the missionary position. (Rather than being tied to a rock and having his liver eaten every day by an eagle, he is punished with syphilis and castration.) If Vasconcelos had only known, maybe he would have stuck with that essay after all.

The abandoned origins of *Prometeo vencedor* still haunt it in the form of a lengthy prose "prologue" appended to the dramatic text. Like his future, far more famous prologue-cum-essay, this prologue to a play that could/would have been an essay sets itself the distinctly unessayistic task of telling the entirety of world history. The text begins by describing a pre-ethical phase of human development—the material, or warrior stage, if *La raza cósmica*'s schema is projected back onto this text, the first line of which announces with pseudo-biblical pomp: "Happily wanders the beast, ignorant of pain."[55] Humans, meanwhile, are lowlier than beasts because although they possess consciousness, they do nothing to alter the injustice they suffer under an unnamed Tyrant. Prometheus steps in to "initiate the order of will over the order of necessity" (10), but after two brief paragraphs he is shuttled off the page and immediately eclipsed by a more intriguing icon of rebellion: Satan. In a strange blend of everyday language and philosophical cant, the text recounts the devil's fall from grace, relays his unsatisfactory encounter with a Tiger (the King of Beasts), and justifies his decision to align himself with death as a means of spurring humans out of their renewed complacency. Adding to the odd mix of registers and cultural referents is a subtle slippage in pronouns, so that by the last few pages phrases such as "*Satan* observed" and "*he* climbed Olympus" have given way to "*I* rest," "*I* meditate," and "*I* was in the valleys of the Ganges." A voice that is identified as the Devil's but might also be the author's breezily ponders the problem of evil, scoffs at imperialist tyrants, and so on, until the storyline with its fictional figures fades away entirely and for long stretches it seems as though the text we are reading is not the prologue to a play but a—well, an essay.

This awkward allegory is no centaur, however. Humans may be shown lapsing into bovine existence, but the goal is to transcend man's creaturely half, not domesticate it. Culture is neither an extension of nature nor its double but rather its antithesis, and at this point, after years of warfare in Mexico and a world "war to end all wars," there is no illusion it already exists. Just a few years later, Vasconcelos would espouse similar notions in a text that, though eccentric, looks enough like a Spanish American essay to be widely (mis)taken for one, but his earlier prologue is clearly uncomfortable in its own skin. Narrative passages sit uneasily alongside essay-like ruminations, the colloquial tone jars with the universalizing intent, and the author's voice never fully emerges from behind its satanic mask. Given his prefatory commentary on the play's origins, its incomplete identity with the essay genre is surely part of its point. It is as if the prologue were meant to exemplify the struggle through which its own ideas sought to free themselves from the essay's morass, as if generic conventions were akin to theoretical concepts and their interplay was itself a kind of argument.

So it is that Satanás, convinced by neither angels nor beasts, decides to join forces with his Greek counterpart and search for "vigor" and "audacity" among men (15). The final paragraph slips back into narrative mode as he surveys the landscape and spots a shooting star whose tail, pointing toward earth, "signals in the direction of Egypt, in the direction of Judea!" (21). He hits the dusty trail, and when the reader turns the page the prologue has given way to a stage and the sight of the Promised Land: not Judea, but the peaks of the mountain chain that joins the volcanoes Popocatepetl and Ixtaccihuatl, with a view of Puebla in one direction and Mexico City in the other. Prometheus sits on a rock, "with his fist under his chin, in the pose of Rodin's thinker and maintaining, to the extent possible, his robust pagan nudity"; by his side is Satan, "with the angular figure the legend has bestowed on him" (23).

The stage is thus set for the events that will usher in a realm beyond good and evil. Yet in keeping with its speculative nature, the bizarre plot about to unfold hardly seems designed to play out on a "material" stage: there is nothing to suggest that Vasconcelos ever desired to see *Prometeo vencedor* performed, and the nondramatic prologue is itself a sign that this is a drama for readers, not a script to be represented by actors for a theatrical audience. The obvious model in this opening scene is Plato's Socratic dialogues—a genre central to Nietzsche's account of the death and rebirth of tragedy. Although Vasconcelos remains strangely mum on the relation in his own genealogy of genres, the Platonic (and Socratic) antagonism toward the flowering of tragedy and comedy that accompanied the rise of democracy in Athens is hard to overlook. Nietzsche lambasts the dialectical logic of

Socrates as the antithesis of the Dionysian spirit of tragedy; at the same time, he grudgingly concedes, Plato's dialogues were the "ark" on which poetry survived in an increasingly rational age. Like tragedy before it, the dialogue was created by "mixing all available styles and forms together so that it hovers somewhere midway between narrative, lyric, and drama."[56] Not only is the dialogue itself a quasi-theatrical form, but Socrates frequently builds his arguments around examples drawn from particular plays. Indeed, the dialogues as a whole subtly parody, revise, and/or overturn a number of tragic and comic conventions. As Andrea Wilson Nightingale argues, "When Plato constructed the specialized discipline of philosophy . . . he did not sequester it. Rather, he staged an ongoing dialogue between philosophy and its 'others.' "[57] To put it another way: the father of philosophy elaborates his theory of ideal forms by at once indulging and disavowing what Nightingale calls a "hankering for the hybrid" (2).

Prometeo vencedor is less bashful in engulfing the dialogue in its own generic blend, and it quickly outstrips its more sedentary predecessor with its elaborate plot, settings, and cast of characters. Among all its other affiliations (modern tragedy, literary symphony, post-Platonic postdialogue), Vasconcelos's text is also *sort of* a closet drama, a term often employed by critics for dramatic texts meant to be read rather than staged. Here again he is working from some obvious (if unacknowledged) models. With all the other metaliterary allusions in this play it is hard not to see its Mephistophelian Satanás and triumphant Prometeo as attempts to one-up Goethe's *Faust* and Shelley's *Prometheus Unbound*, two of the numerous closet dramas by Romantics that put pressure on the Platonic ideal by bringing its dependence on the dramatic to light. Scholars often smile at the derivative, old-fashioned air of Vasconcelos's aesthetics, and his turn to this arcane genre could be seen in such a light; yet the recent renaissance in the study of closet dramas offers reasons for seeing it as a modern(ist) move. As Martin Puchner has pointed out, Mallarmé sought to create his own "total" genre, a goal he pursued in his "theater-book" *Livre* and his poetic dramas *Hérodiade* and *Igitur*. Later figures such as T. S. Eliot, Gertrude Stein, and Ezra Pound would also write awkward plays often classified as closet dramas (even if some were actually staged) because of either a *lack* or *excess* of action that defies what can convincingly be performed. Puchner traces this modernist suspicion of embodied mimesis and the public aspect of art back to Plato, even as he also positions it as a countercurrent to the "total theatricality" championed by the avant-garde and a textual bulwark against new forms of mass spectacle. In his words, the "resistance to the theater also produces a theater, one that breaks apart the human figure and rebels against the mimetic confines of a stage and theatrical action."[58]

Not unlike the essay, the modernist closet drama establishes its autonomy as a textually mediated mode of performativity. As with the essay, however, *Prometeo vencedor*'s formal convergence with the (anti)tradition of the closet drama also marks a discrepancy in social function. Like Plato, Vasconcelos defined himself as a philosopher; like Shelley or Mallarmé, he was also a writer. At the same time, he was an intellectual who had served as a scribe for the leaders of a revolutionary army and was already looking ahead to the possibility of establishing a new cultural order founded on the principle of mass education. He would deliver speeches on aesthetics before audiences in the thousands, build a sixty-thousand-seat "stadium theater" to serve as the stage for mass ballets and political spectacles, and promote the "art of the future" as the only antidote to economic imperialism. *Prometeo vencedor*'s resistance to the "mimetic confines of a stage" also produces a theater, but it is one with a far more instrumental intent.

As is clear from the opening tableau of Prometeo and his satanic sidekick looking down on humanity from their mountainous perch, this modern trag-edy will not be an exact replay of the old defy-the-gods-and-suffer-for-eternity routine. In *The Birth of Tragedy*, Nietzsche invokes Aeschylus's Prometheus as the archetypal tragic hero, a figure born of the struggle between Apol-lonian representation and its Dionysian dismemberment. Like the art of tragedy itself, Prometheus is a redemptive illusion, a constructive force driven by a desire for justice, yet he is ultimately a mask for Dionysius, essence of the primordial unity, god of music and all that eludes figuration.[59] Prometheus is the ideal protagonist of the impossible theater Nietzsche desires—in the words of Puchner, a "theater without representation, actors, and beholders, the hallucination of an invisible theater that isn't one."[60] Inevitably, he has to undergo a transformation in his transposition back to the stage, purely textual though it may be. Vasconcelos's Prometeo is no longer the suffering Dionysian martyr; rather, he is a victorious hero and the perfect picture of Apollonian repose, likened to a sculpture (the sun god's signature art) that is also an oft-parodied image of philosophical (non)activity. The rebel has become a respected member of the classical canon—indeed, the sly instruc-tion that he should "conserve as much as possible his robust pagan nudity" points to his conformity with the conventional mores that circumscribe what can be shown even on a virtual stage (23).

Prometheus triumphs. And then? The tragic hero and mythic maker of men, the West's symbol of knowledge, creativity, and technological progress, loses the ability to embody the eternal contradiction at the heart of the world, and another element is required to set the dialectic in motion again. This is the role of Satanás, the inveterate naysayer who is defined by what he is not, a figure described as a shadow and a "murky liquid"—a demonic character who, were the play ever performed, might prompt the use of cinematic pro-jections or some other technological media. In truth, Satanás only exists *as* mediation: his modus operandi is irony, the product of an incongruity or gap between literal meaning and intent, and so he has no ideal form. Yet he *does* have a genre. Throughout the play, he invokes comedic forms from the Span-ish tradition: "minor" genres such as the theatrical *sainete*, which operate

according to a logic other than that of artistic autonomy. One character calls
him an "old *pícaro*"—the roguish protagonist of a picaresque narrative—and
another a "devil from a *pastorela*"—shepherd's plays that live on in the realm
of Mexican popular performance. Nearly the entire first act consists of long
colloquies in which the two icons of iconoclasm debate the merits of their
philosophical and stylistic predilections:

> PROMETEO: Pleasure is sterile. Suffering is fecund, because it forces
> one to be grave, to struggle and discover power.
> SATANÁS: Have you tried irony?
> PROMETEO: You're the prince of irony, I know, but irony is incapable
> of building anything. However, irony does serve to denounce our
> shady intentions and draw us away from incomplete ideals and
> false gods.

> PROMETEO: El goce es estéril. El sufrimiento es fecundo, porque
> obliga a ser grave, a luchar y a descubrir poder.
> SATANÁS: ¿Has probado la ironía?
> PROMETEO: Sé que tú eres el príncipe de la ironía, pero la ironía es
> incapaz de construir. Sin embargo, la ironía sirve para denun-
> ciar nuestros propósitos turbios, y para apartarnos de los ideales
> incompletos y de los dioses falsos. (26)

Prometeo's analysis of irony as an inferior force that de(con)structs
without constructing any principles of its own is clearly a judgment on the
comedic modes of satire and parody, which rely on imitation and are therefore bound to what they critique. At the same time, it echoes the author's own
description of the essay, that "incomplete" form cultivated by a race whose
"minor brains" and disinclination for "fundamental principles" were also
to blame for George Bernard Shaw and J. M. Barrie—both exponents of an
abominable form of *humor a la inglesa* that "brings ideals down to the level
of buffoons."[61] Vasconcelos's commentary on English humor is only a brief
aside, but it is worth recalling that Adorno describes the essay's tendency to
"devour" ideal theories as parodic; devoted to critique rather than creation,
"the essay does not in fact come to a conclusion and displays its own inability
to do so as a parody of its own a priori."[62] Vasconcelos sought to transform
Latin America into a creative principle, the privileged bearer of universality—
everything the essay is not. Yet the essay is the necessary foil for his literary
symphony, the fragmentary medium through which he projects his own invisible ideal, and in a similar way, his essay-that-becomes-a-tragedy has to pass
through parody. *Prometeo vencedor* can't simply assume the mantle of the
tragic tradition at the outset because its own tragedy is an endpoint, a goal it
hopes to achieve in overcoming this tradition while taking it to a higher—and
bigger—stage. The play allegorizes the aesthetic and objectifies the privileged

symbols of Western culture, exposing them as historical constructs that are no longer and not yet universal, and this incomplete totality, this gap, is the shaky ground on which it founds its own claim to the tragic legacy. Prometeo needs Satanás; in a relation reminiscent of Nietzsche's *Thus Spoke Zarathustra*, one of the inspirations Vasconcelos cites for his play, the tragic ideal and the ironic *ensayo* are not enemies but intimate accomplices.

In fact, only after their tête-à-tête can the play begin to articulate its own nascent "theory." When a noise resembling the vibration of a telegraph interrupts the dialogue, Prometeo explains to a quizzical Satanás that he has received a message via a system of mental communication "more perfect than any device"—impulses of energy shared by those of a like nature, "as the vibrations of a similar order [*un orden afín*] join together in an orchestra: violins with violins, brass instruments with brass instruments, to form phrases and themes" (39). Pythagorean rhythms are clearly in play here, as is a more general association between spiritualist practices and new technologies such as telegraphy.[63] As Vasconcelos stresses in his essay, Pythagoras himself was a believer in metempsychosis, and if souls can transmigrate from one body to another, the literal transference of thoughts should be a simple operation. In this scene, the triumphant hero already resides in the realm of the aesthetic; he already thinks as part of a symphony. Now the task is to extend this community beyond mythic figures and a few mortal mystics to include all men, to generate a genre of thought that the scene encourages us to envision as mass communication with no external mediating device. As if on cue, "a shadow appears, which is at first tenuous and then becomes clearer until its outlines are precise and meld into those of a man in everyday attire" (40). It is a recently defunct Philosopher of the Earth, passing by en route to the afterlife to spread the word: the world war spelled the end of an era, and in the future "empires will not be formed by the sword or commerce but by taste and sympathy," while "nationalisms, which are the work of politics, will gave way to pan-ethnicisms," collectivities organized by languages (44–45). Spanish America, the world's melting pot, is the natural epicenter of this movement: "The men of all races who have gathered there speak of forming a new humanity with what is best of every culture, harmonized and ennobled within the Spanish mold" (41).

This cameo appearance by the Everyman is the only moment in the plot when the play acknowledges its own historical stage, the only thread that ties its philosophical banter and prophetic visions to an identity claim. The Philosopher's predictions are short on details, and some of the details differ (Vasconcelos had not yet been to Brazil or concocted Universópolis), but he already has the gist of the idea that would become the cosmic race. What is missing is the unifying figure. Spoken by a dead man who materializes out of thin air, a feat impossible to perform on the material stage in which humanity is stuck, these words aren't mediated by the authorial voice and incipient institutional apparatus that would shape *La raza cósmica* into what some now perceive as an essay. Their only grounds of justification are the future. The Promethean task of this tragedy over the next two acts will be to bear them out in the mimetic mode—to create the beautiful illusion. First, however, the Philosopher has to contend with Satanás, who mocks the man as naive and asks: How could the future of freedom lie in Spanish America, where "run-of-the-mill despots" (*los déspotas más ramplones*) rule? The scene nearly devolves into an absurd fistfight when the diabolic jester likens the dreamer to an "ape recently come down [*descolgado*] from the tropical forest," evidence that the devil is in cahoots with the English, evolutionist essayists (42).

But in fact, this scene suggests an affinity between Satanás and the phenomenon known as *relajo*, a form of mocking, frequently physical, and sometimes violent humor that is regarded as peculiarly Mexican. Like a similar mode of Cuban humor called *choteo*, *relajo* had become an object of intellectual interest by the late 1920s and early 1930s and was often depicted in ambivalent terms, as a kind of ironic comedy endowed with a critical value but ultimately dependent on what it critiqued and innately hostile to the construction of autonomous ideals.[64] In pseudo-Socratic fashion, Satanás reminds the idealist of the political obstacles that relegate his vision to the realm of fancy, even as he exposes the political dimension of the play's effort to enthrone art as an ideal. Vasconcelos already knew that foundational acts are messy—they always play out on the political stage. Furthermore, unlike most modernist closet dramas, *Prometeo vencedor* is driven by the irreducibly political desire to claim aesthetics as an agent of anti-imperialism. As a consequence, its own autonomy can only be a precarious illusion, which the play registers through the figure of Satanás. It then goes on to prefigure his defeat by excluding all trace of politics from the space of representation. When the second act opens, Satanás has dropped out of the picture, and the rough-hewn naturalism of Rodin has given way to a stylized forest scene, with characters "richly dressed according to the style of Botticelli's *Primavera*. At the same time, there should be details of the most refined *modernismo*, as the action takes place in a future thousands of years from now" (46).

Presumably, this is it: the aesthetic era, when nature is remade in the image of art and the artistic styles of the past are recapitulated as reality. It could in fact be the poetic world of Mallarmé or Rubén Darío: the scene begins with a choir of nymphs who entice Prometeo (now flying solo) with a siren song that touts the advantages of being beautiful but barren. Nowhere else in the play is race linked to phenotype, but these lovely ladies wax poetic about their skin tones, all shades of white: "We are white like the clearest marble . . . Others of us are white with a bluish tint, whiter than the white of a blond woman and more provocative . . . Others of us have been burnished by the sun's golden rays" (47). Evidently some cosmic mixing has occurred through acts of aesthetic gratification, though indigenous cultures must have been consigned to the sphere of nature, just as they are excluded from the play's own generic blend. Stage directions describe Dionysian choirs and dances that look oddly like the mass choirs and dances the author would later organize as secretary of public education—performances that sought to create a "new artistic genre" in which the thousands of participants would be "at the same time, spectators and actors," a fusion that would signal "the triumph of our race."[65] A prophet named Saturnino, a more advanced incarnation of the Philosopher, descends in an airplane and addresses the masses, just like the globetrotting pedagogues of *La raza cósmica*. He recaps the history of how this marvelous new world came to be—the political stage readers were not allowed to see—and urges his people to remain strong in their will to defeat materiality, to deny the instinct that compels procreation and become a truly universal race. Not through force, not through violence—rather, "the resolution of abstinence must well up from the depths of love [or "wanting," *de lo hondo del querer*]" (61).[66] (Vasconcelos frequently associated aesthetic creation with the refusal of biological procreation: it comes up in his essay on Pythagoras, and despite his very public love affairs, he would later recall in his autobiography that on learning his wife was pregnant with their second child, he experienced a "sense of failure" and "physical repugnance" that led him to hole up in his room and write the "hymns to sterility" out of which *Prometeo vencedor* was eventually born.)[67]

No critic has done a better job of exposing the ideological intentions of the cosmic race than its author does here. From now on, readers of *La raza cósmica* can spare themselves the trouble of proving that mestizaje is really a code word for whitening or that Vasconcelos's anti-imperialism is secretly trying to do European universalism bigger and better. All the secrets are on the surface in this allegory. A bystander explains the source of Saturnino's power to Prometeo: the Philosopher's doctrine is nothing special, but "he knows how to state it [*exponer*, also to display or show] with dramatic characters; he takes it to its extreme consequences" (49). Everything is out in the open because here, on a virtual stage, Vasconcelos theorizes with dramatic characters the way ideology works, and as is true of Saturnino's creed, the power of his theory lies not just in its "content" but in its style and its form. On the one hand, *Prometeo vencedor* presents itself as a prefiguration of the aesthetic future it prophecies—within this textually mediated world, millennia are like a day, people can become white by singing the right songs, imperialism is defeated through sheer will, and dead men can reappear. Yet the extravagance of these feats also ensures their impossibility. The cosmic race is so tragically powerful because the illusion can't actually be performed, though it can call forth desire.

But this is only the second act, and no Paradise is ever perfect, especially one that requires a stage. Although the bodies in this play are purely textual, a textual body is still a body of a certain sort, still haunted by the specter of the flesh. As a "theory" that hinges on the metaphor of race, Vasconcelos's cosmic idea also needs the body: racial miscegenation is what enables his identity claim on behalf of Spanish America, but it also stands in the way of the triumphant march toward universality. And so, before long, this fragile illusion begins to break down as the outlines of familiar genres reappear. An Old Man pokes holes in Saturnino's philosophy, Saturnino responds, the Old Man answers back, and suddenly it's a Socratic dialogue all over again! Melodrama is thrown into the mix with a weepy monologue by a mother whose only son has died. And though a choir sings of the "ill-fated tragedy" that is unfolding, the act ends on a comic note when a group of "the ugliest women" threatens to go procreate, to which Saturnino scoffs that they will never find willing partners. Looking back on it now, their response is more than a little ironic: "We'll search for centaurs! Strong centaurs! Beautiful centaurs!" (70).

Act 3 brings us to the grand finale. Flanked by Prometeo and Satanás, perched atop the Himalayas, a now-elderly Saturnino delivers a comically overblown performance of tragic suffering: "Here I sit on the world's highest rock, like a new Prometheus, tormented, no longer by the Olympic furies but by the rigor of my own thoughts!" (71). Surrounding him are "strange apparatuses," among them an audio device and telescope-reflector that allow him to see and communicate with any site on earth, though the only people left are Saturnino, a man in Africa, and a third in the Americas: an untimely Third World alliance whose members toll a bell every midnight to let the others know they are still alive. Saturnino and his mythic companions wait for the hour to arrive. They listen. There is only silence, "the negative signal" (78). This is the prophet's cue. "Oh! Race that suffered such ardor [afán], your final cry will be a cry of triumph, expressed in a vibrating, celestial melody!" He carries on for page after page, proclaiming "the end of the tragedy of man! . . . Nature has concluded its ensayo!" Finally his well of Dionysian exclamation marks runs dry and he drops dead (79).

Surely this ecstatic frenzy is the single moment when the race that does not yet have a name but would later become "cosmic" actually exists. This is the death that gives birth to the synthetic race, the Genre formed from the mixture of every conceivable medium and genre, the moment of agony when Nietzsche's invisible theater seems to be in sight and all the incomplete ensayos give way to a total, tragic performance that will abolish the stage. This is what should take place, in theory, but even in the skewed world of this play it doesn't happen that way. For one, Saturnino's solo still rides the line where tragedy meets its parody. And while he may be the sole representative of the Race whose song he sings, actor and audience can't collapse into the primordial unity, because Satanás and Prometeo are there to witness his show. Indeed, they are still dissertating over his inert corpse when all of sudden a young man clad in kangaroo hides bursts onto the scene, "with a not very intelligent appearance but a strong body and resolute gestures." He commandeers the global speaker system and announces, "We have triumphed, the world is ours!" (84). Lo and behold, it turns out that hordes of lusty women and a few feeble men escaped Saturnino's influence and went to live Down Under, where they bred like rabbits in the forest and created an artificial fog to thwart the guru's surveillance devices. (Note from the author of this book: I am not making this up.) In other words, the technological mediation of the globe was faulty and incomplete; the prophet's achievement of absolute consciousness was an illusion. Even Satanás is dismayed to discover that "this whole beautiful tragedy of Saturnino and his heroic generation has been nothing but a *sainete,* a decadent *entremés* in the majestic and fatal course of life" (86).[68] In a split second, *Prometeo vencedor* falls apart, its title is unmasked as ironic, aesthetic form collapses into "minor" theatrical genres from the Spanish tradition, the universal race falls prey to Anglo-Saxon imperialists, and the sublimation of thought is bested by the body's desire. Tragic pathos is upstaged by the comic.

Or is it cosmic? Prometeo, for one, refuses to concede defeat—he insists that even if it was all just a rehearsal, there is a "yearning that is noble but blind, there is a sublime order of force, a new rhythm we call aesthetic" (91). On the heels of the Australian bushwhacker's scene-stealing debut, his lofty speech seems absurd. What is this if not parody? Even so, maybe Prometeo is right—what takes place onstage may be funny (or trying very hard to be), but tragedy was never meant to be the "content" of the cosmic race. *Prometeo vencedor* mixes genres high and low, conjuring up the possibility of a moment when all distinctions will disappear; it tries to turn the West's symbol of progress against itself; it promises to trump injustice, race, and imperialism through art. It fails, but it does so in a spectacular fashion, and this tragic gap between the universal ideal it evokes and what we see on the virtual stage is Vasconcelos's own "theory" of ideology.[69] But as even Prometeo seems to know, a speculative theory of ideology is not ideology itself, and so he tells Satanás to roll up his sleeves and descend once more among men—not unlike Vasconcelos would do, laying the uncertain foundations of institutions that, over time, transformed all of these contradictions into an identity.

¿Vasconcelos vencedor?

When Saturnino drops out of the sky in the second act of *Prometeo vencedor,* he is already an accomplished orator able to change the course of human desire (or so he thinks). By contrast, there were no crowds of jubilant masses waiting for Vasconcelos when he swooped into Mexico City in July 1920 to become rector of the National University. A few months after his return *Prometeo vencedor* made its appearance in print. The response? Several readers praised the first act, the author wrote to Alfonso Reyes, but they had nothing to say about the second, and only one—one!—understood (or claimed to understand) the third.[70] Over the next year he used his post to drum up support for the vast expansion of infrastructure necessary to carry out the mandate of free and compulsory education in the Constitution of 1917—no small task in a war-torn country where at least 80 percent of the population was illiterate, and where large numbers spoke one of multiple indigenous languages instead of Spanish. In February 1921 the legislature debated his proposal for the creation of a national Secretariat of Public Education (SEP). At this stage the power of the government was precarious, diplomatic recognition from the United States was still over two years away, and foreign investors and lenders were wary because the regime's agenda was not yet clear: after the assassination of Zapata, his followers had aided Obregón in driving out Carranza, and the new president had to negotiate a range of competing interests, including a growing urban working-class movement. Expanding access to culture and education was one of the few things on which most of his tenuous allies, for diverse reasons, could agree.[71]

It easy to forget that Vasconcelos only led the SEP for three years and that it was an "exceptional" time. There are plenty of reasons to think he himself believed he was making a Faustian deal. One thread he returned to in many of his speeches was his support for the socialism of Karl Liebknecht, the cofounder of the Spartacus League who had been murdered alongside Rosa Luxemburg by the new democratic German government in 1919. Vasconcelos was notoriously quixotic in his interpretations of others' ideas, but what drew him to Liebknecht was the latter's critique of militarism and its role as the linchpin of imperialism, nationalism, and the class system.[72] Increasingly hostile toward the tradition of military strongmen in Mexico, Vasconcelos thought culture could act as a check on this tendency and create an alternative basis for national sovereignty—though alas, in order to build the enabling institutions of culture, he needed the generals who ran the new regime. He was uneasy in August 1923 when the government pledged not to nationalize any properties of foreigners acquired prior to the signing of the Constitution of 1917, and even more displeased the following month when Obregón nominated as his successor General Plutarco Elías Calles, another member of his military circle and a man Vasconcelos intensely disliked. As attention shifted toward rebuilding the economy and rejoining the world of international diplomacy, it was also clear that cuts to his budget loomed; he departed his office along with Obregón, and not long after that La raza cósmica was published in Spain.

The mass literacy campaigns Vasconcelos initiated with the help of enthusiastic young volunteers and poorly paid maestros ambulantes are now the stuff of legend, but the gains they made were arduous and slow. He was the Medici of the muralist movement, yet the number of people who saw the murals on a regular basis was relatively small. The performing arts, on the other hand, could involve large numbers of people as both participants and spectators, including those who had no formal education and spoke little Spanish. Like the literacy campaign, the SEP's theatrical activities were inspired in part by the policies of Anatoly Lunacharsky, the Soviet Commissar of Enlightenment (another man with an interest in the occult who had written a strange play about a secular prophet).[73] In Mexico City, the SEP immediately began to sponsor "cultural festivals" featuring choirs, music ensembles, and "popular" dances; it also set about building small open-air theaters in the city's neighborhoods and parks and encouraged teachers setting up new schools in rural areas to lead the locals in building outdoor theaters. In other cases the SEP stepped into fund projects already in the works.[74] The next chapter, for instance, discusses an open-air theater in San Juan Teotihuacán, not far from the Toltec pyramids then in the process of excavation, where it partnered with the Department of Anthropology to fund artist-ethnographers who studied the customs of indigenous people and created short sketches often labeled as *ensayos*—stylized representations of their subjects' daily lives, which indigenous actors performed for their peers and for tourists with the goal of fostering the development of a "national" theater.

Not long after assuming office, Vasconcelos began to concoct an urban counterpoint to these short, modest slices of "real" indigenous life. In February 1922, he took to the pages of *El Universal Ilustrado* to tout his idea for an enormous open-air theater near the Chapultepec forest on the former grounds of Parque Luna, an amusement park built by U.S. investors a few years before the revolution began. A weekly magazine soon to become an outlet for writers linked to the estridentista avant-garde, *El Universal Ilustrado* often devoted articles to the vexing absence of "national theater" and surveyed prominent intellectuals on the topic. Never before, however, had anyone proposed a stadium-theater "with a vast stage like a bullring" where twenty to thirty thousand people would gather to witness "profound dramas, scenes of dazzling beauty, which first drown and then explode in rhythms of jubilation"—and all for little or no cost.[75] Vasconcelos began his full-page article by contrasting his plan with the theatrical endeavors of the ancien régime: the rotunda in Chapultepec park, for instance, only held the five hundred "lackeys of the dictator who attended official ceremonies," though it was referred to as monumental "because everything in that era was measured by the moral size of Porfirio Díaz, which was very small." Even the Teatro Nacional, a lavish building begun in 1904 but stalled by the revolution, would lack sufficient space after it was finished (which was not until 1934, when it was rebaptized the Palacio de Bellas Artes). In fact, *all* modern theaters suffered from the same defect: all were "enclosed theaters" that sequestered spectators from the sun and subjected them to "psychological dramas, dramas of the salon or interior problems" rather than expressing "collective ideals." Never one to waste an opportunity to fan the flames of anti-imperialist sentiment, Vasconcelos decries these indoor, egoistic theaters as "absurd importations" from the cold countries of the North and insists that Mexico must draw inspiration from the Greeks and other Mediterraneans to create a blend of open-air theater and "modern" stagecraft.

Here Vasconcelos made no reference to Soviet mass pageantry, but two weeks later he cited it as a model for Mexico in one of *El Universal Ilustrado*'s surveys, railing against the vulgarity of the "bourgeois" and the "wealthy classes that do no work" and therefore "do not live the intense life that is the mother of art."[76] Eventually some rather hazy invocations of Aztec ritual pageantry would also make it into the mix. In his initial iteration of his idea, however, he relies on the familiar language of tragedy and genre in projecting a plan for the "progress and triumph of our race."[77] The new theater he intends to build will not simply be "a bullfighting plaza where opera is sung" but will give rise to a new artistic genre that will spell the end of both bullfighting and the "conventionalisms" of German and Italian opera. (Bullfighting, he says, is noxious because it encourages the audience to remain passive while taking vicarious pleasure in another person's bravery, and the only operas still worth listening to are Wagner's *Tristan and Isolde* and Rossini's *Barber of Seville*). He boldly declares solos and arias elitist forms destined to disappear—as a matter of fact, he has already eliminated them from all open-air festivals, in accordance with the principle that "the highest things have humble origins." While the stadium will one day host a "great ballet, orchestra, and choirs of millions of voices," these new forms of mass spectacle can only grow out of "popular dances" and "the freshest shoots of popular art."

Puchner notes that avant-garde theatricalism and modernist antitheatricalism converge at the point of their shared resistance to embodied mimesis.[78] Although he never imagines a single person as the site where this convergence occurs, the performance Vasconcelos envisions here is something like his quasi-modernist closet drama turned inside out. If *Prometeo vencedor* resists—even as it represents—the material stage in order to establish the autonomy of its ideal, this is a direct call for a kind of "total theater," the quintessentially avant-garde ideal of an all-encompassing spectacle that revolutionizes the Real by mixing and superseding every known genre and medium. The lingo of totality is there, along with all the motifs common to the European theatrical vanguard, and Vasconcelos draws on the same sources, among them Greek tragedy, Wagner, Nietzsche, Soviet pageantry, and the "people's theater" of Romain Rolland. Two key differences: he held a political office, and unlike the TotalTheater designed a few years later by the Bauhaus architect Walter Gropius in collaboration with Erwin Piscator, his dream of a gigantic theater-stadium would (sort of) come true.

Plans for the project were temporarily delayed by other priorities, including Vasconcelos's diplomatic trip to South America for the centenary of Brazil's independence in September 1922. The Parque Luna site also fell through, but in its place the president gave him a large plot of land in the well-to-do neighborhood of Colonia Roma (a former municipal cemetery from which the remains had been removed). The biggest obstacle was money: given the need to rebuild damaged infrastructure and the lack of access to foreign capital, the Obregón regime was perpetually short on cash. Vasconcelos was set on using reinforced concrete—the most modern material—but the cost was prohibitive, so he had to settle for a metal framework from a foundry in Monterrey, which was then covered in cement. His solution to the budget shortfall was to ask all of the SEP's employees (including teachers) to sacrifice one day's salary, and to urge students to collect contributions. As for the design, he had ideas of his own, which may be why the task of coming up with the initial blueprint went to José Villagrán García, a young draftsman in the SEP's construction division who was still finishing his degree and had never before designed a building for construction. Vasconcelos favored the dominant neocolonial style, but other exigencies, both aesthetic and practical, also influenced the final product. At his request, the simple horseshoe plan and series of arcades gave the structure an appearance similar to a bullring—that vile form of entertainment he aspired to drive out of business. True to his Pythagorean principles, he insisted that its acoustic qualities were more important than sight lines or visual appearance, and rather than relying on electrical amplification (still very new at this time), the design should allow the sound of a single voice to reach each and every spectator.[79] (For this reason the original dimensions of the interior—172 meters long by 90 meters wide—were altered to 172 by 60.)[80] The sculptor Manuel Centurión was hired to design and execute a series of bas-reliefs around the façade, and few were surprised when Diego Rivera was announced as the winner of a contest to paint murals of the figures *Videncia* (Clairvoyance) and *Voluntad* (Will) on either side of the main entrance.

Well before the disastrous rehearsal where dehydrated schoolchildren withered in the weltering sun, the National Stadium was a source of controversy. The architectural establishment was none too pleased about being shut out, and they found fodder for their resentment when, after construction began on March 12, 1923, it was discovered that calculations for the multi-tiered, pyramidal stairway leading up to the stadium were wrong. Vasconcelos sought suggestions from several people, starting with Villagrán García, but every potential solution presented other issues, until Diego Rivera weighed in with an idea, and while he was at it also requested a minor adjustment to the angle of the balustrade to coordinate with his murals. A committee made up of two architects, an art history professor, and two painters declared the new design feasible, but then the real headache began. A member of the local architectural society named Juan Galindo published a series of scathing attacks in the pages of the notoriously conservative *Excélsior*, denouncing the stadium as a "disaster" and accusing Vasconcelos of infringing on the architect's authorial rights by allowing engineers, sculptors, and painters to each add their own little bit, making it a veritable *cena de negros* (a "dinner of blacks," or utter disorder).[81] With the inauguration drawing nigh, all of the key players—except Villagrán García—engaged in an all-out bout of public mudslinging. Architecture, scoffed Diego Rivera, was a plastic art organized around the same essential laws as sculpture and painting—though Galindo could hardly be expected to know this, because he had gained his fancy credentials by copying ancient buildings and designing bad knockoffs of the colonial style perfected by the Yankees in California.[82] For his part, Vasconcelos pleaded guilty as charged. Yes, he said, the National Stadium, like other works of the SEP, had involved painters, sculptors, and lawyers, and even "businessmen would have been able to intervene if by some chance they had good advice, because I have no prejudices of professional caste, nor do I look for diplomas, but only stones and lines that attempt to achieve music."[83]

Two days later, on the morning of May 5, 1924, the director of the SEP stood in his theater-stadium before a sea of sixty thousand spectators and thousands more young performers. Following a few forgettable words by the president, Vasconcelos assured the crowd that the Estadio Nacional was no mere imitation of Greek and Roman amphitheaters, nor was it a nostalgic bid to resurrect the "archaic ceremonies" of "remote" Indian ancestors, because within its concrete walls "stammers a race that yearns for originality." Funded by contributions from students and teachers, designed by architects and engineers, decorated by painters and sculptors, and built by manual laborers, the stadium would serve as the stage for mass choirs, cosmic music, symbolic rites, the recitations of great tragedians—the "art of the future."[84] Judging from the newspaper accounts, the show went off far better than expected. Vasconcelos made sure containers of fruit water were on hand to forestall any unfortunate repeats of the rehearsal; the one thousand couples dancing the *jarabe tapatío* were reasonably well in step; the gigantic human pyramids may have wobbled a bit, but no disasters occurred; and if any of the vocalists belting out the national anthem hit a false note, the other 11,999 choir members must have managed to drown them out.[85] Even the *Excélsior*—after all the business with the touchy architects and hysteria over the fainting schoolgirls—ate its words in a headline declaring the inauguration "a poem of sun, of color, of rhythm" and proclaiming "Never Before Now Has Mexico Contemplated a Similar Spectacle, the Portent of a New Race."[86] Not that all was forgotten: Galindo still managed to get in an occasional jab, and the incident did little to endear the old guard to Rivera, who had been censured in an *Excélsior* editorial for praising unlettered rural folk as more enlightened than the idiotic architects of the bourgeoisie and for fancying himself a *genio estridentista*, or "estridentista genius"—one of those artists from that new "vanguard" movement who felt entitled to spout off about art just because they had a benefactor in the government.[87] Clearly the theater-stadium, in conjoining all of the arts, had touched a nerve among the defenders of disciplinary autonomy, and the threat it posed was perceived to be linked to the avant-garde.

So how is it that the National Stadium came to be deemed the very antithesis of the avant-garde? By the 1930s, Villagrán García would be renowned as the country's foremost theoretician of international modernism, and his design for the Granja Sanitaria de Popotla, a hospital complex completed in

1925, is often seen as marking a shift toward functionalism by virtue of its similarities to the work of Le Corbusier and the Bauhaus school. Yet his first project—finished just one year before—is often omitted from chronologies of his work.[88] The few discussions of the National Stadium tend to attribute its authorship entirely to Vasconcelos, as Salvador Novo did in the early 1960s when he derisively stated that the building "united the Aztec and Conquistador in surrender to architectural neocolonialism."[89] More recently, Rubén Gallo has taken it up a notch by depicting the stadium and its inauguration as a totalitarian expression of the cosmic race *and* a prelude to the seven decades of the single-party state starting in 1929. (Never mind that this event actually coincided with Vasconcelos's defeat in a presidential election marked by fraud and his subsequent exile and marginalization.) Pointing to Vasconcelos's editorship of the journal *Timón*, a journal financed by the German embassy in Mexico for a few months in 1940, Gallo spots striking similarities to the opening ceremony of the 1936 Olympics in Berlin and the Nazis' plans for a 400,000-seat stadium at Nuremberg. What does this tell us? "Fascist ideology" was already at work in his cultural program for the SEP—as evidenced not by anything he said (he roundly rejected fascism at this time), but by the stadium spectacle, with its "perfectly aligned bodies" and "civilized masses, educated in Vasconcelos's schools, who subjected their every movement to the strictest rules of order and reason."[90]

The one problem for Gallo is that avant-garde artists were fascinated by the stadium. The critic traces it across media and genres, spotting troubling signs of Vasconcelos's vision of "order" and "harmony" in Tina Modotti's abstract photographs of its sloped concrete steps and sounding alarm bells over the image of masses of people moved by a "single idea" in Kin Taniya's estridentista ode to the building. Strangely, though, both the man and the architectural object at the center of all this experimental art are anything but: Vasconcelos was a "conservative," and as a classicist he sought to impose a singular, monumental style on a structure he envisioned as a "return to the past" (206). In the end, he failed, and the stadium was a "mishmash" and "hodgepodge," probably because he interfered in the design. The National Stadium cannot be art because it *is* ideology.

This hyperbole has the virtue of highlighting Vasconcelos's ex-centric role in relation to the avant-garde. Vasconcelos acts as a limit case where political and aesthetic power appear poised to converge—a theoretical totality that enables the very notion of "art" as the avant-garde of society but against which the avant-garde must also be defined. This specter of the "aestheticization of politics" also haunts the avant-garde as a whole, and it is little wonder it so often takes a theatrical form, because the idealization involved in envisioning a perfectly coordinated spectacle in which bodies are mere conduits for ideology requires a willful, imaginary transcendence of the material stage. Less than two months after the inauguration Vasconcelos would present his resignation, and he knew as he stood there that day that his window was about to close. He had rushed construction of the building, and on the big day Rivera's murals were only partially done, while half of the grand staircase over which such a ruckus was raised was still missing. Even in his speech Vasconcelos emphasized that the stadium was to be the "cradle" of the art of the future—not the stage on which this totality would be performed. And what actually was to happen that day? In the final lines he told the audience to have faith in this "oppressed race" as they "watch it rehearsing [*ensayando*] the victorious gestation!"[91]

Decades later, critics pick apart his "essay" *La raza cósmica* as though the truth lay within it. Meanwhile *Prometeo vencedor* and the real drama of his theater-stadium have become tragicomedies hidden from sight—not quite philosophy, ideology, or art, but rehearsals and remnants of an invisible stage that correspond to no genre we know.

Chapter 2

✦

Primitivist Accumulation and *Teatro sintético*

When the several dozen members of the American Industrial Mission settled into their seats at the Teatro Olimpia on the evening of September 17, 1924, were they anticipating a reprieve from the wheeling and dealing, or did they still have dollar signs in sight? During the previous few days they had hit all the architectural highlights of Mexico City, talked tariffs and investment opportunities with politicos, and sipped libations on the balcony of the Palacio Municipal as multitudes gathered below to commemorate independence and hear the president reenact the *grito*, or cry of rebellion against Spain. On the itinerary for September 18 was a tour of several factories, where they would admire the facilities and then dine on a light lunch of lobster cocktail and squab as workers performed gymnastics and military drills to the accompaniment of a brass band. At the moment, however, these esteemed representatives of U.S. banking and manufacturing interests were relaxing after an all-day excursion to the ancient Indian pyramids of Teotihuacán while waiting for the curtain to rise on what had been billed as a spectacle in which native customs and rituals would commingle with picturesque scenes of urban life, creating a "synthesis" of the primitive and the modern along with an amalgamation of music, song, dance, painting, and mime. Musicians and dancers from the Tarascan tribe had traveled from their remote village in the state of Michoacán to take part in the debut of the Teatro del Murciélago (which meant "Theater of the Bat," as a short preamble delivered in English helpfully explained); with the aid of several young artists and actors they would distill the country's color and character into a series of brief, nearly wordless tableaux that would fill viewers with an "exquisite emotion," offering them a *tienda de juguetes para el alma*—a toy store for the soul.[1]

Whether or not the industrialists felt the flutter of emotion (exquisite or otherwise) is difficult to say, but the reviews that appeared over the following few days were almost all gushing in their praise of a performance said to have elicited a sense of the "dramatic, the frivolous, the tender, the melancholic, the reminiscence of childhood, everything a man can experience in his passage through life in these times when everything is synthesis."[2] The word "synthesis," so ubiquitous in Mexico (as in Europe) during the 1920s and 1930s, characterizes the Teatro del Murciélago in more ways than one. The project arose out of a collaboration involving artist-ethnographers working in indigenous communities and an international cast of characters affiliated with the avant-garde movement known as estridentismo. Its premiere performance, sponsored by the Mexico City Council and Chamber of Commerce, was part of an effort to (re)establish economic ties following the decade-long revolution and reintegrate the country into circuits of commodity exchange. In fact, for many of the U.S. "missionaries" who saw the show it must have had a familiar air: as the artists openly acknowledged, their project was inspired by (and named after) the Théâtre de la Chauve-Souris, a touring revue of Russian émigrés known for its stylized depictions of Slavic folk customs and tableaux in which humans acted like mechanical dolls. The Chauve-Souris had taken Paris, London, New York, and other cosmopolitan cities by storm. Undaunted, its Mexican double promised to prove that the land south of the Rio Grande boasted even more "color" than Old Mother Russia. Why, then, did the Murciélago vanish almost immediately after its debut, leaving in its wake an elusive ideal summed up by the term *teatro sintético*?

Avant-garde artists engaging with indigenous culture is not unusual in itself, especially in Mexico, where muralists adorned the walls of government buildings with dancing peasants and Aztec warriors, and where intrepid foreigners such as Sergei Eisenstein and Antonin Artaud came to smoke peyote and search for signs of the future in the primitive past. Estridentismo, however, is often seen as an exception: the first movement in Mexico to call itself *la vanguardia*, it is remembered for its "strident" manifestos as well as for its members' early embrace of mass culture and their subsequent attempt to transform the provincial city of Xalapa into a socialist utopia. Art historians have recently muddied the waters by drawing attention to the involvement of estridentistas in the muralist movement, and new archival research continues to shed light on its affiliates' commitment to issues of indigenous and rural labor.[3] But despite the "theatrical" quality of the group, its sole theatrical endeavor looks perplexingly un-avant-garde. In place of either futuristic verve or primitivist passion, Teatro del Murciélago delivered carefully crafted scenes of quaint local color. Rather than standing in solidarity with the proletarian struggle, it modeled itself after a theatrical revue whose charm lay in its nostalgic remembrance of prerevolutionary Russia. And while abstracting or experimenting with indigenous figures in paintings or woodcuts might seem innocent enough, there is something more unsettling about the Italian actress and future photographer Tina Modotti mimicking a Purépecha woman engaged in a mourning ritual on the Night of the Dead. Still more difficult to assimilate is the sentimental, precious quality of Teatro del Murciélago and the way it openly (if also ironically) peddled emotions like products, as if it were indeed a "toy store for the soul."

This curious phrase, which was quick to catch on among critics, epitomizes what Sara Ahmed has written about the operations of "affective economies."

Ahmed argues that although emotions are commonly imagined as dwelling within the interior of the subject (or "soul"), they are relational and socially produced in a process roughly analogous to Marx's model for the creation of surplus value. For Marx, money becomes capital when it not only functions as a medium of exchange but also accumulates value in its movement through the market. Ultimately, this surplus is the new value created by (i.e., extorted from) workers in excess of their own labor cost, yet only in the conversion of money into commodities and then back into money (M–C–M) can it be realized and can capital itself be valorized. Ahmed likewise insists that "emotions work as a form of capital: affect does not reside positively in the sign or commodity, but is produced as an effect of its circulation."[4] In her view, emotions are neither "inside" nor "outside" people or things but are what create the effect of boundaries between bodies and the very sense of the subject's interiority. Just as the fetish of the commodity consists of concealing the labor and acts of exchange through which its value is generated, "'feelings' become 'fetishes,' qualities that seem to reside in objects, only through an erasure of the history of their production and circulation" (11).

Although Ahmed is primarily interested in showing how emotions work *like* capital, her emphasis on their material dimension logically implies that the connection is more than metaphorical. In this chapter I borrow from her approach while also tapping into a different critical trend that focuses on the ways in which affects are implicated in the accumulation of capital itself. Art is often defined in opposition to the realm of commodity relations, as an alternative circuit of exchange where emotions and ideas act as the currency of a more genuine community. Yet as an art form that typically involves people working to produce an affective experience in the presence of a paying audience, theater puts particular pressure on this ideal, even while it serves as one of its most enduring models. In this sense a focus on theater can lend historical perspective to recent claims about the role of "immaterial" labor in our own so-called postindustrial world, where the economy is said to hinge not on the manufacturing of things, but on the production of ideas and affects.[5] Like the schema of surplus value Ahmed employs, these discussions often neglect to factor in the essential *unevenness* of capitalist accumulation. As Marx himself concedes, all of his formulas and equations of capital are theoretical models, and the nature of their truth can only be understood when one turns (as he eventually does) to the historical genesis of capital and to what he sees as its still-incomplete emergence in the Americas. There accumulation occurs not through the seeming magic of the market but by dint of "direct extra-economic force": the brute violence of land enclosures, enslavement, and colonial plunder, but also legislation, taxation, and other forms of state intervention exterior to the "immanent laws of capitalist production."[6] This is what Marx dubs *ursprüngliche Akkumulation*—an accumulation of material resources and labor that is "original," "originary," and "primordial," or "primitive" (as it is typically rendered in translation).

This chapter tracks the circulation of the notion of theatrical "synthesis" across a wide swath of the globe, exploring its connections to the accumulation of capital and emotions alike. The first part skirts the periphery of Europe, starting with the *sintesi* of the Italian futurists and then heading to the heart of prerevolutionary Russia, where out of the bowels of the Moscow Art Theater and a dimly lit basement cabaret fluttered the exquisite animal eventually known as the Chauve-Souris. In following the flight of the Bat from the newly formed Soviet Union to Paris, London, and New York's Great White Way, I show how its self-referential scenes worked through doubts and desires related to the mechanization of living labor, the commodification of the performing arts, and the intimate alterity of cultural repertoires associated with "outmoded" ways of life. This point of comparison is essential to understanding both the similarity and specificity of the Chauve-Souris's less successful, might-have-been Mexican double, the genesis of which the rest of the chapter reconstructs. Like the Chauve-Souris, the Murciélago mimicked the customs of peasants, but it had its immediate roots in an anthropological project and brought indigenous people to the city to perform onstage; and whereas the Chauve-Souris turned a profit by tugging at heartstrings, the Murciélago—though by a certain measure less profitable or "productive"—was more directly connected to the creation of new institutions and labor regimes. Taken together, they trouble both the timeline of capitalist accumulation and the temporality of the avant-garde.

When (or if) does capitalism become complete—a "synthetic," self-sustaining whole? Marx gives conflicting signs as to when (and whether) primitive accumulation comes to an end, and his richly metaphorical language only fuels the interpretative debates. As I read his text, this is part of its point: primitive accumulation is not only an empirical or historical process, and it cannot be separated from questions of culture and representation. Although it is about the creation of markets and the expropriation of the means of production from the true producers (i.e., workers), it is also about how capital comes to be conceived and experienced as distinct from everything and everyone it is supposedly not.[7] The theater is a good place to examine the entanglement of these two seemingly separate problems because it is a place where the metaphorical and the material are especially hard to pull apart. By this same token, I use the term "primitivist accumulation" not as a symbolic or cultural analogue to the "real" accumulation of labor and wealth on which capitalism depends, but to underscore their intimate interrelations.

All Things Small and Synthetic

As fragmentary and fleeting as the spectacles it described, the concept of "synthetic theater" turned up during the early twentieth century and then faded like any other passing fashion. In a four-page leaflet dated January 11,

1915, and titled *Il teatro futurista sintetico*, F. T. Marinetti and his collaborators, Emilio Settimelli and Bruno Corra, announced a new kind of theater capable of mobilizing minds and bodies for Italy's entry into the Great War. In the face of mortal danger, books and magazines slowed people down, and although 90 percent of all Italians (according to their estimate) attended the theater, little could be expected from its "somnolent stages" and "depressing, boring, funereal fare."[8] Reworking motifs from prior futurist manifestos on the virtues of variety theater, the artists took Henrik Ibsen, Bernard Shaw, and other would-be innovators to task for failing to obey the imperative of compression—of "squeezing into a few minutes, a few words and a few gestures, innumerable situations, sensibilities, ideas, sensations, facts, and symbols," all of which were needed to allow theater to conquer the competition it faced from cinema (201). The new "synthetic" theater had to be born out of improvisation; it must ignore the expectations of the audience; and rather than serving as a mere photographic copy of reality, it should aim to tap into a "special sort of reality that violently attacks the nerves" (205). Similar to the scenes performed during their raucous *serata* or soirées, the futurist *sintesi* (staged by professional actors during tours of Italian cities) featured minimal scenery and props, terse dialogue, and few or no dramatis personae. Such is the case of Francesco Cangiullo's *Detonazione*, in which the sole character is A Bullet, the setting is a cold, deserted road at night, and the action consists of a minute of silence punctured by a gunshot. Subtitled "A Synthesis of All Modern Theater," the play allegorizes the idea of a performative action so rapid-fire and absolute it can only be registered as sound, and in eschewing human actors it heightens the sense of the agency of objects.

As John Muse has argued, these futurist microdramas were not entirely novel. During the last two decades of the nineteenth century the rise of cabarets and independent, subscription-based theaters such as Freie Bühne in Berlin and the Théâtre-Livre in Paris had encouraged experimentation with shorter, less costly, and more intimate genres: whereas the oneiric one-acts of the symbolists sought to construct subjective microcosms freed from historical and clock time, the naturalist *quart d'heures* minimalized this difference with their depictions of popular manners and enactments of the snippets of sensationalist news reporting known as *faits-divers*. Muse attributes this impulse toward abbreviation to "widespread exhaustion with various kinds of gigantism," which he pithily sums up as including "imperial expansion, totalizing historical narratives, epic pretensions, multi-volume novels, and melodramatic hyperbole."[9] Perhaps most striking, however, is the way it mimics a certain dynamic intrinsic to capitalist accumulation and commodity production. Long before the futurists, people had written of how new inventions such as the steamboat or the telegraph would bring about the "annihilation of space by time," and in the *Grundrisse*, Marx employs this same rhetoric when he writes of how the development of new transportation and communication technologies is driven by a fundamental tension.

Capital must expand to survive, and its value can only realized by virtue of circulation, yet this very process entails additional costs and labor time. So "while capital must on one side strive to tear down every spatial barrier to intercourse, i.e. to exchange, and conquer the whole earth for its market, it strives on the other side to annihilate this space with time, i.e. to reduce to a minimum the time spent in motion from one place to another." [10]

As a country where industrialization was both recent and rapid, Italy was one place where this experience of "time-space compression" was especially acute. [11] Russia was another. Directors and stage designers such as Vsevolod Meyerhold, Vladimir Nemirovich-Danchenko, and Yuri Annenkov all invoked the notion of synthesis, but it was Alexander Tairov who developed the most elaborate articulation of synthetic theater. Opposed to both the "conscious theatricality" of Meyerhold and to the naturalism of Konstantin Stanislavsky, Tairov encouraged the formation of "master-actors" trained in everything from ballet to fencing and juggling. In his small Kamerny Theater, founded in 1914, he and his collaborators worked from scenarios rather than fully fledged scripts, seeking to create a type of "synthetic scenic construction" that would "fuse the now separated elements of the Harlequinade, tragedy, operetta, pantomime, and circus, refracting them through the modern soul of the actor and the creative rhythm kindred to it." [12] If the end goal of the synthesis sought in many Italian futurist productions was to annihilate the actor (and his labor) in order to turn the time-based art of theater into an instantaneous medium of transmission, Tairov resisted the logics of mechanization and specialization by exalting the agency and artistry of the actor. It was the actor who integrated all elements of production and, through the rhythmic work of his body and his "creative fantasy," constructed not a character but a "scenic figure"—a "synthesis of emotion and form" (77). Rejecting all calls to involve spectators in the spectacle, the director and his collaborators wanted to free themselves from the "general public" (i.e., that "Philistine firmly ensconced in the theaters") and instead perform for a "small chamber audience of *our own* spectators, dissatisfied, restless seekers such as we" (56).

Who was this ideal audience able to affirm the value of the performance while allowing it to evade the usual circuits of economic exchange? Other artists. This was the mystique of Letuchaya Mysh (The Bat), a cabaret-like show performed in intimate cellar-club theaters in Moscow and later known internationally as La Chauve-Souris. Possibly named after the Cabaret Fledermaus in Vienna, Letuchaya Mysh was founded in 1908 by Nikita Baliev, the son of a wealthy Jewish Armenian family who got his start as a secretary and minor actor in Stanislavsky's Moscow Art Theater but found his forte as the master of ceremonies at its legendary "cabbage parties," or *kapustniki*. Held at the end of the winter season and during Lent, when most public performances were prohibited and actors were unemployed, the cabbage parties were private, closed-door affairs that remade the theater into a cabaret where actors and artists were alternately waiters, spectators, and performers. [13] The events had a practical, redistributive function, with profits going to those who were struggling in the off-season; at the same time they allowed actors to engage in send-ups of their more "serious" roles as well as satirical skits featuring in-jokes and a mix of music and dance foreign to the naturalism of the Moscow Art Theater. When Baliev and his partner Nikolai Tarasov first opened Letuchaya Mysh, it maintained this same spirit as an invitation-only club of forty seats where theater artists gathered after hours; in 1912, after moving to a larger space, it opened its doors to all paying customers and started to retire some of the self-referential gags in favor of one-act adaptations of Russian classics (i.e., stories and plays by Chekhov and Gogol) interspersed with theatricalized folk songs and dances. Still, it continued to cultivate the intimate atmosphere of a self-sustaining world of art, with Baliev in his role as emcee cajoling and insulting patrons with a familiarity usually reserved for peers.

Much as in Germany, where cabaret was considered a type of *Kleinkunst* (small art), the increasingly polished, short scenes of Letuchaya Mysh were referred to as *teatr malykh form* (theater of small forms) or *teatr miniatyur* (theater of miniatures).[14] This small size and improvisatory nature served it well during the turmoil of the Russian Revolution, and afterward the club as well as others like it continued to operate, but despite attempts to adapt its repertoire, its intimacy and exclusivity ran against the grain of an era of mass political action and the theatrical pageants advocated by figures such as Meyerhold.[15] In 1919, Baliev left for the Caucasus and then Constantinople before joining several former members of his company in Paris, where he also recruited the prima ballerina Elizaveta Yulievna Anderson, who doubled as choreographer and performer, and Sergei Sudeikin, a set designer who had worked with Meyerhold, Tairov, and Sergei Diaghilev (founder of the Ballets Russes).[16] Retooled and rebaptized as the Chauve-Souris, Baliev's troupe opened on December 23 at Théâtre Fémina, a popular locale for operetta and other "light" fare.[17] In this new context the dramatic numbers shrunk to as short as three minutes, and the dialogue diminished in importance since the scenes were performed in Russian, though music was key: the "soundtrack," so to speak, included snippets of Rachmaninoff and Stravinsky; the latter orchestrated a polka and several other pieces specifically for the show.[18] Baliev filled in details between the acts as part of his jocular repartee with the crowd, drawing additional laughs due to his poor command of French; yet rather than detracting from the performance's effect, this semantic opacity seemed to heighten it. Reviewers praised the group's ability to utilize "all the resources of aesthetics: words, mimicry, music, dances, have been put into play in the Chauve-Souris, and that synthesis always attains the height of the purest art."[19] Even more impressive was the economy of expression displayed in its laconic acts, described by one critic as "condensations, crystallizations, cells"[20]—a depiction reminiscent of Marx's description of commodities as "crystals" or "congealed quantities of homogeneous human labour."[21]

In her remarks on miniature books and other diminutive objects such as dollhouses, mementos, and model trains, Susan Stewart notes that the fascination with miniatures is closely associated with an ethos of craftsmanship and nostalgia for a preindustrial era: in contrast to machine-made products assembled out of disparate parts, small objects are more often made by hand and require an outsized investment of labor-time. By reducing the physical scale, the miniature "skew(s) the time and space relations of the everyday lifeworld, and as an object consumed, the miniature finds its 'use value' transformed into the infinite time of reverie."[22] A dollhouse, for instance, typically re-creates an idealized vision of upper-class domesticity from an earlier era, yet in drawing viewers into its self-contained world it also privatizes the subject's own experience, serving as a mirror for "the realization of the self as property, the body as container of objects, perpetual and incontaminable" (62). On the other hand, the capacity to create an "arrested" or "other" time—"a type of transcendent time which negates change and the flux of lived reality"—also explains the frequent depictions of the lower classes, peasants, and cultural "others" in miniature form (65). Stewart mentions several miniature books with an orientalist bent, but an equally apt example might be the Russian *matryoshka* or nesting dolls, which were first designed in 1890 by an artist at Abramtsevo, an estate near Moscow owned by the railway magnate Savva Mamontov that served as the center of the folk arts and crafts movement and housed a theater where Sergei Sudeikin, the set designer for the Chauve-Souris, first got his start working on productions of Slavophile operas and dramas by figures such as Stanislavsky and Rimsky-Korsakov.[23] The matryoshka's replication of the female peasant figure evokes yet ultimately assuages the anxieties surrounding mechanical (re)production, since each handcrafted doll, though at first glance identical to the others in all but size, turns out to be marked by subtle differences. At the same time, the succession of ever-smaller dolls holds out what Stewart calls the "promise of an infinitely profound interiority" (61).

Much of the lavish praise of the Chauve-Souris's "theater of small forms" revolved around the exquisite, gemlike quality of its scenes and the attention to detail revealed in the choreography, costumes, and set. Similarly, the frequent references to the reduced size of its public served to distinguish it from larger theaters with more mass(-produced) appeal—though as evidence of its "modern" or even "avant-garde" quality, reviewers compared its fast-paced scene changes and synchronization of acting, lighting, and décor with the effects achieved by film.[24] Yet what is perhaps most striking in light of Stewart's observations is its predilection for staging social worlds coded as "other" or increasingly obsolete in an age of revolution and changing class dynamics. In "A Night at Yard's," a scene widely praised for its simplicity, a group of gypsies sang for the pleasure of three patrons dining in a famous Moscow restaurant. The longer "Fountain of Bakhchisarai," an adaptation in two wordless tableaux of a Pushkin poem about murder and passion within

Figure 2.1. Sergei Sudeikin's illustration of the sketch "Katinka." This same image appeared in the program for the fourth run in Paris. From *F. Ray Comstock and Morris Gest Have the Honor to Present Balieff's Chauve-Souris, Bat Theatre, Moscow* (1923).

the harem of a Crimean khan, led one ecstatic critic to offer a rapturous description of the naked torsos and undulating gestures of the women, praising the act as an "oriental miniature."[25] But the undeniable crowd favorite was "Katinka," in which a dancer dressed in the colorful garb of a Russian *muzhik* (peasant) executed a series of angular, abrupt gestures to the rhythm of a polka and the mechanical cues of an older peasant man and woman stationed on either side of her (figure 2.1). Framed by a set designed to look like a music box, it was one of several numbers in which actors played the part of puppets or mechanical dolls. In "The Porcelains of Sèvres," for example, two frozen figures dressed in the style of Louis XV gradually came to life and danced a finely measured minuet, until the large rococo clock dominating the set struck 1 A.M. and they settled back into sculptured immobility.

The stage as a magnified music box, display case, or dollhouse: if miniatures tend to reify the interiority of the subject by eliciting an experience of arrested time, these tableaux of living, dancing dolls also provoke unsettling pleasures and preoccupations surrounding the relations between people and things. Critics often applauded the Chauve-Souris for its "irony," and although the object of this irony always remained unstated, it seems to have had to do with the way the spectacle flaunted its complicity in the very processes of commodification it disavowed. The discrete, decontextualized scenes of the Chauve-Souris mimic the logic of abstraction underlying the commodity, and in their depictions of far-flung places they appear as an accumulation of goods in the no-man's-land of the world market. Yet by its very nature as an "embodied" and ostensibly "ephemeral" art, a theatrical performance is more difficult to disentangle from the process of its production and the living labor on which it depends—a point obsessively underscored in the show by the metatheatrical scenes of singing gypsies, dancing peasants, and serenading shepherds. Marx tended to classify the labor of performing artists as "unproductive" from the standpoint of capital precisely because it seemingly did not produce a commodifiable product distinguishable from itself, and in more recent decades critics such as Peggy Phelan have embraced this as an ontological quality, defining performance as that which exists only in the present and so eludes the "economy of reproduction."[26] But even Marx conceded that the labor of a singer in the employ of an entrepreneur was "productive"—meaning that it "objectifies itself in commodities," or directly creates surplus-value— and while he saw such cases as of negligible importance at the time, this situation had clearly changed by the era of the Chauve-Souris.[27]

Especially pertinent in this regard is the Chauve-Souris's close association with the Moscow Art Theater (MAT), one of the country's first professional companies. In the context of a discussion of Chekhov's *Uncle Vanya*, a play written for the MAT, Nicholas Ridout connects the intense industrialization of Russia during the late nineteenth and early twentieth centuries to what he characterizes as the "incipient Taylorization of the theatrical production process."[28] The MAT ushered in a series of changes that reorganized theatrical labor along lines reminiscent of the factory model: actors were subject to a more formal training method involving longer and more frequent rehearsals (for which they won their demands to be paid), and the stage director took on a more prominent role as a type of "industrial manager" charged with coordinating the diverse labors of his cast and crew in order to achieve a "unified vision." Despite this, Ridout suggests, the new ethos of professionalism also implied certain antimarket principles such as a devotion to the work for its own sake and a degree of autonomy from the strictures of wage labor. As an after-hours offshoot of the MAT, the Chauve-Souris betrays a similar tension, but in even more extreme form. On the one hand, its initial function as a vehicle for artists to exercise their creativity after the workday was done recalls Ridout's definition of the theater artist as a "passionate amateur" whose activity unsettles the distinction between labor and leisure. Yet in transposing the logic of miniaturization into the time-based art of theater, the Chauve-Souris echoed the drive to reduce the turnover time of capital and objectify value. This is most evident in the scenes that raise the specter of mechanization: whereas Stewart sees the common fantasy of toys coming to life as expressing a desire to revivify reified things, what Katinka and the porcelain figurines dramatize is the subjection of the living, performing body to the demands of (re)productivity and the rigors of standardized time (symbolized by the older *muzikh* couple and the rococo clock). In place of concrete objects, these oddly impersonal women and figurative gypsies and peasants are manufacturing affects—along with the very distinctions of gender, ethnicity, and class they perform. Baliev, meanwhile, was hailed for his skill in synchronizing the ensemble work of actors whose virtuosity was measured by their ability to mimic a machine.

The tensions on display in these allusions to the subsumption of the performing arts under capital would become even more pronounced as the Chauve-Souris became a touring troupe, replicating the show in San Sebastián, Spain, and then for a few weeks in London before heading to New York, where it debuted for a select audience on February 3, 1922, at the Forty-Ninth Street Theater.[29] Hyped in advance by Morris Gest, a Russian-born producer who would also bring the Moscow Art Theater the following year, it surpassed all expectations for its success: what was announced as a five-week run turned into fifteen months (with four different iterations of the show), and it became so notorious among the Broadway set that it inspired a parody called *No Siree!*, a revue staged by Dorothy Parker and other members of the Algonquin Round Table.[30] Particularly popular was the "Parade of the Wooden Soldiers," a number in which the performers once again played anthropomorphic objects; based on a story about soldiers rehearsing under the command of Tsar Paul I who marched all the way to Siberia when he forgot to issue orders to halt, it also conjures the specter of the assembly line and the chorus lines of those spectacles-for-the-masses the Chauve-Souris disdained.[31] These portraits of the distinct social sectors of Old Mother Russia were complemented by a growing repertoire of memento from other parts of the world: in addition to orientalist numbers (including "Samurai—An Exotic Japanese Dance"), there were depictions of Baliev's native Armenia ("Alaverdi—Scenes from Life in the Caucasus"), as well as a parody of Italian opera and several pastoral mises-en-scène of "old French songs."

In their fixation on the traditional garb and performative practices of diverse cultural and class "others," all of these tableaux shared a pseudo-ethnographic sensibility that was far from alien to Broadway. The Great White Way was awash in samurais and shahs at this time: just a few years earlier Morris Gest and his partner F. Ray Comstock had produced the wildly successful *Chu Chin Chow*, a musical comedy starring a brownfaced actor in the role of Ali Baba. As for the Chauve-Souris's scenes of the Slavic folk, one possible parallel can be found in the long-standing fascination with rural black life in vaudeville and on the musical stage, where it often took the guise of blackface routines such as those performed by the legendary Al Jolson—a fan and frequent attendee of the Russians' show.[32] The Chauve-Souris styled itself as a more "refined" version of such fare, yet its grab bag of ethnic and regional "types" calls to mind the connections Brad Evans has drawn between the vogue for local color fiction in the United States and what he describes as an "early twentieth-century, modernist trade in exotic objects."[33] Despite their superficial differences, Evans argues, works such as Sarah Orne Jewett's *The Country of the Pointed Firs* (set in a decaying fishing village in Maine) and the stylized, "chic" images of the international aesthetic arts

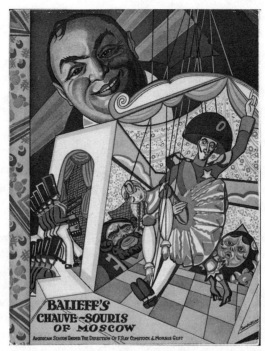

Figure 2.2. The cover of the illustrated handbook produced for the second U.S. season of the Chauve-Souris in 1923, when it returned to New York following a five-month-long repeat engagement at the Théâtre Fémina in Paris. From *F. Ray Comstock and Morris Gest Have the Pleasure to Present Balieff's Chauve-Souris, Bat Theatre, Moscow.*

movement (exemplified by the influence of Japanese woodcuts on illustrators such as Aubrey Beardsley) all contributed to the formation of a popular "ethnographic imagination" prior to the articulation of the concept of "culture" in its current anthropological sense. The sets and costumes designed for the Chauve-Souris by Sudeikin, who had modeled some of his previous work on Beardsley's drawings, vividly illustrate this dynamic.[34] Sudeikin's paintings of the tableaux, which were reproduced in the sumptuous program, also offer visual confirmation of Evans's argument that intrinsic to the appeal of "local" culture was its detachment, decontextualization, and displacement from its original context. Circulated in magazines and the growing book trade (or by traveling theater troupes), the local became "a highly aestheticized global commodity, one that was flung far into a kind of transnational aesthetic where it traded on the visual and visceral pleasures attendant to a dislocation of the self" (113). In this sense, Evans concludes, both U.S. regionalism and movements such as Art Nouveau reveal a "prototypical primitivism" that anticipates the later confluence of avant-garde art and ethnography (23).

As it so happens, an admirer of the Chauve-Souris would act as an instigator of such connections. The Mexican poet and art critic José Juan Tablada, born in 1871, had made his name publishing in journals associated with modernismo, the Spanish American literary movement known for its predilection for exotic settings and highly refined style marked by echoes of French Parnassianism and symbolism; yet over the next few years he would become one of the main promoters of the postrevolutionary avant-garde both in Mexico and New York, where he ran a Spanish-language bookstore and served as a conduit for cultural exchange between the two locales. As a poet, Tablada was most acclaimed for his calligrams and for introducing the genre of the haiku into Spanish. His collection *Un día* (One Day, 1918) is composed of what are referred to on the cover as thirty-eight "synthetic poems," each accompanied by a small illustration resembling a traditional Japanese woodcut. Like calligrams, which seek simultaneity by conflating the visual and the verbal, *Un día* joins two modes of signification and refuses the imperative of specialization. (Tablada was both the author and the artist.) But although the haikus' brevity is in keeping with a futurist impulse, their subject matter (animals and plants) is not, and the illustrations are more apt to recall the aesthetics of Japonisme developed by impressionist painters and the decorative artists of art nouveau.[35]

Coincidentally, one of his haikus is called "El murciélago," or "The Bat":

Does the bat, in the shadows,
Rehearse the swallow's flight
So as to later fly by day?

¿Los vuelos de la golondrina
Ensaya en la sombra el murciélago
Para luego volar de día?[36]

The poem elicits the idea of a rehearsal in the dark for a performance that will likely never take place, since bats are nocturnal. Although Tablada makes no mention of his own poem in the review of the Chauve-Souris he wrote for *Revista de Revistas*, a weekly cultural journal in Mexico City, his entire article is an encomium to smallness, starting with the usual nod to the group's select audience. The poet jokes that "the bulk of the public [*el grueso público*] is unable to pronounce its name and instead says 'Chop-Suey,'" whereas the "more refined public" tries to resist its vaudeville-like charms but eventually abandons itself "body and soul" to a spectacle remarkable for "the most poetic irreality and most modern irony!"[37] Never mind the high price of tickets, or the headshot of the producer Morris Gest in the program, or the reference to Baliev as the "proprietor" of the Chauve-Souris: evidently irony was enough to distinguish the troupe from the world of commercial theater in which it enmeshed. Recalling its origins as a form of entertainment for other artists, Tablada wagers it will teach all the "opulent impresarios," "proud managers," and "greedy magnates" of Broadway that a "small theater, with a company that adds up to fewer than twenty actors, with miniscule decorations . . . with a minimal orchestra, and sometimes only a piano, [can] produce all the effects of colored vision, of harmonious sonority, of atmospheric poetry, of melancholy, of pain, of joy."

The pithy pieces of this petite production open up an enormous spectrum of sensations and emotions able to elude commodification and mechanization. Predictably, however, in the description of select scenes with which Tablada ends his article, it is clear his favorites are the ones in which humans pretend to be mechanical dolls.

Forging Institutions and Emotions

Nowhere in any of the extant programs for the Chauve-Souris does the phrase "synthetic theater" appear. Nor does Baliev seem to have invoked the concept in his dealings with the press, despite some of his artists' close ties to Tairov and others who did. The words *synthétique* and *synthèse* crop up frequently in the program and reviews from Paris, but their equivalents are rare in the ephemera from New York, where a fixation on the outsized personality of Baliev tended to foreclose serious critical reflection on all other aspects of the show. Even Tablada, a man with synthetic intentions of his own, declined to use the term in his review. The verb *sintetizar* occurs in an earlier review of the Parisian show by a French critic that was reprinted (in translation) in the weekly cultural journal *El Universal Ilustrado*, but this hardly suffices to explain how two words circling in the same orbit eventually conjoined to form teatro sintético.[38]

One important factor was Mexico's own special saga with synthesis. If in Europe the idea gained momentum amid the strife of the Great War and Russian Revolution, in Mexico it assumed center stage shortly after the first postrevolutionary president, Álvaro Obregón, took power in 1920. José Vasconcelos, the founding director of the Secretariat of Public Education, had spent the final years of the revolution in exile developing his philosophy of aesthetic monism, a system of "synthesis achieved on the basis of aesthetic pathos" and exemplified by the accumulation of all other genres in a new, future form called the "literary symphony."[39] As the previous chapter detailed, these seemingly esoteric notions were closely tied to his later claim that Latin America was the future birthplace of *la raza cósmica*, or cosmic race—a *raza de síntesis* in which all of the world's races would converge.[40] Vasconcelos had already begun to develop this idea in a philosophical drama published the same year he returned to Mexico, and a similar language of synthesis runs through the rhetoric he wielded in his drive to build schools, organize literacy campaigns, galvanize (and subsidize) artists, and construct an enormous "theater-stadium" to hold mass spectacles.

But while his ideas may have had some part in the genesis of teatro sintético, a more immediate influence was the evolution and increasing institutionalization of anthropology. This process had begun as early as 1887 with the creation of a new division of anthropology at the National Museum, and it gained momentum from 1911 to 1914, when Mexico City was the site of the International School of American Archaeology and Ethnology, a project led by the renowned German-U.S. anthropologist Franz Boas.[41] One of his students at Columbia University, Manuel Gamio, founded the first federal division of anthropology in 1917. Like his mentor, Gamio was a vocal critic of scientific racism and a stated proponent of cultural relativism, but whereas Boas sought to professionalize anthropology within the university as a way of maintaining its autonomy from the state, Gamio openly instrumentalized it as an essential tool of good governance necessary to stimulate the development of "national industry" while placing the nation's indigenous majority on equal footing with their compatriots of European descent. In his 1916 treatise *Forjando patria* (Forging a Nation), he echoes Boas in insisting on the need for "scientific," empirical studies guided by a holistic approach that integrates physical and cultural anthropology with archaeology and linguistics. Yet he does not issue the familiar lament for "dying" cultures disappearing in the face of progress. For Gamio, the main obstacle to the growth of the nation's economy and the reason for its submission to foreign capital is the "material isolation and cultural divergence" of its indigenous elements.[42] His solution is to recast the interdisciplinary imperative of Boasian anthropology as a means of achieving an "ethnic" or "cultural fusion" among the peoples of the not-yet-nation of Mexico. Only by adopting this "integral method" can Mexicans acquire an intellectual and affective understanding of indigenous cultures, and in the process "Indianize" themselves—if only "a bit"—in order to then present their own culture already "diluted with his own" to the Indian (98).

Hovering in the backdrop of this argument is the problem of how to rein in the more radical demands of indigenous forces mobilized during the revolution.[43] On a more abstract level, however, Gamio was grappling with a conundrum Marx had diagnosed:

> We have seen how money is transformed into capital; how surplus-value is made through capital, and how more capital is made from surplus-value. But the accumulation of capital presupposes surplus-value; surplus-value presupposes capitalist production; capitalist production presupposes the availability of considerable masses of capital and labor-power in the hands of commodity producers. The whole movement, therefore, seems to turn around in a never-ending circle.[44]

The answer to this riddle, Marx says, is that the seemingly autonomous system of capitalist production depends on another kind of accumulation—a "secret" stockpiling of wealth and wage labor using the very methods capitalist logic disavows. While the classic examples of what he curiously refers to as "so-called" primitive accumulation are land enclosures and slavery, his list also includes legislation, taxation, and other forms of "extra-economic" coercion that wrest the means of production from the producers in order to create wage laborers and consumers of commodities. Yet as Silvia Federici argues, primitive accumulation does more than just this: the only reason it can function in a systematic way (i.e., as a mode of accumulation) is that it marks off whole groups of people, practices, and ways of life as "primitive," "other," and "outside." According to Federici, primitive accumulation was (is) "not simply an accumulation and concentration of exploitable workers and capital. It was *also an accumulation of differences and divisions within the working class*, whereby hierarchies built upon gender, as well as 'race' and age, became constitutive of class rule and the formation of the modern proletariat."[45] As evidence, she shows how the land enclosures and colonial conquests of the sixteenth and seventeenth centuries went hand in hand with legal and disciplinary measures (including the great "witch" hunts) to divest women of control over their own bodies, "enclosing" them within a naturalized domestic sphere defined in opposition to the realm of commodity production where their task was to *re*produce the waged workforce by performing the unpaid labor of childrearing and housework. In the case of colonial Mexico, too, Daniel Nemser has shown how the policy of resettling indigenous people in towns was not only about facilitating new forms of tribute and labor extraction: it also served to subjectivize and shape the "Indian" into a single racial category.[46]

No wonder Marx seems to waver as to when or if primitive accumulation ends: although capitalism strives for total dominance, it always remains "unfinished" because it has to (re)produce its "primitive" antithesis in order to grow.[47] In *Forjando patria* Gamio rails against the appropriation of indigenous lands under the liberal governments following independence from Spain and insists on the need to raise the living standard of the poor (who will otherwise be unable to buy commodities). But true to his admiration for the protoethnographic work of the early colonial friars, his proposal calls for treating the "extra-economic" force of anthropology as an alternative to the classic forms of primitive accumulation—using it to draw indigenous outliers into a network of capitalist relations, expanding the pool of wage workers and the domestic market in order to turn the country into "one of the foremost industrial producers of the world" (133). In tandem with his excavation of the Templo Mayor pyramid at Teotihuacán, Gamio led an ambitious study of the surrounding valley and its residents, employing anthropologists, engineers, artists, teachers, and laborers to not only collect empirical data but also actively reconfigure indigenous work and life patterns. New schools were opened for children and adults; plans were drawn up for new dams and wells; and collectives were formed to encourage peasants to "industrialize" their agricultural and handicraft production.[48] Although small-scale tourism already existed, a new railroad station and highway from Mexico City led to an exponential increase. In a lecture delivered to the Carnegie Institute in Washington, D.C., and reprinted in the Bulletin of the Pan American Union, Gamio reported that during the winter of 1922–1923, the pyramids had hosted an average of five hundred daily visitors who contributed to the local economy through the purchase of food and crafts such as pottery and obsidian jewelry.[49]

But it would take something else to redeem the Indian from his state of "backwardness" (*atraso*) and turn Mexico into an industrial powerhouse: according to Gamio, economic integration also depended on drawing the disparate sectors of Mexico into a shared circuit of *emotional* exchange. To recall the initial pages of this chapter, Sara Ahmed has argued that emotions are produced through a process of social circulation in a manner akin to Marx's money–commodity–money formula for the creation of surplus value. But what is the genesis of this "never-ending circle"? Is there an affective equivalent to primitive accumulation? In the Valley of Teotihuacán it was the role of the artists employed by the Division of Anthropology and the Secretariat of Public Education to accumulate raw material—to document songs, dances, visual motifs, phrases, and linguistic peculiarities—as a way of jump-starting the creation of emotional and cultural capital. This involved musical notations, in-depth descriptions, transcriptions, sketches, photographs, and dozens of films of indigenous subjects performing dances or typical domestic and agricultural routines. Simple data collection, however, was only part of the point. In the introduction to his dissertation, a collectively authored "synthesis" of findings from the project, Gamio praises the painter Francisco Goitia for his "extreme sensibility and penetrating analytical criterion," explaining that Goitia lived in the valley for several months until, "identifying with the beings and things that surrounded him, he felt his emotion vibrate with the same palpitations that shook that milieu of mysterious contrasts."[50] (Note the similarities to the "vibratory" language of Vasconcelos's Pythagorean philosophy, a connection the art critic Renato González Mello supports in suggesting that Gamio, like Vasconcelos and Diego Rivera, was influenced by Rosicrucian esotericism.)[51] As participant-observers, Goitia and other artists were catalysts for the accumulation of affects, their own bodies serving as both agents and objects of an (uneven) intercultural exchange. This was what allowed them to transmit such "palpitations" in their own work, mimetically reproducing—though with a difference—the visual, aural, and kinesthetic qualities of the indigenous scenes and practices on which they were based. The daily scenes of family life were re-created in paintings and short plays; the steps of traditional dances were standardized; and "typical" songs were arranged for orchestras that incorporated indigenous instruments such as the *chirimía*. When circulated or performed, these proto–works of art acted as "objects" to which the emotions of both indigenous and nonindigenous Mexicans could (in Ahmed's terms) "stick."

The challenge, Gamio later stated, was not just to incorporate indigenous motifs into art, but to "facilitate the fusion, or at least a rapprochement, between the aesthetic criteria" of Euro-descendants and indigenous groups.[52] Underlying this push was the Boasian principle of cultural diffusion, which held that cultures developed historically through the interaction of different populations and the circulation of ideas, institutions, practices, and objects. As Brad Evans points out, cultural diffusion posed a challenge to both Romantic nationalism and doctrines of social evolution by showing that race, language, and culture could not be conflated; individual cultural elements were integrally related to broader, culturally specific systems of meaning-making, but they were also "detachable" in the sense that they could be adopted and reintegrated into other symbolic systems. Evans links this anthropological interest in discontinuity and the "detachability" of cultural objects and practices to the more general logic of cultural objectification and commodification also apparent in the vogue for folklore and local color literature.[53] But whereas for Boas the concept of cultural diffusion was primarily descriptive, Gamio transforms it into a prescriptive call for a "fusion of races, convergence and fusion of cultural manifestations, linguistic unification, and the economic equilibrium of social elements."[54] The joint forces of art and ethnography had the task of objectifying and accumulating cultural products, yet the embodied and embedded dimensions of culture were just as crucial to his economic objectives as detachability.

In fact, it was the "unproductive" nature of performance—the inextricability of the product from the process—that explains its role at Teotihuacán. Indigenous-made pottery and jewelry could be transported and sold in the capital by a handful of intermediaries, but performances required groups of people to come into contact, which drove the expansion of infrastructure and created more opportunities to forge material and affective ties. (The performances themselves, however, were free to the public, and it is unclear whether the performers were paid.) Located in San Juan Teotihuacán, site of the new railroad station and the largest of the dozens of towns in the valley, the Teatro Regional de Teotihuacán was built by the Secretariat of Public Education in early 1922 as the first of what were eventually dozens of such "regional" open-air theaters throughout the country.[55] The theater made its official debut on Saturday, May 20, at 6 P.M., with a lineup that began with a lecture on Mexican theater and Teotihuacán pottery delivered by Esperanza Velásquez Bringas, the daughter of a textile company executive who at the age of twenty-three already had a reputation as a journalist and fervent advocate of popular culture.[56] Following her talk were orchestral arrangements of "typical" songs of the area, a "regional" dance-drama called Los Alchileos, an unnamed "national film," and a play called *Los novios*

b). — Actor indígena que representó el
personaje Enrique en "La Cruza".

Figure 2.3. An indigenous actor in Rafael M. Saavedra's regionalist *ensayo* (play) *La cruza*, staged at the theater at Teotihuacán in 1922. Published in the journal *Ethnos*, founded and edited by Manuel Gamio (November 1922–January 1923). Courtesy of University of Texas at Austin Libraries.

(The Bride and Groom) by Rafael Saavedra with costumes and set design by Carlos González.[57] Like a number of other ethnographic plays created and staged over the following year, *Los novios* was classified as an *ensayo*—a rehearsal, essay, experiment, or unfinished form. No effort was made to correct the actors' pronunciation, and the compression of idiomatic expressions and customs into a few "typical" scenes invited spectators to act as amateur ethnographers. Yet if on the one hand these humble displays of "regional" culture tended to reify difference, they were simultaneously presented as the germ of a "national" theater whose genesis was dependent on the "fusion" of ethnicities and cultures.[58]

This cross-pollination of performance and anthropology was not entirely new. During the late nineteenth and early twentieth centuries archaeology and anthropology had figured prominently in Mexico's exhibits at the World's Fairs, which were designed to attract foreign investment while displaying the country's progress and ability to redress evolutionary deficiencies through sanitation and hygiene. Claims about the abundance of potential workers suitable for diverse types of employment were documented by

a).—Grupo de intérpretes de "Los Novios".

Figure 2.4. Actors in Rafael M. Saavedra's play *Los novios*. Published in *Ethnos* (November 1922–January 1923). Courtesy of University of Texas at Austin Libraries.

studies and even demonstrated by "real-life" *indios* performing "typical" dances and songs along with their daily chores and the mundane rituals of manual labor. Mauricio Tenorio-Trillo explains this overlap between science and commerce by noting that at the time anthropology was defined as "a discipline concerned with the historicization of labor itself, while ethnography was considered the history of progress in material things."[59] A similar logic underlies the performances at Teotihuacán, though some key differences accompanied the shift toward the more holistic notion of "culture" and the creation of a national audience formed by economic *and* affective bonds. Despite the frequent allusions to agricultural work in the *ensayos* performed at Teotihuacán, the scenes enacted before the audience invariably highlighted the labor of social reproduction. Female characters outnumbered males, and the domestic space of the home provided an ideal setting for displaying everyday customs while evoking an air of intimacy. Nearly all of the schematic plots of the extant scripts revolve around romantic relations and end in marriage, with the exception of *La cruza*, in which a young woman shames her family and fiancé by succumbing to the advances of the *patrón*.[60] Some of the plays also allude to and contextualize the songs and dances performed in the open-air theater, as in *La tejedora* when a young man pledges to dance in the annual religious pageant of *Los Alchileos*, in return for which the town's

b.)—Dos payasos con Pilatos, en la danza de "Los Alchileos".

Figure 2.5. A performance of *Los Alchileos*, one of the traditional dance-dramas artists at Teotihuacán studied in order to create more "polished" versions. Published in *Ethnos* (November 1922–January 1923). Courtesy of University of Texas at Austin Libraries.

patron saint miraculously stops his father from drinking so he can tend to his crops.[61]

Because of its ability to incorporate other artistic traditions, theater played an especially prominent role in the "integral" ethnography practiced at Teotihuacán, as it also would in a subsequent spin-off project. Impressed by what he had witnessed at the inauguration of the Teatro Regional, José Vasconcelos hired the writer Rafael M. Saavedra and the visual artist Carlos E. González to undertake similar experiments among the Purépecha (also known as Tarascan) communities in and around Lake Pátzcuaro in the state of Michoacán. Within a few years this area would become a prime destination for folklorists and anthropologists such as Frances Toor, editor of the bilingual journal *Mexican Folkways*, as well as artists and photographers including Tina Modotti and Edward Weston; by the end of the decade a small tourist industry had grown up, and as the home base of the state governor and future president Lázaro Cárdenas, the area would be a focal point for tourism and government development programs.[62] When Saavedra and González arrived in August 1922, however, the lake was still off the beaten path, and its traditions and customs were still unfamiliar to most outsiders. The two men spent five months in the area and then returned in February 1923 with the composer Francisco Domínguez to document the enchanting environment and the customs of its people: the mist-shrouded lake, the distinctive *rebozos* (shawls) of the women, the candlelit vigil at the small cemetery on the island of Janitizio on the Night of the Dead, and performance traditions such as the comic *Danza de los viejitos*, or Dance of the Little Old Men. No longer under the guidance of Gamio, the artists worked without assistance from anthropologists or educators, and there is no evidence anyone in the trio spoke the dominant Purépecha language (though the majority of the locals also spoke Spanish). In spite of such limitations González and Domínguez eventually oversaw the opening of another SEP-sponsored "regional" theater in the town of San Pedro Paracho on June 10, 1923—an event reported to have drawn ten thousand people, including indigenous people from a wide range and intellectuals from the state capital of Morelia.[63]

Yet from the very beginning this trio of artists had its sights set on other goals. In January 1923, the Mexico City–based newspaper *El Mundo* reported that the three were at work on developing a new form of spectacle based on their research in Michoacán and were in discussions with impresarios interested in booking the group at theaters in the capital. All of the performers would be indigenous people, and the spectacle would be divided into three parts: Mexican ballet, indigenous comedy and drama, and *comedia sintética*—a new genre of "very brief scenes in which everything is the result of fine observation. Notes. A landscape, an attitude."[64] Another feature story on the group published around the same time in the weekly cultural magazine *El Universal Ilustrado* makes no mention of this new term, though it quotes Carlos González describing the genre in similar terms, as "very brief scenes" that portray "regional aspects, our things [*cosas nuestras*], passed through the sieve of art . . . perhaps scenes in which the figures are immobilized to emphasize an attitude, a moment."[65] Like the reporter for *El Mundo*, the author gives an account of his visit to the home studio of González, recalling in luxurious detail all of the colorful objects the painter had collected from Michoacán as well as his own vivid mock-ups of the scenes he and his collaborators planned to stage. On his hand-drawn calling cards González described himself as an "orientalist painter of deep thoughts,"[66] and this aspect of his work was at least partially born out in a drawing accompanying the article: it depicts a figure in a fancifully stylized turban and cape performing the Dance of the Moors, a tradition of the Purépecha and other indigenous groups that had evolved out of the reenactments of battles between Christians and Muslims first staged in sixteenth-century Spain and imported to the Americas by evangelical friars (figure 2.6).[67] At once "other" and "ours," indigenous and exotic, these "Moors" visualized a close link between orientalism and *indigenismo* that was also evident in the haikus and Sinophilic poetry of Juan José Tablada and Vasconcelos's passion for Asian philosophy.[68]

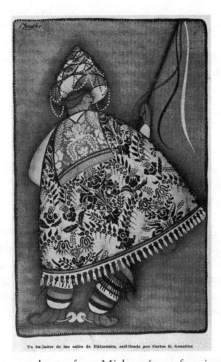

Un bailador de las salas de Pátzcuaro, estilizado por Carlos E. González

Figure 2.6. An indigenous dancer from Michoacán performing the Dance of the Moors, as depicted by Carlos González. Although the dancer's attire closely resembles that of actual dancers, the complex floral pattern on the cape is González's invention. Published in *El Universal Ilustrado*, January 11, 1923. Courtesy of University of Texas at Austin Libraries.

Peasants singing and dancing, references to "synthesis," immobilized actors, the orientalist vogue . . . If all of this sounds reminiscent of a certain Russian revue, observers at the time agreed. The article in *El Universal Ilustrado* ends by citing Tablada, who on learning of his compatriots' activities drew a comparison to the spectacles of the Chauve-Souris he had seen in New York.[69] The stylistic confluences are indeed clear in the one surviving script from this phase of the project. Published in *El Universal Ilustrado* in March 1923, "La Chinita" was identified as an example of *teatro mínimo*—though on a future occasion Saavedra would call it a work of teatro sintético—and is divided into three *instantes*, each of which would likely last about five minutes. The first "instant" takes place on market day in Uruapan, a town on the western edge of the Purépecha highlands. Amid vendors hawking the distinctive foods and products of the region, a man sings and plays a jarabe on the guitar as others dance, until a stranger dressed in the wide hat and white garb characteristic of the warmer coastal region arrives. El de Tierra Caliente (The Man of the Hot Lands) negotiates a deal with El Cantador (The Singer), who tells his customer, "There are songs for every taste, I have passionate ones, sad ones, ones for saying goodbye, ones for disputes."[70] Their transaction is completed in the final instant as El de Tierra Caliente sits on the shore of a river with his ladylove (the *chinita* of the title) while El Cantador sings the song of a rambling man bidding his woman farewell. Money is exchanged, and the play ends in darkness with the sound of a kiss—as if the culmination of the artistic and cultural synthesis enacted over the previous few minutes could only be experienced as sound rather than sight.

As places where distinct groups of people came into contact for the purposes of trade, indigenous markets had been important sites of cultural diffusion since long before the arrival of the Spanish. On the one hand, "La Chinita" emphasizes the personalistic, precapitalist nature of the economic exchange it depicts (El Cantador is first seen playing for pleasure, and the never-named price seems to be decided through informal negotiation), yet the piece also naturalizes its own act of appropriation inasmuch as it imagines the songs it stages as protocommodities. Domínguez's score for the songs (included in the music section of the journal) and two drawings by González contribute to the process of detachment and objectification while at the same time evoking the idea of a performance capable of superseding the commodification of its constituent parts through what the magazine describes as its unique *sintetismo*. Alas, the synthetic bonds joining the playwright, painter, and composer proved too fragile to hold: a few months later the group dissolved due to a dispute over the authorship of a piece titled "Tiene la culpa el cilindro" (It's the Barrel Organ's Fault), which by some accounts was (or would have been) the very first realization of teatro sintético.[71] In short, Saavedra found himself squeezed out by the drive for brevity and compression, which diminished the importance of his "literary" role. The playwright went his own way, and little was heard of teatro sintético until June of the following year, when reports began to circulate that González and Domínguez were collaborating on an upcoming spectacle called Teatro del Murciélago with Luis Quintanilla, a poet affiliated with the estridentista avant-garde.[72]

Born to Guatemalan parents but raised in Paris, Quintanilla had seen the Chauve-Souris on Broadway while serving as an attaché at the Mexican embassy in the United States. On arriving in Mexico City, where he continued to work for the Ministry of Foreign Relations, he threw in his lot with estridentismo, which since the launch of its first manifesto in the final days of 1921 had grown from the one-man show of Manuel Maples Arce into a conglomeration of writers and visual artists who gathered at a spot they dubbed El Café de Nadie and collaborated on the short-lived journal *Irradiador*. Whether or not the Teatro del Murciélago formed part of the movement is a bone of contention: the estridentista label was not officially attached to the project, and seven decades later in an interview Germán List Arzubide, who will play a pivotal role in the following chapter on the afterlife of estridentismo, dismissed the Murciélago as an "aristocratic thing" for *señoritos* (little gentlemen) and derided Quintanilla for passing it off as an estridentista endeavor.[73] But who or what decides where the limits of an ism(o) lie? Quintanilla's public profile was tied to estridentismo, and at least two of the other participants he recruited were active estridentistas at this time: the Swiss anarchist Gaston Dinner had contributed poems to *Irradiador*, and Tina Modotti, who had settled in Mexico a year earlier, would continue to collaborate with the group in Xalapa, where several of its core members relocated in early 1926 to work under the socialist governor of Veracruz until his ouster in a coup in September 1927 led to estridentismo's demise. Prior to this, the cultural politics of the group were more amorphous: odes to the Bolshevik Revolution such as Maples Arce's *Urbe* had no concrete connection to the Mexican Communist Party or labor organizing, and Quintanilla's Dada-esque poem *Avión* (published under his pseudonym Kin-Taniya) made no overtly political claims.

What is indubitably true is that the Teatro del Murciélago might never have taken flight were it not for the connections Quintanilla had made through his day job. On September 3, 1923, the regime of President Álvaro Obregón had received official recognition from the U.S. government after tense negotiations ending in a controversial promise to guarantee the property rights of U.S. citizens and corporations (i.e., oil companies) acquired prior to the revolution. Rebellions were raised and high-profile opponents of the concession met with an assassin's bullet, but the dust had mostly settled by July of the following year when Marcos E. Raya, the mayor of Mexico City, invited the American Manufacturers Export Association to send a delegation of bankers and manufacturers to attend the annual festivities in honor of Mexico's independence on September 16.[74] The group of more than fifty men, dispatched with a blessing from President Calvin Coolidge and led by William Wallace Nichols (president of the Allis-Chalmers Manufacturing Company), arrived in Mexico City by train on September 15 and spent the next five days in the city.[75] What sorts of deals, insinuations, or veiled threats were made behind closed doors and over cocktails as the members of the American Industrial Mission met with government officials and local business leaders? No such details were to be found in the press, but newspapers brimmed with information about the elaborate performances staged for the U.S. missionaries on their pseudo-ethnographic excursions. Evidently a simple tour of factories to observe their protocols and the efficiency—and felicity—of their workers was not enough: at lunchtime managers sought to ease their guests' digestion by arranging for workers to offer a display of gymnastics, military exercises, marches, and songs by a small *orquesta típica* (figure 2.7).[76] On the morning of September 17, the foreigners boarded a special train to Teotihuacán, where a brochure by Manuel Gamio and an on-site talk by an employee of the Division of Anthropology filled them in on the pyramids and the surrounding area. Some of the visitors also checked out the open-air theater (though there does not seem to have been a performance),[77] and at lunch a banquet was set up in a grotto, where a representative of the Ministry of Foreign Relations encouraged the

Figure 2.7. The lunch banquet for the American Industrial Mission during one of their factory tours. The two men seated in the center are William Wallace Nichols, who was the head of the mission (to the left, staring at the camera), and President Álvaro Obregón. The women in the background are part of the workers' orchestra. From the scrapbook of the Mission assembled by William Wallace Nichols. Courtesy of the Manuscript and Archives Division, The New York Public Library, Astor, Lenox and Tilden Foundations.

visitors to feel the "vibrations of the Indian soul" (figure 2.8).[78] Back at the hotel in Mexico City the men must have freshened up before heading to the Teatro Olimpia, eager to enjoy the evening's performance in the company of the *Embajadoras de la Simpatía*, or "Ambassadors of Charm"—women from every state in the republic chosen in a contest by the newspaper *El Universal* to offer a warm welcome to the U.S. industrialists.

This is all to say that the Teatro del Murciélago's big debut was just a small part of the affective labor expended in the campaign to forge new economic alliances and industrialize Mexico. As they waited for the show to begin, the honored guests must have perused the colorful program, and more than a few might have recognized its vivid illustrations and short summaries of each number as reminiscent of the programs of the Chauve-Souris. Nor did the artists make any attempt to deny their debt, as the audience found out when the performance finally got under way at around 8:45 P.M., three-quarters of an hour behind schedule. After the forty-person orchestra (directed by Domínguez) played the national anthem, Quintanilla delivered a short prologue in English explaining how he had dreamed of creating a Mexican equivalent to

Figure 2.8. Members of the American Industrial Mission at the open-air theater during their visit to Teotihuacán. It is not clear whether the women accompanying them are their wives or the women elected as "Ambassadors of Sympathy." From the scrapbook of the mission assembled by William Wallace Nichols. Courtesy of the Manuscript and Archives Division, The New York Public Library, Astor, Lenox and Tilden Foundations.

the Chauve-Souris ever since seeing it on Broadway. As he cheekily noted, "We have titled our spectacle the 'Murciélago,' because '*murciélago*' is the translation of '*chauve-souris*.'" Like the Russian troupe, he and his collaborators "employ almost all the resources of the aesthetic" in order to provoke an "exquisite emotion of art." Then why not call the project Teatro Sintético Mexicano (as some had apparently suggested)? In all likelihood the reason was related to the earlier dispute between González and Rafael Saavedra over the use of this term, but Quintanilla rather vaguely states, "Our Theater . . . is synthetic and something more." Whereas the Chauve-Souris was "international," the Murciélago, despite its pretensions as a touring phenomenon, was resolutely "national": "We want to present to the public, especially abroad, in a synthetic and suggestive form, all those aspects of our national life that are characteristic of our color, our melody, our poetry."[79]

There was another difference, of course. Although the Chauve-Souris drew on repertoires, images, and information amassed during the preceding decades at Abramtsevo and other such colonies, where artists often worked directly with the peasantry, the Russian troupe was one step removed from the process of primitivist accumulation in which the Murciélago was involved. On hand for the performance at the Teatro Olimpia were Purépecha musicians, who

Figure 2.9. The cover of the souvenir program from the Teatro del Murciélago's debut, designed by Carlos González. Luis Quintanilla and Carlos González, *Teatro mexicano del Murciélago* (1924).

played songs arranged by Domínguez between the dramatic scenes and during the Dance of the Little Old Men and Dance of the Moors. As described in the program and relayed in English by Quintanilla from the stage, the Dance of the Little Old Men was accompanied by *jaranitas*, or small guitars, and executed by young men in grotesque masks who wore the wide palm hat and distinctive dress of ranchers from the Tierra Caliente region (figure 2.10). Quintanilla emphasized that the dance, for all its humor, was performed as part of a *manda* or religious pledge—a statement that was only partially correct, since it ignored the role of locals such as Nicolás Bartolo Juárez in disseminating and secularizing the dance.[80] Bartolo Juárez, the only Purépecha mentioned by name in the handbill, had trained a group of students from the capital to perform the dance for this occasion and also took a turn himself in the Dance of the Moors. The description of this scene exclaims, "Gaspar, Melchior, and Baltazar!" and mentions leaders of "Arabic tribes" from the Bible before evoking the veiled dancers and the "black mystery of their slanted eyes."[81] Conveniently, however, this conflation of Mexico with the Middle East and the multicultural fable of the Three Magi obscured its violent origins in the expulsion of Muslims from Spain and the conquest of the Americas.

Figure 2.10. Carlos González's illustration of the Dance of the Little Old Men, from the souvenir program of the Teatro del Murciélago. Luis Quintanilla and Carlos González, *Teatro mexicano del Murciélago* (1924).

Like these two dances, several of the other scenes had been in the works since long before Quintanilla came on board. His one major innovation appears to have been a plan to alternate the indigenous tableaux with urban scenes, though for reasons unknown only one of these (soon to be discussed) made it into the show. The program, however, offered clues regarding these future additions to the Murciélago's lineup. The summary for a scene called "Fifís" explains in a roundabout way this term for well-to-do pretty boys (or forerunners to today's *fresas*)—"mobile ornaments" that serve an "exclusively decorative" function and frequent French sweetshops and American drugstores yet are "distinctly Mexican."[82] Another scene, entitled "Camiones," depicts Mexico City's electric trolleys as "flea nests. They are the antithesis of fifís. Those adorn and perfume. These get in the way and smell. But like fifís, though they dress in the American style, they have an essentially Mexican soul."[83] This coy acknowledgment of the propinquity between originality and imitation had plenty of parallels in the Chauve-Souris, which established its own authenticity as Russian in part through its impersonations of Japanese samurai and Crimean khans. The decision to name the Murciélago after the

Chauve-Souris also played on this paradox, but Quintanilla and company took it a step further by pointing to mimicry as constitutive of Mexican culture itself. If indigenous culture owed its ethnographic value to the imitation of old men from the neighboring lowlands and the impersonation of distant and imaginary Moors, *la mexicanidad* of urban culture (both popular and elite) was inseparable from its simulation of the lifeways of Uncle Sam.

Among the scenes performed, the pleasures and perils of cross-cultural mimesis reached their peak in "La Ofrenda" (The Offering). Singled out by critics as a favorite for its emotional intensity, this reenactment of the Night of the Dead ceremony on the island of Janitzio featured Tina Modotti in the role of a Purépecha woman bringing food and other offerings to the cemetery, with a darkened set illuminated by candles and yellow *cempazuchitl* flowers providing splashes of color (figure 2.11). In foregrounding the role of women and the labor of social reproduction, this scene harked back to the earliest *ensayos* at Teotihuacán. Claudio Lomnitz has noted that the Day (and Night) of the Dead occurs shortly after harvesttime, and in indigenous communities, offerings were traditionally imagined in terms of a debt payment or reciprocal exchange with the deceased, who both signified and ensured the fertility of the soil. During the colonial period communities also gave prolific offerings of money and material goods to priests as a way of negotiating new alliances and the continuation of pre-Hispanic mortuary rituals.[84] The Murciélago's mise-en-scène of this ritual was an early instance of its embrace by artists in the postrevolutionary period and their reimagination of Mexico as a nation whose experience of modernity was marked by a unique intimacy with death. Modotti's act of impersonation also allegorically enacted the "ethnic fusion" Manuel Gamio sought when he recruited artists for his anthropological project: how better to affectively identify with the indigenous than by serving as a surrogate for one of them in the act of mourning? Although this act of "synthesis" was *trans*national in scope, it is unlikely many in the audience were aware of the actress's Italian identity, since the drive toward compression and condensation elided the problem of linguistic difference by almost entirely eliminating dialogue in a push to achieve a pure emotion unmediated by words.

And so it was only fitting that the Murciélago capped off the evening with a wordless scene. In "Aparador" (Store Window), the sole tableaux with an urban setting, a male and a female actor played mechanical dolls representing "typical" figures of the Guadalajara region dancing the *jarabe tapatío* around a sombrero (figure 2.12). Outside, standing under a street lamp, a blind man performed by the Swiss writer Gaston Dinner played popular melodies on a flute as a police officer strolled back and forth. (One review seems to suggest this was a nod to an actual person who played his flute every evening in front of the Teatro Nacional.)[85] Quintanilla and González had always taken pains to distinguish the Murciélago from the already hackneyed celebration of the *jarabe tapatío* (made internationally famous as the Mexican Hat Dance after

Figure 2.11. Carlos González's illustration of the Night of the Dead scene, titled "La Ofrenda" (The Offering), from the souvenir program of the Teatro del Murciélago's debut. Luis Quintanilla and Carlos González, *Teatro mexicano del Murciélago* (1924).

the Russian dancer Anna Pavlova visited in 1919 and incorporated it into her repertoire), but even the businessmen and government officials in the audience might have picked up on the self-reflexive irony of this scene—after all, the Murciélago was presented in the program and the press as a "toy store for the soul." To again cite Brad Evans on regionalism in the United States, the aesthetic charge of the figures in the window, like all of the Murciélago's tableaux, had less to do with their attachment to a particular people or place than with the "dissociation of the aesthetic object from its anthropological origins" and its circulation in an (inter)national art market.[86] In other words, it was through its de- and recontextualization in networks of commodity exchange that their local color accrued its value—an "aura of dislocation" that Evans suggests is not so distant from the avant-garde penchant for juxtaposition and collage (217n4).

Given the context of the performance, it is hard not to detect a note of cynicism in this final tableau. Yet as is often the case, its cynicism contained a seed of hope—and maybe also a little fear. The only sound in this scene was the flute of the blind man, but the text in the program speaks on behalf of

Figure 2.12. Carlos González's illustration of the scene titled "Aparador" (Store Window), from the souvenir program of the Teatro del Murciélago's debut. Luis Quintanilla and Carlos González, *Teatro mexicano del Murciélago* (1924).

the objects in the shop window: "To display their force, men have imprisoned objects in cages of thick glass, as if they could escape. Therefore hides, metals and fabric, *rebozos*, *sarapes*, and saddles are slowly dying of melancholy, and it is in vain that the jewels, sparkling from sorrow, beg for commiseration."[87] Invested with emotions, these sentient commodities have been deprived of their use value and now serve a solely decorative function (like the pretty-boy *fifís*). But the text puts a twist on the animistic fetishization of commodities by asking the audience to look and listen with the eyes and ears of a child in order to hear their silent cry. "—Who will free us from our slavery?—say the poor paralytic things.—Who? and when? when?" The description ends: "But in the shadow of the jewelry stores, like mysterious conspirators, the clocks do not cease to chatter, disorderly, like politicians on the eve of revolution." The Murciélago thus leaves its spectators with an ambiguous reminder of their own—and its own—complicity, and perhaps also with the question of how the fate of the frozen man and woman behind the window might depend on a liberation of things.

A Fuzzy Little Black Mystery

Ten days after its debut for an invitation-only audience, the Murciélago gave a public performance at the Teatro Principal in Mexico City, after which it appears to have folded its wings.[88] Despite calls for the city government to continue funding the project, it either saw no purpose or lacked the resources, and no impresarios stepped up to the plate. Certainly at the level of the federal government it was an unpropitious moment: just a month before the Murciélago's premiere José Vasconcelos had resigned as director of the SEP in protest of the impending presidency of Plutarco Elías Calles, and Manuel Gamio would also soon be on the outs with the new chief executive over his decision to subordinate the Division of Anthropology to the SEP.[89] Meanwhile the members of the American Industrial Mission returned home and declared their experience a success. Although their follow-up report said nothing about the spectacle they had seen—far more pressing, after all, was the fact that Mexico's "supply of raw materials is greatly varied and almost unlimited"—it deployed a similar language of intimacy and ethnographic authenticity, emphasizing the need to go beyond the experience of the tourist in order to learn about the "inner life and attitude of mind of these people."[90] True, the illiteracy rate was around 80 percent, but as compensation there was a large supply of potential industrial workers gifted with unusual manual dexterity, a trait the report attributes to the fact that boys learned from an early age to play the guitar and girls learned to draw.

Teatro sintético had a slightly longer life than the Murciélago. Just two months after the performance at Teatro Olimpia, the poet José Gorostiza published a short play in *El Universal Ilustrado* that he labeled a work of "teatro sintético," though in its bitter portrayal of the anomie of the city it reads like a parody of the preciousness of the Murciélago—and indeed, the following year the same author would publicly lambast teatro sintético as a glorified version of the follies or *teatro de revista* (musical revue theater).[91] A new collective called Grupo de Siete Autores (also known as Los Pirandellos) mounted several short one-acts identified as *ensayos* of teatro sintético during its debut season of 1925–1926, and almost inevitably, the Secretariat of Public Education also got in the game with a project called Teatro Sintético Emocional Mexicano. Luis Quintanilla had been called back to his diplomatic duties and was in Paris, but Carlos González served as artistic director, and the premiere production recycled two of the Murciélago's pieces—including the store window scene—along with an old Purépecha ceremony called "Canacuas" that had been staged by the Saavedra-González-Domínguez trio in Michoacán and reprised a month earlier for a festival in honor of visiting dignitaries from Brazil.[92] Among the new elements were a "very rapid tragedy" by the Yucatec Mayan writer Ermilo Gómez Abreu and a dramatization of the Zapotec story of *la tona*, the special spirit-animal believed to inhabit every baby at birth.[93] According to the press most of the audience members were students and teachers, and although the identity of the actors is unclear, a classical choir of teachers and soloists sang "Mexican" songs, with a violinist and pianist providing accompaniment. None of the musicians from Michoacán appear to have been on hand; yet in keeping with the inclusion of indigenous themes from other regions of Mexico, the goal of the production was described as nothing less than to "embody our racial structure."[94]

So said José Manuel Puig Casauranc, the new director of the SEP, in his opening speech. Puig made an argument for state sponsorship of the arts, insisting that the SEP would fail if it limited its sphere of action to the schoolroom: only by venturing into realms of social life where thought assumed diverse forms could it succeed in "opening new windows onto the comprehension of, and affection for, our national life." Articulating a notion already present, if in more fragmentary form, in the discussions of theater in San Juan Teotihuacán, he lauded theater as an ideal medium for the circulation of ideas, a "passionate spectacle" with the potential to bypass the sterile distinction between intellect and emotion. What the audience was about to see was "barely, in reality, a rehearsal [*ensayo*]," a work-in-progress driven by the desire to learn to love those sights and sounds that "exalt before our own eyes and before the eyes of strangers, our racial character." But while all the elements of the spectacle were Mexican, there was nothing exclusively national about its form. On the contrary, people everywhere were coming to share this desire to shed the baggage of excessively literary drama in favor of forms of *teatro condensado* such as the Grand Guignol. Unlike Vasconcelos, who had imagined his grandiose theater-stadium as supplanting commercial spectacles, his successor saw the role of the SEP in more modest terms, as a force responsible for inspiring the public to demand similarly "national" scenes from theater impresarios.

Yet in this case too "our racial structure" seemed to resist full embodiment: for all the fanfare, there is no record of a second performance of the Teatro Sintético Emocional Mexicano. If the repertoires of racial synthesis were effective, it was in the form of fragments. Carlos González, Rafael Saavedra, and Francisco Domínguez continued to work for the SEP over the following decades, and many of their scenarios, set pieces, and songs reappeared in the context of other (often short-lived) performative projects. At the end of 1926, a few scenes from the Murciélago, along with others from the Teatro Sintético Emocional Mexicano, were performed at the Casa del Estudiante Indígena, a new boarding school in Mexico City where promising indigenous children and youth from around the country were brought to be assimilated and educated to serve as future teachers; González was apparently involved, as was Guillermo Castillo (another Murciélago collaborator) and the composer Tata Nacho, but it is unclear how long the project lasted.[95] A few years later in 1932, when the National Dance School was founded, its director Carlos Mérida cited the Murciélago as its "only precedent,"[96] and the material collected in Teotihuacán and Michoacán would serve as the basis for what Manuel Gamio praised as the choreographers' labor of "synthesis, polishing, and stylization."[97] Meanwhile the Dance of the Little Old Men and the Night of the Dead quickly became national icons and not only continue to draw tourists to the Pátzcuaro region today but have also moved with the waves of migration from this region and are performed throughout the United States.[98]

Shortly after its ephemeral run, Luis Quintanilla evoked the story of the Murciélago in a curious text published in a publication of the PEN Club of Mexico. Divided into a series of short segments resembling the brief "instants" of teatro sintético, it begins as follows: "Bat, little bat. I brought it from New York without paying customs duties. But on its first Mexican night it died from the light. It was killed by the light!"[99] Quintanilla carries this conceit throughout the entire text, describing the experiences of the bat on its transnational journey, which shadows the flow of capital yet continually eludes its reach. From New York, the bat travels with Quintanilla through Cuba, where a "mulatta wanted to hold him in her chest, between her swollen, warm breasts"; when they arrive in Mexico (the writer reminds the animal), "The businessmen paid to see you. The businessmen paid two thousand pesos to caress your wings, but the black mystery of your little velveteen body must have filled them with fright" (31). This "black mystery," it seems, is something like the longed-for "Mexican" theater—a theater that is both art and an expression of the popular, both an agent and outcome of cultural diffusion. The bat arrives with Russian snowflakes on its wings, but the author imagines that when it returns to Russia from Mexico, fleeing the death-dealing light of the stage, "you will carry pineapple and lemon snow. Tell Nikita [Baliev] you now know how to speak Tarascan and Spanish" (32). Quintanilla imagines the prodigal bat's return in a distant future that sounds more like a postapocalyptic scenario than the futuristic fantasy of Estridentópolis, the technological wonderland invented by his fellow avant-garde artists: "When you return you may not find so much as my cadaver among the bills from the Union of Stagehands Set Designers Electricians and So on of Mexico City" (33).[100] Neither human nor machine, its elegant flight unable to be assimilated as commodified labor, only the primitive bat remains as witness after the final synthesis occurs.

Chapter 3

◆

Radio/Puppets, or The Institutionalization of a (Media) Revolution

Listeners who tuned into station XFX in Mexico City at around 10 A.M. on February 19, 1933, were greeted with a cacophonous clangor and clatter of brass instruments, strings, cymbals, and xylophones—an avant-garde mélange of dissonant sounds interspersed with the fragmented melody of a familiar children's song. Then at a certain point a voice intervened and said something close to if not exactly like this:

> Hear my sonorous song ascend through my crystal throat and amplify in the magnavox of my mouth. I am TROKA the Powerful. The man of metal moved by electricity. So big, so strong, so resistant am I! My body is formed out of hard, shiny, polished planes. My arms and legs are made of aluminum to give them agility; my joints rotate on steel balls. My chest is of iron and in its interior hums my heart, an electric motor. Hear it! *(A buzz is heard.)* My head is made of bronze; in it I enclose my brain, made of electromagnetic apparatuses; from this brain my nerves emerge and fan out like metallic threads that run all over my body and transmit the orders that make me act.

> Oíd mi sonoro canto que asciende por mi garganta de cristal y se amplía en el magnavoz de mi boca. Soy TROKA el poderoso. El hombre de metal que se mueve por electricidad. ¡Qué grande, qué fuerte, qué resistente soy! Mi cuerpo está formado de duros planos pulidos y brillantes. De aluminio son mis brazos y piernas para que sean ágiles y flexibles; sobre balas de acero giran mis coyunturas. Mi pecho es de hierro y en su interior zumba mi corazón, motor eléctrico. ¡Oídlo! *(Se oye el zumbido.)* Mi cabeza es de bronce; en ella encierro mi cerebro hecho todo de aparatos electromagnéticos; de este cerebro salen y se distribuyen mis nervios, hilos metálicos que corren a través de mi cuerpo y transmiten las órdenes para que yo actúe.[1]

Who or what is the subject of this Voice—this strange "spirit" cobbled together out of sheet metal, electrical impulses, and mechanical parts? Troka speaks in the stilted syntax favored by deities and commands his audience to *hear* his song, a song of the body electric that is simultaneously the "industrial song of the world." Over the next few years, as the host of a popular "children's hour" on the official station of the Mexican Secretariat of Public Education, he would spin stories in which modern machines conquer space and time while flaunting their strength and speed in the face of the older technologies they claim to supersede. In this initial apparition, however, he simply beckons his young listeners to *listen* to the myriad manifestations of his power. Troka (says Troka) is present in the "solemn murmur" of motors and the "impatient panting" of machines, in the whistle of locomotives and the "cry" of sirens summoning men to work in factories. He is the synthesis of all elements and the efforts of all men: of the ironworkers whose hammers send sparks flying, the engineers who build bridges out of cables and steel plates, the scientists who unlock the secrets of nature, the white men who fell the Canadian forests, the yellow men who sow the Chinese plains with rice, and the black men who tap rubber trees in the Amazon. His eyes are streetlights; his nerves are telegraph wires; his arms are radio towers. And his voice? It is the medium of radio itself. Troka is the ghost in the machine, the self-authorizing subject of technology that conjures its own power into existence and boxes in its own brain.

Or is he? In fact, it is likely some of the listeners who tuned into Troka heard echoes of other voices in his bombastic (or reassuringly avuncular?) timbre. At least a handful of the adults knew there was a reason he sounded so similar to Germán List Arzubide, a man (made of flesh and blood) whose notoriety extended back a decade to his days as one of the most visible and vocal estridentistas. During the early 1920s the estridentistas were notorious for their raucous odes to revolution and embrace of radio and other new technologies—though as was revealed in the previous chapter, several members had also turned their attention to indigenous culture with their short-lived Teatro del Murciélago. The movement "died" well before the end of the decade, crushed by the forces of reaction in the prime of its youth (or so the story goes), but it is conceivable some listeners could discern a few "strident" strains in the didactic declarations of this aural automaton. Still, probably fresher in the mind of most was the fact that less than a year and a half earlier, List Arzubide had been accused of hijacking Mexico's most powerful radio station and broadcasting an antigovernment speech in commemoration of the Russian Revolution. So who really was this character now commanding impressionable young ears in the name of the Secretariat of Public Education? Did it occur to anyone that something about Troka was a little out-of-joint—that not all of his mechanical parts fit? As it happens, even some of the children might have had an inkling about one other curious detail: he was also (and perhaps originally) imagined as a marionette. The

Voice of Troka was not his own, and his song—"the industrial song of the world"—was shadowed by the specter of a small stage on which object bodies move to the motion of hidden hands.

This chapter sets out to resurrect Troka el Poderoso, a radio/puppet born in the afterlife of estridentismo and at the forefront of a fraught alliance among the artistic avant-garde, the communist Left, and the cultural bureaucracy of a "revolutionary" state. In doing so, it also counters the common narrative of an estridentista "radio revolution" and taps into an ongoing wave of interest in media that are ostensibly "old," "residual," "dying," or "dead." Carolyn Marvin's *When Old Technologies Were New*, often cited as a prescient example of this trend, challenged what she called an "artifactual" perspective, in which new social practices are seen as emanating from the object itself, and offered an account of the telephone and the electric light as "constructed complexes of habits, beliefs, and procedures" emerging out of a "pattern of tension created by the coexistence of old and new."[2] More recently, Lisa Gitelman has shown how digital networks are acquiring their own "coincident yet contravening logic" vis-à-vis an existing textual economy by drawing comparisons to the phonograph, whose novel ability to record and replay sound was initially understood in relation to practices of writing and reading.[3] Like Jonathan Sterne, who traces the "one hundred year history" of the MP3,[4] Gitelman suggests that "the introduction of new media . . . is never entirely revolutionary: new media are less points of epistemic rupture than they are socially embedded sites for the ongoing negotiation of meaning as such" (6).

This self-reflexive trend in new media studies is premised on the idea that technologies no longer regarded as agents of progress and productivity can illuminate the ways in which media become constituted as historical subjects implicated in complex social, economic, and material relations. One of my aims is to show that these critiques of new media discourse—like efforts to reimagine the temporality of the avant-garde—have much to gain by redirecting their attention to regions of the world regarded as "backward" and "behind." One might assume that the "mysterious spirit of mechanical things" would be born in the bowels of industry, but Troka the Powerful was a belated offshoot of an avant-garde movement in a largely agricultural country where relatively few people owned radio receivers and the transmitters were all imported from his imperial neighbor to the north. Artists are often intimately involved in the early, experimental stages of emerging technologies, and people in the role of technicians are often guided in part by aesthetic concerns; but these boundaries tend to be more obviously uncertain in times and places where the intellectual field is less divided and dominated by "experts" or "specialists," and where access to the necessary knowledge and instruments is constrained by geopolitical inequalities. Contexts such as these can help estrange commonplace assumptions about what media are and what they can and cannot do—especially when the context is one where the relevant institutions are in the process of highly politicized change. A lot hinged on the modernizing promises of technology in Mexico during the 1930s, but the illusion that it possessed its own agency and could erase the inequalities of the present and past had to rely more openly on the fiction-making and desire-inducing powers of "art."

There is no hard evidence a puppet named Troka ever existed in physi-cal form, and the character who spoke on and *as* the radio apparently never acknowledged his alter ego. But who knows? Despite an abundance of memos, proposals, and a collection of stories whose connection to his broadcasts is unclear, there are no recordings of his voice—and even if such aural evidence existed, it is unwise to take a radio puppet at its word. Instead, I glean the archival remains to piece together the tale of how Troka acquired his Voice, reconstructing him as a figure for the (partly) imaginary agent of technological progress and the protagonist of a fantasy of liberation via industrialization that fueled the expansion of capitalism in the 1930s. Rather than heed his siren song, I seek to (over)hear something similar to what Mladen Dolar calls the "object voice"—a voice which "does not go up in smoke in the conveyance of meaning, and does not solidify in an object of fetish reverence, but an object which functions as a blind spot in the call and as a disturbance of aesthetic appreciation."[5] Troka's power was always precarious, uneven, and vexed, yet I argue that this radio/puppet born in the afterlife of the avant-garde in an "underdeveloped," (post)revolutionary country can offer insight into a series of questions that are genealogically linked: How do media acquire and exercise power, and how is their agency enabled and bound by material strings? In what sense, if any, can art act as the avant-garde? And finally: what does it mean to make a revolution?

Avant-Garde Remediations

Nowadays, in our so-called postindustrial era, Troka's hymn to the might of machinery is apt to elicit a wry smile, and his utopic vision of radio as the über-medium capable of orchestrating the labors of all mankind seems curiously archaic. Yet there is also something uncannily familiar about his lusty proclamation of power. Take for example the open letter from Louis Rossetto to his children Orson and Zoe in the May 2008 edition of *Wired*, where the founding editor of the journal cast a retrospective eye on the pub-lication of the first issue in 1993 and recalls that "the Digital Revolution was ripping through our lives like the meteor that extinguished the dinosaurs. Practically every institution that our society is based on, from the local to the supranational, is being rendered obsolete."[6] It was good old Dad and his fellow techies who had predicted the "Long Boom," which began with the introduction of the personal computer and was leading to the spread of liberal democracy, rising literacy rates, a decline in armed conflicts, and an "unprecedented increase in material well-being for most of humanity" that was sure to continue "until at least 2020." Nor did their powers of prophecy stop there, for they had also foreseen the emergence of a "new planetary consciousness" arising from the use of "ever-more-powerful" computers—an early intimation of what would come to be called the One Machine. As the folks at *Wired* envision it, the One Machine has no eyes, ears, arms, legs, or even an audible voice; instead of organs or appendages its constituent parts—MP3s, PDAs, PCs, DVRs, digital cameras, cell phones, webcams, data servers—are all "portals" leading directly into a single enormous brain. The One Machine, Rossetto tells his tykes, already has a million times as many transistors as the neurons in one human brain (HB), and by 2040 it is set to surpass 6 billion HB, exceeding the "processing power" of all humanity.

But alas, even before this declaration of triumph hit the web the subprime mortgage crisis was in the works, and within months the global financial meltdown would expose the Long Boom as a bubble that had burst. Now, as the Great Depression makes room for the Great Recession in the annals of history, perhaps it is a good time to reflect on what a radiophonic robot can tell us about the power and precarity of a digital brain. Like Troka, the One Machine vividly illustrates and accidentally allegorizes what Lisa Gitelman describes as a deeply entrenched "tendency to treat media as the self-acting agents of their own history"—and not only of *their* history but of History itself.[7] These invisible automata are depicted as the causal forces of economic and political progress, spectral figurations of the Hegelian Spirit driving development toward some rational and always imminent end. As Paul Duguid noted more than twenty years past in a critique of claims about the demise of the book in the electronic age, this mode of media speak relies on the "futurological tropes" of supersession and liberation, which fuel two related assumptions: (1) each new technology subsumes and supersedes its predecessors and (2) each offers more transparent access to information by freeing it—and by extension *us*—from the constraints of materiality.[8] Troka tells of how the typewriter trounced the pen and pencil and the elevator rendered the stairs a labor for fools, though his own Voice trumps them all because only *it* has the capacity to make man and machine one: "I am the radio that traverses the seas and resounds in all latitudes; the electric message that tells us of what the men of the world do; the voice of time; the universal clamor; the human cry . . . All is in me."[9] Seventy-five years later, his digital counterpart has shed even this vocal vestige of the body and (via its human proxy) augurs the end of analogue and every other alternative to his own reign.

One maxim of media studies is Marshall McLuhan's famous dictum that "the 'content' of any medium is always another medium."[10] In recent years, scholars have picked up on David Bolter and Richard Grusin's use of the term "remediation" to show how the very "newness" of new media can be seen as a surplus-effect produced through remediation processes: emergent technologies establish their own difference and acquire their cultural significance by imitating, refashioning, rivaling, and (only ever partially) incorporating the "old" media they are said to replace.[11] Early photographers billed their art as an improvement on painting; film directors borrowed genres and other conventions from the theater; common wisdom claims digital media obey an entirely new logic distinct from books, television, or radio, but in fact they draw on many of their predecessors' rhetorical conventions and techniques.

If the connection between radio and theater seems less intuitive today, it is in part because discussions of theater tend to privilege its visual element. Yet there is plenty of anecdotal evidence to suggest that during the 1920s and 1930s, theatrical performance was a frequent foil for what was imagined as its aural other. Like theater, early radio was "live": not until the late 1920s did stations acquire the capacity to air prerecorded programming, and throughout the 1930s most broadcasts were performances transmitted to distant listeners in real time. Theater halls also set the scene for several early, experimental broadcasts, as when Guglielmo Marconi relayed a concert by the soprano Nellie Melba at a New York theater on May 19, 1920, or a few months later when Radio Argentina began regular transmissions from the Teatro Coliseo in Buenos Aires with a performance of Wagner's *Parsifal*. Commercial stations continued this trend by broadcasting operas, dramas, and musical comedies straight from the stage. Articles from the early 1920s often treat the broadcast itself as the main event, delving into technical details about the proper placement of microphones, scrutinizing the sonic effects of the actors' movements, and weighing in on which plays or genres are most suited for the radio. A *New York Times* article from March 1922 begins by announcing, "There is much the same fascination in going behind the scenes of a great broadcasting station as is found behind the curtain of a theatre"—only the fascination is greater, the writer implies, because what lies hidden isn't just the mechanics but the performance itself. He invites listeners of an unidentified station near New York to "visualize the unseen stage from which they are being entertained," describing the studio setting in minute detail and recounting every action taken by the technicians from the moment the program begins until it concludes and his theatrical metaphor runs up against a wall: silence. "The audience listening in is doubtless the largest ever assembled, but there is not the faintest whisper of applause."[12]

This chasm separating performer and public wasn't necessarily seen as a limitation. Radio's isolation of the aural was just as likely to be hailed as a triumph over space, an idealistic challenge to the tyranny of the material realm, and an exhilarating "emancipation from the body." Such is how Rudolf Arnheim describes it in his widely read *Radio* (originally published in English in 1936), which devotes nearly as much ink to theater as it does to the medium referenced in its title. Time and again the German media theorist illustrates the specificity of this new aural art by way of comparison and contrast with the stage. Like radio, he explains, theater unfolds in and through time. The two art forms differ, however, because in the theater, particularly in the case of naturalistic drama (Arnheim's true bête noire), the spectator's impressions are always subject to a split between the ear and the eye, a contradiction between the world conjured up by "the word" and the action realized onstage. Radio banishes the visual, allowing auditors to immerse themselves in a purely subjective realm of sound:

> Although wireless, when it wished to, could beat the theatre at sound realism, yet those sounds and voices were not bound to that physical world whose presence we first experienced through our eye, and which, once perceived, compels us to observe its laws, thus laying fetters on the spirit that would soar beyond time and space and unite actual happenings with thoughts and forms independent of anything corporeal.[13]

This passage, right down to its rhapsodic tone, exemplifies a particular type of radio speak. Radio was (and still is) said to be immaterial and disembodied; it offers a shortcut to the spiritual realm, yet the experience it engenders is more intimate, immediate, and "real" than any ocular impression. Arnheim vehemently objects to the transmission of live performances and sporting events, because in such cases radio serves as a mere relaying apparatus instead of creating a self-referential "acoustic world." His preferred model, the type of broadcast he believes best realizes its potential to transcend rather than transmit actuality, is the radio play. When radio dramas are done right, he argues, they reveal words to be sensuous sounds rather than mere conduits of semantic meaning; they recall a "primeval age" prior to language, when expression was limited to the mating calls and warning cries of beasts and "the word was still sound, the sound still word" (35). Such comments mark this radio enthusiast as a modern-day metaphysicist, heir to a tradition that locates the voice at the origin of ideality, prior to writing or even the advent of language. Indeed, Arnheim posits the possibility of radio dramas in which all trace of materiality has been effaced, "fantastic spirit-plays in the realm of thought with symbols and theories as characters" (20). This, then, is the real drama to which radio listeners are privy: the epic struggle for abstraction, the effort to wrest pure thought from flesh and have done with the specter of the stage—the same stage this discourse must evoke in order to cast its unrepresentable ideal into relief.

A similar dynamic riddles the notion of "auditory mysticism" evoked in the late teens and early 1920s by the Mexican minister of education José Vasconcelos, whose ambivalent relationship to theater was the subject of the first chapter. Although Vasconcelos left office before he was able to implement his radiophonic designs,[14] Arnheim reveals himself to be a kindred spirit when he hails the "wireless as educator!" (269). Broadcasting, he suggests, offers the prospect of a new and improved mode of aesthetic education, not only because it reaches beyond the lecture hall to the common man but because it does so through the ear, "the tool of our understanding, of the brain, the receiver of what is already formed" (279). Its pedagogical value has less to do with the specific content it conveys than with its capacity to engender the "right attitude," to mold the listening subject's mind and desires to an onto-logical form. By eliminating the "distractions" posed by visual phenomena, radio heightens the auditors' powers of imaginative concentration, unifying them in their simultaneous contemplation and aural enjoyment of a single aesthetic object. Even better, it has a "disciplinarian effect": because listen-ing is a solitary activity (a dubious assumption Arnheim shares with many other commentators) no one else censors listeners' responses, so they learn to internalize responsibility for their own reactions to what is beautiful and good (269). Suffice it to say, such a powerful force cannot be left to the whims of commerce but should be guided by "teachers, educators and *lit-térateurs*" (286).

Arnheim echoes a common call among intellectuals in the early 1930s to institute more cohesive regulatory regimes. As his own biography suggests, this desire for the state to take on a custodial role in radio cut across the era's growing ideological divisions: an exiled German Jew living in Fascist Italy, he refrains from criticizing the Nazis' centralization of broadcasting and even concedes that this "authoritative form" of radio may at times plant the indispensable seed of a more democratic, "organic wireless." In countries where national sentiment is weak, radio can both prefigure and produce it by means of carefully crafted cultural programs, the goal of which is "leveling the taste and education of the different classes of people" (248) and "bringing art and philosophy and the people into accord" (251). Unified with the aid of technology, the radiophonic voice can stand in for and as the promise of an organic national body.

This effort to isolate radio's singular nature refashions a long-standing discourse on theater even as it declares the theatrical stage an obstacle to be overcome. Friedrich Schiller had hailed the stage as a "moral institution" with the capacity to transcend contingencies of class, geography, and gender; 140 years later, Arnheim argues for the superiority of an ostensibly "immate-rial" art, yet his desire to hypostasize the voice and banish the body is also a move to salvage the notion of culture-as-enlightenment from the crisis of liberal democracy and the systems of representation to which it was tied. In a short text from 1932, Arnheim's compatriot Walter Benjamin takes this logic to task and insists that precisely because theater is the site where the crisis is most keenly felt, radio must engage it in collaboration and debate. Radio, Benjamin acknowledges, has most of the advantages on its side: not only is it far less encumbered by tradition, it can also reach larger masses of people, and both its "material" and "intellectual" elements (i.e., programming) are more closely intertwined with the interests of its audience. In comparison, what does theater bring to the table? His answer is unequivocal: "the use of a living medium, nothing more."[15]

In the current context, Benjamin states, there are two possible ways one can grapple with theater's dependence on people as the medium and material of signification. The first persists in portraying man as the all-powerful representative of "humanity," laboring to compete with newer media by employing multitudes of extras and ever more complex machinery, or by re-creating distant times and places that radio and cinema can more convincingly simulate in a studio. Regardless of its subject or style such theater "always perceives itself as a 'symbol,' a 'totality,' a 'total work of art'" (366). The alternative is Bertolt Brecht's epic theater, and in particular the Brechtian acting technique of *gestus*, which is based on the principle of interruption and aims to achieve an effect similar to the critical method of montage employed in radio and film. What this re-remediation or "retro-transformation" of a mechanical medium by human actors does is to draw out "man in the present crisis, man eliminated by radio and film, man, to put it somewhat drastically, as the fifth wheel of technology." Epic theater subjects this "diminished" remainder of humanity to examination as if in a laboratory and replaces culture-as-consumption with the "training" of judgment; or to invoke the more familiar Benjaminian lingo, it dissolves the aura of organicity (367).

But theater is not the only one with something to learn from its encounter with radio. As a counterpart to epic theater, Benjamin suggests that radio should also undertake adaptations of plays—not, as Arnheim desires, in order to fashion itself as an autonomous art or to create a world all its own, but to illuminate its own specificity *and* its limits. Although Benjamin briefly alludes to the dramatic "listening models" he himself had written and broadcast over the previous few years,[16] it is once again Brecht who provides the main model, this time with works such as *Der Flug der Lindberghs* (1929), a radio play in which listeners were meant to follow the printed score and intervene in the action by singing designated parts. By its author's own account, the piece was designed to put pressure on the existing apparatus of radio, revealing the need to transform it from a device for the simple distribution of prepackaged goods into a "vast network" capable of facilitating true communication.[17] In commenting on the play, Benjamin concludes that only in this way can the apparatus "remain free from the halo of a 'gigantic educational enterprise' . . . and scaled back to a format fit for humans" (368). In the end, theater's weakness is also its strength; only when it concedes that it is not larger than life can it cut technology down to size, help strip away the aura it too has accrued, and force the question of how to (re)construct human agency in a critical relation to these new media machines.

Despite the stark differences between Arnheim and Benjamin, both write from within and respond to a historical crisis that registered most acutely in the realm of art as a crisis of the bourgeois stage. In Mexico, on the other hand, the theatrical "naturalism" against which Arnheim defines his radio art had never taken hold; "theater" had never achieved the status of a "symbol" or "total work of art," and while efforts were under way to make the stage a "moral institution," they were still highly contested and politicized. Theater was less often invoked as a metaphor for a stage of development to be overcome than as an elusive goal the country had yet to attain.

What Mexico could lay claim to was a vibrant tradition of popular puppet theater. The legendary Rosete Aranda company, whose roots reached back to the 1830s, regularly crisscrossed the country and had even ventured into Texas and Central America by the end of the nineteenth century. With its collection of more than five thousand marionettes (often referred to as *autómata*), the company staged comic skits of local customs and regional "types," re-creations of historic events such as the "grito" of independence from Spain, adaptations of classical literature, and picaresque tales involving characters such as the rural trickster Vale Coyote. According to most accounts, the upheaval caused by the revolution and the rise of new mass-mediated modes of entertainment spurred the decline of the Rosete Aranda puppets and other similar enterprises. In 1923 the family sold the use of the company name, though their puppets would continue to circulate for several decades, even appearing in some instances on the radio.[18]

Perhaps it is the image of the Rosete Aranda marionettes that hovers in the backdrop of the following text:

Twentieth-century guignol.
To be more precise: Radio-guignol.

Guiñol siglo XX.
Para llamarlo mejor: Radio-guiñol.[19]

So begins an article in the July 7, 1924, edition of *Antena*, a short-lived literary journal sponsored by a cigarette company that had founded Mexico's second radio station the previous year. Following his opening salvo, the author of "Al pie de la antena" introduces himself to readers as Maese Pedro, the itinerant puppeteer in *Don Quixote* whose performance goes awry when the novel's protagonist intervenes to save the life of a beautiful marionette. On this occasion, however, the legendary impresario hasn't come to beguile his audience with medieval tales of damsels held captive by the Moors; his purpose is to offer a backstage glimpse of a new kind of show that has made his own art obsolete.

No longer, as in times gone by, do people gather round to watch amusing puppets perform for them on the farcical stage; from faraway points, united by the miracle of air, people, distant from one other, sit down to listen.

But the puppets are the same. Those that used to travel the land in their humble carts performed a primitive, enthralling, entertaining art. These modern marionettes present a new art, more entertaining and no less enthralling, from their distant studio, where they stand before the microphone, scattering the notes of their rhymes, of their songs or serenades to the four winds.

And at the foot of the antenna, which serves on this occasion as a curtain, the puppeteers in charge of moving the figures await the moment to commence the show for their imaginary audience.

Ya no, como en los tiempos idos, se reunen las gentes para mirar lo que en el tablado de la farsa les presentan las graciosas marionetas; desde lejanos puntos, unidos por el milagro del aire, las gentes, distanciadas, se sientan a escuchar.

Pero las marionetas son las mismas. Un arte primitivo, subyugador y divertido, representaban aquellas que en los carros humildes hacían su recorrido por la tierra. Un arte nuevo, más divertido y no menos subyugador, presentan estas marionetas modernas, que desde el estudio lejano, frente al micrófono, lanzan a los cuatro vientos las notas de sus rimas, de sus canciones o de sus serenatas.

Y al pie de la antena, que hace en esta ocasión las veces de telón de boca, los titiriteros encargados de mover las figuras, esperan el instante de dar principio a la función ante el imaginario auditorio. (18)

The analogy is arresting in part because it doesn't entirely add up, because it evokes the specter of a subject that never quite coalesces in the mind's eye. If the radio performers are puppets, who or what are the puppeteers? The conceit unfolds as the narrator begins to elucidate the invisible infrastructure that makes Station CYB tick, introducing the key players by name and explaining the duties each one performs. Take the sonorous voice that welcomes listeners at the start of every show, he says: it might sound like the sad clown Pierrot, but in truth it belongs to Fernando J. Ramírez, a general in the Mexican army who doubles as the station's announcer and technical manager. One Guillermo Garza Ramos operates the machinery from the wings, Mariano Ramírez keeps tabs on the "puppets," and Ofelia Euroza de Yañez, the official pianist, plays the part of the organ grinder that once accompanied the guignol. The real wizard behind the curtain, however, is the stage director, a young man named Juan de Beraza who "holds in his hands the multiple strings that move the marionettes." It is he who tells the performers when to make their entrances and exits, when to launch into their tales of love and jealousy, what to sing, or how to pluck a plaintive melody on the harp.

But Maese Pedro has one last trick up his sleeve, because the stage director's power turns out to be incomplete; the real locus of control is even further removed from the bodies whose voices float through the ether and enter the listener's ear. Only toward the article's end does he shine the spotlight on CYB's director, who is also the general manager of El Buen Tono cigar factory and an illustrious senator of the republic. The *alto Jefe* gives a veritable laundry list of the wondrous benefits of radio: by broadcasting concerts of music by Mexican artists, it fosters greater unity within the country's own borders; it facilitates closer intellectual relations and inspires "profound sympathy" between Mexico and its neighbors to the south; it instills a greater sense of purpose in the nation's artists. Most importantly, however, it lures listeners away from less edifying diversions by offering them one that is new, free of charge, and "cultural." Indeed, station CYB—like the puppeteers of yesteryear—devotes special attention to its youngest audience members, encouraging them to save their pennies and awarding prizes for those who build receptors. Wireless, like its primitive precursor, has the capacity to educate even as it entertains, just as the analogy Maese Pedro has drawn in such detail is meant to intrigue and instruct readers in the workings of this mysterious new medium. While the puppets perform their show, he explains, "the public listens, it divines their indispensable presence"—a presence whose power derives from the fact that it cannot be seen, even though we all know it *must* be there. In the end, "Al pie de la antena" delivers a lesson about the benefit of close collaboration between private enterprise and the state, about art's proper role as an agent of social cohesion and the need for a well-defined hierarchy to keep the machinery of modernity running on track; at the same time, it teaches listeners to hear the radio's voices as though they emanated from an imaginary stage.

Media theorists often refer to these uncanny voices unhinged from their bodily source as "acousmatic," a word borrowed from the disciples of Pythagoras, the pre-Socratic mystic (and inspiration for Vasconcelos's "theory" of rhythm as well as his even hazier auditory mysticism) who schooled his followers in the secrets of knowledge from behind a curtain or screen.[20] The intent was to conceal the Master's physical idiosyncrasies, his material props, the worldly setting of his words—and the theatrical element of which no lecture is entirely devoid—allowing the uninitiated to immerse themselves in the sound of his Voice and what it said. Two millennia later Maese Pedro evokes a similar aura of authority surrounding the acousmatic voices produced by the rise of radio. But this is 1924, a mere fourteen months after broadcasting made its Mexican debut, and what takes place on the other end of the antenna is not the theater of man but the diminutive farce of the guignol. Any power these voices possess isn't truly their own because it only exists by virtue of a disjuncture between the sound and its source. What occupies the space of this gap, dividing even as it connects those on either side, is the medium itself: not just the stage or the technological apparatus but the web of political, social, and economic relations in which the embryonic apparatus is enmeshed. Even the *jefe*, the illustrious representative of the national bourgeoisie, is just another character in the farce, and the quotation marks framing his words serve as a reminder that the acousmatic voice belongs to the Master/Maese, a fictional figure who has been regarded as a vestige of bygone days from his very first appearance in print. This baroque allegory may hail radio as the singular voice of modernity, but the medium of its message reanimates those "humble" figures whose power crumbled when a renegade member of the emerging gentry fancied himself a medieval knight-errant and charged the stage.

Of course, some readers must have been aware that CYB was financed by French capital; many if not most surely knew that the station's transmitter had been purchased from their imperial neighbor to the north.[21] But just as the charm (and terror) of puppetry lies in seeing an object move and hearing it speak, Maese Pedro beckons readers to pretend there is magic in the machine.

(Media) Revolutions and Peripheral Avant-Gardes

Despite its allure, the posthumous voice of the puppeteer plays no part in most accounts of the origins of Mexican radio. A far more common narrative revolves around what Rubén Gallo characterizes as "the other Mexican revolution: the cultural transformations triggered by new media in the years after the armed conflict of 1910 to 1920."[22] In his book *Mexican Modernity: The Avant-Garde and the Technological Revolution*, Gallo paints a picture of two separate and consecutive upheavals—one violent and the other "cultural"—a commonplace of Mexican historiography with roots in the postrevolutionary regime's own efforts to cast itself as the culmination of the military conflict while simultaneously mobilizing support for its institution-building drive. For Gallo, however, the subject of this stirring saga is not the Mexican state or *el pueblo*; writing not long after the ouster of the Institutional Revolutionary Party, which had ruled the country since 1929, and amid ongoing optimism over the ability of the internet to dissolve national borders deemed oppressive and obsolete, he hails the "new media" of this earlier era as the prime mover of an aesthetic revolution carried out by a "cosmopolitan," "international-ist" avant-garde. The iconic images of peasant insurrection and ancient Aztec civilization painted by Diego Rivera on the walls of government buildings are entirely absent from this revisionist account, and even the artist's *Detroit Industry* murals come under fire for propagating an "old" medium rather than opening up the process of artistic production to the "transformative powers of technology" (11). By contrast, the Italian-born photographer Tina Modotti is lauded for eschewing pictorialist representations of "premodern" themes (i.e., peasants) in favor of images of technological artifacts that draw attention to the indexical quality and mechanical reproducibility of the photographic medium itself.

Mexican Modernity succeeds in destabilizing a certain canonical view of the *vanguardias* by shifting attention to works of art that seem to defy the familiar framework of cultural nationalism. At the same time, it uncriti-cally echoes the rhetoric of rupture implicit in both the avant-garde and new media discourse and reinscribes a unilinear conception of development all too amenable to the imperatives of *Wired*'s One Machine. Gallo relies on the language of revolution to bolster his claims for the radicalism of avant-garde art, but in doing so he actually *divorces* media technologies in the 1920s from the issues at stake in the armed struggle. Ignoring the unmet demands of the more radical, popular forces defeated by the leaders of the new regime and the ongoing opposition to the new social "order" (assassinations, strikes, and major revolts were hallmarks of the decade), he depicts the early 1920s as a clean slate, a time when "a new chapter in Mexican history was to begin—an era marked by peace, reconstruction efforts, and a technological frenzy that one writer called 'the madness of radio' " (141).

Radio is in many ways the ideal artifact around which to construct this narrative of an entrepreneurial avant-garde unhindered by either class warfare or a strong state. During the dictatorship of Porfirio Díaz, the government and military had conducted experiments with radiotelegraphy, which also played a strategic role in the revolution, but public broadcasting did not begin until the early 1920s.[23] In Mexico, the new government lacked the resources and organizational capacity to create the sort of centralized broadcasting system that was adopted in most European countries, and while a few branches of the bureaucracy set up stations to relay official information, private capital was encouraged to take the lead.[24] The first station to receive a permit, like several following it, was affiliated with a print publication, in this case the illustrated weekly *El Universal Ilustrado*, known for keeping readers abreast of everything from vaudeville to the latest academic tome. The magazine was also a frequent forum for figures linked to the estridentista avant-garde, and when station CYL made its debut on May 8, 1923, the long lineup of performers was headed by the group's front man Manuel Maples Arce, a brash twenty-three-year-old who initiated listeners into the ether with a reading of his poem "TSH" (short for *telegrafía sin hilos*, or wireless telegraphy). "TSH" evokes the schizophonic experience of tuning into a cacophonous space where geographical borders and the boundaries of subjectivity collapse as "transatlantic addresses" cross paths with "international pentagrams" and the "Jazz-Band of New York" pulsates in place of the speaker's own heart.[25] Other elements of the broadcast, however, point to the power relations in which the emerging medium was enmeshed: the "onstage" audience present at the event included the national secretary of communications, and the very first voice listeners heard belonged not to Maples Arce but to Raúl Azcárraga, co-owner of the station and a retailer of U.S. radio receivers whose family would go on to build the communications conglomerate now known as Televisa.[26]

Carlos Noriega Hope, the editor of *El Universal Ilustrado* and director of station CYL, depicted estridentismo and radio as two *hermanos de leche*, or foster brothers nourished by the same breast, triumphantly declaring, "They're vanguard things!"[27] Rubén Gallo completes the chain of associations by citing the event as evidence of a "technological revolution" authorized and enacted by the artistic avant-garde. But in fact, the word "revolution" doesn't appear in either the poem "TSH" or press coverage of the broadcast, no doubt because its own meaning was still so unstable and subject to debate. Just a week after CYL took to the air, the Mexican government entered into talks leading to the Bucareli Accords, which aroused opposition from diverse sectors of the population by forfeiting the right to expropriate foreign oil and mineral holdings acquired prior to the Constitution of 1917. Signed in return for diplomatic recognition from the United States, the treaty was also part of a campaign to quell the concerns of foreign corporations and increase the influx of capital needed to spark the development of industry and technology. As negotiations were under way, President Álvaro Obregón liquidated one potential source of unrest when he either orchestrated or at least facilitated the assassination of Pancho Villa, who still enjoyed strong popular support in the North; shortly afterward he defeated a major rebellion led by his ex–minister of finance, Adolfo de la Huerta.[28] According to the historian J. Justin Castro, Obregón's opponents routinely sabotaged radio stations or commandeered them to broadcast their message and coordinate forces, prompting the government to implement stricter regulations and control over radio.[29] Even before this, however, stations such as CYL avoided reporting on anything deemed "political" in the interest of developing a mutually beneficial relationship with the state.[30]

Despite this injunction, the estridentista romance with radio runs right through the complex cultural constellation surrounding the rearticulation of Mexico's role in the world economy. The visual artists Fermín Revueltas and Ramón Alva de la Canal designed ads for station CYB, some of which push the fragmentation of form so far they seem to subvert their ostensible function. Arqueles Vela wrote articles on radio, and Luis Quintanilla (writing under his phonetic nom de plume Kin Taniya) sought to re-create the experience of station surfing in "IU IIIUUU IU," part of a longer "wireless" poem. Quintanilla also seems to have had plans to develop a sketch revolving around radio for the Teatro del Murciélago, though the group dissolved before it came to fruition and there is no evidence of what it might have looked like onstage—no clues, for instance, as to whether the radio listeners would have been indigenous, or whether this would have been one of the "urban" numbers.[31] Most likely the latter, given the "inaugural broadcast" of the estridentistas' ephemeral journal *Irradiador*, which points to radio as a model for reimagining the work of art in an era of "installations, electric generators, gears, and cables" and in a place where the "entire city crackles, polarized by the radiotelephonic antennas of an implausible station."[32]

In fact, the industrial infrastructure in Mexico was limited, radios were still a rare commodity, and for all their allusions to the medium, there is little evidence the estridentistas were involved in broadcasting in the years following the inauguration of CYL. Yet as the Soviet leader Leon Trotsky argued in 1924, the same year Maples Arce published his "Bolshevik super-poem"

Urbe, an ode to skyscrapers and submarines can be written with a pencil on
a scrap of paper at the far ends of the earth. As I note in the introduction,
Trotsky saw the appearance of futurism in Russia and Italy, two comparatively underdeveloped countries on the periphery of Europe, as evidence of
the uneven and combined nature of development: in a world where capitalism draws distant regions into connection with one another, growth and
change in any one place is partially contingent on what takes place elsewhere,
and art is never simply a reflection of its immediate surroundings. Indeed, he
argued, history had shown more than once that the "backward" countries
"reflected in their ideology the achievements of the advanced countries more
brilliantly and strongly."[33]

Technology was key to Trotsky's rejection of the assumption that all countries must (or can) proceed through the same series of developmental stages,
just as it was central to his sympathetic critique of futurism and its desire
for an immediate fusion of art and "life." In a speech delivered to the First
All-Union Congress of the Society of Friends of Radio in 1926, the Bolshevik
leader hammers home the challenges facing the Soviet Republic, a geographically immense territory divided by linguistic and cultural differences and
lacking in basic elements of infrastructure such as schools and roads. His
assessment, repeated like a litany: "We are a backward country." Here again,
however, he views backwardness dialectically as both an impediment *and*
a spur to progress, just as he views the medium of radio as both an instrument *and* object(ive) of revolutionary struggle. "Socialism presupposes and
demands a high level of technology," but radio transistors and airplanes alone
do not possess the power to establish a socialist society.[34] Although science
and technology (like art) possess their own logic, this logic is itself condi-
tioned by social forces, and in the present, their meaning and materiality are
still up for grabs. This may be why elsewhere Trotsky expresses no regret
over the fact that the focus on rebuilding "old" infrastructure damaged during the war has stymied the realization of proposals such as Vladimir Tatlin's
Monument to the Third International, a constructivist radio tower designed
to double as headquarters for the Comintern: the delay will allow the social
struggle time to transform the relations of production, and in the meantime
(he suggests) it is unwise to entirely relinquish the *relative* autonomy of art.[35]

A year and a half after his speech on radio, Trotsky was expelled from the
Communist Party; in 1929 he would be forced into exile as Stalin consolidated power, and the vanguard movements he both defended and critiqued
would crumble as artists committed suicide, faced repression, or came to
terms with new realities. Yet at the end of 1936, he accepted an offer of asylum secured with the aid of Diego Rivera and arrived in a country where the
trajectory of the postrevolutionary avant-garde was bound in curious ways
to the one he had left behind.

In January 1926 Maples Arce was conscripted to serve as secretary general
to Heriberto Jara, the socialist governor of his home state of Veracruz, and

in turn he lured some of his crew to the city of Xalapa. By most accounts, Xalapa marks the high point of estridentismo: it was here where they concocted plans for Estridentópolis, an absurdist city set in the distant future of 1975. Its principal landmarks? A people's university and a gigantic radio tower.[36] In more immediate terms, however, the group took charge of the government-run press, with the truculent writer Germán List Arzubide at the helm and Ramón Alva de la Canal and Leopoldo Méndez in the role of official illustrators; in addition to experimental works by estridentista writers, they put out political tracts, didactic pamphlets on topics such as hygiene, free editions of texts by Mexican and foreign writers, and a journal called *Horizonte* dedicated to a wide array of topics including culture, local labor issues, and news of Jara's reforms. Some members of the group took up educational posts, others were involved in the newly created Department of Popular Aesthetic Culture or participated in the inauguration of the new stadium (a counterpart to Vasconcelos's *teatro-estadio*), and although there is no evidence estridentistas appeared on the air during their time in the city, Maples Arce oversaw plans for the construction of a state-run radio station.[37] In the end, however, the institutional volatility of the 1920s, the very factor that facilitated this rapprochement between avant-garde art and political power, also precipitated the movement's dramatic demise. In September 1927, amid a dispute with foreign oil companies and under pressure from workers and peasant groups demanding more radical change, Jara was ousted in a legislative coup backed by the federal government and the radio tower sending signals from the future became one of the era's seemingly utopic, never-to-be-realized plans.[38]

Strictly speaking, this is where the story of estridentismo ends. In the wake of Jara's ouster, Maples Arce (though a persona non grata among the new officials) was elected to the state legislature of Veracruz for a two-year term, after which he wound his way through Cuba, New York, and Spain before settling in Paris to take courses in history and international law with an eye to a career in the diplomatic service. Luis Quintanilla, who had served in Brazil as a secretary to the ambassador from 1927 to 1929, was already in Paris, as was Arqueles Vela, recently returned from a spell in Germany teaching Spanish.[39] The sculptor Germán Cueto and his wife Lola (an artist known for her textiles) spent the entire period from 1927 to 1932 in Paris and participated in a collective of abstract artists known as Cercle et Carré whose members included the Uruguayan constructivist Joaquín Torres García, Wassily Kandinsky, and Le Corbusier.[40] Meanwhile back in Mexico some of the visual artists, including Ramón Alva de la Canal and Fermín Revueltas, formed a short-lived splinter group in Mexico City called *¡30–30!*, and Leopoldo Méndez illustrated various journals and joined the Communist Party.[41] List Arzubide, an old anarchist who had joined the Communist Party in 1926, stayed in Xalapa and was active in labor organizing until 1929—right around the time of Vasconcelos's failed presidential run and the formation of the National Revolutionary Party (forerunner to the PRI), which coincided with a crackdown on the newly outlawed Communist Party. According to List Arzubide's own account, he beat the heat by heading for the second World Anti-Imperialist Congress in Frankfurt; on his arrival he received an ovation from Jawaharlal Nehru, Madame Sun Yat-Sen, and other attendees when he presented a U.S. flag captured by Augusto Sandino in his struggle against the U.S. military intervention in Nicaragua. During his time in Germany, the ex-estridentista accepted an invitation to the USSR and spent several months palling around with the likes of Sergei Eisenstein and Vladimir Mayakovsky before heading back to Mexico by way of Paris, where he met up with the Cuetos and other old comrades.[42]

It takes a little digging to find these details, because right around 1929, the grand narratives of the avant-garde tend to fall silent: from the *vanguardias* of the 1920s the spotlight skips ahead to the alliance between the Left and the progressive presidency of Lázaro Cárdenas (1934–1940), when collectives such as the Liga de Escritores y Artistas Revolucionarios (League of Revolutionary Writers and Artists) and its art school, the Taller de Gráfica Popular—spearheaded by the ex-estridentista Leopoldo Méndez—put art to work in the fight against fascism and in support of the government's land reforms.[43] Meanwhile, those missing years in the early 1930s lurk like a historiographical black hole.[44]

Object Voices and Institutional Strings

Yet out of this abyss emerges the echo of a "strident" voice. Shortly after 9 P.M. on November 7, 1931, three self-identified members of the Mexican Communist Party walked into the operations hub of the country's most powerful radio station, tied up the technician, and then cut into a remote broadcast of a concert featuring the classical choir of the Secretariat of Public Education. Listeners all over the continent who tuned into XEW—the "Voice of Latin America from Mexico"—heard a man extol the Soviet Union as an example for capitalist countries wracked by mass unemployment and then denounce the "military dictatorship" of Plutarco Elías Calles as an agent of Yankee imperialism, guilty of aiding and abetting the murder of Julio Antonio Mella, a Cuban communist gunned down two years earlier in Mexico City while in the company of Tina Modotti. The speech lasted all of ten minutes and the technician was released unharmed; yet over the following weeks the federal police conducted a sweep of the local Reds before identifying the two accomplices as Valentín Campa, a member of the party's central committee, and the muralist David Alfaro Siqueiros. As for the man behind the mike, the daily *Excélsior* relayed the official report: "The One Who Led the Assault Was Germán Litz Arsuvide [*sic*], Expert in Radio and Man of Rare Audacity" (figure 3.1).[45]

Figure 3.1. A front-page headline claims that the perpetrators of the attack on XEW are in hiding in Veracruz and points to Germán List Arzubide as the ringleader. *Excélsior*, November 13, 1931.

Who was this audacious man? Although the papers offered few facts, surely some readers recognized him as the former first lieutenant of the estridentista avant-garde, author of a quixotic "history" of the movement and a longtime political militant who had recently returned from a sojourn in the Soviet Union. *El Machete*, the Communist Party newspaper, offered alibis for all three of the accused in its November 10 issue: Campa was said to be representing the party at its official commemoration of the Russian Revolution in downtown Mexico City, Siqueiros was holed up with a serious illness in the mountain town of Taxco, and List Arzubide was at a rally back on his old stomping grounds in Xalapa, delivering a speech much like the one read over the radio by a voice that clearly couldn't be his.[46] The federal police paid no heed and ordered the state governor to close in on the prime suspect, but in an odd twist he was saved by an opportune invitation from Lázaro Cárdenas, the future president who was then governor of Michoacán. "Here you will have the freedom to do everything you want," List Arzubide would later recall Cárdenas saying as he offered him refuge until the furor died down. Several years later as president, Cárdenas would turn against the "military dictator" derided in the broadcast that led to this encounter; at the time, however, Calles was still a crucial ally, and Cárdenas himself would continue to be a target of the communists through his first months in office.

List Arzubide, however, sealed the deal with a statement that may (or may not) have been accompanied by a sly wink: "I didn't give that speech. I would have liked to, but it wasn't me."[47]

The brief seizure of the XEW's transmitter turned the indeterminacy of the radiophonic subject into a tactical tool, giving an illegal party with dwindling numbers fleeting access to a broader public while making it loom all the larger for the fact that its voice had no face. The federal government, rushing to defend capital, seized on this same uncertainty to fuel paranoia and put the squeeze on an errant intellectual, precipitating a pact that allowed him to secure a space of "liberty" under the protection of an emerging political power. Yet it was just over a year later—and a full twenty-one months *before* Cárdenas assumed the presidential office—when a certain mechanical spirit began to animate the airwaves of the radio station of the federal Secretariat of Public Education. Troka the Powerful promised to lead listeners into the future by dint of his invincible strength, and from the vantage point of the present he appears as a figure for the forces driving the institutionalization of class conflict and consolidation of the single-party state. But Troka was more fractious and disjointed than he let on, and among the scraps of information, oblique references, and odd bits of bureaucratic prose in which he is named one can catch hints of an "object voice."

Mladen Dolar associates the object voice with the *objet petit a*, the Lacanian term for the unattainable object of desire sought in the other. Like the gaze, it is a partial object that appears as an object-cause or remainder of the Real, though it is actually a surplus produced by the subject's formation and incorporation into the Symbolic order. The object voice is that part of the voice that does not interpellate a subject and cannot be fetishized as an object of art but instead occupies "the space of a breach, a missing link, a gap in the causal nexus."[48] It is the medium of the voice, the material and mechanical aspect of signification that signals its (partial) presence when the movement of meaning catches on the hitch of what cannot be said. In my account of the fantasies of liberation via industrialization Troka enabled, it was the interference, the part of the radiophonic voice listeners had to learn to hear past in order to believe the promise of its power: the struggles and calculated compromises, material and organizational infrastructure, and all the other still-visible strings that made the "wireless" medium of radio work (or not, as the case may be). Did some listeners recognize a resemblance between Troka's voice and the one that had interrupted the sweet sounds of a SEP choir with a call to revolution? Why do his appearances in the archive always seem to be shadowed by a puppet?

Just over a year after List Arzubide had his first encounter with Cárdenas, at the beginning of 1933, this Man of Rare Audacity joined a committee charged with revamping XFX, the radio station of the SEP, which had been deemed lackluster and in need of bold new ideas after years of leadership by a woman named María Luísa Ross.[49] Nearly a year earlier a cross-section of the Mexican intelligentsia—seemingly all men—had been invited to offer recommendations. The roster reads like a future who's who of Mexican culture: in addition to Maples Arce (newly elected to the federal legislature),[50] the group included Rufino Tamayo, a Zapotecan migrant to the capital who was to become one of the country's most celebrated painters; Agustín Yáñez, a PRI politico-in-the-making who had recently arrived from Guadalajara and would later write one of the canonical "novels of the Mexican Revolution"; the concert pianist and music professor Salvador Ordóñez Ochoa, a native of the state of Hidalgo; José Gorostiza, a poet from Tabasco and newly named head of the Department of Fine Arts; and Xavier Villaurrutia, a poet and member of the newly created Teatro Orientación who (like Gorostiza) was affiliated with the Contemporáneos, an experimental group often at odds with the estridentistas.[51] The committee was active throughout 1932 and early 1933 and exchanged preliminary drafts before submitting individual reports. When all was said and done, Agustín Yáñez had been named the station's new director, with List Arzubide second in command.[52]

The proposals submitted by the committee members vary widely in content and style: Maples Arce, for example, insists with manifesto-like bravura that the radio's "socializing" effects must take the form of "immediate action," and he lambasts the other proposals for focusing on the petty details of programming while failing to see that "strictly speaking, it is not a program, a microphone, or a machine that will constitute the radiophonic action of the Secretariat, but rather that superstructure which will make its euphonic diction effective."[53] Still, like nearly all of the other members he concedes that the station faces two imposing obstacles: its transmitter has a very limited range, and the vast majority of its potential listeners in rural areas have no access to the medium. (Alas, the "superstructure" does in fact require a material base.) In cities, on the other hand, common folk listened to the radio in bars, which in the opinion of List Arzubide only encouraged their predilection for "coarse" music.[54] In light of such constraints, List Arzubide contends that programming should be primarily directed toward the small middle class, "the group that has historically been the one to guide the masses."[55] Here, in plain language, he reveals his adherence to the stagist view of development Trotsky critiqued: his statement implies that "backward" nations such as Mexico must follow in the footsteps of their forerunners and pass through the phase of capitalist accumulation and consolidation before achieving the desired but always distant socialist utopia. And so in the very last lines of his text he conjures Troka the Powerful, a "dramatic type" and "mysterious character who incarnates the spirit of man's mechanical creations." It is the task of Troka—an unlikely amalgam of media and machines—to arouse the interest of middle-class children in modern technologies.

In February 1933, this invisible spirit began to speak through the lungs and larynx of List Arzubide. Although there are no recordings, clues to his pedagogical methods can be found in a later collection of short stories called

Troka el poderoso, which appear to be lightly revised scripts of his broadcasts.[56] In his Second Appearance, Troka el Poderoso introduces Anselmo and Raymundo, two schoolchildren who heard his first broadcast and have now come to the Radio Station to meet him firsthand (23). When this originally aired, were these voices actual children, or projections of List Arzubide's own voice? Quite possibly they were "real": memos in the archive refer to children being invited to come and speak on air, though it not clear if they were given scripted lines or allowed to speak extemporaneously. In the text, at least, these untutored voices model the ideal relationship to their teacher Troka by exploring the interior of his body. Troka describes them going up an escalator at the station (his legs) and then riding in an elevator (his stomach) before finally entering his mouth, where they become like actors on a stage inside his body. They describe his brains, which look like a telecommunications center. They ask him questions about some wires, which he explains are electric cables that run from different Mexican cities to his center (24–25). These descriptions probably bear little resemblance to the actual appearance of the station's operations, but empirical accuracy is beside the point. Through their two proxies, children listening from home can imagine themselves within the spectral body of radio, a technologically mediatized manifestation of the big Other.

But some of the children listening in on these tales might have had an inkling of the media monster's more tactile, diminutive double. Troka's very first appearance in the archive dates from August 1932, several months prior to List Arzubide's involvement in the overhaul of XFX, and it comes in the form of a memorandum submitted to the director of the Department of Fine Arts by the ex-estridentista printmaker Leopoldo Méndez, who had been hired on as head of the Section of Drawing and Plastic Arts at the beginning of that year. Méndez includes a brief proposal for a radio character called Troka whom he envisages as a tool for teaching children to draw: primary school students will listen to his broadcasts and sketch his mechanical body as well as the stories he tells.[57] The document describes the musical component of the program ("a song of motors, sirens, and metallic sounds") and concludes with a short script for Troka's opening speech. It also offers an explanation of the character's name, which is graphically—though not phonically—marked as foreign by the letter *k* (nonexistent in Spanish). Troka, the proposal states, is an adaptation of the English word *truck*—a "word of universal industrialism" used in Mexico to refer not only to large vehicles but also "the wheels of locomotives, etc. etc."[58] Yet a reader attuned to the political sympathies of Méndez and List Arzubide might also note that "Troka" sounds suspiciously similar to *troika*—the traditional three-horse carriage that was an iconic symbol of prerevolutionary Russia and later, under the Soviet system, referred to a powerful triumvirate of bureaucratic leaders.

In fact, it was in the Soviet Union where List Arzubide had been inspired by the efforts of intellectuals to transform folk puppetry into a revolutionary medium of mass pedagogy.[59] Although the proposal makes no mention of puppets, it suggests children should learn to draw Troka and then represent the episodes he relates in school theater productions. As other archival documents reveal, Méndez was waging a contentious campaign to reorient school theatrics toward puppetry as a way of integrating manual arts such as drafting, design, and carpentry into the curriculum.[60] Over the previous few months he and List Arzubide had begun to work with a number of their old cohorts including Ramón Alva de la Canal and Fermín Revueltas as well as Germán and Lola Cueto, who had a long-standing interest in puppetry possibly fueled by their time in Paris among the artists of the Cercle et Carré collective.[61] The couple had recently returned to Mexico accompanied by Angelina Beloff, a Russian artist (and ex-partner of Diego Rivera) who assisted in translating a number of Soviet pamphlets and puppet plays. Other newcomers to the group were Graciela Amador, the ex-wife of David Alfaro Siqueiros and a communist activist and artist in her own right; Elena Huerta Muzquiz, another communist activist and artist who was connected to Siqueiros through marriage; and Dolores (Loló) Alva de la Canal, the sister of Ramón, who along with Roberto Lago would continue to work as a puppeteer for decades. They all met in the Cuetos' patio workshop, an old estridentista haunt, where according to several accounts they began to experiment with marionettes, though the difficulties involved in making and manipulating stringed dolls eventually led them to opt for hand puppets—small figures devoid of details that betray an impulse toward formal abstraction and technical simplicity.[62] A month after Méndez submitted the proposal for Troka, his higher-ups in the Secretariat of Public Education approved the puppet project for funding, and Méndez hired List Arzubide in the Section of Drawing and Plastic Arts, giving the former fugitive an institutional foothold from which he quickly branched out into radio.[63]

In the months leading up to Troka's radio debut, the ex-estridentistas and their collaborators organized three puppet troupes and made the rounds of public parks and schools, performing short shows featuring talking animals and fantastical characters such as The Giant, as well as one of the most popular: the Everyboy character named Comino, created by List Arzubide and "animated" by Loló Alva de la Canal, who starred in plays such as *Comino Goes on Strike!*, *Comino Brushes His Teeth*, and *Comino Beats the Devil*. During the presidency of Lázaro Cárdenas these troupes ventured into other regions as part of SEP-sponsored literacy campaigns, and today they are credited with ushering in the golden age of *teatro guiñol*, a "popular" tradition seldom recognized as a second-generation offshoot of the country's most irreverent avant-garde. Closely associated in popular memory with the Cárdenas era, the puppet troupes remained active for decades until 1985, when the Center for Children's Theater of the National Institute for Fine Arts was destroyed in the 8.0 earthquake that shook the city that year—an event that not only caused thousands of deaths but also sparked widespread opposition to the Institutional Revolutionary Party.[64]

Figure 3.2. A SEP *guiñol* (puppet) troupe in an outdoor performance, ca. 1933. Courtesy of the Archivo Histórico de la Secretaría de Educación Pública.

Troka the Powerful is a tenuous link between the avant-garde and this more popular (and populist) past, and for years his infrequent appearances in accounts of this period have been dogged by the (unsubstantiated) claim that he once was or was first imagined as a puppet.[65] In 2003 the puppeteer Pablo Cueto, grandson of Lola and Germán Cueto and son of the puppeteer Mireya Cueto, was invited by the University of New Mexico Chamber Orchestra to stage a show for their performance of a recently rediscovered piece by the modernist composer Silvestre Revueltas—a "dance pantomime for children" called *Troka*, said to have been written for a performance involving marionettes. Two years later Cueto's company Teatro Tinglado shed the marionette strings and created a toy theater version.[66] Billed as a celebration of estridentismo, its miniature set features the famous woodcut of the Estridentópolis radio tower by Ramón Alva de la Canal, framed by black-and-white images of factory whistles, tools, and angular buildings. The puppeteer composes the set before the eyes of the audience as Revueltas's percussive, brassy composition plays over the speakers; when the dialogue begins, it is not Troka who first speaks but an image of Maples Arce that pronounces his poem *Urbe* while his arm—replaced with a mechanical hook—is moved by the partially hidden puppeteer. After this prelude, little by little, Troka the Powerful materializes onstage as the puppet master constructs his tiny figure out of cardboard cranes and paper trains. The audience hears the grating sound of a siren, the lights go out, and a flashlight intermittently illuminates his small body as he declares, in a voice mediated by a device, *Yo soy Troka el poderoso* (I am Troka the Powerful). Yet after only a minute or so the lights go on, his human helper takes him apart, and only occasionally does he reappear in the interludes between a melancholic ode to Revueltas (who died young from alcoholism), snippets of other estridentista texts, and a glimmer of a warning about environmental damage. In its hyperawareness of its own history and constant juxtaposition of a human and diminutive representations of machines, the piece exemplifies what Rebecca Schneider (drawing on Fred Moten) describes as "inter(in)animation"—a term for the way in which "live" art and technological media "cross-identify" and "cross-constitute" each other, and in which the past and present coexist in the "syncopated time" of theater.[67]

In 2007, Mexico's newly established (and not yet inaugurated) Fonoteca Nacional, a sound archive and center dedicated to preserving the nation's "sonorous patrimony," collaborated with a Spanish intermedia artist on its first audio production: a podcast re-creation of a Troka broadcast, with the puppeteer Alejandro Benítez from Teatro Tinglado once again lending his voice.[68] Like the very idea of an "avant-garde" in an "underdeveloped" country, this radio/puppet link poses a potential quandary for the developmentalist logic to which Troka himself subscribes. Radio is a "modern" mass medium whereas puppetry is an "ancient" art that has existed in some form for millennia. But it is more than just a question of chronology: the partial figure of a radio puppet that keeps peeking into view throughout the record of the reorganization and expansion of the cultural apparatus also confounds the very concepts and categories we use to talk about media and art. If radio is often imagined as immaterial and ethereal, puppet theater revolves around the manual manipulation of objects on a physical stage. Whereas radio is a sound technology, puppetry appeals to both the eye and the ear. Radio broadcasts emanate from a fixed source across a wide radius of space, drawing together listeners in distant locales, but the SEP's *teatro guiñol* troupes were peripatetic, staging repeat performances for discrete audiences at different moments in time. And while broadcasting requires a complex mechanical apparatus, the hand puppets and stage sets used in the guiñol (like Teatro Tinglado's toy theater version of Troka) were purposefully simple, designed for easy transport and assembly and with the hope that children who started out as spectators could eventually learn to play the part of puppeteer.

Where does the link lie? Like puppetry and other forms of theater, early radio was "live" as opposed to recorded—although phonograph recordings were often played on the air, just as they were often used in puppet shows.[69] Yet both radio and puppetry also complicate and unsettle the sense of plenitude and embodiment associated with the live. Just as Rudolf Arnheim idealized radio as an "emancipation from the body," Edward Gordon Craig and others during this era argued for replacing actors with marionettes in order to liberate the theater from its dependence on the human body. Sounds and voices heard over the radio are acousmatic—the listener cannot see their originating cause—and in a guiñol show the puppeteer typically remains hidden behind a curtain or beneath the stage in order to create the illusion that his or her voice belongs to the visible body of a doll. In each case, the efficacy of the medium (or is it an art?) hinges on a disjuncture between the body and the voice, which is also a split between sight and sound. The human voice, often imagined as the direct expression of subjectivity, is overtly mediated by a nonhuman element—in the case of puppetry, by the presence of the stage and the puppet itself, and in the case of radio by an invisible yet no less material technological apparatus. This mediation of the live by the material and mechanical explains the uncanny, spectral quality often attributed to puppets as well as to radio, especially in the latter's early days. Indeed, in the figure of Troka—the "mysterious spirit of mechanical things"—the medium of radio becomes something akin to what Scott Cutler Shershow calls the puppet: an "inanimate object invested with histrionic 'life.' "[70]

Radio is not the only histrionic object that looms large in Julio I. Prieto's woodcuts for *Troka el poderoso*, the collection of short stories that List Arzubide published in 1939, after Troka went off the air (figures 3.3–7).[71] In the book's preface, List Arzubide explains his use of a robotic spirit as a pedagogical tool by comparing the psychic life of children to the phenomenon of animism among "primitives," an analogy he seems to borrow from Freud's *Totem and Taboo*. Freud associates animism—the tendency to see spirits in plants, animals, and fetish objects—with the narcissistic stage of child development preceding self-awareness. (Later on Lacan would dub this the mirror stage, which hinges on the gaze or *objet petit a*.) List Arzubide simply explains that both children and savages lack the capacity to exercise critical reason; instead, their instinctive response when faced with the violent, mysterious forces of nature is to "project onto the horizon their own astonished and terrorized spirit, and [in doing so] animate, give life, their own life, to everything around them" (7). In the past, pedagogues and priests exploited this tendency in order to lure children into the realm of superstition, the prerational world of "totems and taboos." In contrast, the ex-estridentista proposes to redirect those animistic energies toward the mechanisms of modern life, the instruments of technology and progress that constitute a "new nature" controlled by men. Children cannot be initiated into reason all at once, and thus the goal should be to "lead the child toward reality, give him real elements so that he can reflect on them animistically" (8–9). In other words, Troka's mission is not limited to communicating information about technologies; his power derives from the process, the formation and aural interpellation of subjects suited to meet the demands of a modern industrial society.

What is surprising about this is not the turn to animism as a way of theorizing new media. Sergei Eisenstein, whom List Arzubide reportedly met in the Soviet Union, explained the appeal of Disney cartoons based on their ability to tap into a system of "prelogical," "sensuous" thought; his desire to

Figures 3.3–3.6. Woodcut illustrations by Julio I. Prieto from Germán List Arzubide, *Troka el poderoso: Cuentos infantiles* (1939).

Figure 3.7. The hammer talks to the sickle. Woodcut illustration by Julio I. Prieto from Germán List Arzubide, *Troka el poderoso: Cuentos infantiles* (1939).

direct this primitive vision toward revolutionary ends was what drew him to Mexico in 1930–1931 to film his unfinished epic *Que viva México*.[72] Walter Benjamin, too, drew on anthropological studies of the "mystical," "mimetic" mentality of non-Western peoples to speculate on the insurgent energies latent in commodities (most notably children's toys), and he argued that new technologies had the (still unrealized) potential to liberate the forces condensed in things.[73] Between 1927 and the beginning of 1933 Benjamin also scripted and delivered more than eighty radio broadcasts, the majority of them for the Youth Hour on Radio Berlin and Radio Frankfurt, among which was a radio play starring Kasper, a familiar slapstick character from German puppet theater.[74] Despite their differences, both of these men saw animism as a way of imploding the commodity fetish; in contrast, List Arzubide openly instrumentalizes animism and turns it into a model for ideology, the grease that turns the wheels and sets seemingly self-acting machines into motion so that they can act as agents of progress and productivity and lead Mexico away from those "primitive" totems and taboos. (Of course, List Arzubide neglects to mention that Freud also associates animism, or the "omnipotence of thought," with neurosis and obsessive thinking:[75] parents might have balked at a theory of neurotic pedagogy.)

Despite his general aversion to "old" technologies, Troka makes an exception for the hammer and sickle, whose story begins with an argument over which sound—the clang of the hammer or the swish of the sickle—is more effective in inspiring men to work. At the end the two talking tools realize each needs the other and they join forces, preserving the symbolic integrity of revolutionary communism while offering a tacit nod to the agrarian reforms that Lázaro Cárdenas began to implement after assuming the presidency at the end of 1934. In the preface, List Arzubide cites a passage from Friedrich Engels's *Socialism: Utopian and Scientific*, in which the author counterpoises the French Revolution to the "less noisy" but no less transformative Industrial Revolution that kicked off in England around the same time. Implying that his (Mexican) readers are now following in the footsteps of their English predecessors, List Arzubide goes on to argue that the machine has created a "new social form . . . a social form that will very soon impose a society of free men." This statement hints at the need for Troka's own invention: the idea of radio as a revolutionary agent hinges on a series of contradictions that can only be resolved in the form of a fictional figure. Men make machines, but it is the machine (and *not* men?) that has made this new social form, which will paradoxically "impose" freedom—just as the seemingly autonomous movements of a puppet are controlled by a hidden hand. This discussion of animism, then, is an attempt to grapple with a single question that was driving debates about the nature of development as well as disputes over the role of culture and art in relation to the economic "base": who or what actually pulls the strings?

Nowhere in this text does List Arzubide mention puppets, and yet it is hard not to see their specter, especially since the very puppets for which he wrote some of the most popular plays were often referred to as *muñecos animados*, or "animated dolls."[76] At least one reference in the archive confirms the connection: in a letter to Méndez following a guiñol troupe's visit to her school, a teacher praised the play *Un viaje a la luna* (A Trip to the Moon, by List Arzubide) for the way it "satisfies the animism of children" (*satisface el animismo infantil*) by personifying natural forces such as the sun and wind as well as the telephone and radio.[77] Finally, the only remaining aural evidence of Troka seems to clinch the case: the theme song played at the beginning of his broadcasts, by the modernist composer and estridentista affiliate Silvestre Revueltas, is classified as a "dance pantomime for children," and notes on the score indicate that it was written for a piece involving marionettes.[78]

Presumably this was the same piece that turns up in a discussion of the Escuela Nacional de Danza, or National Dance School, an academy the SEP started in 1932. The school sought to develop a form of ballet it called *teatro coreográfico*, which drew inspiration from experiments in the Soviet Union and the recent staging of its own choreographer Nellie Campobello's "symbolic proletarian ballet" *¡30–30!* at the Estadio Nacional.[79] In an unpublished text written sometime during its first few years, the director Carlos Mérida (himself a painter) emphasizes the potential of dance as "a complete medium [*medio*] of artistic expression in which all of the fine arts are joined."[80] One of the most ancient of all artistic expressions, it is the "concretion of all the arts," and as such it has "its own essence, absolute autonomy, it exists for itself" (129). In Mexico, however, this essence and autonomy has yet to achieve concrete form. Although the school has started to rectify the long-standing neglect of the country's rich "aboriginal" traditions by collecting, cataloguing, and studying dances (160 to date), Mérida stresses that the ballets it develops are not designed to "strengthen a spirit of nationalism" and must avoid at all costs "offering the tourist a gift" (142–143). Like the national dance school in Moscow—and (he says) like the Teatro del Murciélago, whose composer Francisco Domínguez was one of the collaborators—he and his fellow artists treat this folkloric material as a "plastic element" to be realized through rigorous "technique" (140).[81] Rhythm is the key, and Mérida gives his due to Émile Jacques-Dalcroze, the inventor of eurythmics and the system of "rhythmic gymnastics" introduced into Mexican schools under Vasconcelos (see chapter 1). Ultimately, though, he critiques Dalcroze for his method's excessive "automatism" and praises the "freer" and more "human" rhythmic technique taught by Mary Wigman, an important influence on German expressionism and (apparently) the new piece the dance school had just begun to rehearse: a "ballet pantomime" called *Troka*, with music by Silvestre Revueltas, stage set designed by Leopoldo Méndez, and dramaturgy by Germán List Arzubide.

Mérida divulges few other details, opting to defer to a quote from List Arzubide:

> *Troka* is the spirit of mechanical things that have made many of man's ancient dreams possible. In this danced pantomime, *Troka*—who is **perhaps** radio, the synthesis of our era—calls the children of the world to dance with him in a solemn, grandiose spin uniting people and desires; so that beyond the bitterness of a present of war and hunger will rise the hope of a better day that begins with the new generations and goes toward a horizon of redemption through universal effort.

> *Troka* es el espíritu de las cosas mecáncias que han hecho posible muchos de los antiguos sueños del hombre. En esta pantomima bailable, *Troka*—que **acaso** es la radio, síntesis de nuestra época—llama a los niños del mundo a danzar con él en un giro solemne y grandioso que une pueblos y afanes; que sobre la amargura de un presente de guerra y hambre levanta la esperanza de un día mejor que principia con las nuevas generaciones y va hacia un horizonte de redención por el esfuerzo universal. (141–142)

Dance is envisioned as the "coordination" and "concretion" of every other art. Yet at the institutional origins of "Mexican" ballet are children circling around the medium of radio represented in concrete form as a puppet. Dance achieves its status as a "complete," "autonomous" art by remediating radio, which in turn is imagined as the aural "synthesis" of the era. Furthermore, this dance is also theater and clearly has a symbolic, representative function: it suggests that this mechanical agency is what links individual human bodies to the social collectivity. Here, it would appear, is where the radio puppet's parts all come together. The catch? Neither Mérida nor List Arzubide mentions a puppet. And then there is the semantically ambiguous *acaso*: this word could mean "perhaps," but depending on the context it can also function simply as a kind of embellishment added for rhetorical effect. It might not mean anything at all. In either case the reader of this passage is left to ask: did the children dance circles around a puppet? Around an actor who might represent radio? An actor representing a puppet who might be radio? Or was there nothing at the center of the circle at all?

There is no known script for this performance, though the scattered trail of Troka does (or rather did in my case) lead to multiple mimeographed copies of a dramaturgical outline for a "dance pantomime for children" with the title of *Troka*.[82] The copies are buried in the archive of Leopoldo Méndez, the prose reads like the work of List Arzubide (though the document is unsigned), and throughout the text are numbers that sync up the action with Revueltas's musical score. According to the schematic two-page text, the piece begins with a brief musical introduction—most likely those same dissonant notes heard by radio listeners at the start of every broadcast by Troka. When the curtain opens the stage is in darkness, and only little by little does the title character appear—not in his entirety, but "disarticulated, shapeless [*informe*], a suggestion of the character (a hand, an arm, the head)," each illuminated by some type of "phosphorescent substance." There is a dramatic crescendo from the orchestra, a gong is struck, and then a little boy and girl watching from the wings come forward with "surprise" and "fear," examining Troka as if in astonishment and wonder. Like a fetish object, or a work of auratic art, he remains motionless as other children flood the stage, calling to their "invisible companions" (other radio listeners?) to join them in dancing circles around the silent cipher while singing the traditional children's tune "A la víbora del mar," one of the recurring leitmotivs in the aural automaton's theme song.

What is the object around which they dance? A mind prone to paranoia might start to suspect that the artists engaged in the project all conspired to conceal the answer to this question, because there is no indication of what (in concrete terms) Troka is meant to represent or how (if at all) he was incarnated onstage. There is no mention of a radio, and at no point is it hinted he could be a marionette. Logistics would also seem to work against this scenario: a small doll with throngs of children circling around it would have been difficult to see, and the puppeteers would have had nowhere to hide, since the performance was clearly intended to take place on a human-sized stage. And then there is the question: would such a small object inspire awe? It could be that the artists planned to use an oversized doll maneuvered by puppeteers hiding in rafters above the stage, though given the technological and financial limitations the new dance school faced this solution seems unlikely. Or perhaps Troka would have been embodied by a human actor—a man (or woman) playing the part of a marionette whose voice was radio. (*Petrushka*, the ballet by Stravinsky in which a traditional Russian puppet comes to life only to be tragically slayed, was a common reference among the artists involved in the project.)[83] The paradoxical figure of a wireless marionette is compelling precisely because it is so difficult to envision its incarnation onstage. How was mechanical versus human agency depicted? Once again: who or what pulled the strings?

But in fixating on an (absent) object, the viewer or auditor (or critic) can become blind and deaf to the action around it. Whether or not he had yet read Freud, this opening scene illustrates something similar to the theory of animistic pedagogy List Arzubide would later lay out in the preface to the print version of *Troka el poderoso*. Troka first appears as an inert object, and the children (along with the audience) struggle to glean what lies hidden within, piecing together the individually illuminated parts in an effort to discern the whole, the self-acting agent in the machine. In truth, however, its anima or spirit is a projection of their own inner selves, their deepest desires and fears, and their movement is the motor making him act. Suddenly, Troka wakes as if from a slumber and breaks through their circle with "excessive" or even "insolent" gestures (*gestos desmesurados*), dispelling the reverie as he greets a group of children carrying a "ridiculous" puppet or doll identified as the "corpse of imperialism." As the orchestra plays an ironic lament, the children unceremoniously toss the puppet on the floor and recommence their dance with "frenetic," "crazy" joy, perhaps resembling those "savages" whose primitive psychic state List Arzubide would later describe as analogous to their own. The action is interrupted once more by the sound of a gong, the stage goes dark . . . and then the mysterious spirit of mechanical things speaks. He launches into a story about "what the Chinese are currently suffering" (an allusion to the civil war between the communists and the Nationalist forces of Chiang Kai-shek), and then, as if to warn that the effigy lying at his feet might have life in it yet, he concludes his story with the proclamation, "'and that is what happens on account of this puppet'" or—the text offers as an alternative—"any other such silliness" (*o cualquier tontería semejante*) (figure 3.8).

All of the action leading up to this moment has prepared the reader to hear a serious, ideologically charged message; instead the text casually undercuts the mood of solemnity and suggests that it may not matter exactly what Troka says. This "silliness" marks a hermeneutic limit: like the historian who scours the archive, critics too tend to desire an object, words on a page or bodies on a stage that can be picked apart and pieced together in order to

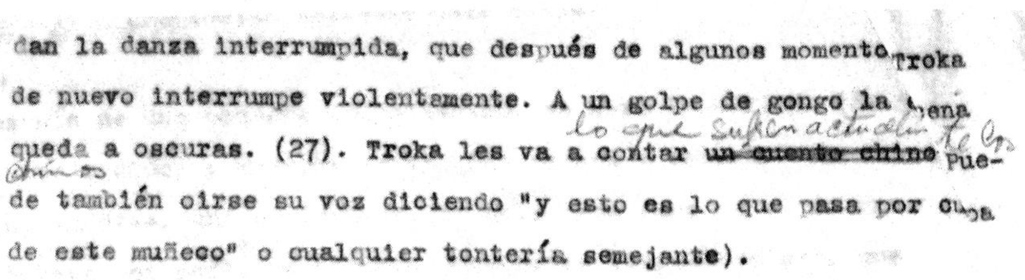

dan la danza interrumpida, que después de algunos momentoₜroka
de nuevo interrumpe violentamente. A un golpe de gongo la ṭₑₙₐ
queda a oscuras. (27). Troka les va a contar un cuento chino pue-
de también oírse su voz diciendo "y esto es lo que pasa por cu‿ₐ
de este muñeco" o cualquier tontería semejante).

Figure 3.8. From the dramaturgical outline of *Troka* (dance pantomime for children). Archive of Leopoldo Méndez, Centro Nacional de Investigación, Documentación e Información de Artes Plásticas (CENIDIAP).

illuminate their inner anima. But this is an outline for a performance still in the stage of rehearsals, still being shaped by its collaborators' competing desires and ideas, not to mention the complex confrontations and concessions taking place within the cultural bureaucracy at this time. Despite Troka the Powerful's seemingly simplistic and deterministic view of development, what ultimately drives his mechanical heart is the art of theater, with its reliance on stagecraft and the element of contingency performance always entails. As Troka stands over his imperialist enemy, a somber tableau of "poor, sad children, looking desolate, miserable, etc." is illuminated behind him by means of spotlights, "or whatever else occurs to you/them to use" (*o por lo que se les ocurra*); soldiers arrive and engage in a tumultuous battle, which then dissolves through the use of "silhouettes or some other trick" in an effect possibly inspired by the medium of film. In the distance, the march of Troka is suddenly heard. The children listen attentively, until finally it is revealed to be the march of the *niños obreros* or "working-class children" who have come to join their (implicitly) middle-class allies onstage: "The stage is flooded with light and the working-class children enter and are received with overwhelming joy and they begin the dance of labor. Of the workers' labor that will make the new sun rise [*o no, como se quiera*]" (figure 3.9).

The interpretation of this passage hinges on the odd parenthetical remark at the end—"o no, como se quiera"—a subjunctive phrase with an impersonal, unspecified subject that has multiple meanings and in this case could signify "or not, as the case may be" *or* "or not, as is desired." Immediately following this the text cuts to an abrupt ending: "The dance ends, all sing the march (or hymn) of Troka. March of optimism and hope." All is well. Dancing around the voice of radio, or a puppet, or a radio puppet, or whatever this mysterious spirit of mechanical things is, will bring a brighter day. And yet this ending cannot erase the instability and uncertainty that *o no, como se quiera* creates. The intention could be to offer a dramaturgical option: perhaps the dance of labor is superfluous and the performance can cut straight to the concluding march or hymn if the choreographer (or someone with

En estos momentos se oye, muy lejana la marcha de Troka. Todos

los niños escuchan con ansiedad: Son los niños obreros que llegan

(43). Se hace luz completa en escena (43) y entran los niños obre-

ros que son recibidos con júbilo desbordante (44) y empiezan la

danza del trabajo (45) Del trabajo obrero que hará surgir un nuevo

sol. (o nó, como se quiera).

Terminada la danza todos cantan la marcha (o himno) de Troka.

Marcha del optimismo y la esperanza (56).

Figure 3.9. From the dramaturgical outline of *Troka* (dance pantomime for children). Archive of Leopoldo Méndez, Centro Nacional de Investigación, Documentación e Información de Artes Plásticas (CENIDIAP).

bureaucratic oversight?) so desires. An equally plausible interpretation, however, is that the workers' dance will not necessarily bring forth the new sun. Perhaps in order to make the new day dawn these children will need to perform another *giro* or turn, one that does not involve circling around the voice of technology or revering an object of art—a performance that will not occur in the orbit of a "revolutionary" state but will require a revolution of some other kind.

An Unfinished Medium (Or Is It an Art?)

Troka makes no appearances on any of the programs for performances of the dance school.[84] Perhaps in the end the ex-estridentistas themselves, when faced with the exigencies of the stage, were unable to decide how to represent Troka; or perhaps they never got the knack of manipulating a marionette. Most likely this was one of the many projects from this era that never came to fruition, one of the many "unfinished" performances that were instrumental in re-creating both the conceptual and organizational infrastructure of all the old and new media and arts. There is an extant program for the Department of Fine Arts' "Cultural Series" from 1933 that makes mention of a future performance of *Troka* with choreography by Gloria Campobello, Nellie's half-sister (figure 3.10). Once again, however, there is no mention of a puppet, though it seems plausible since the SEP's puppet troupes did often perform in conjunction with displays of dance in the context of what could be regarded as "multimedia" shows for festivals, held in parks and the many open-air theaters built during the 1920s. In some cases as many as twenty-five hundred programs were printed, which invites the question of

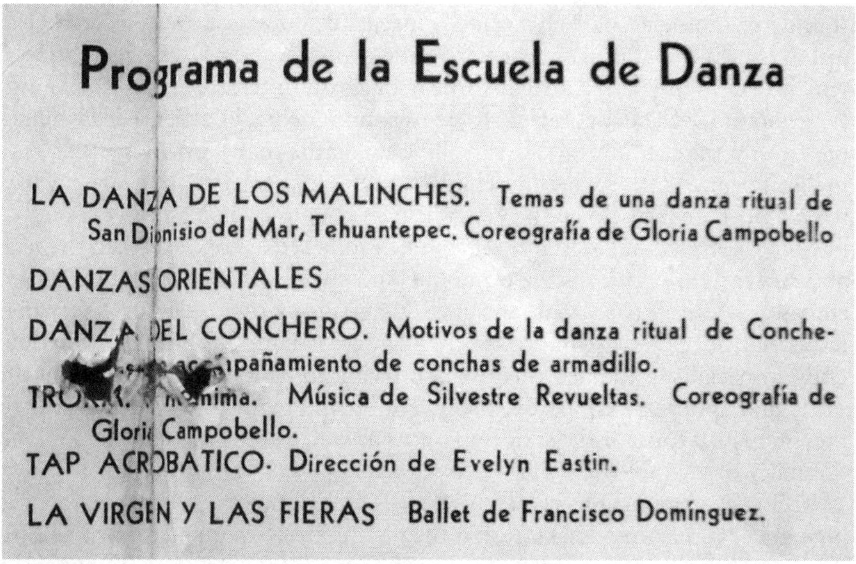

Programa de la Escuela de Danza

LA DANZA DE LOS MALINCHES. Temas de una danza ritual de San Dionisio del Mar, Tehuantepec. Coreografía de Gloria Campobello

DANZAS ORIENTALES

DANZA DEL CONCHERO. Motivos de la danza ritual de Conche-....acompañamiento de conchas de armadillo.
TRO... ánima. Música de Silvestre Revueltas. Coreografía de Gloria Campobello.
TAP ACROBATICO. Dirección de Evelyn Eastin.

LA VIRGEN Y LAS FIERAS Ballet de Francisco Domínguez.

Figure 3.10. Fragment of a poster announcing the 1933 Cultural Series organized by the Fine Arts Division of the Secretariat of Public Education. Fondos Especiales de la Biblioteca de las Artes del Centro Nacional de las Artes (CENART).

how everyone in the audience could have seen and heard the show, especially the part involving the small hand puppets. Internal memos in the archive suggest the auditory issue was resolved: microphones and amplifiers were used, and the festivals were often broadcast over the radio.[85]

So let us imagine *this* performance did take place (despite the lack of evidentiary proof), and let us even imagine it was broadcast over the radio. What did young listeners hear? Possibly nothing, given the irony behind Troka the Powerful's name: XFX, the Secretariat of Public Education's radio station, was notoriously faulty and weak. In the report he drafted during the station's reorganization in 1932–1933, its future director Agustín Yáñez prefaced his ambitious plan for the station to become the be-all and end-all of Mexican education by noting that his proposals "revolve around the idea that the voice of the SEP can be heard clearly in the entire country and even during the months of the worst atmospheric conditions."[86] Yet he also acknowledges this is a fiction. His plan is premised on an *idea* of a "mass" audience that was precisely that: his own speculative ideal. The Voice of radio, the Voice of technological progress, the Voice of the state, Troka's voice, was apt to cut out and was inaudible for some listeners from time to time. Troka the Powerful, in other words, was no less of a fantasy for his creators.

Of course, fantasies can have very real effects. In fact, if Troka was successful, it was in some sense because of his failings: as Jonathan Sterne argues, sound technologies have historically been accompanied by a pedagogical discourse that encourages listeners to develop certain "audile techniques," which usually involve learning to hear past any interference to distinguish "pure sound."[87] The ideological force of sound media, in other words, hinges on turning the medium into a vanishing mediator that must be present only to disappear. Again, what the children were supposed to be learning was to *not* hear Troka's voice, if one considers the voice not as the content of meaning but as the materiality of signification. Troka tried to teach them to abstract technology from the economic and social practices in which it was embedded—an illusion that sustained his creator's own seeming belief that industrial development under the tutelage of a national bourgeoisie could undo imperialism. At the same time, in trying to hear Troka through all the static and spotty transmission, they were being taught to turn a deaf ear to the unfinished form of the state apparatus as well as the inherent fragility and fallibility of technology.

Troka, it is important to remember, was called into existence to create the power he claimed to possess. Just as the puppet troupes aimed to involve children in the productions, he formed a Friends of Troka club that sponsored social events and invited individual children to come to the radio station and appear on air. And just as the puppet troupes asked children to draw the scenes they saw, Troka frequently asked his listeners to draw the events he narrated, to envision and draw the figure of Troka, and then send their drawings to the radio station to be judged by—who but Troka himself? According to memos the station sometimes received as many as two thousand drawings in a single contest, and at least one public exhibition was planned, though only a dozen or so remain in the station's archive, all from his initial broadcast.[88] What do they reveal? I refuse to say or show, because regardless of what is or isn't there, it was through these new practices and institutional relations that Troka's power became partially real.

Brazil

Chapter 4

✦

Parsifal on the Periphery of Capitalism

The city of São Paulo is noisy, chaotic, and larger than life, but few would describe it as elegant. Still, it seems oddly apropos that one of the most recognizable landmarks in this megalopolis of soaring skyscrapers and favelas is an opera house known simply as the Theatro Municipal. Postcards disseminate images of its façade, a jumble of neobaroque and art nouveau styles with nubile sylphs, delicate stained glass, and hoary atlases who shoulder columns crowned by the words *Música* and *Drama*. Tourists wander down the stepped terrace along the building's edge, stopping to gaze up at the mustachioed visage of Carlos Gomes, the Brazilian composer whose opera about the love of a noble savage and a Portuguese colonizer's daughter was once the toast of Milan. Only a handful of the metro area's 21 million inhabitants will ever enter the door, let alone see the stage, yet the small plaza where it stands is a popular spot for political protests to begin or end, a site where the destitute often congregate in the middle of the night like an ironic comment on the beauty wrought by the bourgeoisie.

Although the stage of the Theatro Municipal has seen its share of opera stars, one of the principal reasons for its renown is its status as the birthplace of the Brazilian avant-garde. The tale has been told many times: over the course of a week in the middle of February 1922, a group of artists and writers came together in São Paulo's premier performance venue to overthrow the *passadistas* of the old imitative order. Emiliano di Cavalcanti and Anita Malfatti set up easels in the foyer, turning crystal chandeliers and gold filigree into a backdrop for canvases awash in rude colors and unconventional lines. Victor Brecheret's bust of Christ with his hair in braids sent the classicists scurrying away in disgust. Meanwhile, in the sumptuous auditorium where Enrico Caruso had wowed the crowds just five years earlier in *Carmen* and *Tosca*, all semblance of decorum disappeared amid a cacophony of whistles, hoots, and catcalls.[1] Graça Aranha, a man far too old to plead youthful folly as an excuse (he was pushing fifty-four), scandalized his colleagues in the Brazilian Academy of Letters when he walked onstage to give the opening speech. The next day Menotti del Picchia upped the ante in a rousing defense of the new art, illustrated with readings of poetry and prose by a lineup that included Sérgio Milliet and Oswald and Mário Andrade as well as a dance by one Yvonne Daumerie. At some point the composer Heitor Villa-Lobos showed up with a shoe on one foot and a slipper on the other: he later chalked it up to gout, but critics were so appalled by his attire that they nearly forgot to comment on the "African" and "indigenous" elements in his dances for piano. The only part of the program on which the upstarts and their naysayers could agree was Guiomar Novaes—the essence of pianistic perfection as always, even if she did obstinately insist on playing a few numbers by Debussy, that old Romantic.

Some who tell the tale of the Week of Modern Art miss the irony entirely, but for scholars of theater it sticks in the craw: Brazilian modernismo was "born" in a theater, yet it engendered no new theater of its own. Sábato Magaldi and Maria Thereza Vargas attribute the absence of *teatro modernista* to the fact that, "being a synthesis of artistic elements, it presupposes the prior renewal of the arts that compose it."[2] By this logic, avant-garde theater can only ever be belated. Even so, the lack might be felt less keenly if the Theatro Municipal didn't loom so large in narratives of modernismo, if the participants and later critics didn't continually return to the primal scene, and if the stage at its center hadn't been built for an art so irrevocably tied to the Belle Époque. The artists later known as modernistas chose to make their break from within the carapace of the established order, but perhaps theater would have spoiled the tenuous illusion of a rupture between the old and the new; maybe something about the sight of bodies trying to enact experimental forms on an operatic stage would have confirmed a nagging doubt among the artists and their heirs as to whether Brazilian modernismo was really as modern as it claimed.

Indeed, the truly orphic moment, the scene history is most apt to recall, took place just beyond the designated space of performance, on the sweeping staircase leading up from the lobby to the auditorium doors. It was here that Mário de Andrade stood before a crowd and said . . . what did he say? There is no hard evidence, and an aura of ambiguity surrounds the speaker and his words. Some later critics say he read parts of the preface to *Paulicéia desvairada*, the lyrical panegyric to the city he would publish later that same year. It is amusing to imagine him—tall and gangly, every bit the bespectacled professor—framed between the graceful feminine statues on either side of the stairs, declaiming in his coy, self-ironizing fashion: "I am a *passadista*, I confess. No one can liberate himself all at once from the grandmother-theories [*teorias-avós*] he has imbibed."[3] Most, however, insist he read from an early draft of *A escrava que não é Isaura*, a whimsical critique of futurism in which he defines modernist poetry as The Slave Who Is Not Isaura—*not* the nearly white protagonist who is born into bondage in Bernardo Guimarães's Romantic classic *A escrava Isaura* (1875), but a slave who can only be named in the negative, by evoking the colonial legacy and shame of servitude one might expect the avant-garde to disavow. In fact, eyewitness accounts indicate this is *not* what he read, yet if the claim persists perhaps it is because it seems a fitting performance for an intellectual who was not quite white and not openly gay, but by all accounts queer—a man described as "peculiar," "elusive," and an "enigma," as if he were the half-hidden secret of modernismo. Over time Mário's speech has come to be regarded as one of the movement's defining manifestos, though it is a manifesto of a curious sort because its performative power hinges on the refusal to give itself to be seen.

The very idea of the avant-garde posits the possibility of a rupture with the immediate past and privileges art as an agent of change. In this chapter, however, I draw out a divergent logic (partially) hidden at the heart of this future-oriented impulse by turning to an avant-garde that flaunts its dependence on pseudo-secrets and an art often said to be dead. Unlike the Mexican *vanguardias*, which arose in the wake of a decade-long revolution, Brazilian modernismo emerged at a more ambiguous moment of transition and in a place where the transformations associated with modernity owed an obvious debt to the continuity of social and economic practices typically conceived as backward and behind. Despite this, canonical accounts of the Week of Modern Art depict it as a watershed in the quest for cultural autonomy, a performative break that ushered in the "heroic" decade of modernismo and presaged the (top-down) Revolution of 1930. But situating the event on an operatic stage troubles this tale. After the dawn of the twentieth century, writes Mladen Dolar, opera becomes "a huge relic, an enormous anachronism, a persistent revival of a lost past, a reflection of the lost aura."[4] Rendered irrelevant by the rise of mass culture, its corpus ever more moribund as the same old classics are rehashed time and again, this holdover from an earlier era is said to epitomize the conventionalism and hollow pomp that the vanguard set out to destroy. Even in Europe this narrative is riddled with contradictions, but it runs into particular problems in Brazil, where in 1922 most opera performances were imported from Europe. To borrow a phrase from Roberto Schwarz, opera was very conspicuously "out of place." Then again, so was Mário de Andrade when he said whatever it was he said on the stairs of the Theatro Municipal.

This chapter demonstrates how an avant-garde on the semiperiphery of capitalism emerged out of a "peculiar" temporal lag manifesting in the guise of operatic drag. As a point of departure, I turn again to Marx's discussion of the "secret" of "so-called primitive accumulation"—a secret he argues is exposed when the language of liberal political economy ventures out of its "natural" habitat in Europe and into regions of the world where its artificiality becomes transparent. A similar dynamic is at work in Schwarz's well-known description of liberalism in late nineteenth-century Brazil as an "idea out of place." Drawing out the feelings of backwardness and shame that Schwarz sees as formative of Brazilian identity, I show how this "peculiar" mode of ideology rooted in the experience of incongruity also created an odd aura around intellectuals tainted with the "sins" of racial mixture and nonreproductive sexuality. The heart of the chapter traces these associations in the actions and words seen or heard on- and offstage in the lead-up to and during the Week of Modern Art. By foregrounding the role of the Theatro Municipal in the staging of the event and in the debates it provoked, I argue that the contradictions Schwarz pinpoints converged around the "anachronistic" art of opera and the characterization of Mário de Andrade as the modernistas' own Parsifal: a vaguely queer, visibly mixed-race version of the chaste knight who wanders the primeval forest in Richard Wagner's opera of the same name. The chapter draws to a close with early efforts to memorialize the Week of Modern Art, including a "profane oratorio" by Mário in which he textually restages the event as an operatic song contest between competing choirs with some 550,000 singers.

A saintly air has long clung to Mário (he was dubbed the "pope of modernismo" by his peers), and until recently it has been something of a taboo to speak of such subjects.[5] Of course, people *do* talk. From the time he appeared on São Paulo's literary scene there were vague allusions; his friend and fellow modernista Oswald de Andrade, ever eager to push the envelope, was known to make indiscreet jokes and eventually brought their friendship to its bitter end with his off-color innuendos about Mário's sexuality and race. Memoirs and testimonials by fellow intellectuals, written long after Mário's untimely death, speak of his repressed desires and speculate on the causes, often as if in hushed tones.[6] My reconstruction of the Semana de Arte Moderna sheds light on how Mário de Andrade's queer mode of publicity emerged, and how his status as a figure who is vaguely "out of place" came to acquire a kind of symbolic power—though symbolic in an odd sort of way because it operates as an open secret, a shared knowledge of something that can never be entirely seen or said.

Primitive Accumulation and So-Called Secrets

In the first volume of *Capital*, Marx saves his discussion of "so-called primitive accumulation" for the very end, as if he wanted readers to work their way through abstract considerations of value and an excess of empirical details about wages and machinery only to discover that the secret is all too simple. What is it? If the answer remains opaque (as his frequent use of scare quotes implies), it is in part because our words do not always mean what they seem to say. A "free" workforce ostensibly refers to wage earners who are at liberty to sell their own labor power; yet in a more profound sense these workers have been set free *for* capital by being stripped of their own means of production and left with no option other than to work under conditions determined by their despoilers. Unevenness, in other words, is integral to capitalist development: freedom from serfdom goes hand in hand with dependence on capital, and the creation of wealth is always also an act of dispossession. In

Europe, where capitalist relations have already penetrated most sectors of society, those who use the language of liberal political economy can ignore its strange slippages in meaning, but when they attempt to transport it beyond these safe shores, its contradictions come to light and the "beautiful illusion is torn aside."[7] In the Americas, the separation of the producer from the means of production has to be "artificially" achieved through physical force, enslavement, coercive laws, the outright theft of land—acts of "primitive" barbarism that are speciously cast back onto the people who suffer them as if their impoverishment were divine punishment for some "original sin" (873). Yet for Marx, the obvious artifice of capitalism in the colonies simply reveals its innermost logic. This, the very last sentence of the book proclaims, is the "secret discovered in the New World by the political economy of the Old World": not some font of originary value to be extracted from capitalism's ever-receding periphery, but the logic of savagery and expropriation that remain hidden in Europe, in the belly of the beast (940).

This initial installment of *Capital* appeared in 1867, and the Civil War and abolition of slavery in the United States hover in the background of Marx's reflections, repeatedly referenced if never explicitly addressed as a subject in their own right. But the emergence of this former colony as an industrial power, clearly anticipated in the book, would only further accentuate the "primitive" elements of countries entering into what is commonly referred to as Latin America's "Export Age."[8] In an essay originally published in 1973, Roberto Schwarz drew attention to the peculiar status of liberalism in late nineteenth-century Brazil, where ideals such as liberty, equality, and economic rationalization sat uneasily alongside the "impolitical" fact of a slave system that would endure for two and a half decades after it ended in the United States.[9] While slavery was the fundamental relation of production, the ideological nexus around which the society of "free" individuals converged was access to patronage, or *favor*—a practice directly at odds with individual autonomy, "disinterested" culture, and the universality of law. And yet liberal ideology could hardly fail to hold sway, given its dominance in the sphere of international trade, in which Brazil's own slave economy played an integral (though structurally dependent) role. Bourgeois culture and ideas possessed ornamental value as markers of modernity and hence prestige, often serving to legitimize the "backward" systems of patronage and latifundism they derided as obsolete. Of course, liberal ideology was also a false description of European realities, as Schwarz (like Marx) is quick to concede; and yet in Brazil, where industrial capitalism couldn't even be said to exist, this incongruous complicity between liberalism and its ostensible object of critique meant that "thought lost its footing" and ideas qua ideas were perceived as "out of place" (155). Patently lacking any claim to generality, grafted onto a system grounded in the *exception* to the rule rather than the principle of representation, liberal ideas in Brazil were plagued by an air of inauthenticity, anachronicity, and lack.

Schwarz's essay assembles a striking repertoire of terms to describe the
psychic toll this situation exacts on those who claim "Brazilian ideas" as
their domain. Time and again he highlights the intense shame the Brazilian intellectual expresses when faced with the "impropriety of our thought"
(152); citing literary and historical sources, he remarks on the bitterness,
irony, and sense of inadequacy the local literati betray when describing their
own apparent irrelevance and the egregious disparity between the imported
luxuries of the elite and the squalid quarters of their slaves (160). His point,
however, is not to simply add another voice to the chorus of woe, but rather
to show how this experience of incongruity and the negative affect it entailed
came to form the crux of a distinctive ideological dynamic. If theory was
unable to reconcile these incongruities, the arts could more easily transform
what was and would continue to be regarded as a "national shame" into
a "national originality" (160). If Brazil had no choice but to reckon with
"modern" styles, literature and its like could "adore, cite, ape, plunder, adapt
or devour all those manners and styles, so that they reflected, in their flaw, a
kind of cultural torsion [torcicolo cultural] in which we recognize ourselves"
(159). In short, Brazilian culture is founded on this "flaw"; the contradiction
becomes content and acquires symbolic value as self-affirmation and negation become inextricably bound. As Schwarz briefly notes, both modernismo
and the Tropicália counterculture movement under way at the time he was
writing achieved resonance for the very reason that they register and put into
play these dislocations and disharmonies "for which there was nevertheless
no name, because the improper use of names was its nature" (159).

Although slavery is his point of departure, Schwarz is strangely silent on
the question of race and how it relates to this symbolic recuperation of dependency and degradation *after* 1888–1889, when the "abominable institution"
came to an end and Brazil swapped the title of empire for the trappings of a
republic. He remarks on the hollow nature of a liberal constitution enacted
by regional slave-owning elites, but he never explains how the last country in
the Americas to declare abolition could give rise to the myth of "racial democracy" in only a few decades' time. He cites retrospective accounts of slavery
still suffused by shame and inferiority, yet he never explicitly states how the
idea of liberty hangs together once its linchpin, the condition against which it
is defined, no longer has an institutional existence. Following emancipation
came four decades of mass immigration from the peripheries of Europe (primarily Italy), subsidized by states such as São Paulo in order to drive down
wages while also "whitening" the population. Blacks were disproportionately
displaced from the realm of "free" wage labor or relegated to its margins in
service jobs and the armed forces, even as the need for raw materials to fuel
industrialization drove capital deeper into the Amazon and drew its inhabitants into the export economy in the guise of "primitive" labor. Schwarz
provides one of the most incisive critiques of this push-and-pull, yet there is
something he either doesn't see or declines to say; something that might make

his own quasi-theoretical language seem out of place, because it has to do with the "impolitical," "moral" fact that several of the intellectuals he refers to were slightly brown.

Such was the case of Machado de Assis, the first president of the Brazilian Academy of Letters (founded in 1897) and the writer whose ironic take on the fin de siècle inspires many of Schwarz's own reflections.[10] In his essay, Schwarz never mentions that Machado was regarded as mulatto—but then again he has no need to, because his intended readers already know. Nor does he allude to the ambiguous racial identity of Mário de Andrade, whose "harlequin" method of poetic composition he cites as another example of the national penchant for dissonance and decontextualization. Only by extrapolating from his insights about the affective idiosyncrasies of cultural discourse in Brazil will one ask whether the canonical status of these and other "mulatto" writers in the decades following abolition might have something to do with the historical process by which the "exception" came to (imperfectly) incarnate the law and the stigma began to double as an emblem of national pride.

Both Machado and Mário played instrumental roles in founding cultural institutions with national claims. Both on occasion held bureaucratic posts, a coincidence explained in part by the fact that unlike their peers from the landed elite they had to earn a living—no small feat for an intellectual in a country where only a small fraction of the population could read. Both were highly visible public figures, yet Machado stuttered and was notoriously shy, while Mário was said to have abandoned hopes of a career as a concert pianist because his hands uncontrollably trembled whenever he walked onstage. Machado refused to take a public stance on slavery, just as Mário betrayed discomfort when faced with political issues related to class or race. Neither had children, though accounts often emphasized how devoted Machado was to his wife. Yet if Mário's sexuality was a frequent subject of speculation it should not come as a surprise, because the dynamic Schwarz describes bears some striking similarities to a mode of (dis)identification often defined as queer.[11]

Schwarz, to be sure, never draws this connection, and he is a frequent critic of the deconstructionist trends out of which queer theory in the United States has grown. Even so, his essay offers ways of thinking through the rhetorical repertoires and affective affinities linking the love that dare not speak its name to a phenomenon whose nature is the "improper use of names." Queerness, too, is said to register as a vague sense of ontological instability, or of something *fora do lugar*. Like the mode of national belonging Schwarz describes, it is often defined in terms of its deviation from the manifest logic of capitalist (re)production. Cast as counter to economic and political rationality, both are figured as an excess of affect or style, as a failed or flawed (pro)creation, always already a parody or pastiche; both are associated with the language of melancholia, abjection, shame, and anachronicity, giving rise to an impression Elizabeth Freeman describes as "temporal drag."[12] Nor is it irrelevant that the very period Schwarz singles out in explaining how ideas out of place became a symptom of "Brazilian" identity also saw the emergence of the category of homosexuality. In the United States, where the *Plessy v. Ferguson* decision of 1896 ushered in the era of Jim Crow segregation that would prop up its system of racial capitalism, Siobhan B. Somerville has shown how "the simultaneous efforts to shore up and bifurcate categories of race and sexuality . . . were deeply intertwined."[13] In Brazil, too, scientific discourses on sexual identity were steeped in evolutionary and eugenicist narratives of progress, and interracial and same-sex desire often overlapped in the cultural imaginary; but just as the country had no legal equivalent to Jim Crow, it also had no sodomy laws like the ones that contributed to the codification of homosexuality in the United States.[14] In a country where racial mixture was acquiring a symbolic charge, and where "unproductive" relations of patronage formed the basis of the social bond, it is perhaps unsurprising to find figures such as João do Rio, the celebrated flâneur and journalist whose chronicles of Rio de Janeiro offered a glimpse of everything from candomblé rituals to the lifestyles of the lettered elite: a light-skinned mulatto notorious for his liaisons with other men, he easily overcame opposition to win election to the Academy of Letters in 1910 at the age of twenty-nine.[15]

Indeed, Schwarz's thesis that Brazilian modernism arises out of (and not despite) the experience of backwardness resonates with Heather Love's more recent description of a queer mode of modernism invested in "feeling backward." Reading the work of authors such as Walter Pater and Willa Cather, Love sees their gestures of refusal and attachments to failure and loss as a mode of resistance to the emergence of more public and explicit forms of homosexuality. Whereas Schwarz counters the developmentalist teleology on which liberal nationalism rests by pointing to economic dependency as a precondition and enabling element of (rather than obstacle to) "Brazilian" identity, Love emphasizes queer identity's ties to a history of social exclusion and the contradiction at the heart of homosexuality, which can be "experienced as a stigmatizing mark as well as a form of romantic exceptionalism."[16] Schwarz concludes his essay by pointing to "the global reach that our national peculiarities [*nossas esquisitices nacionais*] have and can have," arguing that the precarity and irreality of liberalism in Brazil casts its contradictions into relief in a way less likely to occur in places where ideology's illusions rest on a more solid base (159). In a similar way, Love argues that "reading for backwardness calls attention to the temporal splitting at the heart of modernity" (6). And while Schwarz invokes musical metaphors (*dissonância, desacordo, desafinação*) to describe the off-kilter relationship between representation and its referent in Brazil, Love rejects the quintessential modernist icon Prometheus and instead makes a case for Orpheus, who descends into the underworld and secures the release of his wife Eurydice with his music, only to lose her again when he disobeys the divine injunction against looking back and turns around on their ascent to assure himself of her presence.

Love does not mention it, and perhaps it is only a coincidence that most critics consider the first opera to be Monteverdi's *L'Orfeo*, composed in 1607 for the court of Mantua. But Theodor Adorno would surely affirm the logic of this connection. Writing in 1955, Adorno noted that opera, reified and rendered irrelevant by new modes of mass culture such as cinema, had come to seem "peripheral" and "indifferent," a symptom of a more general malaise afflicting the entire institution of the stage.[17] With the exception of Alban Berg's atonal *Wozzeck* and *Lulu*, opera had resisted all efforts at innovation and was now a parody of its former self. And yet the parody, the German critic insists, simply unveils the true nature of this extravagant art, because in essence "all opera is Orpheus": while its rise in the seventeenth century coincided with the ascendancy of the bourgeoisie, what it portrayed were feudal relations already on their way to becoming obsolete (33). Opera fosters attachments to outmoded ways of life, transforming the past into the lost object of desire, so that "what happens on the operatic stage is usually like a museum of bygone images and gestures, to which a retrospective need clings" (41). At the same time, however, this backward-looking form prefigures the mass medium whose invention would signal its demise; the "conventionality" and "freakishness" that lend the libretti of so many nineteenth-century operas a dated air are signs of their commodity character, and in this respect as well as in their mobilization of all the technological trappings of stagecraft they act as "placeholders for the as-yet-unborn cinema" (34).

Adorno makes another crucial connection when he notes that the "retrospective need" for social structures no longer on the cusp of capitalist production and development is often linked to a desire for those on the geographical or cultural periphery of capitalism. A "bourgeois vacation spot," opera since at least the nineteenth century "has shown an endless love for those who are of foreign blood or otherwise 'outside' "—whether for the gypsies of Bizet's *Carmen* or the Africans in *Aïda*, Verdi's love story about an Egyptian general and Ethiopian slave, which was commissioned by the ruler of Egypt in 1871 and debuted at the Khedivial Opera House in Cairo two years after the building's inauguration in honor of the opening of the Suez Canal (35). Edward Said has situated the opera's genesis in the context of Egypt's deepening dependency on European finance, a process spurred by the Napoleonic invasion of 1798 and accelerated by the U.S. Civil War, when the supply of cotton from the United States to Europe was interrupted and the Nile Delta region picked up the slack. Emphasizing the opera's debt to orientalist archaeology and musicology as well as universal expositions, Said describes its formal qualities in language similar to Roberto Schwarz's depiction of liberal ideas in Brazil, remarking on its "unevenness," "falsity," "anomalies," and "incongruities" and characterizing it as a "peculiar" and "composite work, built around disparities and discrepancies."[18] At the same time, he argues (in a critical move that by now should strike readers as familiar), its eccentricity is exemplary of the genre as a whole, since "*Aida*, like the opera form itself, is a hybrid, radically impure work that belongs equally to the history of culture and the historical experience of overseas domination" (123).

Despite his insights, there is one detail Said neglects to note: grand opera found its most fertile ground not among the imperial powerhouses of England and France but in Germany and Italy, where political consolidation of the nation-state had occurred relatively late and the race for foreign territories was still incipient. In a footnote to his ruminations on opera's posthumous survival and growing popularity, Mladen Dolar speculates on the success of Wagner and Verdi and posits that in Germany and Italy, "the opera assumed the place of the missing state, as it were,"[19] playing a role not unlike it had for the absolute monarchy, acting as a lever or the "grain of fantasy needed to constitute the real community" (4). The grandiloquence of operatic art, his statement suggests, should not be seen as a direct expression of political and economic power but rather as a response to the experience of uneven development *within* Europe: much as Schwarz claims in the case of Brazil, aesthetic excess or overproduction compensates for the weakness of material and institutional ties. According to Dolar, people now recognize the fictitious aspect of the nation-state; nevertheless, opera lives on and even thrives as what he calls a "redoubled or mediated fantasy" (3). The lost object of desire is no longer the mythical community but the fantasy itself, a time in the past when people are said to have believed in and been united by the beautiful lie, a time when ideology was "in place."

And so it is that through a curious temporal twist, São Paulo's Theatro Municipal now appears all the more operatic in its (lack of) essence, strangely ahead of its time—and maybe even kind of "avant-garde." Like other opera houses built in Brazil around the same time, it was always already a redoubled idea-out-of-place, always a desire to believe in a bourgeois fantasy regarded as rightfully belonging to someone else. Although there is evidence of occasional opera performances as early as the mid-eighteenth century, the local allure of the art is tied to the year 1808, when the Portuguese royal court resettled in Rio after fleeing from Napoleon's invading army.[20] During its thirteen years as the seat of the empire, the city became a hub of operatic activity, with musicians and singers arriving from Europe to perform in the multiplying theaters and staff the new conservatory. After independence the new imperial government would continue to subsidize opera productions, but most of the companies were Italian (even if some of the singers and musicians were local), and although a series of attempts to create a national opera company between 1857 and 1863 could count the great Carlos Gomes as a success, the emperor quickly awarded the young composer a stipend to study in Italy, where he would spend most of his illustrious career.[21] Meanwhile, during the Belle Époque, the flow of opera from Europe to the Americas only increased.[22] A few of the iconic opera houses that dot the principal cities of

Brazil are early exemplars of neoclassicism, such as the Theatro São Pedro (1858) in Porto Alegre and the Theatro da Paz (1878) in Belém, where the local composer José Cândido da Gama Malcher succeeded in staging several of his own operas (with libretti in Italian); but a number of other theaters were completed during the age of imperialism's twilight, among them Fortaleza's Theatro José de Alencar (1910), with its art nouveau façade, and Natal's Theatro Alberto Maranhão (1904). The Theatro Municipal do Rio de Janeiro (1909) keeps company with the national library, the supreme court, and the municipal palace on the famed Cinelândia square; its counterpart in São Paulo is now hemmed in by a sea of newer high-rises, but even as these take on the air of relics, periodic renovations keep the theater looking preternaturally young. And then there is the Teatro Amazonas (1896), a neoclassical monument painted pink and crowned by a dome covered in bright yellow, green, and blue ceramic tiles—a gaudy homage to the Brazilian flag. Built in the jungle city of Manaus at the height of the rubber boom, it was in use for just over a decade before the boom started to bust, and no operas were performed again until the 1990s, when the government of the state of Amazonas created a standing ballet corps, choir, and orchestra—with most of the musicians contracted from Russia, Germany, and Belarus—and began to host an annual opera festival.[23]

São Paulo is not the jungle, but it too was a place where the incongruities of the postemancipation period were on dramatic display. Looking back on the origins of modernismo in 1942, Mário de Andrade would prefigure Schwarz in arguing that the movement could only have taken shape in Brazil's "second city"; Rio de Janeiro was more worldly and its artistic scene more mature, but São Paulo was more open to the modern, in part because it was still so provincial.[24] For most of the nineteenth century it was a rustic outpost of mineral prospectors, a frequent butt of jokes among the residents of Rio, home to the Portuguese royal family following its escape from the Napoleonic invasion and later the seat of the imperial court. The winds began to change in the second half of the century with the shift away from the cultivation of sugarcane to coffee in São Paulo State, which would provide half the world's supply by 1900. With coffee plantations came more slaves, and later on waves of immigrants from countries including Italy, Portugal, Spain, Greece, Germany, and (after restrictions on Asians and Africans were lifted) Japan.[25] The abundance of cheap labor and coffee export earnings also attracted foreign investment and drove the development of railroads and light industry. In 1870, the first official census counted 31,385 residents in the city; by 1920 it had swelled to around 580,000 (over a third of them foreign-born) and it would more than double over the next twenty years.[26] Economic power also gave the state political clout; throughout this period the presidency alternated between politicians from São Paulo and Minas Gerais in accordance with a pact known as *a política do café com leite* (coffee with milk politics), an allusion to the primary products of these two states.

By the dawn of the century civic leaders had begun to talk of building a new theater worthy of a city on the rise and able to accommodate the increasing numbers of European companies arriving on tour. The municipal government put out the first call for proposals from entrepreneurs in 1895, offering long-term tax exemptions as an incentive, but proposals were slow in coming, and then there were several false starts as plans were derailed by an economic crisis, failed deals, unexpected deaths, and other contretemps.[27] Eventually the state senate deliberated on whether it was proper to invest huge sums of public money in a project likely to benefit a single class.[28] Apparently its answer was yes, because it set about purchasing and expropriating land in the Nova Cidade, an area opened to development in 1892 when a viaduct was built across the Valley of Anhangabaú, a ravine formed by a river whose name means "demonic spirits" in the language of the indigenous Tupi and Guarani. The site chosen for the theater was on the Morro do Chá (Tea Hill), a high point overlooking the vale, which at the time was half-wild. This would change as the opera house, like other theaters built in Brazilian cities at this time, became the anchor for an urban expansion plan. In 1903, the state ceded the land to the municipality; the city council voted to foot the bill for construction and granted the contract to a group of architects led by Francisco Ramos de Azevedo, whose name now graces the small plaza on which the theater stands.

Ramos de Azevedo was Brazilian, his two partners were Italian, and their design was inspired by the Ópera de Paris, though the building in São Paulo is one-third the size in terms of total square footage and the similarities (at least to my untrained eye) are slight. A forty-two-page booklet distributed on opening night concluded with a list of materials used in construction, along with the companies from which products were purchased and their geographical location: statues from Paris, stained glass from Stuttgart, ventilation equipment from Frankfurt, mosaics from Venice, plasterwork from Milan, marble sculptures from Florence, electrical installations from Berlin, paving tiles from New York, ironwork from Düsseldorf . . . and São Paulo's Lyceum of Arts and Crafts filled in the holes.[29] The Theatro Municipal was "out of place," but clearly part of its purpose was to serve as a concrete display of São Paulo's integration into international commodity circuits. According to a commemorative plaque handed out on opening night, some 90 percent of the laborers and craftsmen involved in building the theater were either from Italy or of Italian descent—so who was to say it was not "authentic"?[30] Construction took eight years, and as the final touches were finished, the city began to transform the Valley of Anhangabaú into a sweeping pedestrian walkway lined with imperial palms and statues in accordance with a plan by the Parisian architect Joseph Antoine Bouvard.

After a one-day delay when props failed to arrive on time, the theater opened on September 12, 1911, with a performance of Ambroise Thomas's *Hamlet* starring the celebrated baritone Titta Ruffo. As a concession to

Figure 4.1. The Theatro Municipal shortly after its construction. From R. Severo, *O Theatro Municipal de São Paulo* (São Paulo, 1922). Courtesy of Harvard University Library.

nationalist sentiments, it was decided the orchestra would first play the overture to *Il Guarany*—the grand opera about a heroic Indian who risks his own skin to save his white ladylove from his less civilized cousins, which had assured the fame of local boy Carlos Gomes when it debuted at La Scala (the epicenter of Italian opera) in 1870.[31] Only after this would the Italian cast commence with its rendition of a Frenchman's remake of a Shakespearean play. Theatergoers must have arrived early to linger in the grand foyer and partake of edibles and libations in the elegant bar–cum–tea salon. Perhaps they debated the merits of the Venetian mosaics in the vestibule at the top of the "noble" staircase, which depict the Ride of the Valkyries and a scene from *Das Rheingold*—a bold homage to Wagner that must have rankled the diehard Italophiles. Eventually they were allowed to enter the lavish, horseshoe-shaped auditorium, where depending on whether they were in the orchestra or in a box they would have looked up or down at the proscenium stage, ringed by medallions inscribed with the names of Verdi, Bizet, Bellini, Rossini, Mozart, Gounod, Beethoven, Weber, Wagner, and Carlos Gomes. According to all accounts, the crème de la crème turned out in full force to fill the 1,816 seats: unlike the Colombo, another city-owned theater (though leased and managed by private interests), the Theatro Municipal charged prices well beyond the means of most residents and dispensed with the standing-room area that in many theaters offered more economical access.[32]

Backward Futurisms

Ten years and change is hardly a long time when it comes to a building that took eight years to construct and at least as long to conceive. In other words, the Theatro Municipal wasn't exactly a relic of a bygone era when the soon-to-be-modernistas stormed its stage, nor were all of their own faces as fresh as some claimed. Twenty years later one critic, echoing what was by then already a cliché, would describe the Semana de Arte Moderna as an event that "left the path clean and clear for the following generations," opening up a new era of creativity "in poetry, in the novel, in essays, in all of the genres except theater."[33] A more accurate assessment is that the Semana de Arte Moderna was at once a testament to the intensity of the changes São Paulo and Brazil as a whole had undergone *and* a vivid illustration of how familiar categories continued to set the terms. Many of the participants were members of the so-called *paulista* oligarchy,[34] but some came from the growing middle class, and a few were foreigners (e.g., the Polish architect Georg Pryzmbel and the Swiss painter John Graz) or first-generation immigrants, in most cases of Italian origin such as the sculptor Victor Brecheret and visual artists Zina Aita and Anita Malfatti (whose mother was from the United States). The presence of several women also signaled a change from the past. Yet as others have noted, financial backing for the Semana, as for the modernista movement as a whole, came not from the emerging industrial class but from the landed elite, namely from Paulo Prado and Olívia Guedes Penteado, heirs to two of São Paulo's great coffee fortunes.[35]

This connection became a sore spot even before the event itself, with the much ballyhooed "futurist" debate.[36] São Paulo's opera house was less than a year old when Oswald de Andrade returned from his first trip to Europe with a copy of the Italian futurists' first manifesto in his bag, but the term gained traction only after Anita Malfatti's controversial solo exhibition at the end of 1917, and what really put it on the map was when Oswald wrote an article around the middle of 1921 hailing Mário as "O meu poeta futurista," or "my futurist poet." Oswald was one of the afore-mentioned scions of the elite; Mário was one of what Sérgio Miceli refers to as modernismo's "poor relations," a professor of music history at the con-servatory and son of a mulatto typesetter/bookkeeper/journalist/self-made man.[37] Oswald heaps compliments on his friend's forthcoming collection of poetry, linking the "strange" but beautiful rhythms of *Paulicéia desvairada* to "the daily, formidable alteration of the very physiognomic grace" of an "uncontained [*incontida*], absorbent, diluvial metropolis of new people."[38] In a particularly florid passage he describes the lanky poet as a "livid and long, well-mannered Parsifal," the local counterpart to Wagner's virgin knight, and evokes the opera's vaguely Christian overtones of self-renunciation, sacrifice, and chastity—all traits still commonly attributed to Mário (229). It is an excessive and effusive but presumably sincere paean, a glowing endorsement from a well-connected insider of an unknown. Readers must have been taken aback, then, when the object of homage published a piece titled "Futurista?!" in which he vehemently rejected the honor.

The cordial but visibly tense tête-à-tête between the two Andrades is one of modernismo's milestones and an early harbinger, many say, of the differences that would later bring its "heroic stage" to an ugly end. For one, it marks Mário's turn against "futurism" (a term he, like many other protomodernistas, originally embraced), which is typically seen as a sign of his desire to distinguish a movement he was coming to view as national in its aspirations from a foreign (or as he describes it, "international") trend—a trend led, moreover, by Filippo Marinetti, whose sensationalism and fascist politics Mário abhorred.[39] Some also depict his response as a desperate attempt to mitigate the emotional and financial damage caused by his public outing. (Supposedly he lost students at the conservatory after being labeled a futurist.)[40] Evidence for all of this exists, but perhaps the key to this brief text lies in what is *not* said and cannot be definitively proven. Is the reader expected to recognize a connection between the "physiognomic grace" of the city and the "livid" or dusky physiognomy of the poet? Is Mário being coded as gay?

Such suspicions find fodder in the strangest aspect of this encounter, which is all the more intriguing because literary historians rarely mention it: neither Oswald's original article nor Mário's rebuttal names the poet in question as Mário himself. Oswald dangles the identity of his subject before his readers saying, "He is called . . . I can't tell you his name. He forbid it, the chaste, good, timid man. I will recount for you his figure and his art."[41] Mário subsequently claims to respond on behalf of their mutual friend and perpetuates the ruse of anonymity with a sly wink: "The parity that exists between me and my friend, the 'futurist poet,' is well known; it will be understood, therefore, that my ideas published here are *exactly* the same as those of the unhappy author of 'Paulicéia Desvairada.' "[42] What is this all about? A question mark hangs over the affair just as it hangs over the acrimonious end of their friendship in the late 1920s, when Oswald publicly ridiculed Mário as "Miss Macunaíma," a feminized version of the race-changing, childlike "hero without any character" of his now-classic novel *Macunaíma*. In "O meu poeta futurista," Oswald appears to be forcing Mário into a position of prominence, capitalizing on his status as an outsider—an eccentric Parsifal *and* an Everyman—as a way of opening up the insular literary scene. For his part, Mário recognizes and responds to this interpellation, which is also an implicit offer of patronage (surely there is a hint of condescension in the possessive *meu poeta*), only to deflect its force by distancing himself from the persona imposed upon him. From the very first, in other words, his relationship with the public is characterized by obliquity and evasion, a dual movement of revelation and self-effacement. Critical acuity, ethical judgment, chastity, and an ambiguous racial identity are all linked in a figure who (to borrow Schwarz's words) has "no name, because the improper use of names was its [his] nature."

"A livid and long, well-mannered Parsifal . . .": given the frequent references to Wagner in the writings of the Brazilian intelligentsia at this time,
certain readers might have picked up on the complexities involved in this
depiction of Mário as an (improper) version of a fictional figure born four
decades earlier on a European stage. The protagonist of Wagner's last work
also first appears as a mysterious stranger, a young hunter wandering through
the medieval forest of northern Spain who is unable to say who his father
is or where he is from and cannot recall his own name. He is also at a loss
to explain how he arrived at the castle occupied by the Knights of the Holy
Grail, whose king suffers from an incurable wound caused by his own Holy
Spear during a tryst with a witch-turned-temptress sent by the evil magician
Klingsor, who seeks revenge after castrating himself in a misguided ploy to
gain admittance to their elite gentlemen's club. This man-child of dubious par-
entage, a.k.a. Parsifal or the "pure fool," dutifully complies with his destiny
by recovering the Spear after valiantly resisting the charms of nubile women,
weeping copious tears of guilt for abandoning his mother, and searching for
years until he finds the path back to the Grail. In one of Wagner's character-
istically overblown finales, he arrives at the castle and, touching the Spear to
the sovereign's side, cures his wound and thus absolves him of his guilt before
commanding the unveiling of the life-giving Grail as the Chorus hails him as
the Redeemer and new King.

Oswald de Andrade was a member of the opera-going elite who had spent
several years in Europe, and as a musicology professor with a keen interest in German culture and Wagner in particular, Mário de Andrade likely
knew that all this brotherly love and jostling of phallic weapons had not
gone unremarked by contemporary observers. In the decades following its
debut at Bayreuth in 1882, critics had openly debated whether *Parsifal* was
a "homosexual opera"; meanwhile, Nietzsche condemned its celebration of
chastity as contrary to nature even as he warned readers not to succumb to
the "decadent" sensuality of the music lest they wind up like the protagonist and end up "forgetting [their] manhood under a rosebush."[43] According
to Nietzsche, the sterility of Wagner's main men was simply the dramatic
counterpart to the "dissonant," "fragmentary" quality of his music, which
was evidence of his incapacity to create an organic work of art—a failure
caused by the desire to theatricalize all of the other arts and pander to the
abject instincts of the womanish masses. Wagner was an "incomparable *his-
trio*" who debased music by attempting to make it "visible," forcing sound
into the service of semantic signification and subordinating it to the logic of
corporeal gesture (172). The composer himself, however, drew on the same
organicist metaphors to depict his "theater of the future" as the culmination
of a heterosexual act in which the "procreative seed" of Poetry impregnated
that "glorious loving woman, Music."[44] As Wagner saw it, the "unnatural"
genre of opera degraded drama by turning it into a mere pretext for the display of vocal virtuosity rather than acknowledging music's proper (feminine)

function as an "art of expression." His proposal to join all the arts into a *Gesamtkunstwerk* or "total work of art" was also a call to slay this "majestic mummy" in order to restore the marriage of music and word found in the songs and dances of the German folk (41).

By the time Oswald anointed his nameless friend a Parsifalian futurist, Wagner himself had been dead for four decades, yet his cult continued to grow. Marinetti derided the phenomenon in a 1914 manifesto titled "Down with the Tango and Parsifal!," a missive addressed to certain "cosmopolitan women friends" known to host tea parties where guests collectively cooed over the "mystical tears" of a "forty-year-old virgin" and performed affected imitations of a dance that simulates unconsummated sex (no wonder "inverts" like Oscar Wilde love the tango, Marinetti suggests).[45] It is reasonable to assume that some inkling of this antagonism found its way to Brazil, though the paulista vanguard may have also recognized that like many other "revolutionary" artists of the era, the Italian futurists were themselves dogged (and driven) by the Wagnerian specter of a total artwork able to subsume every other medium and genre. "O meu poeta futurista" plays up this dynamic of disavowal and dependence by collapsing the figure of the avant-garde poet with the late Romantic knight, creating a character who is anachronistic but oddly apt in a country where Wagner is not yet yesterday's news and cultural development all too obviously deviates from the temporal (and sexual) logic it supposedly follows in Europe. *Parsifal* depicts a "conquering race" whose rituals of purification have lost their performative power because the cult objects around which they revolve have been stolen or concealed, and by recovering the Spear and restoring the Grail to the realm of sight the hero reactivates their aura and restores their devotees' "virility": heterosexual desire is sublimated into religious devotion in an allegory of the composer's attempt to impregnate Music with the Word in order to re-"consecrate" the stage and redeem the German *Volk* from the corrupting influences of modern culture (including Jews). In contrast, São Paulo is said to be an "absorbent" city of "new" people, and rather than progressing toward redemption and revelation Oswald lavishly veils the identity of his reluctant hero in purple prose, transforming him *into* a tarnished relic. The opening line reads, "He is long like a taper and to my recollection evokes the chalice of the Grail suspended before the avid lips of the Babylonian *girl* that is this city of a thousand doors" (22). Oswald picks up on the queer subcurrent of *Parsifal* and plays it to the hilt: instead of the active agent who reunites the Spear and Grail, Mário *is* the impossible object of desire, both taper (an ineffectual phallus) and chalice (a womb-like vessel of *mixed* rather than pure blood). Although he serves as an intermediary between the vanguard knights and the city (not the folk but a flapper/fag hag), sublimation is incomplete, and what results is nothing so holy as a symbolic bond.

It is obvious why Mário might find this offensive, but parsing his response is complicated by his complicity in creating his Parsifalian persona. Although

Paulicéia desvairada does not directly cite *Parsifal*, a scattering of other Wagnerian allusions points to its protagonist as one of many models for the lyric pseudo-subject that reappears throughout the collection of poems as a wise fool, a modern-day harlequin and mercurial flâneur (identified in several instances as "Mário") who paints impressionistic scenes of the equally "harlequin" city and lives out the doctrine of *desvairismo* (delirium or disorientation) proclaimed in the preface.[46] Just a few years later Mário would begin to argue for the need to form a single *raça brasileira* from the synthesis of Brazil's diverse cultural traditions, an idea most fully developed in the unfinished libretti he produced in collaboration with composers who shared his desire to develop a truly "Brazilian" opera (a topic I discuss in the following chapter). Although the accent falls more heavily on divisions and disparities in *Paulicéia desvairada*, here too musical motifs are racialized and endowed with popular value. The harlequin is also a "Tupi Indian strumming a lute,"[47] an indigenous troubadour whose musical madness allows him to pass freely through the city, while in the poem "Nocturno" a guitarist strolling through the immigrant district of Cambuci is described as "a golden mulatto / with hair like lustrous wedding rings [*alianças polidas*]" (55). Whereas *Parsifal* revolves around metaphors of purity and primeval origins, Mário emphasizes the eclectic racial makeup of a city characterized as a site of incongruities and impurities, a quality obliquely reflected in the motley attire and mental vagaries of the harlequin, who has no discernible objective and never assumes the symbolic mandate of authority and reason. Instead he occupies a position José Miguel Wisnik identifies as the purview of the mulatto—a figure "on the frontier between exclusion and inclusion, the part that is neither rejected nor granted admittance but which guards the unspeakable secret [*o segredo inconfessável*] of the whole."[48] At the heart of this secret are the "primitive" processes of which Marx wrote—the extraction of gold from the New World mines and experiences of enslavement and sexual violence, transformed into aesthetic value via a musical mulatto with wedding rings for curls.

This move to reclaim racial mixture as a source of poetic authority was paradoxical and precarious, not least of all because the rhetoric of race was so unstable at this time. In November 1921, just a few months after Oswald and Mário crossed swords, the writer Menotti del Picchia devoted his column in the *Correio Paulistano* to a lineup of the rising stars (himself included) of what he boldly dubbed *futurismo sensacional*. Del Picchia was already well known as the author of *Juca Mulato*, an epic poem about a mixed-race ranch hand who pines for his boss's daughter but heroically resigns himself to a life of labor and a wife of his own standing. Here, too, a similar logic seems to be at work in his choice of a protagonist: first on the roster of this round table of "futurist" knights is Mário de Andrade, whose name is followed by a cryptic "definition" that likens the poet to the "fair at Tiradentes Square, with its stunning cosmopolitanism of unsettled races [*raças mal acampadas*] and long Parsifalian lilies mixed with Leghorn and Carijó hens."[49] The reference to the famous plaza in Rio, named for an eighteenth-century martyr of independence, could be related to Mário's editorial collaborations with intellectuals in the capital city, though a suspicious reader might wonder at the implicit analogy between the "unsettled races" who gather there for market and the merchandise on display: Leghorns originally came from the Italian city of Livorno and are white, as opposed to the speckled Carijós, whose name comes from an indigenous group enslaved and exterminated by the early Portuguese colonizers. Once again Mário is not openly identified as mulatto, but those in the know can be expected to recognize the meaning behind his metaphorical depiction as a medium for cross-racial encounter and economic and cultural exchange. (Tiradentes Square was also the site of two theaters where operas were often performed.) His imagined link to this eclectic public space operates as a source of symbolic capital for his fellow *futuristas*, yet Del Picchia also puts a nasty spin on the Wagnerian motif with his juxtaposition of poultry and Parsifalian lilies, which reads like a parody of the harlequin-like juxtaposition of high and low culture in *Pauicéia desvairada*.

The tension between these two writers was an open secret, and like many of the other alliances among artists who took part in the Week of Modern Art, their mutual membership in the so-called Group of Five (also composed of Oswald, Tarsila do Amaral, and Anita Malfatti) would later give way to open animosity. It is not hard to see why. Just two days prior to the inauguration of the Semana de Arte Moderna, Del Picchia wrote a column in which he attributed the region's cultural vitality to its role as a racial melting pot, boasting that "São Paulo—cradle of a racial, industrial, economic futurism—is the cradle of cultural futurism."[50] Writing under the pseudonym Hélios, he wields the triumphant tone of those who have emerged victorious from the "fecund violence" of São Paulo's "clashing racial characteristics"—as beneficiaries of a uniquely dynamic form of entrepreneurial capitalism that broke with the ancestral customs of the "patrician" North. As evidence he invokes the *bandeirantes*, early colonial prospectors who also led expeditions to capture indigenous slaves and whom Del Picchia euphemistically credits with achieving the "fixation of nationality," leading to a natural "weakening" of the nation's "first ethnic stratum" that in turn helped fertilize the ground for the new waves of "Latin" immigrants.[51] Even at this stage, in other words, the writer was voicing ideas later linked to the protofascist faction of modernismo known as *verdeamarelismo*, or "green-goldism" (in honor of the national flag). With the influx of people from elsewhere and the disappearance of Indians (there is no mention of blacks), he boasts that it is "as if a piece of the world had moved [*se deslocasse*], geographically, to America." As a result, São Paulo was the site of a cultural vanguard "as modern, as alive as the most evolved in the rest of the world"—as would be seen in the upcoming events at the Theatro Municipal.

In the Shadow of the Operatic Stage

There are no detailed accounts of the negotiations leading up to the Week of Modern Art; history did not record how or why Oswald backpedaled from "futurism," although presumably Mário's opposition and the troubling connotations it acquired in the hands of Del Picchia played a role. It is clear that the participants must have come to some kind of last-minute accord, because when the big day arrived, several of the speakers felt the need to clarify that this motley crew was *absolutely not* "futurist." At this point, however, no alternative had yet been proposed. What did they have in common, despite all their differences? For starters, most of them had whiled away many an hour in the Theatro Municipal: some had attended political meetings held in the auditorium and many were no doubt regulars at the bar, but at some point most had also come to catch the latest production of *Rigoletto* or perhaps *Manon*. Thus it should come as no surprise that they articulated their call for the "new" in and against the idiom of opera.

That the artists themselves saw the setting as significant is evident from the fact that on day 2, Menotti del Picchia concluded his speech and prefaced the afternoon's performances with an allegorical coda about an "unheard-of thing" [*coisa inaudita*] that had taken place only a few months earlier on the very stage where he stood: the fourth act of Arrigo Boito's *Mefistofele*, an opera said to have sparked a riot at its debut at La Scala in 1868 over its obvious affinities with the mythic music-dramas of Wagner.[52] Del Picchia doesn't cite this detail, but he does offer a blistering description of the grand finale as a "ridiculous" *comparsaria*, a preposterous hodgepodge of Faust, ancient Greece, and Roman gods. The lawyer-cum-journalist-and-poet heaps scorn on the opera's eclectic aesthetic and blithe disregard for chronology while lambasting the artificiality of the mise-en-scène, scoffing that the regal crowns on the heads of the gods were cobbled together out of cans while the mighty sword of Mars was tin and the "gold" adorning their togas was only flimsy painted paper. Of course, he may be embellishing a bit to prove his point, namely that the "Parnassian" decadence on display in this shoddy spectacle is precisely what the vanguard is out to overturn. The language of his critique conjures the very specter that *l'art pour l'art* seeks to keep at bay, portraying Boito's revue of "readymade gods" (*deuses de fancaria*) as an accidental allegory of the decline of the aura.[53] Grand opera musters all of its performative power to create a sense of ritualistic presence; yet this is opera "designed for reproducibility" (to borrow Walter Benjamin's description of art in the age of mechanical reproduction), not only because so many of its constituent parts are mass-produced but also because it is opera for export, an Italian company playing another gig on the South American circuit.[54]

What is the solution? Give up the ghost and actualize the aesthetic, make art reflect reality, write poems relevant to the age of automobiles, and recognize that "the modern nymphs dance *maxixe* to the sound of jazz."[55] Del

Picchia wants to update the objects art represents, but he indicates no need to change the social form or function of representation, nor does he suggest artists actually take up the new cultural practices he extols. If anything, his digression on the performance of *Mefistofele* is a call for reform to prevent the lines between cultural spheres and social classes from collapsing. Throughout his speech he is at pains to prove that he and his comrades are *not*, as some would have it, a "band of Bolsheviks of the aesthetic," not "outlaws [*cangaceiros*] of prose, verse, sculpture, painting, choreography, music, mutineers in the banditry [*jagunçada*] of the literary Canudos of Paulicéia Desvairada."

One wonders how the audience responded to this jumble of allusions: was the mention of Mário's (still-unpublished) collection of poems meant and/or taken as a dig? The speaker compares the hallucinatory vision of São Paulo conjured in the book's title to the colony in the northern backlands of Bahia where a millenarian sect of former slaves, landless peasants, and uprooted Indians held out against the authority of the republic for several years before being massacred by the military in 1897. From the context it is clear Del Picchia regarded Canudos as a sign of the disorder and backwardness Brazil had to overcome, and in light of his earlier allusions to Mário's race this comparison of Canudos to *Paulicéia desvairada* seems like an effort to quiet fears of a connection between Mário's literary "madness" and challenges to established social hierarchies. The "century of discoveries" led by Wagner, Cézanne, Rodin, and Rimbaud is over, Del Picchia says. This is the century of construction, and it has fallen to those assembled in the theater to achieve the "foundational fixation [*fixação basilar*] of a new aesthetic, in which we will be, in the future, the neoclassicists." "Desvairada"? On the contrary, this is a vanguard ready to lay down a new law.

If Del Picchia's protomodernista parable begins by conjuring (only to critique) a prior performance of an operatic scene, it ends with a gesture of abstraction, divesting opera of its ties to the physical stage in order to redeem it as an ideal. In an indirect allusion to the protagonist of his novel *Juca Mulato*, Del Picchia evokes "the national *cow-boy*" who, in the Rio Preto region of São Paulo State, "reproduces the equestrian odyssey of Orlando Furioso" just as Edu Chaves (a famed local aviator) "reproduces with *paulista* audacity the dream of Icarus." But the star with top billing is the city of São Paulo itself, depicted as a modern industrial polis composed of neatly defined classes and corporatist groups: "the worker claiming his rights" shares a stage with "the bourgeois defending his coffer," "functionaries gliding on the tracks of regulations," "the industrialist fighting the struggle of competition," and even "woman breaking the bonds [*algemas*] of her age-old slavery." Nothing is awry in this fully rationalized system; everyone sings his or her designated part. African slavery has left no legacy, clientelism has ceded to free competition, and we get no glimpse of any coffee planters or pickers, the agricultural basis of the export economy on which São Paulo's industrial growth relied. For Menotti del Picchia, liberal ideas aren't out of place in

Brazil; the country can successfully replicate the classic stages of capitalist development (just as it can reproduce its classic myths), and the role of the avant-garde is to consecrate its golden age. And so he concludes by presenting the "revue" of artists who will illustrate his words and banish the specter of *Mefistofele*'s tawdry gods by turning the stage into the site of avant-garde music, dance, poetry, and prose—all of the old arts, except theater.

This vision of São Paulo as a heroically operatic metropolis surely appealed to the interests of the festival's financial backers, who billed it as an event of international import as well as proof of São Paulo's unique character as a place of self-made men.[56] But not all of the participants played to the audience's sense of self-importance with such an utter lack of irony. Oswald de Andrade was more tied to the money than most: it may have been due in part to his family connections that the audience on opening night included Washington Luís, the state governor and future president of Brazil.[57] Perhaps for this very reason Oswald felt at liberty to turn his scathing humor on one of the local gods—Brazil's sole claim to operatic fame, and the only national composer who appeared alongside Verdi, Wagner, Bellini, and all the rest in the list of names inscribed above the stage of the Theatro Municipal. There is no record of the exact words Oswald uttered onstage, but they were apparently of the same tenor as a column he wrote for *Jornal do Commercio* the day before the Semana began, in which he cut to the quick:

> Carlos Gomes is horrible. We've all felt it from the time we were small. But since he's one of the family's pride and joys, we swallowed the whole jingle of *Guarani* and *Schiavo*—inexpressive, fake, heinous. And when someone speaks to us of the absorbing genius from Campinas, we wear a smile like a stage trap, like someone saying: "It's true! Better for him not to have written anything at all . . . A talent!"

> Carlos Gomes é horrível. Todos nós o sentimos desde pequeninos. Mas como se trata de uma glória da família, engolimos a cantarolice toda do *Guarani* e do *Schiavo*, inexpressiva, postiça, nefanda. E quando nos falam no absorvente gênio de Campinas, temos um sorriso de alçapão assim como quem diz: "É verdade! Antes não tivesse escrito nada . . . Um talento!"[58]

Leave it to Oswald to poke his finger in the wound. Gomes's operas, he suggests, do act as a kind of cultural glue, but not because the music evokes genuine emotion or because anyone actually believes the trite stories are good. Au contraire! The family's pride and joy is also its secret shame. "Conventional opera" (he specifies: "Italian opera") had its "era of legitimate affirmation," but it was back in the days of Monteverdi and Scarlatti, back when those "tenors covered in rouge" and "sopranos strangled by lyrical hypocrisy" were false yet still in sync with the ideology of the times and opera "went with the era, marked it, honored it" (77). That moment was long past when Gomes came along and hitched his wagon to Polichinelli and other lackluster Italians rather than following the lead of Wagner, whose "revolution of Bayreuth" joined poetry and drama to music and in doing so "brought to the theater an unknown vigor and corrected it, intellectualized it" (78). If Del Picchia cites Wagner as a master whose era has been overcome, Oswald hails the German as the vanguard of his day and credits his "union" of the arts with granting theater a theoretical validity it had hitherto lacked.

By the time he began to write for the stage in the early 1930s, a period marked by his turn toward communism, Oswald would view Wagner's notion of the total work of art with far more ambivalence. As I argue in the final chapter of this book, his sprawling "spectacle" *O homem e o cavalo* (Man and the Horse) satirizes the Nazis' appropriation of the composer's legacy and grapples with the rise of mass spectacle as a tool of authoritarian regimes by opposing a dialectical vision of world history to the logic of immediacy and "total" theatricality. Here, however, he echoes the admiration of Wagner shared by many modernizers in Brazil. The medieval knights of *Tristan und Isolde* and the Norse giants who lumber through *Die Götterdämmerung* and *Die Walküre* (says Oswald) succeeded in making the Völkisch spirit visible. In contrast, Carlos Gomes "succeeded in profoundly defaming his country, making it known via Peris wearing gourd-colored bathing suits and gaudy feather dusters on their heads, roaring indomitable strength on terrible stage sets." (Peri is the indigenous protagonist of Gomes's opera *Il Guarany*.) Gomes gave audiences in Paris and Milan the spectacle of the exotic other, and its artificiality only makes visible a cultural and racial divide that is all too real.

Still, Gomes is "our man," not despite but by virtue of his operas' egregious flaws. "We" swallowed it whole, we hum the discordant tune, we carry the contradiction deep within. The basis of "our" bond isn't our common identification with an exemplary scenario onstage but our sense that what we hear and see is a sham—something *nefando*, or abominable, atrocious, unspeakable, morally wrong. (Note, though, that Oswald avoids saying *why* dressing white actors up as Indians and calling their resistance to the colonizer "ours" is wrong.) How do we register "our" recognition? By mouthing words that mean the opposite of what they say while exchanging a complicitous smile— the hidden hole in the stage, the gap in the ground of representation through which bodies pass. Oswald exposes the lie at the core of high culture in Brazil, yet the "we" to and of whom he speaks is ambiguous. While his critique of the cult of the *maestrino nacional* accurately diagnoses the cultural malaise of the postcolonial elite, he performs the ideological sleight of hand Schwarz describes by projecting the shame of one class onto the country as a whole. And as is so often the case, he does so in order to justify his own "national" cure: as it turns out, his lampoon of Gomes is a lead-in to a plug for Heitor Villa-Lobos. The composer of *Kankukus* and *Kankikis*,

Oswald argues, is in touch with the times, on par with Stravinsky and Italian contemporaries including Malipiero and Castelnuovo-Tedesco, working in the same vein as experimental artists such as Jean Cocteau. Villa-Lobos *is* from Rio (no one is perfect), but Oswald confidently predicts, "São Paulo is going to hear him. And since São Paulo is the city of miracles—heir to migrations and *entradas*—it is going to accept him."[59] Funny how an article that begins by cutting paulista pride to the quick ends up reaffirming the region's exceptional status, invoking São Paulo's violent history as a colonial frontier as evidence of its capacity to assimilate its "others." Funny, too, how for all his differences with Menotti del Picchia, Oswald also solves the issue of opera-as-national-embarrassment by eliding its theatrical component, which conscripts human beings as the material matter of representation. The "terrible stage sets" of Gomes's allegories of racial miscegenation will give way to Villa-Lobos's African-inspired "dances" for piano; São Paulo will hear the *carioca* composer's music, and if it resonates as an authentic expression of "Brazil," that is because it spares its listeners the shameful sight of a white man in Indian drag. Whereas Wagner strove to stage the social totality by conjoining all the arts, the musical ingénue of modernismo eliminates all but the drama's aural trace. There can be no counterpart to *Lohengrin* and *Die Walküre* in a country imperfectly forged in the fires of conquest and slavery.

But the Brazilian vanguard did have a Parsifal. Mário de Andrade—that chaste, good, timid man—did not pillory the family's pride and joy or even mention opera at all, at least not as far as the record shows. On the afternoon of the second day, as part of the lineup following Menotti del Picchia's speech, he was called onstage to give the audience a preview of *Pauliceia desvairada*, but he apparently spent little time onstage, and his words were inaudible above the crowd's—cheers? Or boos? The one vivid depiction of this moment in the local press mocks the hype with which he was introduced and claims that after reciting two poems, "there was so much applause and so many 'encores!' and cock-a-doodle-doos that the incommensurable poet refused to say any more. . . . He was satisfied. For his glory it was sufficient! And he fell silent [*embatucou*]." This reticence comes across as doubly ironic because the writer pegs him as one of the "two Andrades of Futurism, *bandeirantemente!*"[60] Recycling a trope from "O meu poeta futurista," the text emphasizes the disparity between his intensely public persona and his aversion to the limelight, which is seen as a sign of arrogance. In contrast, most modernistas attributed it to shame, shyness, or fear. Three decades later, Oswald recalled the caustic jibes he himself endured—jibes that continued when his sidekick took the stage. But whereas Oswald had ignored the crowd (or so he claims), "Mário, with that saintliness that sometimes distinguished him, shouted: 'I won't recite any longer like this!' ['*Assim não recito mais!*'] There was enormous laughter."[61]

Who knows what mix of emotions made Mário exit the stage in a rush? Still, it is hardly a stretch to imagine he felt uncomfortable in his role as a poster boy for racial "futurism," especially given that people coded as mulatto or black rarely appeared on such a prominent stage as the Theatro Municipal. No eyewitness accounts allude to these factors, and it would pose a problem for the argument advanced in this chapter had the audience been so indiscreet. In retrospect, however, the premature conclusion to his debut in the hallowed halls of São Paulo's operatic elite lends significance to the setting of his second solo performance, which occurred later that same day following a recital by the celebrated pianist Guiomar Novaes. The program makes note of a "Talk [*palestra*] by Mário de Andrade in the foyer of the Theater" during the intermission of the main-stage show; according to accounts by two fellow participants he spoke on painting and theories of modern art amid "heckles and sarcasm," though other observers simply summarized his subject as "modern art" and made no note of the audience's response.[62] Over the decades, however, the work of critical commentary and commemoration has transformed this moment into one of the defining "manifestos" of modernismo, and in the process it has become ever more nebulous and opaque. Some critics couch their claims as speculation, but others boldly state that Mário read a draft of his "very interesting" preface to *Paulicéia desvairada*. Far more often, however, it is said that he read an early version of *The Slave Who Is Not Isaura*, a text published two years later with the subtitle "A Speech [*discurso*] on Some Tendencies of Modernist Poetry."[63] Yet in another speech delivered twenty years later, Mário referred to his earlier talk as a "lecture on plastic arts"—a solution that has the virtue of simplicity, since it confirms all other available evidence while also explaining his decision to stand on the stairs leading from the foyer up to the auditorium doors, where he could command a view of the spectators gathered below while gesturing by way of illustration to the paintings and sculptures on display (figure 4.2).[64]

Why the discrepancies? Given all the hype for Mário's collection of poetry during the Week of Modern Art, it is easy to see how its preface could come to usurp the place of his untitled talk. But the later speech in which he offers a conflicting story is a well-known text, so why the refusal to take the speaker at his own word? Is there meaning in the mistaken identification of his performance as a reading of *The Slave Who Is Not Isaura*? A now-canonical text often invoked in passing but rarely discussed in detail, the essay is regarded as the first formulation of modernismo, a concept its author defines not only in reference to Brazil but as a zeitgeist evident in figures as diverse as Amy Lowell, Francis Picabia, and Vladimir Mayakovsky, whose desire for a "leap into the future" he recognizes as salutary in a revolutionary society but impossible—and undesirable—to achieve because it ignores the utility of the old in constructing the new.[65] This sympathetic critique of Russian futurism (which in some ways echoes the one Trotsky was making at this very same time) is part of a broader argument about the partial and *relative* nature of poetry's autonomy from its historically accumulated conventions and its immediate social contexts.[66] Mário summarily grants the legitimacy of "free"

Figure 4.2. The "noble staircase" where Mário de Andrade gave his speech. Photo by Sylvia Masini and courtesy of João Malatian at the Theatro Municipal de São Paulo.

verse, comparing it to the "infinite melody" of Wagner, but in an obvious jab at Marinetti's call for the total destruction of syntax ("words in freedom") he declares, "Subject and predicate will eternally exist" (234). Arguing that new media and modes of transportation have made us "simultaneous inhabitants of all lands," he notes his passionate identification with other cultures and countries, yet he also states that while he could live in Germany or Austria, "I live in a patchwork way [*remendadamente*] in Brazil, crowned with the thorns of ridicule, vanity [*cabotinismo*], ignorance, madness, stupidity" (266). Ultimately what he proposes is "poetic polyphony," which seeks to capture the simultaneous existence of contradictory facts and sensations—though unlike the superimposed melodies of polyphonic music, it is textually mediated and can only be apprehended retrospectively as a "TOTAL FINAL COMPLEX SENSATION" (269).

None of this explains the significance of the essay's title. In fact, neither Bernardo Guimarães's novel nor the institution of slavery is mentioned in the text, and other than the half-mocking nod to his own martyrdom cited above, there is little to mar its breezy, cosmopolitan tone. Nevertheless, the title clearly creates an interpretive frame for the elaborate allegory with which the essay begins. A comic parable, it tells the story of the "slave of Ararat," a woman Adam "tore from his tongue" (or, alternatively, "from language") and then displayed atop the mountain where Noah's Ark had come to rest until the discovery of sin leads him to cover her parts with the proverbial leaf; over the subsequent centuries each generation and each new "race" adds on an item of apparel (a Roman tunic, a Chinese fan, etc.) until one day a wayfarer by the name of Arthur Rimbaud comes along and clears away the heap of frippery only to discover her "nude, anguished, ignorant, speaking in musical sounds, unaware of the new languages, savage, coarse, free, guileless, sincere" (201–202). *This* is the slave who is not Isaura—not the classically beautiful slave (phenotypically white but part African by blood) who is smothered in the sentimentalism of Romantic abolitionism and ultimately liberated into marriage by a bourgeois crusader, but the slave known as Poetry who is emancipated from the burden of cultural tradition by a symbolist boy-poet notorious for his colonial adventures and embrace of the Paris Commune, not to mention his (homosexual) love affairs. Yet by the very virtue of her conspicuous absence, the slave who *is* Isaura haunts the metaphors of freedom versus bondage to which Mário repeatedly returns in his ensuing exploration of the paradoxes of artistic autonomy. An oblique critique of liberalism's whitewashing of race, the essay also enacts its own ironic debt to this tradition by overtly avoiding the topic, with one notable exception: after elaborating his theory of simultaneity, the author tentatively offers himself up as its embodiment when he notes that "three races meld [*se caldeiam*] in my flesh . . . Three?" (266).

Although it is unlikely that these were the words Mário spoke as he overlooked the lobby of the Theatro Municipal, they are all the more resonant given the one tenuous clue connecting his performance to *The Slave Who Is Not Isaura*. Emiliano di Cavalcanti's design for the posters announcing the Week of Modern Art and the cover of the catalogue of works included in the art exhibition depicts a woman on a pedestal against a "primitive" background of lush vegetation, her head hung in shame and her nudity partially covered in an apparent evocation of Eve's expulsion from the Garden of Eden (figure 4.3). No other image is so closely associated with the modernista movement or so often reproduced in the context of discussions of the Week of Modern Art; yet it typically appears without commentary, as if there were nothing noteworthy about an image of abjection so seemingly antithetical to the ethos of the avant-garde.[67] Never is it linked to the opening parable of Mário's essay, nor does anyone note its resemblance to another iconic scene of original sin: that of a slave woman standing on the auction block.

Finally, there is the curious caricature published in a local satirical weekly the day after the festival ended (figure 4.4). A startled observer stands before a statue of a nude with women's breasts and male genitalia; the caption below reads "aesthetic disequilibrium and ecstatic disequilibrium," suggesting a link between sexual perversion and the avant-garde's stylistic deviations from

Figure 4.3. The cover of the program for the Week of Modern Art at the Theatro Municipal, designed by Emiliano di Cavalcanti. Courtesy of the Instituto de Estudos Brasileiros and Elisabeth di Cavalcanti Veiga.

classical norms. Could onlookers have associated this image with the figure of Mário standing at the top of the stairs? Is the ecstasy to which it alludes a result of glimpsing the forbidden sight—the impossible union of taper and chalice (to refer back to Oswald's characterization of him in "O meu poeta futurista")?

Retrospective Need and the Harvest of Remembrance

There is another scene hovering in the background of Mário de Andrade's solitary silhouette. On September 7, 1822, just outside of what was then the small settlement of São Paulo, Prince-Regent Dom Pedro is said to have stood before his men and renounced all fealty to the Portuguese sovereigns (i.e., his parents) with the not-exactly-original proclamation "Independence or Death!" Although the location was probably a coincidence, this *Grito* or "Cry" of Ipiranga (named after a nearby creek) provided a historic pretext for proud paulistas to claim supremacy in national affairs. In Rio, the

Figure 4.4. Caricature in *A Garoa*, February 19, 1922. The accompanying headline reads, "Desequilibrio estethico e desequilibrio extatico" (Aesthetic Imbalance and Ecstatic Imbalance).

yearlong celebration of the centennial was interrupted in July when junior army officers stationed at a fort in Copacabana led a failed revolt demanding changes in the electoral process and an end to the corruption and cronyism of the oligarchic federalist system. Although São Paulo would explode two years later as the epicenter of a more far-reaching *tenentes* revolt, dissent was held in check for the time being, and the carousing carried on with little more than a hiccup.[68] In the months before and after the Week of Modern Art, the Theatro Municipal played host to patriotic speeches, gala balls, and an extra-extravagant opera season that included the local premieres of *Die Götterdämmerung* and *Die Walküre*, a clear sign of Wagner's growing appeal.[69] Meanwhile, representatives of the Italian community colonized the terrace leading down to the Valley of Anhangabaú with an elaborate ensemble of bronze sculptures consisting of allegorical figures representing Italy and Brazil, along with characters from the operas of Carlos Gomes, all of them clustered around a towering likeness of the man himself.

In the midst of this operatic pomp and circumstance, and only a month or so prior to independence day, Mário's *Paulicéia desvairada* made its long-promised appearance in print. In all likelihood, most of those who purchased

it had already heard or read a number of the poems; the closing piece may
have come as a surprise, though for different reasons it, too, must have elicited
a sense of déjà vu. "As enfibraturas do Ipiranga" (translated as "The Moral
Fibrature of the Ipiranga") is a script for a "profane oratorio" featuring a cast
of 550,000 singers—roughly the population of São Paulo in 1922—clustered
into four competing choirs radiating out across the city from the Theatro
Municipal.[70] Standing at the theater's windows and on its balconies are the
Conventional Orientalisms (Orientalismos Convencionais), described as a
"large, imposing, finely-tuned chorus" of mixed voices belonging to "writers
and other praiseworthy artisans" (escritores e demais artífices elogiáveis). The
Palsied Decrepitudes (Senectudes Tremulinas) are millionaires and bourgeois
castrati who sing their primly measured lines from other loci of economic and
political power, including City Hall, the Hotel Carlton, the Automobile Club,
Weisflog Printing Company, and "even the Alves Book Store in the distance."
Seated on the terrace are around five thousand musicians, and just below
them, standing in the soil of the Valley of Anhangabaú, are the Green-Gilt
Youths (Juvenilidades Auriverdes)—untutored tenors identified in the cast
list as nós, or the collective "we" of the Brazilian avant-garde. These three
choirs engage in a battle of operatic manifestos before an "onstage" audience
made up of the Indifferent Pallbearers (Sandapilários Indiferentes), workers
and poor people who shout their lines in baritone and bass voices from the
viaduct that overlooks the valley and connects the older part of the city to the
newer development anchored by the Theatro Municipal (78–79).

As if to preempt any doubt as to whether this farce was an allegorical
depiction of the Week of Modern Art, its author had alerted potential readers to the connection in the pages of a newspaper just two days before the
festival began. Framed as a rebuff to a critic's attack on São Paulo's "futurists," his brief note mentions the title and peculiar generic classification of
the unpublished piece but withholds all details about the plot, revealing only
that the cast includes a choir called As Juvenilidades Auriverdes.[71] As proof of
how distant from futurism the "lads" of the Week of Modern Art are, Mário
rattles off a list of the real-life members of this juvenile group. The poet Guil-
herme de Almeida, he says, is a "marvelous aristocrat" and a "fan of Wilde"
who "would be scorned by futurism"; Menotti del Picchia is a "prosodist" (in
his latest book "the best of d'Annunzio persists") and would be "insulted by
the futurists"; another Brazilian "aristocrat," Sérgio Milliet, was educated in
Switzerland and wrote his recently published poetry collection (which Mário
hails as a masterpiece) in French. The list continues as the author fires off one
dubious compliment after another, pointing to the persistence of outmoded,
imitative social structures and styles—a gesture almost certainly meant to
pull the rug out from under Del Picchia and others who, even at this late date,
were still flying the futurist flag. These Green-Gilt Youth, Mário concedes,
may "lack rehearsals," but one thing is clear: "They bandeirantemente refuse
the baton of Marinetti."

If the Italian futurists sought to create spectacles "born of improvisation, from a spark of intuition,"[72] this reference to rehearsals invokes a different theatrical logic in which both artistic creation and national identity arise out of repetition and the reworking of prior experiences. The title of the oratorio, with its allusion to the Cry of Ipiranga, superimposes the vanguard's struggle for cultural autonomy onto the ritual reenactment of an earlier (and incomplete) political break. The classic device of metatheatricality affords ironic distance from the haphazard performance that results: as the stage directions explain, the four choirs and five thousand musicians (directed by "maestros . . . from abroad") have gathered to perform a profane oratorio called "As enfibraturas do Ipiranga," a play-within-the-play that shares the same name and genre as the frame text (79). All 550,000 singers clear their throats and take "exaggeratedly deep breaths"—yet when the Green-Gilt Youth kick off the concert it is with trepidation, declaring their existence in hushed tones (the "libretto" is marked *ppp*) and rolling off a litany of tropical flora and fauna in irregular rhymes and mellifluous alliterations:

> We are the Green-Gilt Youths!
> The fringed banners of the banana trees,
> the emeralds of the macaws,
> the rubies of the hummingbirds,
> the lyricisms of the *sabiás* and the parakeets,
> pineapples, mangoes, cashews,
> long to station themselves triumphantly,
> in the thundering glorification of the Universal! (81)

> Nós somos as Juvenilidades Auriverdes!
> As franjadas flâmulas das bananeiras,
> as esmeraldas das araras,
> os rubis dos colibris,
> os lirismos dos sabiás e das jandaias,
> os abacaxis, as mangas, os cajús
> almejam localizar-se triunfantemente,
> na fremente celebração do Universal! (80)

It could be that some of the items in this catalogue of exotica had grown in the soil where the singers stand before the Valley of Anhangabaú was converted into an elegant esplanade, but others originate in parts of Brazil where few if any of these "aristocrats" (to recall Mário's earlier depiction of them) had ever set foot. As if to drive home this point, the effect of their soulful *rubato* is undercut as instruments play off-key and strings snap at inopportune intervals. But if the naïveté of their nationalist aspirations is the object of humor, the more polished performance of their opponents comes across as equally absurd. Comfortably ensconced in the Theatro Municipal, the

Conventional Orientalisms also commence with an act of self-identification, though unlike the Green-Gilt Youth they follow official grammar rather than popular usage in omitting the redundant pronoun *nós*, and their verses end in comically contrived rhymes:

> We are the Conventional Orientalisms!
> The foundations must never fall again!
> No ascents or verticals whatsoever!
> We love the boring flatness!
> We hack down peroba trees with uneven branches! (83)

> Somos os Orientalismos Convencionais!
> Os alicerces não devem cair mais!
> Nada de subidas ou de verticais!
> Amamos as chatezas horizontais!
> Abatemos perobas de ramos desiguais! (82)

The Conventional Orientalisms occupy the epicenter of performative power, yet their name marks them as an idea out of place—and is perhaps meant to redefine Europe (their cultural model) as the Eastern periphery of a Brazil-centered world. Guardians of the ideology of order and progress, these cultural mandarins disavow their natural environs and call on science to classify and pacify the "irregularities" that the vanguard aims to enshrine as the essence of a national art. As the oratorio progresses it becomes clear that the Conventional Orientalisms are in cahoots with the Palsied Decrepitudes, who sing their short lines to the tempo of a courtly minuet and later a gavotte. A parasitic elite, these castrati are unwilling to invest in infrastructure ("Widen the streets? And the institutions? . . . Can't be done!") or incorporate the masses into the national imaginary (87). Wagner's chromatic innovations hold little appeal for such philistines, who only value art for its cultural capital and attend the opera because it offers "elegance by precept! / But what a bore [*paulificância*]" (85).

Despite the lighthearted tone, there are occasional hints of the historical violence underlying this cultural conservatism. Hermann von Ihering, founder of São Paulo's natural history museum and an advocate of exterminating the indigenous population, is among the local icons of positivism the Conventional Orientalisms invoke, and the shadow of slavery hangs over their threat to punish those who commit the crime of dissonance: "Our choruses are all on the note of 'do'! / For those off-pitch a lesson with the whip!" (83; *Temos nossos coros só no tom de dó! / Para os desafinados doutrina de cipó!* [82]). Even so, the avant-garde's promise of radical change fails to win over the vox populi—the Indifferent Pallbearers, whose name in Portuguese (Sandapilários) refers to the men in ancient Rome who carted the bodies of slaves and the poor to their graves. In their only chorus, immediately following the opening number by the Green-Gilt Youth, the pallbearers fire back with a five-line salvo, bawling down from the viaduct overlooking the valley to stop with the "noise" (*Vá de rumor!*) and professing their desire to snooze in peace. Even Puccini's "E lucevan le stelle," they say, is preferable to this racket—quite the insult given that the famous aria from the final act of *Tosca* was often dismissed by opera connoisseurs as hackneyed and trite (80–81).

For the critic Benedito Nunes, who interprets *sandapilário* as a pejorative neologism based on the root word *sandeu* (fool), this depiction of the plebes as hostile to artistic innovation is a symptom of the residual elitism of Mário and his fellow modernistas.[73] Yet in his desire to witness an imaginary reconciliation between the vanguard and the masses, Nunes overlooks the critical charge of the oratorio's quasi-operatic form. For slightly different reasons, Vicky Unruh makes the same slip in her reading of the piece as a "performance manifesto," one of a number of dramatic works by Latin American vanguard writers that "display the type of art that they espouse, portray art as a 'doing process' that incorporates its recipient into the doing, and dramatize the desired spectator's participation in an encounter of conflicting artistic positions within a context of cultural affirmation."[74] Unlike Nunes, Unruh appears untroubled by the possible elitism reflected in the disinterest of the Pallbearers, nor does she detect any hint of irony or self-deprecation in the depiction of the Green-Gilt Youth; despite her own observation that "As enfibraturas" is "fundamentally not performable," she persists in reading the oratorio as its own defiant "performance" of the modernista spirit (47). But one might also ask what the apparent failure of the avant-garde performance represented within the text—that is, the youth's inability to impress any of their audiences—has to do with the ostentatious "unperformability" of the text itself.

Unruh's own investment in the project of "cultural affirmation" may explain why she, like Nunes, ignores the oratorio's obvious spoof on *Die Meistersinger*, Wagner's only comic opera—a detail clearly announced in the cast list when the Green-Gilt Youth are identified as "Tenors, always tenors! Just ask Walter von Stolzing!" (79; *Tenores, sempre tenores! Que o diga Walter von Stolzing!* [78]). Frequently interpreted as an allegory of Wagner's own compositional practice, *Die Meistersinger* revolves around a song contest held among the famed guild of Mastersingers in sixteenth-century Nuremberg to determine who will win the hand of the town goldsmith's daughter. Walther von Stolzing is the aristocratic young knight who, driven by his desire for the woman offered as the prize, enters the contest only to find his inspired but unschooled singing rejected by some of the Mastersingers, middle-class burghers whose craftsman-like approach to art hints at the bourgeois division of labor Wagner railed against. With the help of the cobbler-poet Hans Sachs, Walther composes a song that weds romantic self-expression with socially consecrated norms and wins over the people because "it sounded so old / and yet it was so new."[75]

It is telling that Wagner resorted to comedy in depicting this rejuvenation of the body politic through art, and even more so that in São Paulo it cannot be staged. Mário adopts the plot of the song contest, but instead of opera he opts for the oratorio, a genre that is closely related but distinct in two key regards: first, the subject matter is sacred rather than secular, and second, the music is usually performed as a concert piece with little to no costuming, props, or dramatic action. Oratorios first gained popularity in early seventeenth-century Italy and often served as a substitute for operas during Lent, when the Catholic Church enforced a ban on public spectacles.[76] By the mid-nineteenth century, however, their religious subject matter was no longer in vogue, and their lack of dramatic display seemed weirdly outdated in the context of the era's ever more expansive theatricalism. In his *Art-work of the Future* (1849), Wagner denounced oratorios as "the sexless embryos of Opera" and an "unnatural abortion" of the "true" drama, in which "each separate art can only bare its utmost secret to their common public through a mutual parleying with the other arts."[77] Their failure to visualize the action aurally evoked was a symptom of social fragmentation; in contrast, the theater of the future would create a synthesis of the senses, and with it, a fusion of all classes with the Folk.

In a critique of Wagner, written at a time when his operas were being assimilated into the official repertoire of the Third Reich, Adorno argued that the aim of this drive toward synesthesia was to create the illusion of a self-generating work of art. Like the commodity form, this "phantasmagoria" dissimulates the social relations involved in its production in order to foster the fiction of communal integration—a dynamic dramatized in the reconciliation of the feudal and bourgeois orders enacted by Walther's winning song and its acclamation by both the guild of master singers and the *Volk*.[78] By contrast, what "As enfibraturas do Ipiranga" dramatizes is the failure of the phantasmagorical illusion in Brazil. The title recalls the foundational act of independence, yet in lieu of the univocal *grito* (cry), it depicts the collectivity as a composition of competing and ultimately irreconcilable "fibratures." Instead of ending on a rousing song extolling the virtues of German culture, the piece concludes as the vanguard is lulled to sleep by My Madness, a shadowy figure who surfaces at odd intervals throughout *Paulicéia desvairada* as both the internal mistress and muse of the poet's demented "school." In the final lines, "the Green Gilt Youths and My Madness sleep eternally deaf; meanwhile, from the windows of the palaces, theatres, print shops, hotels—wide-open, but blind—there comes the enormous derision of whistles, cat-calls, and stamping of feet" (99). Deaf or blind: the fragmentation of the senses corresponds to a fragmented social order, just as the unfinished form of the oratorio indexes the incomplete embodiment of national culture in Brazil.

As a point of fact, however, readers do not see *or* hear the Conventional Orientalisms and Palsied Decrepitudes' noisy disapprobation (except in the mind's ear), because "As enfibraturas" is not actually an oratorio but a seemingly unstageable libretto for a nonexistent score. Like *Prometeo vencedor*, the philosophical drama by José Vasconcelos discussed in chapter 1, the text resembles what Martin Puchner refers to as an "exuberant" closet drama—a play written-to-be-read that "willfully exceed(s) the limits of theatrical representation" and in doing so casts those limits into relief.[79] Puchner contrasts the closet dramas of modernists such as Stéphane Mallarmé and Gertrude Stein with the Wagnerian imperative of total theatricality and the performative politics of the European avant-garde. Yet if, as he argues, this modernist antitheatricalism is deeply ambivalent—the hyphen betrays its dependence on the theatricalism it critiques—its ambivalence was even more marked among the Brazilian futuristas-cum-modernistas. Mário's over-the-top oratorio does indeed lampoon Wagnerian and futurist fantasies of immediacy (only in a metaphorical sense is it possible to perform a play with 550,000 actors).[80] But part of the joke is that the material and ideological infrastructure needed to sustain those fantasies is lacking in Brazil. One could even read the Shakespearean epigraph to the piece as a comment on the *disavowal* of theater at the Week of Modern Art: "O, woe is me / To have seen what I have seen, see what I see!" Spoken by Ophelia after she witnesses Hamlet's apparent unraveling, the line evokes a traumatic sight that turns the seer mad by exposing the lie at the heart of social "reason"—a sight, perhaps, such as white actors wearing fake Indian headdresses and colored tights.

But if the antitheatricalism of Brazilian modernismo is partly imposed, it also enables a curious kind of agency. As Puchner and others have noted, modernist closet dramas are often sites for the imaginative enactment of nonnormative modes of sexuality: sheltered from the strictures of society and liberated from the exigencies of the physical stage, male characters can change into women (and vice versa), or gender identification can be left ambiguous or undefined.[81] Such is the case of My Madness, the coloratura soprano and figure for the author's own broken but would-be lyric voice who comes crawling toward the Green-Gilt Youth across the Valley of Anhangabaú. In *Die Meistersinger*, the song contest is capped off by nuptials: heterosexual desire drives artistic innovation and institutional change, inheritance is bequeathed on the basis of Walther's hereditary as well as natural nobility (his innate musical talent), and his marriage to Eva assures the controlled reproduction of the race. In "As enfibraturas," however, the star soloist is an epicene subject who sees the social contradictions and is split, just as the oratorio (that "sexless opera-embryo") is split between sight and sound.[82] The strange, mystic recitatives of My Madness send the song contest spiraling into a shouting match between the Conventional Orientalisms and her followers, who (whether by coincidence or design) are gathered on a site that the historian James N. Green notes was a well-known cruising-spot for men in search of same-sex relations.[83] The cautious innovations of the Green-Gilt Youth devolve into a frenzy of neologisms and exclamations of

desire for self-immolation before the singers lose their last shred of coherence, "shouting in irregular cadence" and "screaming" one-word epithets
at their opponents (93). Finally, even their capacity for insult runs dry and
they can only utter a blank space, which according to parenthetical instruc-
tions should be completed with "the filthiest word that the reader knows"
(95). So much for the phantasmagorical illusion of a self-producing work
of art.

The oratorio comes to a close as the Green-Gilt Youth shed tears of repen-
tance and My Madness sings them to sleep with a lullaby. "Weep! Weep!
Then sleep! . . . Your final kisses, your first tears / for the white fecundation!"
Her voice convokes a brotherhood of intellectuals, off-key singers whose
shared experience of failure sows the seeds of the future: "But in twenty
years the sown fields will blossom! . . . You will have the harvest [*cultura*]
of remembrance!" (97). This is a community constituted through a deferral
of its promise to represent the totality, an avant-garde whose performative
power works in retrospect. In a final flare of irony, the author often called the
"pope" of modernismo interrupts the catcalls of the operatic elite and concludes his profane oratorio with the exclamation "LAUS DEO!" (99).

In Anima Nobile

As it turned out, the fecund tears of the modernistas did indeed reap a rich
harvest of remembrance. By the end of the 1920s, the warring factions of the
avant-garde had lionized the Week of Modern Art through their competing
claims to its legacy, and in the 1930s the involvement of many modernistas
in the expanding cultural and educational apparatuses helped endow it with
the aura of a foundational myth. In 1942, when Mário addressed a group of
intellectuals gathered in Rio to commemorate the twentieth anniversary, he
referred to scenes he clearly assumed were familiar to his audience:

> How did I have the courage to participate in that battle! It is true
> that I've been scandalizing my country's intelligentsia for a while now
> with my artistic experiments [or experiences], but only ever exposed
> in books and articles, which means those experiments aren't executed
> *in anima nobile*. I'm not present in body, and that softens the shock
> of stupidity. But how did I have the courage to say those verses in the
> face of jeering so rowdy I was unable to hear what Paulo Prado was
> shouting to me from the first row? . . . How did I manage to give a
> lecture on plastic arts, on the stairs of the Theater, surrounded by
> strangers who were roundly mocking and offending me ?

> Como tive coragem para participar daquela batalha! É certo que
> com minhas experiências artísticas muito que venho escandalizando

a intelectualidade do meu país, porém, expostas em livros e artigos, como que essas experiências não se realizam *in anima nobile*. Não estou de corpo presente, e isto abranda o choque da estupidez. Mas como tive coragem pra dizer versos diante duma vaia tão bulhenta que eu não escutava no palco o que Paulo Prado me gritava da primeira fila das poltronas? . . . Como pude fazer uma conferência sobre artes plásticas, na escadaria do Teatro, cercado de anônimos que me caçoavam e ofendiam a valer?[84]

On the one hand, these scenes enact the quintessential vanguard move of establishing an adversarial role with the public; even the heavy-handed overtones of martyrdom and sacrifice recall the Promethean ethos of the avant-garde. Yet Mário is not the aggressor in this encounter. Far from adopting an assertive stance, he expresses disbelief at his own ability to withstand the audience's ridicule, acknowledging his vulnerability and dwelling on the image of himself frozen before a crowd of hostile strangers who see and judge. Out of place on the operatic stage, this Brazilian Parsifal looks across the chasm to Paulo Prado, the coffee baron who just a few years later would publish his famous *Retrato do Brasil* (Portrait of Brazil), where he attributes the country's "melancholic" character to the avarice and extravagance of slavery and the shameful "vice of our mestizo origins."[85] Prado (it appears) tries to offer Mário encouragement but he fails because the lines of communication are cut off, because all the money in São Paulo can't silence the noise of the old order separating a not-quite-white intellectual from the rogue aristocrat whose money and prestige facilitate his appearance on the city's premiere stage. Refusing the injunction to perform, Mário abandons the inner sanctum of representation in a move toward the emerging mass public beyond the theater's doors, though he doesn't leave to go perform in the street and what he reads isn't a "manifesto," the favored genre of the futurist avant-garde; instead he delivers a lecture on art, a more scholarly, conventional genre, "exposing" himself once again to mockery in the lobby, *o entre-lugar*, or space in-between. Standing on the stairs leading to the vestibule adorned with the Venetian murals of Wagner's operas, he enacts something similar to what Heather Love, in her readings of Walter Pater, calls an "epistemology of the vestibule," convoking a community of subjects who occupy a "liminal, semipublic space" defined by way of "indecision" and "delay."[86]

Why did this moment strike such a chord? Why were so many people invested in imagining a grown man quaking in fear? If Mário's fellow participants and Mário himself continually retold the tale, I suggest, it is because the constitution of modernismo as an intellectual public and the paradoxical authority of modernismo's pope are bound up in—and bound together by—a sense of backwardness and shame. In recalling his experience Mário demurs and insists, "My merit as a participant is the merit of others. . . . I wouldn't have had either the physical or moral force to look into the eyes of that tempest of humiliation. . . . If it had been up to me, I would have given up."[87] He renounces his individual agency, transferring it to the emerging avant-garde, and it is his body that takes the hit: his visually striking physique coded as racially mixed and queerly asexual is where the lines separating stupidity from intelligence are drawn.

Chapter 5

✦

Phonography, Operatic Ethnography, and Other Bad Arts

Werner Herzog's avant-garde classic *Fitzcarraldo* (1982) is a film about a man who undertakes an absurd quest to build an opera house in the Amazonian jungle. Its eccentric protagonist is also a phonograph fanatic. For all viewers know, Fitzcarraldo's only experience of "live" opera consists of a few furtive minutes during the opening sequence when he arrives at the Teatro Amazonas in Manaus, Brazil, to see Enrico Caruso perform the final death scene from Verdi's *Ernani*. Back in his home base of Iquitos, Peru, an even more remote outpost on the capitalist frontier, he lugs around a Victor Talking Machine and plays recordings of Caruso for the local indigenous children, a parrot, and a pig. For the blond, blue-eyed maverick, these recordings fuel the desire to repeat the feat of the operatic entrepreneurs in Manaus and lure his idol ever deeper into the Amazon—to reattach the Voice to a visible body in another far-flung place. His audience, on the other hand, has no experience or knowledge of the operatic ideal, and what they hear (or so the film suggests) is not the aural reproduction or representation of a prior performance on a distant stage, but the auratic voice of a divine machine.

The phonograph, however, fails to convince the local rubber barons who control the capital on which the realization of Fitzcarraldo's dream depends. Perhaps they know the boom is about to bust—rubber production had begun to shift to Asia by this time—or perhaps they sense that the apogee of opera has already passed. Whatever the reason, they would rather feed dollar bills to their carnivorous fish than invest in a lasting monument to art. So Fitzcarraldo sets sail down a tributary of the Amazon on an improbable mission to establish a rubber plantation deep in the heart of a region known as Cayahuari Yacu—"the land where God did not finish Creation." As the ship advances into the territory of headhunting *jíbaros*, the intrepid explorer and his crew are surrounded by the beating of drums and ritualistic cries, sounds whose source is enveloped by the thick foliage and invisible to the eye. His terrified men abandon the ship, and out of desperation Fitzcarraldo fights fire with fire: he mounts the phonograph on the prow and projects His Master's

Voice into the vast unknown. Just as he is about to concede defeat and turn around, his observers emerge from the trees in canoes and approach to offer him their labor, having taken him for the white god of their legends who has returned to finish his work—or so Fitzcarraldo believes, though he has an inkling that something is amiss, a suspicion that the only mind ensnared by this fantasy of a god who needs no means of coercion other than a beautiful voice might turn out to be his own. Sure enough, the indigenous crew cunningly foils his plan, leaving it unlikely the opera house will ever be built. The film, however, redeems this failure in one final twist when Caruso and his fellow cast members arrive all the way from Manaus and sing a Bellini opera from the deck of the battered ship for the rubber barons, children, pig, and all.

On the evening of May 11, 1927—two decades or so after Fitzcarraldo's spectacular failure, if fictional and factual chronologies can be compared—another man with an affinity for opera embarked on a journey up the Amazon. In the previous chapter, which revolved around the Week of Modern Art held at the Theatro Municipal in February 1922, the rising stars of São Paulo's self-declared vanguard hailed Mário de Andrade as the Brazilian counterpart to Parsifal: a mixed-race, vaguely queer variant of the hero of Wagner's last opera who wanders the wild forest in search of the Holy Grail. Now, as if to make good on his sobriquet, the knight-errant of modernismo joined a group of locals and foreign tourists aboard a steamship on a three-month-long excursion that set sail from Rio de Janeiro and skirted the northern coast before venturing into the interior. Along the way he recorded his impressions of Belém, Solimões, Maceio, and Manaus—though strangely, he took no note of the Teatro Amazonas, perhaps because the opulent opera house had fallen into disuse and disrepair. Nor did he enrapture the natives with the otherworldly sounds of a U.S.-made machine. Armed with nothing but a pen and paper, he transcribed the tunes of the *toadas*, *bumba-meu-boi*, and other "popular" performances he heard and saw as the vessel traveled upriver all the way to Iquitos and then just past the Bolivian border before doubling back and heading for home.

On his return to São Paulo, Mário followed in the footsteps of his cinematic predecessor by taking on the role of cultural prophet. Selling the local tycoons on the virtues of high opera was not his concern: just ten years earlier Caruso himself had sung at the Theatro Municipal, the local equivalent to the Teatro Amazonas, built with the profits of the coffee boom that was fueling the city's rapid expansion and incipient industrialization.[1] In the pages of the *Diário Nacional*, a daily newspaper and official organ of the recently formed Democratic Party, Mário entertained his urban readers with anecdotal accounts of his travels, piquing their curiosity about the unfamiliar sounds he had encountered, but also issuing a dire warning: "Our popular music is a prodigious treasure, condemned to death. Phonography imposes itself as a remedy of salvation."[2]

Several years later, as the founding director of São Paulo's Department of Culture, Mário de Andrade would carry out his own injunction by sending researchers far afield with phonographs and cameras and establishing one of the largest archives of ethnographic recordings in the Americas. At the time he sounded his clarion call, however, the international economic crisis that would bring Latin America's Export Age to an end was still a year away; the top-down Revolution of 1930 had not yet installed the populist Getúlio Vargas in power; and the cultural infrastructure Mário and some of his fellow modernistas would help create only existed in the form of unfulfilled desires and increasingly audible demands. In its absence, Mário drew on his own fieldwork as well as the collections of friends to create a homegrown equivalent for the operatic art that the elite imported from the Old World. Toward the end of 1927, while finishing revisions of *Macunaíma*, he drafted an outline of scenes for an operatic version of his novel, which features a race- and shape-shifting "hero with no character" who undertakes an epic journey out of the Amazon to São Paulo. The following year he completed a libretto for a comic opera about a folklore figure named Pedro Malazarte known for his perpetual wandering, penchant for trickery, and evasion of manual labor. Plans for the musical component of *Macunaíma* never came to fruition, but *Pedro Malazarte* was scored by Camargo Guarnieri, a young composer who shared Mário's desire to create a legitimately "national" opera by weaving together performance traditions of the disparate races and regions of Brazil. Over the next few years Mário would also begin drafts for an operatic ballet and a three-act opera about the collapse of the coffee economy. But although his collaborators' music was publicly performed, he failed to finish most of the libretti, and even during his tenure at the Department of Culture, when he oversaw programming at the Theatro Municipal, this Parsifal never sought to see his own operas staged.

The last chapter revisited one of the foundational moments of the modernista avant-garde. In explaining the simultaneous centrality of the operatic stage and the absence of theater at the Week of Modern Art, I drew on Roberto Schwarz's notion of "ideas out of place," which traces a peculiar sense of dissonance at the core of Brazilian identity back to the late nineteenth century, when the country's increasing integration into global commodity circuits cast into stark relief the incongruity of ideals such as liberty, equality, and economic rationalization in a society founded on slavery and the practice of patronage.[3] The late 1920s, though, was a time of impending crisis when long-standing tensions within modernismo flowered into open animosity. If opera had originally served as a lingua franca among modernista artists, it now became a prism for refracting their growing ideological differences; and if references to race had once reinforced the modernizing claims of paulista exceptionalism, the geographical diffusion of modernismo set the stage for debates over the symbolic value of the "primitive." These shifting conceptions of national culture were connected to changes in the global economy—a dynamic evident in the efforts of recording companies to expand their operations in Brazil by opening local studios, building factories, and supplementing their imports of classical music (such as opera) with more recordings of "popular," "Brazilian" genres.

In what follows I tease out a sinuous, shared logic linking Mário's national opera project to his passion for the phonograph, a technology with the ability to record and reproduce sounds at a different time and in a distant locale, or "out of place." The first part of the chapter offers a synoptic account of the early phonograph industry in the United States and Brazil, laying the groundwork for the subsequent sections by tracking common concerns of temporality, ephemerality, and race across the realms of ethnographic, operatic, and "popular" recordings. Central to this narrative is the Victor Talking Machine Company, not only because it was the industry leader and was especially known for its opera selections, but also because Mário had close ties to its personnel in Brazil. I delve into these details in the following section, which connects the modernistas' turn toward the "primitive" to the mass culturalization of the *malandro*: a trickster-like folk figure who lives by his wits (rather than "productive" work) and became notorious in samba songs for his womanizing, quasi-criminal ways. Finally, the last part of the chapter considers how all these elements coincide in Mário's project to create a national opera, namely in his libretto for *Pedro Malazarte* and discussions surrounding a never-drafted opera of *Macunaíma*.[4]

Though partly based on ethnographic fieldwork conducted in situ, Mário's operas de- and recontextualize cultural traditions, incorporating Amazonian dance-dramas into plots set in other parts of Brazil and integrating *emboladas* into arias. Malazarte (Bad Art) and Macunaíma (Great Evil): the protagonists of his first two operatic experiments are itinerant figures, moving agents and mediums of exchange whose names also indicate their deviation from the "good," or "fine" arts (*belas artes*). Both exemplify what Esther Gabara characterizes as Mário's "errant modernism"—a term she derives from his predilection for the verb *errar*, meaning "to wander" but also "to err."[5] Gabara, like many critics, sees such "erring" in positive terms, as both an ethical and aesthetic strategy that allows Mário to formulate a kind of "critical nationalism." This chapter, on the other hand, resists the impulse to redeem these two malandros and explores their role in circulating all the "bad" feelings Schwarz associates with ideas out of place. My readings show how Malazarte and Macunaíma's conflicted stance toward capital plays out not only in their aversion to physical labor, but also in the implicit aversion to performance at stake in Mário's would-be operas, which seem to have been written for the archive—as though the archive were a spectral stage.

Fugitive Sounds

In a discussion of the phonographic face-off between red men and white conqueror in Herzog's film, Michael Taussig identifies this scene as an example of what he describes as one of the "frontier rituals of technological supremacy."[6] In the United States and parts of Europe, the image of naive natives entranced by the talking (or singing) machine became a staple during the early decades of the twentieth century, turning up in everything from ethnographic field notes and docudramas to popular travel narratives and advertisements for the phonograph. Taussig turns the anthropological tables and asks: why was (and is) the white man so fascinated with the fascination of the other? Pointing to a primitivism interwoven into the Western rationalization of technology, he argues that what is really at stake in staging such encounters is a desire to replenish the magical power of mechanical mimesis. If the first public demonstrations of the phonograph following its invention in 1877 had been greeted with a sense of wonder and awe, the later replication of this scenario on the far edges of empire serves to "emphasize and embellish the genuine mystery and accomplishment of mechanical reproduction in an age when technology itself, after the flurry of excitement at a new breakthrough, is not seen as mystique or poetry but as routine" (208). But he neglects to mention that *Fitzcarraldo* adds another twist: although the film underscores the irrationality of its title character's passion and his ironic affinity with those he exploits, what their apparent reverence restores for him is not only the primitive power of the modern machine but also the enchantment of an increasingly "outmoded" art.

Released in 1982 (the same year the first commercial compact discs were produced), *Fitzcarraldo* revels in a counterlogic of capitalist development driven by the energy of the residual and soon-to-be obsolete. Adorno is not the only critic to note that even in its heyday opera almost always depicted the feudal relations of an earlier era; obsessed with the political intrigues of medieval counts and the ill-fated loves of ancient Ethiopian princesses, it resembled "a museum of bygone images and gestures, to which a retrospective need clings."[7] The phonograph, in contrast, was initially tied to an emergent mode of managerial capitalism due to Edison's original decision to market it as a dictation device for use in offices and tout its potential to boost productivity. Yet it too was imbued from the very beginning with an air of déjà vu: in borrowing the name of his invention from a system of shorthand called phonography (sound writing) first introduced in 1837 and subjected to numerous revisions, Edison also echoed a long line of promises to offer a more accurate means of capturing what he fancifully referred to as "sounds hitherto fugitive."[8] The earliest tinfoil recordings were so fragile they perished when removed from the machine, and even wax cylinders quickly wore out. Despite this, one of the most common claims for the phonograph's novelty and technological prowess was its ability to permanently preserve the voices of the dead. Jonathan Sterne situates its emergence in the context of changing attitudes toward death in the late Victorian era and likens sound recording to a process of "embalming" the voice. Just as the embalmment of bodies for funereal display (a relatively new custom at the time) chemically transforms and fixes the tissues of the body in order to maintain its outward appearance, sound recording "preserved the exteriority of the voice while completely transforming its interiority," detaching it from the living subject and nexus of social relations out of which it arose in order to preserve—or rather re-create—the semblance of its original sound.[9]

This capacity to artifactualize aural experience also explains the phonograph's appeal for those seeking to save the sounds of "dying" cultures. Throughout the nineteenth century there had been numerous attempts in the United States and in parts of Spanish America to circumvent the limitations of the Roman alphabet by devising phonetic systems of notation for indigenous languages. (Strangely, there is little evidence of such efforts in Brazil.) Unsatisfied with the results, the Harvard ethnologist Jesse Walter Fewkes transported a phonograph and a box of wax cylinders up to the coast of Maine in March 1890 to record the songs and speech of the Passamaquoddy. He later repeated the experiment among the Zunis of New Mexico, and within a few months he had published a spate of articles announcing that the marvelous invention offered new hope for "preserving the songs and tales of races which are fast becoming extinct."[10] As Brian Hochman has pointed out, Fewkes's insistence on the scientific value of the phonograph was not fundamentally about its accuracy; in fact, the range of frequencies the early machines could capture was relatively restricted. Rather, it had to do with the possibility of eliminating errors of interpretation and minimizing the mediation of fickle ears. Just a year earlier the anthropologist Franz Boas had explained the problem of "alternating sounds," or seeming variations in the pronunciation of indigenous words, by arguing that the issue lay not with the speakers or singers, but with the faulty perception of their nonnative listeners. In keeping with the paradigm of cultural relativism for which he became known, Boas contended that culture shaped the senses, leaving people prone to a form of "sound-blindness" when it came to distinguishing the unfamiliar phonemes and inflections of other groups.[11] Hochman shows how dialect writers and ethnomusicologists, too, drew attention to the fallibility of human hearing and the inadequacies of print while imagining the phonograph as an "ideal cultural listener: as an unmediated medium that could objectively record the auditory data of difference."[12]

Race was no less of a factor in the first commercial recordings, which frequently evoked an impression of ephemerality by drawing on listeners' experiences of the popular stage. Although blackface minstrelsy had been popular in the United States for decades, it gained a new lease on life right about the same time as the Passamaquoddy experiment when several fledgling companies started to record music to be played in the new "automatic phonographs," coin-operated machines with earphones located in hotels, train stations, saloons, movie theaters, circuses, and eventually in "phonograph parlors." The improvisatory ethos of minstrel shows, with their lively exchanges between actors and audience, may have helped to underscore the

relative fixity of recordings versus the contingency of what would later come
to be called "live" performance. The remediation of blackface minstrelsy in
coon song recordings is only the most striking example of how the phonograph destabilized what Lisa Gitelman calls the "visuality of music" and
its connections to the vexed visuality of race.[13] Noting that the height of
the "coon craze" coincided with the *Plessy v. Ferguson* case of 1896, when
the U.S. Supreme Court upheld the constitutionality of segregation laws and
established the so-called one-drop rule, Gitelman contends that "on the heels
of the *Plessy* decision, which had determined 'blackness' to be a matter of
blood, not skin color, the meaning of music thickened" (134–135). Specific
melodies, dialects, and musical traits such as syncopation came to bear the
burden of signifying an intrinsic racial or ethnic difference; paradoxically,
the split between sight and sound facilitated a kind of "aural essentialism"
while also allowing elements of blackface and other working-class forms to
enter the parlor rooms of the middle-class (136). Karl Hagstrom Miller, too,
argues that between the 1880s and the 1920s both the music industry and
the newly professionalized discipline of folklore studies engaged in a process
of "segregating sound" that willfully obscured the hybrid origins of the blues,
hillbilly music, and other "southern" genres.[14]

An important if underacknowledged aspect of this dynamic was the geopolitical pretensions of Uncle Sam. The U.S. intervention in the Cuban war
of independence and the subsequent conflict in the Philippines were a boon
for the nascent recording industry, which had started to market the phonograph as a home entertainment device only two years earlier. The top hit of
1898 was "A Hot Time in the Old Town Tonight," a coon song adopted as
the quasi-official anthem of Teddy Roosevelt's Rough Riders. Ragtime numbers said to be favorites of the troops acquired a patriotic flair in recordings
by military brass bands, and a new genre called the "descriptive selection"
purported to re-create the cacophony of notable battles.[15] The consolidation
of the industry coincided with the U.S. occupation of Cuba and Puerto Rico
(and later Haiti), the construction of the Panama Canal, and an influx of
U.S. investments in mining, railroads, and export agriculture, all of which in
conjunction gave rise to what O. Henry—in a novel that grew out of a short
story about a phonograph—first called the "banana republic."[16] Early on,
companies realized that although there was money to be made in import-
ing phonographs and records of U.S. and European music, customers also
desired to hear the voices of prominent local musicians and more familiar
"national" styles. Columbia started to make recordings in Mexico City in
1903, and Edison and Victor quickly followed suit; within a few years all had
established a presence elsewhere in Latin America, with Havana and Buenos
Aires the prime spots.

Brazil, in this respect as in many others, marched to a slightly different
drum. Although the first documented exhibition of the phonograph took
place in Rio de Janeiro in February 1878, just six months after its invention,

it was not until 1889 that a local representative of Edison's National Phonograph Company undertook a systematic effort to popularize the machine.[17] Among its most eager enthusiasts was the emperor, Dom Pedro II. Over the course of several days leading up to the proclamation of the Brazilian Republic, which would force them into exile, Edison's agent made recordings of Dom Pedro and other members of the royal court speaking and singing. As Flora Süssekind writes, "The recordings had a somewhat ambiguous effect: at the same time that they preserved and reproduced the voices, they also seemed to divest them of their earlier aura, in a cruel way. The voice of the emperor, recorded on November 9, was the voice of a deposed monarch only one week later."[18] Yet nostalgia for the empire lingered, as Fred Figner discovered nearly two years later when he arrived in the northern coastal city of Belém. Figner, a Czech emigrant naturalized in the United States, had spent fifteen months organizing phonograph exhibitions throughout the rest of Latin America before deciding to try his luck in Brazil. In Belém he played recordings he had brought from the United States and made cylinders of *lundus*, modinhas, and songs from operettas, as well as (amid other miscellanea) a humorous diatribe against the republic delivered by a local lawyer.[19] Following a lengthy detour up the Amazon River to Manaus, he returned to the coast and headed south to Fortaleza, Natal, Recife, and Salvador, arriving in Rio on April 21, 1892.

The ventures of Figner offer a glimpse into the dizzying geographies of culture and capital out of which the industry emerged. For several years he continued to tour through Brazil, making forays to Montevideo and Buenos Aires and eventually to Milan, where he recorded opera stars at La Scala and reportedly gave Verdi his first introduction to the apparatus.[20] In 1897, when a Canadian engineer resident in Rio began to import phonographs to Brazil, Figner went into business selling cylinder recordings and discs. His first catalogue (issued in 1900 under the name Casa Edison) was made up entirely of imports, but just two years later it featured many selections he himself had recorded, including fifty modinhas, eighty-one lundus and *cançonetas*, fourteen speeches, sixteen *polcas* (polkas), and five maxixes. These were released on seven- and ten-inch discs under the label of Zonophone, a short-lived, Berlin-based company that established a partnership with Casa Edison. In fact, Figner worked closely with all the major foreign firms operating in Brazil: in collaboration with an Englishman named Bernard Wilson Shaw, he started a series of graphophone clubs to help popularize the Columbia brand, and he engineered many of the early Brazilian recordings released under the Columbia and Victor labels.[21] His closest relationship, however, was with Odeon, another Berlin-based company founded in 1903 by a group that included Fredrick M. Prescott, the former head of Zonophone—now under the control of the U.K.-based Gramophone Company. Odeon's Brazilian discs were originally fabricated in London by the Italian-based Fonotipia Company, but at the end of 1912 it opened the first major record factory in

South America in the Tijuca neighborhood of Rio on land owned by Figner, who oversaw its construction and management.[22]

For more than a decade thereafter Odeon would continue to dominate the Brazilian market with the aid of Fred Figner and Casa Edison, which opened branches in São Paulo as well as a number of other cities and acted as the exclusive distributor for Odeon until 1927. But while none of its rivals came close to matching the quantity and diversity of its "Brazilian" recordings, Odeon faced stiff competition from the Victor Talking Machine Company with regard to imports of opera and other classical music recordings. Victor had grown out of the failed business ventures of Emile Berliner, the Prussian-born inventor of the gramophone (which played discs as opposed to cylinders).[23] In 1901, after a legal dispute forced Berliner to fold his operations, he sold his U.S. patent rights to Eldridge Reeves Johnson, a machinist in the company who reorganized the business under the name of Victor and quickly formalized his already close working relationship with the Gramophone Company of England, an entity established a few years earlier to license and market the Berliner technology in Europe. As part of their agreement Victor acquired the right to share Gramophone's trademark image of the little dog Nipper, along with the caption "His Master's Voice."[24] But what would prove even more significant was their deal to share recording matrices and divvy up the world market, with Victor laying claim to North and South America and parts of Asia, while Gramophone staked out Europe, the British Empire, Russia, and Japan.[25]

There is a reason that the phonograph Fitzcarraldo hauls with him on his sylvan trek is a Victor. Among its competitors the company was known for its carefully crafted image, the fruit of a dual strategy involving an unprecedented emphasis on advertising and a concerted campaign to distance the phonograph from what one historian calls its "honky-tonk past."[26] Until then the apparatus itself had been a functionalist affair, with its mechanical parts on display for all and sundry to see; in a bid to rebrand it as a marker of domestic gentility, Victor shrouded it in ever more elaborate wood casings and billed it as better than a box seat ticket at the Palais Garnier or La Scala. Opera had been popular in the United States for much of the nineteenth century, with works (or liberal adaptations) often performed in translation and on the same playbill as farces or minstrel shows. During the Gilded Age, however, what Lawrence W. Levine refers to as the "sacralization of culture" enthroned it as the epitome of "highbrow" art.[27] Although the Metropolitan Opera House in New York opened its doors in 1883—just a year before construction began on the Teatro Amazonas in Manaus—the genre came to owe much of its cachet to a medium that denuded the music of its hyperbolic gestures and sumptuous settings. In 1903 Victor signed the Italian tenor Enrico Caruso to an exclusive contract, and over the next two decades he would anchor their Red Seal line of records, which were sold at inflated prices to assure their prestige. In truth, most listeners only learned the three-minute excerpts featured on discs, and many of the songs recorded by opera stars weren't opera at all: Victor records often included both arias and popular tunes performed in an operatic style, such as the Romanian soprano Alma Gluck's version of "Carry Me Back to Old Virginny" (written by the African American minstrel composer James A. Bland) or the Irish folk songs sung by the U.S. tenor John McCormack.[28]

Although the company sold three times as many records under its cheaper Black Label (including everything from minstrel numbers and turkey trots to white Dixieland jazz), fewer of these discs seem to have made it to Brazil.[29] Victor registered its name there in 1904, but it had started to sell its wares even earlier through Casa Edison; in 1907 one of its representatives (perhaps Figner) held a session with local artists such as João Barros and Cadete, and the former circus clown and future opera singer Mário Pinheiro recorded dozens of discs at Victor's headquarters in Camden, New Jersey, in 1910.[30] Almost all of the singers were white, though some of the composers were not, and a number of the songs were rhythmically or thematically marked by race: notable titles included "Mulata vaidoza," or "Vain Mulatta" (a lundu), "A abolicionista" (by the female soloist Medina de Souza), and "Imitação d'um batuque africano" (an imitation of an "African" percussion session, though the piece features a male vocalist and guitar). Still, Victor's local recordings paled in number to those put out by Odeon. To an even greater extent than in the United States it put its stock in the operatic anxieties and classical predilections of the elite and a small but aspiring middle class: advertisements featured the same drawings of Caruso or genteel couples envisioning distant orchestras while seated before a Victrola, and the text was often a direct translation from ads in English.[31]

This situation would undergo a major shake-up in the 1920s. During World War I the disruptions to the market in Europe opened up opportunities for recording companies in both the United States and Brazil, but by late 1924 the entire industry found itself in a crisis provoked in part by the arrival of broadcast radio. Salvation came in the guise of what one Brazilian magazine called the "Revolution of 1925"—the conversion from acoustic or "mechanical" recording to a new electrical era.[32] Before this time recording had involved no microphones or other means of amplification; sound waves were simply funneled through one or more metal horns to the recording diaphragm, which was linked to a stylus that cut grooves into the surface of a wax master disc. Amid great secrecy Victor and Columbia cut a deal with Western Electric, which had developed a new microphone-based electrical system that resulted in a dramatically sharper sound and accurately reproduced a much wider range of frequencies. Victor took the lead in promoting the new technology, particularly in Brazil, where the enthusiasm was fanned by the formation of phonograph clubs sponsored by Casa Paul J. Christoph, an importer with stores in Rio and São Paulo and the sole distributor for Victor during this period. In its inaugural edition, dated August 15, 1928, the Rio-based journal *Phono-arte* explained its own appearance by declaring that yesterday, the phonograph was a "simple machine, looked on with curiosity and disapproval by 'cultured people' and people 'of judgment.' " Yet due to the vast improvement in sound quality, it now "gathers around itself an elite of amateurs, artists, musicians, and critics. A noisome fairground instrument with a twangy sound of old tin, suitable for augmenting the vulgarity of popular joys, the phonograph presently delights the most delicate and demanding ears."[33]

Surprisingly, the contents of the magazine were not quite as stuffy as such rhetoric might lead a reader to expect. To be sure, there were articles on opera and classical music, along with updates on new developments in the industry. But the serious attention and space the journal dedicated to "popular" music suggests that the category of "art" was in flux. In the United States, even Victor had ceded to the trends by making tentative incursions into the market for "race records" made by and marketed toward African American audiences: although the company was better known for its hillbilly music and white jazz orchestras, it began a successful campaign in 1926 to record black blues and jazz artists, signing stars such as Jelly Roll Morton and Bennie Moten. In Brazil, on the other hand, the absence of any equivalent to Jim Crow laws (or a codified tradition of blackface performance) contributed to a more diffuse configuration of musical "authenticity," embodiment, and race.[34] The first electrical recordings made in Brazil, released in 1928 by Casa Edison in association with Odeon, were of Francisco Alves (a white songster) singing a new, more syncopated style of samba from the favela of Estácio in Rio, an area commonly known as Little Africa; just a few months later two of the composers, Ismael Silva and Alcebíades Barcelos, were among those who founded Deixa Falar, the first of Rio's legendary samba schools. The following year Almirante and his Bando de Tangarás (also white) scored a hit for the Parlophon label with "Na Pavuna," the first studio samba to abandon orchestral accompaniment in favor of the percussive *batucada* instrumentation of *samba de morro*. Rather than segregating sound, the rise of samba and its popularization via radio and recordings fostered the emergence of a so-called national rhythm celebrated as the common patrimony of a people defined as racially mixed.[35]

Samba was also a prime factor in the nationalization of a new cultural icon called the *malandro*: a street-smart, womanizing hustler who enjoys the good life and flaunts his consumption of wealth but refuses to commit himself to a steady, "honest" job. Marc Hertzman has connected this figure to antivagrancy campaigns in the postslavery period and struggles over social mobility in the context of an emerging mass culture industry. Following abolition and the declaration of the republic, new penal codes required individuals to dwell in a fixed residence and made it illegal to exercise occupations deemed offensive to good morals; although applicable to all, the laws were selectively applied and accompanied by rhetoric stigmatizing Afro-descendants as lazy and ill suited to a modern labor regime. Musicians were frequent targets—not only because their profession lacked the "discipline" of wage work, but also because sound recording and other new cultural forms such as *teatro de revista*, or musical revues, aroused elite anxieties by affording black and mixed-race musicians greater visibility (as well as audibility) and alternative means of monetary gain. Circulated in song lyrics and adopted as a persona by singers, the malandro put a positive—or at least ambivalent—spin on the negative stereotypes associated with the *ideologia da vadiagem* (ideology of idleness). The first high-profile, self-declared malandro, a black musician named Eduardo das Neves who recorded "O malandro" for Odeon in 1910 and was a featured performer for Casa Edison, wore a blue suit jacket and silk hat, flouted his disdain for manual labor, and boasted of his prowess with white women. Yet in contrast to a tendency to stress the malandro's pre- or anticapitalist qualities, Hertzman highlights Neves's efforts to secure authorship rights to his songs and style himself as an "audacious entrepreneur who embraced wealth, capitalism, and the promises of republican citizenship."[36]

Samba was not the only game in town: *Phono-arte* also commented on, carried advertisements for, and published the lyrics of toadas, maxixes, *marchas, ranchos carnavalescos, côcos nortistas, canções sertanejas,* and *choros,* among others. Some were urban genres, but others were "folk" traditions from rural regions whose mutation into mass cultural commodities was the result of migration and urbanization, the growth of folklore studies, and the expansion of the recording industry. Odeon, which had long had a corner on the market for "national" discs, soon discovered it had company. Brunswick, the second-largest U.S. phonograph company, gained a license to sell its products in 1927 and quickly established recording facilities and a factory in Rio. The following year the German company Parlophon followed suit, while Columbia switched it up by building its pressing plant in Rio but basing its studio in São Paulo. Victor did the reverse: although it opened a factory and secondary studio in São Paulo, it located its main studio in Rio, where the acclaimed black composer and flautist Pixinguinha led its house orchestra. The company continued to brandish its operatic image, but if Caruso (who died in 1921) had once been its public face, it now courted Carmen Miranda (who later gained fame in the United States as the "lady in the tutti frutti hat") and pioneered the practice of sending musicians out on trucks to play its artists' new tunes before Carnaval and drum up demand.[37]

Michael Denning has used the phrase "noise uprising" to describe the sudden surge in recordings of vernacular music genres in Brazil and other (post)colonial countries around the world at this time.[38] Yet to hear Victor tell it, its mission was anything but making noise. On October 21, 1928, the *Diário Nacional* of São Paulo carried an article on the Victor factory, which was still under construction, and related a conversation with W. G. Ridge, the inspector general of Victor's operations in Brazil. Putting a new spin on a familiar discourse, Ridge begins by stating that the progress of a people depends on art, and in modern society there is no better "stimulus" than the phonographic disc.[39] During a live performance errors can be forgiven, but a recording immortalizes every defect, demanding nothing short of perfection from the performers. In explaining why the company chose to locate its headquarters in São Paulo, he shamelessly panders to the residents' sense of self-importance, giving kudos to all the (unnamed) artists in the city who earn applause at home and abroad, and praising the local music organizations over and above those in Rio, which are said to suffer from a paucity of government support, cohesion, and (he puts it bluntly) "artistic spirit." Nor is this all: along with its "perfectly organized, complete orchestras" and other musical institutions "perfectly prepared to record a series of magnificent discs," the city boasts "skilled, diligent workers." São Paulo is a place where "artistic advancements run parallel with material advancements," and where people "can distinguish good art from bad."

In other words, São Paulo was a place where capitalism was *in place*. This dream of a modern music factory where the division of labor was an "obligatory rule" (as it was at the Victor headquarters in Camden) seems to have impressed the reporter for the *Diário Nacional*, but there was evidence of unease from other quarters. José da Cruz Cordeiro Filho, one of the editors of *Phono-arte*, would take a job with Victor in 1931, two years after it was sold to the Radio Corporation of America amid a series of mergers and acquisitions in the industry. Despite this, and despite its own obsession with the ins and outs of the business, the journal occasionally got its nationalistic feathers in a bunch. Not long after the new factory in São Paulo started pressing records, an editorial on the changing nature of audition took a curious flight into science fiction as it envisioned a future in which "American *managers* will rationalize musical production, just as they have done with the automobile and agricultural machines."[40] The "Yankees," it predicted, would reduce the "truly fantastic" quantity of musical material and limit the number of orchestras, leaving only as many as were required to carry out the diffusion of all remaining works across the globe. The "elite figure" whose sensibilities had been entirely formed by recorded sound would of course live apart from the "inferior races"— yet contrary to what one might expect, and "as a curiosity, in certain picturesque countries deprived of easily exploitable natural riches, some primitive tribes will be authorized and even invited to live according to antiquated forms of civilization, out of historic interest and as a pastime for scholars [*os sábios*]."

Progress depends on the persistence of the primitive. The editorial ends in the same bitterly ironic tone, with its authors imagining that "once in a while a civilized person, summoned by ancestral memories, will ask himself with a certain apprehension if the industrialization of art constitutes an unalloyed benefit." If his answer is no, the editors of *Phono-arte* suggest, he would be wise to remain silent lest the "eugenic judges" sentence him to sterilization.

Wayward Primitives

It is amusing to imagine the expressions of horror and disgust the scholars in this scenario might make if in their travels they encountered a primitive like Macunaíma—the improbable, grossly inappropriate protagonist of Mário de Andrade's novelistic masterpiece and could-have-been (but wasn't) dramatic dance and opera. This "hero without any character" is inspired by a legend of the Pemon people, and his name in their language means "Great Evil," but the novel is a ribald pastiche that mocks any pretense of anthropological authenticity. Born in the Amazon to the fictitious Tapunhama tribe, Macunaíma is an aberration, a black man-child who morphs (temporarily) into an elegant white prince. He is rude, crude, lazy, infantile, amoral, and lascivious—a primitivist fantasy gone epically awry. Unlike Fitzcarraldo, and in contrast to his own creator, he journeys out of the jungle to São Paulo in search of the *muiraquitã*, an amulet given to him by his lover but later lost and now in the possession of a man-eating Peruvian capitalist. After outwitting his enemy and traipsing through the strange flora and fauna of the city, Macunaíma returns to the forest with the *muiraquitã*, only to lose it again when he is seduced and dismembered by a *iara*, or river mermaid, at which point he decides to call it quits and turn himself into the constellation of Ursa Major. Before ascending to the heavens, he tells his story to a parrot, which—as readers learn in the epilogue—repeated the tale to the author one day when he came upon the place where Macunaíma and his tribe had lived. The Tapunhamas and their language are now extinct, leaving only a bird to record and replay the sounds of their dying culture: "In the silence of the Uraricoera only the parrot had rescued from oblivion those happenings and the language which had disappeared. Only the parrot had preserved in that vast silence the words and the deeds of the hero."[41]

If the modernista movement was São Paulo–centric in its origins, it became more dispersed as the 1920s progressed and clusters of artists and writers in other parts of the country established ties to the paulistas through personal correspondence, the circulation of journals, and visits to the city. Meanwhile the loose coalition convoked for the Week of Modern Art in 1922 dissolved, and more of the participants began to look outward to the diverse regions and cultures of Brazil. One early milestone was the "modernista caravan" of 1924, when a group that included Mário and Oswald de Andrade and the painter Tarsila do Amaral escorted the French writer Blaise Cendrars on an excursion to the old colonial mining towns of Minas Gerais during Holy Week. A stranger case was the embrace of indigenous mythology by the conservative wing of modernismo known as *verde-amarelismo* (a reference to the green and gold colors on the Brazilian flag). It was at the end of 1926 that Menotti del Picchia, Plínio Salgado, and Cassiano Ricardo issued their first call for the "Revolution of the *Anta*," adopting as their emblem the tapir, a short-snouted ungulate said to serve as a totem for some Amazonian groups. An herbivore that ingested indiscriminately, the tapir stood for the lack of racial prejudice in Brazil, its capacity to absorb waves of immigrants, and the desire for a "Tupi nationalism" that was not "intellectual" but "practical" and "sentimental."⁴² The Tupi were the only race that had "objectively disappeared"—less than half a million indigenous remained—yet in doing so they lived on in the assimilationist spirit of Brazil, becoming "the only race that subjectively exercises over all the others the action that destroys their characteristic traits."

It was partly in response to this bizarre "school" that Oswald de Andrade and his collaborators launched their infamous *Revista de Antropofagia*. Whereas the Tupi nationalists recycled the image of the passive Indian whose destiny was to disappear, the Anthropophagists put a new spin on the stereotype of the cannibalistic Indian who bites back. The original inhabitants of Brazil had ritualistically consumed their enemies in order to absorb their strength; according to Oswald and company, the way for modern-day Brazilians to escape the cycle of cultural dependency was to follow their predecessors' lead and not simply reject influences from Europe or the United States, but rip them to shreds and creatively digest them to generate something new. The avant-garde writer set the tone for the movement's campy primitivism in his manifesto, published in the inaugural issue of the journal in May 1928 and dated "in the 374th Year of the Swallowing of the Bishop Sardinha"—an allusion to the fate of the first Catholic bishop of Brazil. Playing on the fact that Montaigne had drawn inspiration for his "noble savage" from the egalitarian customs of the Tupinamba, Oswald flippantly declared, "We already had Communism. We already had surrealist language. The Golden Age." Back in 1922 on the stage of the Theatro Municipal, he had mockingly evoked the embarrassing spectacle of *Il Guarany*, Carlos Gomes's opera (based on a novel by José Alencar) in which white actors wearing feather dusters enacted a foundational fiction all the more implausible for being sung in Italian. In a further twist on that motif, he now boasted that in contrast to Europeans, "we were never catechized. What we really made was Carnaval. The Indian dressed as senator of the Empire. Making believe he's Pitt. Or performing in Alencar's operas, full of worthy Portuguese sentiments."⁴³ The movement was all about the "anthropophagist in knickerbockers and not the operatic Indian,"⁴⁴ yet in shrugging its shoulders at logic and making mincemeat of Romantic notions of authenticity, it also paradoxically redeemed the incongruous image of the white man in Indian drag.

As one of the few modernistas (and certainly the most prominent) who was clearly of mixed race, Mário de Andrade stood in an awkward relation to all of this. Menotti del Picchia and Plínio Salgado had made innuendos about his skin color since the Week of Modern Art, but Mário would have his bitterest exchanges with the Anthropophagists. Oswald too had a penchant for making jests about his skin color and sexuality, and the tensions between the two friends came to a head in 1928–1929. From the outset Mário had been wary of the new movement's aggressive irony, and perhaps also of the way it dragged the figure of the Indian into the middle of increasingly ideological battles: following the Revolution of 1930, Oswald would join the ranks of the Communist Party, and Plínio Salgado would found the fascist Integralist Party. The straw that broke the camel's back seems to have been when the *Revista de Antropofagia* took to identifying Mário as "our Miss São Paulo translated into the masculine" and "Miss Macunaíma."[45] Based on extensive (if still mostly secondhand) research into indigenous and Afro-Brazilian cultures, *Macunaíma* had been hailed as an unrivaled masterpiece of modernismo, and the Anthropophagists had been quick to claim it as a realization of their principles. Its author's decision to break with their leader sent ripples far and wide, prompting even writers and artists in distant cities such as Recife to declare their allegiance to one or the other.

The "humor" of the Miss Macunaíma jab had to do with the contrast between Mário's absurdly lewd, hypersexual savage and his own famously discreet, virginal persona. It also took aim at a certain purchase on the primitive that he enjoyed as a result of his ambiguous racial identity as well as his scholarly expertise and recent firsthand experience. The copious references in his novel to indigenous mythology and Amazonian flora and fauna had mostly come from the writings of the German ethnologist Theodor Koch-Grünberg, and his depiction of a *candomblé* ritual in Rio drew on information from the musician Pixinguinha.[46] But not long after finishing his first draft, in May 1927, the author himself embarked on his three-month journey up the Amazon River. Much to his chagrin (or so he claimed), he showed up to the dock in Rio to find himself the lone gentleman accompanying Olívia Guedes Penteado, daughter of the first (and last) Baron of Pirapitingui and a wealthy patron of the arts, who was traveling with her twenty-year-old niece Margarida and Dulce, daughter of Tarsila do Amaral. The Brazilian president had alerted officials in cities and towns along the way to the arrival of the "Coffee Queen," as Mário jokingly called his esteemed companion, and lavish receptions awaited them at their major stops. In his quixotic diary of his travels, Mário blatantly blends fantasy with fact and depicts himself as an awkward *turista aprendiz* (apprentice tourist), parodying the scientific pretensions and conventions found in the writings of earlier explorers, including Koch-Grünberg and the Brazilian *sertanistas* who led government-funded expeditions in charge of surveying the interior.[47] Rather than a redoubt of absolute otherness like the one burlesqued in the *Phonoarte* editorial, his Amazon is one where the same U.S. film is showing in every little cinema along the river. Yet it is also a sonorous place, and in addition to his diary and hundreds of photographs, Mário returned to São Paulo with notes on songs and other performance traditions he had read about but never before heard or seen.

Not until several years later, with the creation of the University of São Paulo in 1934 and the arrival of visiting professors such as the young Claude

Lévi-Strauss, would anthropology in Brazil start to acquire the outlines of a formal academic discipline. Mário himself would play a pivotal role in this process: along with Lévi-Strauss and his wife Dina he established a Society of Ethnography and Folklore within the Department of Culture, and he is still acknowledged as a founder of the field of ethnomusicology for his copious writings in this area and his commissioning and collecting of ethnographic recordings.[48] As early as 1921, however, he had started to amass notations and observations of popular music genres in and around São Paulo. Following his return from the Amazon, while finishing revisions to *Macunaíma*, he completed his landmark *Ensaio sobre música brasileira*, which proposed to systematize the study of Brazilian music and provide a catalogue of melodies he and his growing network of correspondents had notated. He also started to write for the *Diário Nacional*, the new newspaper of the Partido Democrático (PD). Founded in early 1926, the PD comprised members of a growing middle-class of liberal professionals with key allies among the coffee planters. Its principal demands were the secret vote, the independence of the judiciary, and an end to the corruption associated with the Partido Republicano Paulista (PRP), which had held a tight grip on the state's political scene for half a century.[49] For Mário, who on multiple occasions throughout his life confessed his discomfort with politics, the appeal of the party lay in its national outlook and emphasis on expanding government action in the areas of education and culture. Along with a handful of other modernistas including Sérgio Milliet and Antônio de Alcântara Machado, he formed part of a small cultural wing of the party that gathered at the home of Paulo Duarte, one of its founders, to discuss their shared interest in folklore, draw up hypothetical plans for new institutions devoted to Brazilian culture—and listen to phonograph recordings.[50]

The *Diário Nacional* allotted ample space to all of these preoccupations. Shortly after Mário's return from the Amazon the newspaper interviewed him about his trip,[51] and a few months later he recounted his experience as a spectator at a *ciranda*, a dance-drama revolving around the death and resurrection of a *carão* (the limpkin or crying bird).[52] According to Mário, he and other tourists happened upon the scene in a small settlement of *tapuios*, or acculturated (often mixed-blood) Amazonians, near the town of Tefé on the Solimões River. Dressed in "extravagant" apparel and looking like explorers in their "pull-overs" and "colonial hats," the outsiders observed a jovial parade of young women and men in equally odd attire, with hats inspired by native headdresses and shirts and trousers of those "same crude colors with which Tarsila do Amaral so wisely Brazilianized her paintings." A buffoonish figure playing the part of a priest led the procession to the home of a Syrian rubber trader, where the ciranda took place. All of the action, Mário notes, was narrated by soloists, whose role he compares to the *Testo*, or *Istorico*, in classical oratorios—a genre closely related to opera (as the last chapter explains), though the drama is only sung rather than fully staged. Tellingly, he dismisses the dramatic aspect of the performance as a poor knockoff of the *bumba-meu-boi*, a ritualistic dance-drama from northeastern Brazil in which a bull is killed and brought back to life. The ciranda's dance, much like a children's circle dance, was similarly "monotonous, without any originality, primitive." Yet the poverty of these elements only highlights the fact that "what is really of value is the music." Mário singles out for its particular beauty the chorus's lamentation over the death of the *carão* bird, one of the two motifs he was able to notate. Finally, he ends with a revelation: this music is astonishingly similar to Scandinavian folk songs, differing only in certain "rhythmic deformations." Deep in the Amazon, "among people absolutely untraveled and isolated," are sounds that seem uncannily out of place.

This amateur ethnographer's desire to separate out and redeem the musical dimension of the performance from both the dance and the drama also sheds light on another new passion he shared with readers. Printed under the bold heading "O PHONOGRAPHO" and sandwiched between obituaries and brief updates on the theater world, his column in the February 24, 1928, edition opens by hailing the "extraordinary perfection" the latest models of the machine had achieved.[53] Just a year earlier the Italian government had established a discothèque, or phonographic "museum," to preserve "regional" or "popular" songs that were essential to the ongoing formation of a national musical tradition but would soon (according to Mário) be "abandoned in the voice of the people."[54] And in Brazil? The author cites the case of Edgar Roquette-Pinto, an explorer of the Amazon whose rare recordings of indigenous music had been entrusted to the National Museum only to be worn out or broken through misuse and neglect.[55] Folklorists had collected tunes from other regions in the form of handwritten notations. But in a near-exact echo of an argument voiced almost four decades earlier by Walter Fewkes following his recording sessions with the Passamaquoddy, Mário insists that the hand is unable to keep pace with the speed of song; it cannot register the nasal intonation of the vocalists, nor can it record the irregular *rubatos* and rhythmic fluctuations unique to certain styles. Unlike in Italy, however, there was little hope government institutions would take on the task of archiving these traditions. Vacillating between the prospect of loss and the promise of technology, Mário warns of the imminent demise of a "prodigious treasure" and states that civic organizations must step up and mobilize the potential of the phonograph, which "imposes itself"—or alternatively, "is imposed" (*se impõe*)—as the "only remedy of salvation."

That curious turn of phrase hints at the contradictions in which Mário's newfound enthusiasm was caught. Like audio ethnographers in the United States, he invokes what Jonathan Sterne calls the "nostalgic language of anthropological mourning" while proposing as a solution a technology indebted to the same "modernizing" forces responsible for these cultures' ostensible death.[56] In Brazil, this discourse was even more vexed given the dominance of foreign corporations in the recording industry—an industry that would play a prominent role in mediating the emergence of a "national" music tradition. As a follow-up note in the paper revealed, Mário's article prompted an invitation from the Paul J. Christoph Club in São Paulo, where he spent more than an hour listening to Victor recordings and left even more convinced that with the advent of the electric era, the medium had achieved the status of a "perfectly legitimate and pleasant musical manifestation of art."[57] On this occasion the recordings in question seem to have been of European music, and given Victor's catalogue as well as Mário's predilection, opera was no doubt in the mix. By the end of the year, however, the company had opened its factory in São Paulo and the boom in "Brazilian" recordings had begun.

The Victor Talking Machine Company would have an outsized influence on Mário's relationship to this changing soundscape. Several letters in his archive reveal his attempts to procure a reasonably affordable and portable phonograph to take with him on his second "ethnographic voyage," a more scholarly expedition to the northeastern states of Pernambuco, Alagoas, Rio Grande do Norte, and Paraíba from December 1928 to February 1929. Although apparently unsuccessful, he acquired one shortly after his return— most likely with the assistance of his friend Paulo Ribeiro de Magalhães, a local Victor representative and a fellow member of the Partido Democrático who also frequented the nocturnal gatherings at Paulo Duarte's home.[58] Over the next few years Magalhães would give Mário more than 250 Victor discs for his personal collection, which eventually grew to more than five hundred recordings of various labels, including a wide range of opera and art music (from Verdi and Wagner to Schoenberg), Brazilian popular and "folkloric" music (sambas, choros, *toadas nortistas*, *batuques de macumba*), and equivalent genres from throughout the Americas and Europe (among them jazz, the foxtrot, son, bolero, fado, and milonga).[59] Magalhães also occasionally assisted Mário in collecting ethnographic data, as he did in November 1930 while in Piracicaba, a town in the interior of the state of São Paulo where he was recording *duplas caipiras* as part of a project led by the folklorist Cornélio Pires.[60] A few months later, for reasons related to his job, Magalhães relocated to Rio, where he became a friend and eventual flatmate to Mário's close confidante, the poet Manuel Bandeira. In a letter to Mário, the Victor rep complained that "yankee capitalism" was "sordidly exploiting" him: due to a downturn in business, Victor had cut his and other employees' salaries.[61] Yet both he and Bandeira often wrote about new recordings in their missives to Mário, and their frequent allusions to communal listening sessions leave little doubt that Magalhães's Victrola was the hub of their (homo)social circle of intellectuals and artists.

In his contributions to the *Diário Nacional*, as in his annotations of the recordings in his personal archive, Mário leveled his fair share of critiques. The confusion of the U.S. recording engineers at Victor when faced with the new sounds and styles of singing in Brazil was to blame for some lamentable "errors,"[62] and at best only around 30 percent of all commercial recordings could be said to "escape awfulness" (*escapam do ruim*).[63] But Mário was willing to risk the *ruim*—a word often used as a close synonym of *mau* or *mal* to mean "evil," "harmful," and "morally corrupt," though it can also carry the connotation of counterfeit, inartistic, and of poor quality. By the late 1930s, he would grow far more skeptical of the music industry's effects on urban genres such as samba. Yet in contrast to the claims of many critics and historians, he was far from a purist at this earlier point, when the industry itself was more fluid and open to innovation.[64] In 1930, for example, he contributed the lyrics for "Canção Marinha," a song composed by Marcelo Tupinambá and recorded by Edgard Arantes for Brunswick.[65] A composer and pianist whose great-uncle had composed the first opera written in Portuguese and debuted in Brazil, Tupinambá had a background in "erudite" music but found his calling playing in cafés and writing tunes for teatro de revista (musical revues) and film; the French modernist Darius Milhaud had quoted a number of his maxixes and tangos in his own work, later passing them off as "folkloric" music, and Mário praised his imminently popular melodies for capturing the "heterogeneous indecision of our racial formation."[66]

Radio, which started to steal the show in the early 1930s, was a medium toward which Mário was always ambivalent.[67] In these early days broadcasts were all "live," meaning that listeners shared a temporal if not physical space with the performers and each other. Sound recording, on the other hand, had affinities with Mário's own compositional practice. In an unpublished preface to *Macunaíma*, written shortly after he drafted the novel during two weeks in December 1926, he explained his allusion to the protagonist in the subtitle as an *herói sem nenhum caráter*—a hero without any character. Voicing a common refrain in his writings from this time, he argued that unlike other groups (the French, the Yoruba, or even the Mexicans), Brazilians were a composite people who lacked their own "civilization" and "traditional consciousness." His response to this situation in the novel was to "disrespect geography and geographical flora and fauna" in order to "deregionalize my creation to the greatest extent possible at the same time as I achieved the merit of literarily conceiving Brazil as a homogeneous entity = a national and geographical, ethnic concept."[68] Just as the phonograph seems to detach sounds and songs from their source in order to replay them in distant locales, *Macunaíma* uproots not only plants and animals but also myths and other cultural references from their original contexts and transplants them to other parts of Brazil—or combines them in the impossible person of its itinerant race-changing and shape-shifting antihero. Registering but also working against the strong regional identities Mário saw as a cause of the country's political woes and institutional deficiencies, both the recording industry and his novel created the conditions for a shared national culture by acting simultaneously as archive and agent of a process of cultural diffusion regarded as incomplete.

In some respects, this was similar to the *teatro regional* and *teatro sintético* movements discussed in chapter 2, which involved artist-ethnographers documenting and drawing on indigenous traditions as the basis for the creation of "synthetic" pieces to be performed for (and eventually by) Mexicans of all classes, regions, and races. In both cases the ethnographic impulse to particularize and preserve a multiplicity of traditions existed in tension with the desire to reshape and subsume their objectified elements into a new national, homogeneous "race." Even in his call to save dying songs, Mário values such music primarily as raw material for the creation of "national music schools"; for all its differences, his archival logic shares the assimilationist impulse of the Anta group in consigning indigenous life ways and embodied practices to disappearance. Technology was central to this process: far from assuming the transparency of recordings, Mário increasingly came to insist that the phonograph was not simply a "reproducer of alien sounds" but an instrument that *re*-presented prior performances with a timbre and "special sonorities" of its own.[69] Whereas in Mexico the anthropologist Manuel Gamio and others saw the documentation and subsequent stylization of indigenous songs and dances as a way of standardizing or "fixing" repertoires, Mário recognized that "it is the great phonograph houses that now take charge of the fixation and evolution of our dance songs."[70] In a country where there had been no revolution and no government agencies existed to fund performance (or large-scale anthropological) projects such as the one at Teotihuacán, the accumulation and integration of culture was dis-placed into the virtual theaters of literature and commercially recorded sound.

Roberto Schwarz (readers will recall) argues that national identity in Brazil hinges on an ambivalent attachment to "ideas of out of place," a strange sense of discord and dislocation that he sees as symptomatic of economic and cultural dependency. Schwarz traces this dynamic to the late nineteenth century and the air of inauthenticity surrounding the liberal discourse of the new republic: ideals such as equality, individual autonomy, and the universality of law defied all credulity in a country where slavery was just ending and where the boom in exports of raw materials continued to fuel relations of patronage and forms of labor deemed by liberalism as obsolete.[71] These contradictions were still in play during the late 1920s but were experienced differently among intellectuals making a push to nationalize cultural production—to bring ideas "into place." Mário never quite put his finger on the paradoxical role of international capital in the "fixation" of a national music tradition, at least not in this moment. He never remarked on the Taylorist fantasies associated with the new Victor factory in São Paulo, or on how its efforts to rationalize the production of art might have jarred with the "backwardness" of Brazil—and all the more so given that most of the genres it helped "nationalize" had historical roots in rural regions or among communities of slaves. In *Macunaíma*, however, he (partially) redeems incongruity and anachronicity as artistic principles and as hallmarks of an unfinished Brazilian identity, employing a practice of "deregionalization" that also conveniently coincides with the avant-garde predilection for unexpected juxtapositions and collage. Backwardness and futurity meet, and a "national shame" becomes a "national originality" (to cite Schwarz) in the guise of the celebrated protagonist—a charming if self-centered cipher who lacks any psychological or moral character but is often characterized by critics as a malandro.[72]

It was Antonio Candido, an important influence on Schwarz, who first pointed to *Macunaíma* as the novel in which the malandro was "elevated to the category of a symbol."[73] In a now-classic essay from 1970, Candido identified a national novelistic tradition initiated by Manuel Antônio de Almeida in his *Memórias de um sargento de milícias* (1854), a text unusual for its era in its use of colloquial language and its reckless, charmingly amoral protagonist who owes obvious debts to the tricksters of Brazilian folklore, such as Pedro Malasarte. Contesting the notion that the novel was a precursor to realism, Candido notes that it omits almost any mention of the ruling classes or slave labor; instead it works by capturing a "general rhythm" of Brazilian society that he dubs a "dialectic of *malandragem*," an oscillation between order and disorder characteristic of a system in which slaves were the axis of production and almost all others "abandoned themselves to idleness, repeating the surplus of parasitism, of contrivance, of munificence, of fortune, or of petty theft" (95). As Schwarz writes in his gloss on Candido's essay, the novel "gives general relevance to the experience of one sector of society, the intermediate one, which lacks regular work, does not accumulate wealth or issue orders and which in this sense seems the least essential of all."[74] Not by coincidence, this is the same sector Schwarz himself would single out in explaining the peculiar cast of Brazilian ideology: legally free yet dependent on the patronage of the rich, it was poor men whose experience most clearly showed up the discord between Brazilian reality and liberal ideas.

But while both Candido and Schwarz cite the modernista movement as the moment when this dynamic became predominant, neither remarks on the racialization of vagrancy or the mass cultural metamorphosis of the malandro at around the same time. For both, the malandro (like other free men of his class) is either explicitly or implicitly white. What this overlooks is that *Macunaíma* responds most immediately to a context in which this "unproductive," mediating figure was becoming mixed-race or black.

A Peculiar Badness

Although Mário was attuned to the racialization of the malandro, he also discerned that this figure's deviation from moral and aesthetic norms had correlates in other cultural realms. Over the course of September 1928, he waged a relentless campaign in the pages of the *Diário Nacional* against an annual opera series staged at the Theatro Municipal (with the help of subsidies from the city government) by the privately owned Empresa Theatral Ítalo-Brasileira. His evaluation of the performers was favorable overall, but he had a long litany of other critiques: the repertoire (*Manon, Tosca, Traviata*) was predictable and stale, too much money was spent on showy sets, the exorbitant ticket prices excluded the vast majority of the city's residents, and there were no operas with national themes or musical influences that might appeal to a broader audience. Outraged by this use of public funds for the entertainment of a philistine elite, he went so far as to proclaim that the "false flower it produces has been systematically unfurling since aspirations of vanity led to the construction of that architectonic trifle [*quinquilharia*] that is the Theatro Municipal. Useless, false, hypocritical luxury of an unhappy city in which the people count for nothing."[75] For Mário, there was no reason why opera had to be elitist, and if it was a "foreign" art, the same could be said of every other tradition (including indigenous music) in a country where a national culture did not yet exist. In his *Ensaio sobre música brasileira*, he notes the similarity between an old toada (or popular tune) from Minas Gerais and a melody from *Il Guarany*; asking if Carlos Gomes might have taken his inspiration from this regional song, he suggests that even in Gomes there is an "indefinable something, a badness that isn't exactly bad, it's a *peculiar badness* . . . a first fatal sign of a race ringing from afar" (um não-sei-quê indefinível, um ruim que não é ruim propriamente, é um *ruim exquisito* . . . uma primeira fatalidade de raça badalando longe).[76] In addition to "peculiar," other possible translations for *exquisito* (now spelled *esquisito*) are "weird," "eccentric," or "queer"—in the dated, not necessarily sexual sense of "queer," though depending on the context it can carry this connotation.[77] Notably, Schwarz also uses the nominal variant of the word when he refers to the oddity of ideology in Brazil *as nossas esquisitices nacionais*, or "our national peculiarities."[78]

In fact, the process Schwarz describes is right here, in this recuperation of the *ruim* as the seed of something "ours," a source of shame but also pride. For Mário, this would become a deliberate strategy in his effort to create a national opera. Sometime toward the end of 1927, while still revising *Macunaíma*, the author sent scene descriptions for an operatic version to his friend Oscar Lorenzo Fernández, a professor at the Instituto Nacional de Música in Rio and a composer known for drawing on indigenous, Afro-Brazilian, and "folkloric" motifs while maintaining a devotion to classical technique. Fernández frequently wrote to Mário requesting information and transcriptions of melodies, and his best-known vocal piece from this period, "Toada pra você" (1928), was a collaboration with the writer. His response to this particular proposal, however, was decidedly mixed.[79] Fernández waxed enthusiastic over *Macunaíma* but sheepishly suggested that the theme might be a bit "monochromatic" for an opera, which in his view should be based on a "universal" legend endowed with local color. What it really came down to, he confessed, was that "I'm very afraid of sticking Indians in any operas. You understand, after Carlos Gomes . . . I wouldn't make an Indian sing Italian melodies." In order to avoid repeating this traumatic absurdity, he proposed to minimize the theatrical element and go the route of a symphonic poem, or better yet, a dance, which as a "modern art" was more suited to the "atmosphere of fantasy" the indigenous subject matter evoked. Even then, he said, Mário might want to reconsider the first scene, where Macunaíma drags the Queen of the Icamiabas (or Amazons) across the stage by her foot and has to appeal to his brothers to save him when she tickles him into submission with her spear. In a novel this was one thing, but in the theater it would be "ridiculous." The solution? Eliminate the brothers and reduce the scene to an elegant "stylization of Instinctive Love" in which Macunaíma defeats Ci with his "virile beauty." Needless to say, it should end in a long kiss—though Fernández admits to not knowing if Indians actually kissed, "and much less if they kissed in the style of American cinema."

If the composer found this first scene gauche, one can only imagine what he thought of the five following it. Mário's proposed opera skips over most of the novel, eliminating the character's journey out of the jungle to São Paulo to recover the *muiraquitã* given to him by Ci before her death but lost during his dalliance with a talking waterfall and pursuit by the mythic elf Capei.[80] As a result, there is no face-off with the capitalist cannibal Venceslau Pietro Pietra, the jarring juxtapositions of the "primitive" and the "modern" are gone, and rather than a symptom of a contradictory and characterless nation, Macunaíma returns to being the mythic Makunaíma (*maku*, "evil," + *ima*, "great"), who appears in the stories related by Koch-Grünberg as the creator of the Taulipang, or Arekuna, people. But while tame in comparison, the would-be opera still includes a few eyebrow-raising moments. Mário notes in his description of the second scene that "it will be necessary to stylize" the part where Macunaíma and Ci engage in vigorous lovemaking in a hammock, though he reassures his reader this will be "easy to do without shocking anyone, I'll take charge of that." Presumably he also had something up his sleeve for the moment when a black snake slinks in during the night and sucks on Ci's sole breast, leading her to unwittingly poison her infant son. He is equally vague as to how he would stage Ci's death and transformation into a twinkling star, and while Fernández was perhaps correct that modern dance offered more ways of rendering such scenes "poetic," it is hard to see how even dance could redeem the sight of Macunaíma wailing and childishly sucking his thumb. The scene outline ends on a dark (but perhaps grotesquely comic?) note, with the bloodied protagonist dragging himself out of the pool of water into which he had been seduced by the *iara*, and then dying as she and her mermaid companions sing a "joyful chorale." On this point, however, the author proves flexible and states that if a more "apotheotic" ending is desired, Macunaíma can climb up a vine and become a constellation, as he does in the novel.

Fernández evidently failed to convince the writer to set aside his operatic aspirations in favor of an art less bound by historical baggage and mimetic expectations. Nor did Mário jump at a proposal from Heitor Villa-Lobos, who wrote to him from Paris following the publication of *Macunaíma* expressing a desire to compose a dramatic dance based on the "Macumba" chapter, where the protagonist is possessed by the *orixá* Exú at a candomblé ceremony at the home of the famed *mãe-de-santo* priestess Tia Ciata.[81] Villa-Lobos, who had little formal training and boasted of his early explorations of Brazil, had already gained celebrity among the Parisian avant-garde for his eclectic blend of Afro-Brazilian and indigenous themes, urban street music such as choro, and elements of Romanticism and impressionism. In his letter, he told Mário that for more than a year he had been working on a dance "nostalgic [*saudoso*] of the fetish music of our fanatical macumbeiros." No title had come to mind, and inventing plots was not his area of expertise, but this could be solved by calling his dance *Macunaíma* and basing the storyline on the novel's relevant scene. He had already used several of Mário's poems to "complete" his own "sonorous ideas," so why not continue the collaboration?

No such dance was ever composed (at least not under the proposed title), and although Villa-Lobos had written a few operas earlier in his career, there is no evidence Mário tried to talk him into an operatic version of *Macunaíma*—perhaps because the composer was too well known and had already developed his own signature style, or because Mário had decided to swap out his race-changing protagonist for a slightly more manageable substitute. Drafted between August 27 and 29, 1928, just a month after the publication of *Macunaíma*, *Pedro Malazarte* (originally titled *Malazarte*) is a libretto for a comic one-act opera written expressly for Mozart Camargo Guarnieri, one of many young composers and writers Mário would mentor over the course of his life. A twenty-one-year-old student of Lamberto Baldi, an Italian who had first arrived in Brazil as the conductor of a touring opera company, Guarnieri (the son of an Italian barber-cum-musician) had no formal conservatory training and perhaps for this reason was an optimal candidate to compose an imperfect opera of "peculiar badness."[82] Pedro Malazarte (sometimes spelled Pedro Malasartes) was in many ways a predictable protagonist for such a work. A folk figure of Iberian extraction in a series of stories told throughout much of Brazil, he is a perpetual wanderer, an unscrupulous trickster who lives by his wits, and the very character Antonio Candido cites as a model for the novelistic malandro. The initial story of the cycle presents Pedro Malazarte and his older brother João, the two adult children of elderly parents who have fallen on hard times; to support the family João goes off to work as a hired hand on a plantation, where the avaricious *patrão* forces his employees to sign contracts impossible to fulfill and subjects them to cruel abuse. After his brother returns home empty-handed, Pedro exacts revenge on the plantation owner—in one tale he tricks the *patrão* into shooting his own wife—and all of the subsequent tales revolve around his outrageous schemes to make an easy buck. For the anthropologist Roberto da Matta, the character's restlessness is motivated by the desire to evade the relations of dependence and patronage in which the Brazilian worker is trapped. Malazarte refuses to treat his labor power as a commodity, relying instead on his own inalienable cunning. Yet rather than participating in any collective, systematic resistance, he operates as a highly individualized "man of the interstices who keeps returning to the existing order to exact his revenge."[83]

Mário was not the first to try corralling this rambling man within the confines of the theatrical stage. Graça Aranha, the honored elder of the Week of Modern Art and a man Mário held in low regard, had written a three-act drama called *Malazarte* in 1911, during his days as a diplomat in Paris. Staged by the famed symbolist director Lugné-Poe, the play universalizes the malandro as a Dionysus-like force who is by all indications white, and although the plot gives a nod to some indigenous myths, the use of formal, written Portuguese even in the dialogue marks its distance from the popular realm to which it alludes. In 1921 Heitor Villa-Lobos composed a three-act opera that appears to have been an adaptation of Aranha's play (though it was never performed and is now lost), which would also serve as the basis for an opera by Oscar Lorenzo Fernández composed in the early 1930s and debuted in Rio (in Italian) in 1941. Mário himself had begun to put his own spin on the character in a series of chronicles he wrote for the journal *América Brasileira* between 1923 and 1924. Here Malazarte forms part of a trio along with the author himself and a figure called Belazarte whose name translates as "fine art" (literally "beautiful art")—a dialectical counterpoint to Malazarte's bad, popular art. Belazarte has a constructive spirit and seeks to put down roots but frets that Brazilian civilization is no match for microbes or the forces of nature; his peripatetic antagonist responds that Brazilians are "proudly savage," and that this "innate and historical savagery of a people without traditions, without a past of twenty centuries of critical intelligence" should be the object of envy by Europeans.[84] Both positions, the author concludes, are "illusions" and "lies," and his own role is to mediate between them—though notably, it is Malazarte who lends his name to the title of the chronicles.

Mário's operatic *Pedro Malazarte* allegorizes this struggle to synthesize the *malas* and *belas artes*, not only at the level of the plot but also in its style and form. Instead of opting for the pomposity of grand opera, the Brazilian Parsifal chose to pursue his nationalist ambitions in the minor mode of comic opera, a genre that was originally performed in the interludes between more "serious" works and revolved around relatively ordinary characters rather than nobles and gods. In a letter to the poet Manuel Bandeira, he gleefully referred to the text as his *libretinho-merda*, or "shitty little libretto," and the simple, unpolished dialogue lends credence to his claim that he dashed it off in just two days.[85] The outlines of the plot come from one of the most commonly told episodes in the Malazarte cycle as related in a collection of folk tales from Minas Gerais published by Lindolfo Gomes in 1918.[86] In Gomes's version, the eponymous protagonist sets off on foot after the death of his father and stops at the first house he passes to ask for food, only to be turned away by an adulteress wife who is preparing a feast for her illicit suitor. Malazarte climbs onto the roof to eavesdrop on the woman and her black maid, and when the man of the house unexpectedly returns home he knocks on the door again, this time garnering an invitation to join them for a simple meal. Eager to partake of the elaborate dishes the wife has stashed in the cupboard, the vagabond claims his pet vulture has told him that the wife learned in advance of her husband's early return and has prepared a banquet in his honor. The guilty woman is forced to play along by revealing the hidden food, Malazarte gets his sumptuous meal, and the clueless husband is so taken with the magic powers of the vulture that he buys the animal for a generous sum.

Mário was at least nominally familiar with the Teatro del Murciélago, the short-lived collaboration between members of the estridentista avant-garde and artist-ethnographers who had worked under Manuel Gamio at Teotihuacán and later in Michoacán: from 1927 to 1929 Luis Quintanilla, the artistic director of the project, served as a secretary to the Mexican ambassador in Rio, and just a month after Mário dashed off the libretto for *Pedro Malazarte*, Quintanilla mentioned to him in a letter that the top theater impresario in Berlin had asked him to organize an "indigenous theater" similar to the Murciélago that would also include scenes from Brazil.[87] Like the Murciélago, Mário's opera has a self-consciously quaint and old-fashioned air, though its objectification and decontextualization of "primitive" traditions coincides with compositional practices typical of the avant-garde. Whereas the Mexican revue juxtaposed scenes of indigenous culture with urban tableaux, *Pedro Malazarte* integrates disparate elements from far-flung parts of Brazil into a single plot, enacting the same gesture of deregionalization found in the novel *Macunaíma*, though absent in its would-be operatic adaptation. (Significantly, however, Mário added the qualifier *texto regional* to the subtitle of the libretto in his second draft, explicitly acknowledging that his work of deregionalization remained unfinished.)[88] Although the source story comes from Minas Gerais, the dairy capital of Brazil and a region with a long history of slavery, Mário's libretto transposes the action to Santa Catarina, a state in the extreme south of country known for its large population of German and Austrian descent and its small, family-owned farms. The feast the wife prepares also defies any regionalist conception of authenticity: although the main dish is beans with beef tongue from Rio Grande do Sul (a cattle state bordering Santa Catarina), the more exotic treats later revealed include *doce de bacuri* (a dessert made with an Amazonian fruit), *tacacá com tucupi* (a manioc soup eaten in the Amazon), and the alcoholic *caninha de Ó*, or cachaça (made from sugarcane most likely grown elsewhere in Brazil). Even more significant, however, is the mishmash of musical genres indicated in the libretto. The chorus, sung by children playing outside the house, is a ciranda, the Amazonian dance-drama revolving around the death of a totemic bird about which Mário had written for the *Diário Nacional*. The young wife (a soprano) plays the guitar and sings a modinha, a type of sentimental love song common in both Portugal and Brazil, and her husband (a tenor) sings a toada, or simple regional tune. At one point Malazarte (a baritone) hums a maxixe, a genre that originated in Rio and mixes elements of polka with the Afro-Brazilian lundu, but his major recitative is an embolada, an improvised prose poem from northeastern Brazil:

> I am Malazarte. My part is in every part,
> And my land is in every land
> Where the saw of my art errs.

> Sou Malazarte, minha parte é em toda a parte
> Minha terra é em toda a terra
> Em que erra a serra da minha arte. (62)

The strange depiction of his art as a "saw" (*serra*) evokes associations of manual labor and construction, but this is immediately followed by the information that his art "errs" (*erra*), which can simultaneously mean to wander, to go morally astray, and to be wrong. In the source story collected by Lindolfo Gomes, the house symbolizes stability and fixity, though the adulterous intentions of the young wife threaten to undermine its role as a site of social reproduction; paradoxically, it is the wily wanderer who restores order (or at least its appearance) by passing off the feast as a sign of her devotion to her husband while selling him a "magic" animal able to divulge any future transgressions. Mário's opera gives this domestic drama a twist by racializing all of the characters and depicting each as "out of place." Gone is the black maid who lets Malazarte in on her mistress's secret. Gone too is the absent, anonymous adulterer: here the illicit lover is Malazarte himself. Although his provenance is never specified, Malazarte is described as *moreno*, an ambiguous term that can simply mean dark-haired but often means dark-skinned. Dressed with "foppish elegance" (*elegância almofadinha*), he cuts a striking figure in a short black jacket and long pants, casual shirt unbuttoned at the chest, white shoes, and jaunty checkered hat. The wife, clothed in a pink house dress and referred to as The Baiana, is a "legitimate *branca-rana*," or light-skinned mulatta, and her name identifies her as being from Bahia, a northeastern state known as the most "African" part of Brazil. Her "very blonde, ruddy" husband is called The German, though he turns out to be the son of immigrants (59). Of the trio, he is the most buffoonish in his velvet green tunic, yellow knickerbockers, yellow shoes, and velvet brown hat adorned with wildflowers. His absence is explained by a trip to the city to sell his agricultural wares, and his unexpected return is made all the more comic when Malazarte tumbles out of the rafters where he is hiding and lands at the alpine traveler's feet.

Here the specter of adultery not only calls into question the purity of lineage and property rights (since another man is enjoying the fruits of the breadwinner's labor); it also represents a potential deviation from the racial whitening promised by the union between the mulatta and her Teutonic mate. Strangely, however, this particular incarnation of Malazarte is uninterested in either sex or food. When he arrives he embraces the Baiana with indifference, and even after he wriggles his way into the German's good graces, he only pretends to eat great quantities of the delicacies served. So what does this shifty character really want?

In chapter 2 I noted that in his work on turn-of-the-century regionalism in the United States, Brad Evans traces a connection between the anthropological principle of cultural diffusion, which emphasized the "detachability" and circulation of cultural elements, and the contemporaneous vogue for local color fiction. The appeal of local color, he argues, has less to do with its roots in a particular people or place than with the "aura of dislocation" it accrues when it enters into circulation in an (inter)national art market.[89] As in *Macunaíma*, the deregionalization of culture in *Pedro Malazarte* mimics the logic of objectification and commodification endemic to mass culture. Despite its operatic trappings and rural setting, the libretto could also lend itself to an adaptation in the guise of comic opera's twentieth-century successor, teatro de revista, which featured many of the same singers and songs whose voices circulated on phonograph records. The absurd foreigner or country bumpkin (in this case the German) was a common figure in revistas, and the whitening of the historically black *baiana* seen in Mário's light-skinned mulatta was being performed around this time by the Portuguese-born Carmen Miranda, who was known for her exaggerated portrayal of the same figure. Shades of Eduardo das Neves and other recording and revista stars who styled themselves as malandros are also apparent in the dandyish Malazarte, who disdains physical labor but reaps the rewards of capital—not by making music for a talking machine, but by selling the story of a talking animal (in Mário's version, a black cat).

The sale of the cat marks Malazarte's complicity in the system he mocks. An incongruous act of bad faith, it compounds the negative feelings that undercut the hilarity of the action. Years earlier in his first chronicle about Malazarte, Mário had written that "happiness is a monotonous thing, full of itself, disappointing even, because it is an end, a 'goal.'"[90] Malazarte's constant movement instead evokes a sense of *saudade*—a nostalgic, melancholic longing for someone or something no longer present. In the opera he wears black because his father has recently died, and his devil-may-care demeanor is interrupted on occasion by moments of somber distraction. The other two characters share this sadness. At one point, the German wistfully notes that he has forgotten the songs of his father's homeland. The Baiana, too, is alienated from her roots (not a single culinary dish from her home region appears on her table), but she is most bitter about the domestic cage keeping her in (her) place. When her inebriated husband falls asleep at the table, she desperately begs Malazarte to take her with him, because although the German is a good man, "every single day in this house is the same as the one before." Hinting at her racial bond with the protagonist, she notes that while "the German has hair the color of corn, you have black hair like mine" (66). Malazarte tells her to stay with her husband, and his subsequent swindling of the man adds insult to injury, even if her tears lead him to lower his asking price. At the end of the opera, the couple stands at the door and slowly waves goodbye as the malandro moves on.

Behind him he leaves a vivid impression of absence and loss, just as phonograph recordings of popular performances "condemned to death" generate a sense of absence and loss. There is no phonograph in this picturesque little home, or any other sign of "modern" technology; yet it seems possible, perhaps even likely, that if this opera had been staged at the time, a hidden phonograph would have been used during those moments when the audience hears but does not see the children outside, dancing the ciranda and singing of the death of the totemic bird.[91] In the creation of a Brazilian culture the flesh must be sacrificed, though the tradition is resurrected in song.

A Necessary Tradition

Mário gave his "shitty little libretto" to Camargo Guarnieri immediately after finishing the draft, without bothering to edit it. The young composer sat with it for a while but concluded he was not yet up to the task. He came to the same conclusion when he went back to it three years later, and so over the course of 1931 he studied the libretto and all the relevant musical genres, until in the very first days of 1932 he threw himself into the project and completed the score in just over a month.[92] Guarnieri was still relatively unknown, and not until early in 1935 was the orchestral overture to *Pedro Malazarte* publicly performed; the full score was first heard in public at the opera's debut in Rio in 1952, seven years after Mário's death, and again in 1959. Reviews were mixed: one deemed it a "failed," "frustrated opera," though another considered it charming, if hardly a masterpiece.[93] One of Mário's other collaborations from this period achieved more success: Francisco Mignone's *Maracatú do Chico-Rei*, inspired by his outline for an operatic dance about a legendary slave who rose to become a mine owner, was composed in 1933 and debuted in Rio the following year. The piece was never choreographed, however, and so the dramatic element remained unrealized. A decade later Mário would write his second and last libretto, *O café*, with Mignone in mind, but the composer was unable to finish the music before Mário's death in 1945.

The subject of this second opera—the collapse of the coffee economy—points to the momentous changes that occurred during the handful of years when Guarnieri was sitting on the libretto for *Pedro Malazarte*. The international crisis prompted by the stock market crash on Wall Street not only brought an end to the Export Age; it also set the stage for the Revolution of 1930 and the rise of Getúlio Vargas. Like many other members of the Partido Democrático, Mário was cautiously optimistic that this turn of events would foster the development of a national culture and rein in the regional oligarchies that had ruled the republic. A discouraging experience assisting his friend Luciano Gallet in an effort to reform the National Institute of Music was among the factors that led his enthusiasm to wane, and when the Partido Democrático joined forces with the Partido Republicano Paulista in a revolt against the new central government, Mário lent his support.[94] The paulistas were defeated in the Constitutionalist Revolution of 1932, but they managed to regain some of the privileges the region had lost. Three years later Paulo Duarte led several other members of the now-defunct Partido Democrático in creating a municipal Department of Culture and undertaking a multifaceted effort to "democratize" access to "culture"—a project that would be brought to a halt after the declaration of the Estado Novo dictatorship at the end of 1937.[95] Mário was asked to take the helm of the Department of Culture, Sérgio Milliet became head of its Division of Historical and Social Documentation, and Paulo Ribeiro de Magalhães was assigned to Theater and Cinema. Mário lost his pipeline to the Victor company (which had become RCA Victor amid a great wave of mergers in the late 1920s and 1930s), but with the new resources at his disposal he established the first public audio archive in Brazil—a collection including European classical music, the works of Brazilian composers, and ethnographic recordings such as the 1,299 tracks collected by a team of four researchers he sent out on a "folkloric mission" to the hinterlands of the Northeast.[96]

Thirteen years after the Week of Modern Art, when Mário cut his poetry reading short and fled the stage, he became the man who (in conjunction with Magalhães) oversaw programming at the Theatro Municipal. One of his first decisions was to create a standing orchestra and appoint Camargo Guarnieri as its director, a move that led to the first performances of the composer's major works. Throughout his three years in office he worked to open up the theater to nonelite audiences by offering free concerts of classical music and the works of Brazilian composers, among them Guarnieri and Mignone.[97] Yet there is no indication he ever attempted to see his own opera performed.

Why write an opera destined for the archive rather than the stage? The opposition is familiar, and by now has been subjected to thorough critique: whereas archives are associated with permanence, stability, and material remains, performance is imagined in terms of ephemerality, disappearance, and loss. In her attempt to destabilize this opposition, Rebecca Schneider emphasizes the way "the archive itself becomes a social *performance* of retroaction. The archive performs the institution of disappearance, with object remains as indices of disappearance and with performance as given to disappear."[98] Mário was obsessed with archiving not only songs, but also his own activities, and his voluminous archive (now partially digitized) holds his handwritten text of *Pedro Malazarte* as well as two typed copies. Part of the issue may have been logistics, because while he managed to organize a standing choir and orchestra during his three years with the Department of Culture, coordinating an opera production takes time. Still, as his casually disparaging reference to his libretto suggests, he seems to have thought of it from the first as a mere prompt for the production of music. Onstage he would have had to clarify certain ambiguities, such as Malazarte's physiognomy; the allusions to racial mixture might have acquired a political edge and provoked dissension among an operatic audience; and perhaps its affinity with commercial theatrical revues would have become more readily apparent. If Malazarte uses his wiles to avoid lending his body to the production of capital for another, Mário's disinclination toward performance also has to do with the desire to maintain the possibility of an alternative mode of deregionalization and nationalization, one independent from the circulation of international capital. Deterritorialized and integrated into the increasingly "outdated" genre of opera, his "dying" traditions are restaged as the "bygone images and gestures" Adorno described, and the aura of the archive cloaks them in a sense of nostalgia or *saudade* for a foundational performance that never occurred.

But Mário knew that the creation of a national culture was dependent on more than unfinished operas and experimental novels. In 1939, at a point when the major multinational recording companies had long since consolidated, he attended an annual song contest sponsored by the music industry in the lead-up to Carnaval. More than 300,000 people, "from the whiter-than-white well-to-do, to stray mulattas and lanky malandros" (desde a granfinagem mais de branco até as mulatas desgarradas e os malandros esguios), streamed into a fairground in Rio over several days to hear the new releases performed live and cast their votes for the hits.[99] In reflecting on the experience, he drops the glib irony to which he was prone and comes as close as he ever did to laying it on the line. On the one hand, he says, samba has become a species of "submusic"—"flesh to feed radios and discs, an element of romance and commercial interest with which factories, businesses, and singers sustain themselves, stirring up the cheap sensuality of an entranced public" (281). Yet he also acknowledges, and goes on to describe, how beautiful it was to see such a range of Brazilians gathered, all at the same time and in the same place, and all so passionate over the same thing. With unabashed romanticism, he reflects on the melodic characteristics responsible for the melancholic quality of *samba do morro*, the samba from the hillside favelas that can still on occasion be heard. "Such is the current sadness of samba," he concludes, though within a few years this could all change, "because all urban music . . . is imminently unstable and transforms easily, like things that have no basis in a necessary tradition." He pauses for a beat, takes a paragraph break, and then ends on an ambivalent note: "And, in that case, our national character, undefined, shot through with internationalisms and fatal foreign influences, would be that necessary tradition" (282).

Despite its wistful tone, this is not so far from what Roberto Schwarz would make explicit decades later in his analysis of ideas out of place: "Brazilian" culture owed its existence to the same forces of international capital that condemned it to remaining incomplete.

Chapter 6

✦

Total Theater and Missing Pieces

During the early days of 2005 a perplexing rumor began to wind its way through the artistic community in São Paulo. For over two decades José (Zé) Celso, the notorious director of an avant-garde theater company now nearly half a century old, had waged a relentless campaign against the even more notorious Sílvio Santos, a TV variety show host and entrepreneur who was systematically buying up the historic neighborhood of Bixiga. In interviews Celso stressed that the land where Bixiga stood had once been inhabited by Tupi Indians; during the colonial period it served as a refuge for run-away slaves, and in 1961, when Teatro Oficina built its first theater, it was still a working-class district made up of descendants of Italian immigrants. A few years later the theater was destroyed by fire, and in its place the group constructed a theater in the round with a revolving stage, where in 1967 it created history of its own with its controversial production of *O rei da vela* (The Candle King), a never-performed play from the early 1930s by Oswald de Andrade that raised the ire of the military dictatorship and helped spark the counterculture movement known as Tropicália. By 1979, Teatro Oficina had outgrown this structure, and so Celso enlisted the modernist architect Lina Bo Bardi to design a new corridor-like addition resembling an alleyway or a narrow city block. This building was now protected by its status as a national historic landmark. Yet the theater, one of several in the area, found itself hemmed in on all sides by properties belonging to Grupo Sílvio Santos, a vast conglomerate with interests in banking, agribusiness, cosmetics, hotels, and media whose owner was eager to further diversify its portfolio by build-ing a vast shopping and entertainment complex—right on the doorstep of Teatro Oficina.

Imagine, then, the shock of Celso's supporters when the wizened rebel announced he had cut a deal: Mr. Santos would build his megamall, but he would also fund the construction of a thousand-seat "stadium theater" inspired by Walter Gropius's 1927 design for the TotalTheater in Weimar, complete with a ceiling made of retractable movie screens opening up to the tropical sky. Here, in the heart of Bixiga, Teatro Oficina would fulfill its direc-tor's dream of developing a new mass dramaturgical form based on Oswald de Andrade's *O homem e o cavalo* (Man and the Horse)—another unper-formed play from the 1930s, described by Celso as the "total surmounting" of Russian constructivism "blended with the Great Rituals that shape the Brazilian Mixed Races culture."[1] The deal between Celso and Santos quickly collapsed, and it is possible the whole thing was just another "performance." In an interview at the time, however, Celso betrayed no hint of irony. After decades of neoliberalism and defunding of the arts, the country was on the cusp of an economic and cultural renaissance with the socialist president Lula at the helm, the Tropicalist musician Gil Gilberto was the new minister of culture, and Brazil was at the forefront of a movement to create "another kind of capitalism . . . a revolution within capitalism itself [*uma revolução no próprio capitalismo*]." Imperialism still had to be defeated, as the U.S. inva-sion of Afghanistan and Iraq showed. But in Celso's ecstatic vision, "it is only through a total cultural experience, an experience that is not just cerebral but of the body and lived, the experience of another dimension of the individual human and collective human body—all of which the stadium can provide—that this revolution will be achieved."[2]

This specter of a "total," radically transformative performance dogs almost every discussion of and attempt to create "avant-garde" theater, and it shadows the very title of this book. In the opening scene of the first chap-ter, José Vasconcelos surveys a rehearsal for the inauguration of a "theater stadium" far more immense than anything Zé Celso could ever hope to construct (even with a little help from corporate capital). Using strikingly similar language, the founding director of the Secretariat of Public Educa-tion in Mexico also evoked the idea of a synesthetic experience in which the division between mind and body blurs and all the races converge as actors and audience become one. The actual performance he oversaw at the stadium's inauguration fell far short of this goal, as he well knew; but even so, mass theater had its historical moment in Mexico, and its intimate association with state power has tended to make it a foil for subsequent efforts to define the avant-garde. No such moment ever occurred in Bra-zil. Only in the 1960s did a new avant-garde generation make a push to create a theatrical performance so "total" it would retroactively subsume the stage that the modernista movement had been unable to transform and simultaneously catapult the country into the front ranks of the international avant-garde. *O rei da vela* was raucous and irreverent, and Teatro Ofici-na's production spilled off its revolving stage and aggressively assaulted the spectators' senses. But a far greater challenge remained: the first theatrical text Oswald de Andrade wrote after his turn to radical politics, *O homem e o cavalo* was a shocking, colossal "spectacle" that might have changed the course of (avant-garde) history had its performance not been repressed by the law. Celso first organized a dramatic reading with 150 participants in 1985, the year the military dictatorship came to an end; yet despite his periodic efforts to stage the piece, he and others continue to deem its performance incomplete.

In his introduction to the 1990 edition of O *homem e o cavalo*, the eminent theater critic Sábato Magaldi echoed the view already popularized by Celso when he wrote that the play represented Oswald de Andrade's most ambitious attempt to create a "total theater"—a visionary project that, "by virtue of being at the forefront of its era, hardly even seems to belong to the reality of Brazilian theater."[3] From this vantage point, Oswald's drama appears to be the harbinger of a theatrical revolution that never made it across the Atlantic, the missing piece of a movement that shook the aesthetic ground of literature, music, architecture, and visual art but left the nineteenth-century stage intact. Magaldi, Zé Celso, and others insist that Oswald's reputed plan for a "stadium theater" capable of closing the gap between art and action was of a piece with Max Reinhardt's expressionist experiments, the Bauhaus TotalTheater project, Vladimir Mayakovsky and Vsevolod Meyerhold's constructivist montages, and the theater of cruelty imagined (if never enacted) by Antonin Artaud. Invoking a discourse endemic to critical accounts of the European and Euro-American avant-garde, they celebrate O *homem* as a valiant effort to mobilize the masses by blending popular performance traditions with the erudite genres of the elite and opening up the hallowed halls of bourgeois theater to new artistic media such as film to create a performance that would be nothing less than "total."

This chapter reverses the terms of such interpretations by examining the ideal of total theater through the optic of Oswald de Andrade's ill-fated spectacle and the events leading up to its nonperformance. Discussions of total theater almost invariably start by tracing a genealogy of the phenomenon, and this one is no exception: after a brief reflection on its importance for more recent iterations of the avant-garde, I retread the well-worn trajectory of artists and projects associated with this nebulous ideal in order to tell a different story of diverse and often divergent attempts to reconfigure the agency of art in relation to the new technologies of mass culture, mass political movements, and the expanding powers of the modern state. These issues came to a head in the 1930s, not only in Europe but also in Brazil, where the "Revolution" of 1930 led to the rise of Getúlio Vargas and deepened the ideological rifts among artists identified with the modernista movement; yet unlike in the Old World, factors including race, the relative weakness of state institutions, and the limitations of capital on the semi-periphery continued to stand in the way of avant-garde theater. Following my exploration of this absence and its legacy, I delve into the archives of the political police and make recourse to other ephemera in order to reconstruct the story of the "modern artists' club" where O *homem e o cavalo* had its genesis. Only then, after telling the tale of the dramatic shutdown of the club's experimental stage, do I venture a reading of Oswald's stymied "spectacle."

Pushing back against the total theater narrative, I argue that this awkward, obstreperous work is more akin to Walter Benjamin's interpretation of the Trauerspiel.

Benjamin published his rejected dissertation on the Baroque Trauerspiel, or "mourning play," only a handful of years before *O homem e o cavalo* failed to appear onstage. Like total theater, the Trauerspiel of the late sixteenth and early seventeenth centuries was imagined as stylistically eclectic and geographically expansive in scope; in fact, later German critics regarded Shakespeare and Calderón de la Barca as its most brilliant exponents while shrinking in embarrassment from the bombastic and overly extravagant examples of their compatriots, whose texts were so unwieldy it was assumed they were only intended to be read. Benjamin disagreed, and he insisted that far from being a remake of Greek tragedy (as his predecessors had claimed), the Trauerspiel should be understood as an attempt to wrest a secular drama out of the medieval mystery pageants and reenactments of the Passion of Christ staged by the Jesuit evangelists. In the works of the German dramatists this process remained uneven and incomplete: unable to transcend the mundane materiality of the stage and resolve the vertiginous contradictions of the Baroque with a stunning apotheosis, the minor masters of Saxony and Silesia were embarrassingly unsuccessful in the quest to create a modern-day miracle through the power of spectacle. Yet in failing to overcome the condition of immanence, their hyperbolic, strangely morbid plays also remain true to a certain "allegorical intuition" characteristic of the era; in them, the exuberant pomp of baroque art betrays its own transience and lack of freedom, and "the false appearance of totality is extinguished."[4]

Although Benjamin neglects to mention it, the Passion plays he cites as sources for the Trauerspiel were also important in the colonization and Christianization of the New World—a fact that partly explains why *O homem e o cavalo* adopts this same genre as a model. But Oswald de Andrade (like Benjamin) was not only concerned with the dramatic specters of centuries past: he also had his sights set on the changing politics of mass culture and the moves toward what the legal scholar Carl Schmitt would theorize as the "total state." Contrary to Zé Celso and others who rescued this play from oblivion, I argue that in bringing the aesthetic paradigm of total theater head-to-head with a historical narrative of imperialism, *O homem e o cavalo* redeploys many of the formal and thematic traits associated with the avant-garde in order to posit a very different model of art—one premised on the work's incompletion and its incompatibility with a "revolution within capitalism itself." Benjamin argued for the world-historical significance of a group of ungainly, overwrought plays by forgotten writers far from the main metropoles of international empire and commerce; in a similar spirit, this final chapter suggests that the best place to begin to revise the vexed legacy of total theater might be in a country where what is most notable about it is the missing pieces.

Making Theater "Total" / Theatricalizing Totality

For months, over the summer and fall of 1933, the unusual cross-section of intellectuals, entertainers, and political instigators who frequented a certain "club for modern artists" in São Paulo had observed preparations for the new Teatro da Experiência, a project its participants trumpeted as the most daring theater experiment the country had yet seen. On the program for the opening night was *O homem e o cavalo*, a "Spectacle in Nine Tableaux" by Oswald de Andrade. It was an ambitious undertaking for a group of amateurs: the dramatic action ranged from St. Peter's pearly gates to a Soviet tribunal, while its huge cast of characters included Cleopatra, talking horses, Madame Jesus, the Voice of Stalin, Fu Manchu, and a Poet-Soldier who casually announces Hitler's imminent genocide of the Jews. As fate would have it, the author failed to finish the script in time, and the theater made its debut with *O bailado do deus morto* (Dance of the Dead God), a ritualistic drama created by the architect and artist Flávio de Carvalho in collaboration with the samba composer Henricão and performed by an almost entirely black cast. (Only the titular dead god was white.) On November 16, 1933, after an entire battalion of police officers showed up uninvited for the third performance, the premises were shut down and placed under armed guard. *O homem e o cavalo* never made its debut, and the might-have-been revolutionary masses never got their chance to witness the grand spectacle of world history on a small São Paulo stage.

What exactly did they miss?

In identifying what would and should have occurred as a singular act of "total theater," latter-day critics and directors not only claim Oswald's work as a missing link to the international avant-garde of its own era but also conscript it as a predecessor to the experiments of subsequent artists who claim the avant-garde mantle. The language of totality was a recurring motif among the "historical" avant-gardes, but only in the 1960s did the term "total theater" gain momentum as a way of lending coherence to disparate projects and creating continuity in the avant-garde tradition of rupture. The concept was embraced by groups such as the Living Theater, which collaborated with Teatro Oficina during an extended sojourn in Brazil in 1970–1971 (cut short by its members' incarceration and eventual deportation): invoking the legacy of Artaud, the Living Theater took its act into the favelas as part of its effort to push theater beyond its limit to the point where it became "life."[5] According to the performance studies guru Richard Schechner, figures such as Jerzy Grotowski, Richard Foreman, Laurie Anderson, and the Mabou Mimes fulfilled the dream of total theater—a dream first articulated by Richard Wagner—by sidelining the text and dissolving all distinctions among media and arts.[6] More recently, it has become a buzzword in scholarly work on African theater, and figures such as the Chinese expat and Nobel laureate Gao Xingjian have also used the phrase as a means of framing their own incorporation of non-European (often ritualistic) performance traditions into the trajectory of the international avant-garde.[7]

But if the desire for intercultural communication represents one vector of total theater, another is its association with the drive for national sovereignty. Like Schechner, most who invoke the idea trace it back to the Wagnerian Gesamtkunstwerk, a "total work of art" in which music, poetry, and dance were imagined as merging to form an organic unity. Wagner's "theater of the future" arose out of the convergence of nationalism and popular politics that George Mosse has called the "nationalization of the masses"—a process that "transformed political action into a drama supposedly shared by the people itself"[8]—and its development followed the twists and turns this phenomenon took, as the composer joined the failed democratic-republican revolution of 1848–1849 and then threw his weight behind the movement of conservative nationalism that culminated in the establishment of the German Empire in 1871. Man's mind, Wagner warned, had been "fragmented" by the mechanization and commodification of modern life; his own Völkisch productions at the Bayreuth Festspielhaus (which had been liberated from the constraints of the market by royal patronage) were designed to heal these rifts by crafting absorptive illusions through the use of elaborate stage mechanics, all carefully concealed so that "the public, that representation of daily life, forgets the confines of the auditorium, and lives and breathes now only in the artwork, which seems to it as Life itself, and on the stage, which seems the wide expanse of the whole World."[9]

In his humbler moments (which were rare) Wagner conceded that his works never achieved such expansive aims. Still, in the decades following his death, the *idea* of the Gesamtkunstwerk quickly breached the bounds of the theater as figures such as Mallarmé, Schoenberg, and Kandinsky sought to turn cinema, painting, poetry, sculpture, architecture, music, and even the novel into an arch-medium for the total work of art.[10] Often, it is said to find its most fertile ground at the cusp of new media technologies: Max Horkheimer and Theodor Adorno derided television as a synthesis of radio and film that would take the commodification of culture already at work in Wagnerian opera to an apocalyptic level, and recent genealogies of the Gesamtkunstwerk point to videogames and virtual reality as its latest frontier.[11] But theater has always been its ground zero—the site where the drive to integrate all elements of production and reception has to contend with the agency of actors and the obstacle of a physical and/or conceptual stage. In Russia, the triumph of the Bolshevik Revolution in 1917 initially opened up new arenas of action for formal experimentalism: mass dramas and reenactments such as *The Mystery of Freed Labor* and *The Storming of the Winter Palace* were performed by thousands on the streets, while the playwright/director duo of Mayakovsky and Meyerhold sought to create an "October in the theater" by incorporating elements of the circus, commedia dell'arte, and medieval mystery pageants into the production of futurist-inflected plays such as *Mystery-Bouffe*, a farce about the proletariat's rise to power. Meyerhold's protégé Sergei Eisenstein staged Sergei Tretyakov's *Gas Masks* in a gasworks factory, where the "element of actuality" became so palpable that, as the director later stated, it "finally had to leave an art where it could not command" and pushed him over the brink, "through theater to cinema" (and eventually on to "the phase of socialist realism").[12]

All of these artists were influenced by Wagner, but none used the term "total theater" on a consistent basis (as a matter of fact, neither did Wagner), and the drive to assimilate them into a single teleological tradition overlooks the fact that not all "totalities" are alike: competing conceptions of totality proliferated among the European avant-gardes, and even similar ideas and techniques had different implications depending on the offstage reality in which they were meant to intervene. In France, Antonin Artaud envisioned his metaphysical theater of cruelty as a "total spectacle" that would "make space speak," though he was notoriously unsuccessful in bringing his projects to fruition.[13] A similar fate befell the TotalTheater project developed during the late 1920s in Weimar Germany by the director Erwin Piscator and members of the Bauhaus school—the utopic plan that inspired Zé Celso's as-yet-to-be-realized celluloid stadium in São Paulo. The Bauhaus's emphasis on craft and design was a socialist-inspired attempt to wed functionalism and beauty, but it also gave the school a pipeline to Weimar's bourgeoning industrial class and thus a degree of autonomy from unreliable state funding. Piscator's "proletarian theater" drew on elements of popular musical revues, the mass pageantry of early Soviet theater, and technological innovations including mobile footways and stages, loudspeakers, and film projections. A key component was the reconfiguration of theatrical space: architect Walter Gropius drew up plans for a monumental hall for two thousand spectators seated on movable blocks of chairs, an arrangement intended to facilitate performances that would spread throughout the entire auditorium and incorporate the spectators. Like its predecessor, this radicalized version of the Gesamtkunstwerk was conceived as an organic whole, though its constitutive elements were manifestly mechanical and the object of its impact was the intellect; according to Piscator, his goal was to "dematerialize the stage by means of a total technique, to make it a light and flexible instrument destined to serve mind and not sentimentality."[14] Jeffrey T. Schnapp explains that for Piscator, "the revolution was embedded somewhere in the real itself. The theater's task was simply to strip away all externals and to place that rough and ready reality directly onstage." Totality, in other words, meant an immediately perceptible "totality of effect."[15]

The 1929 stock market crash put a halt to construction plans, and as the 1930s wore on TotalTheater became an ever more fraught strategy for the Left. Even before Hitler became chancellor in 1933, the Nazis laid claim to the legacy of Wagner and the infrastructure of civic performance to develop their own mass rituals, open-air theaters, and choreographed parades—aspects of the "aestheticization of the political" that Benjamin identified as the modus operandi of fascism. Schnapp traces the TotalTheater model's migration to Italy, where it was embraced as kindred in spirit to Mussolini's proposed "theater of masses," and as theoretical confirmation of futurist experiments as well as state-sponsored traveling pageants involving hundreds of performers and up to fifteen thousand spectators. His narrative ends in Rome in October 1934 at a conference held by the Italian Academy and attended by such diverse figures as Edward Gordon Craig, Jacques Copeau, Alexander Tairov, Filippo Marinetti, W. B. Yeats, and the special guest, Walter Gropius himself, all speaking a shared language of total theatricality. Noting the "ideological drift and blurring" that facilitated surprising "cultural convergences" across national boundaries (83), Schnapp suggests that artists on opposite sides of the political divide responded to a perceived crisis of bourgeois theater by creating new forms of mass spectacle that fueled what he calls a "modernist politics of immediacy" (89).

Schnapp attributes the search for "total" aesthetic solutions to a postwar milieu in which religion was on the wane and the new technologies of war and peace were calling humanist assumptions into question. As he might also agree, however, these factors were in turn linked to the instability of the global market as well as a shift in the dynamics of capital accumulation marked by the rise of the United States as an axis of economic power. In Brazil, as the two previous chapters detailed, the emergence of the modernista vanguard took place on a stage set by the coffee export boom of the late nineteenth and early twentieth centuries, which transformed the city of São Paulo and its surroundings into a mecca for immigrants from Italy and other countries suffering the fallout from their own economic adjustments. The storied Week of Modern Art in February 1922 was held in the same opera house where the local elite customarily converged—a decision that in hindsight accentuates the ambivalence of the artists' break with the past and the absence of theater (experimental or otherwise) among the arts on display. For many of the participants, Wagner was not a specter to be shaken or surpassed but a sign of what (despite advances in the other arts) Brazil had never achieved: almost all the operas and singers who performed at the Theatro Municipal came from Europe, and the one famous Brazilian opera composer from the nineteenth century had debuted his foundational romance about white-settler-on-indigenous love in Milan. Like the stark divides of class, region, and race, these cultural displacements were imposing obstacles to any illusion of immediacy or totality; so too was the lack of institutional support for culture, as Mário de Andrade and others argued as modernismo splintered into opposing factions and its "heroic" first decade came to a close.

This would begin to change after the Wall Street debacle triggered the near-collapse of the coffee economy and the weak republic gave way to the Revolution of 1930. Prompted by the breakdown of the "coffee with milk" alliance between the elites of São Paulo and Minas Gerais, the revolution was a bloodless coup d'état led by military officials who ousted the president Washington Luís (a former governor of São Paulo) and prevented the inauguration of the president-elect (another paulista) before handing over power to Getúlio Vargas, an opposition candidate from the southern state of Rio Grande do Sul. Vargas set up a provisional government and immediately made moves to rein in the regional oligarchies by replacing state governors with federally appointed *interventores*—one of many infringements on the privileges São Paulo had come to acquire that led its squabbling elites and some sectors of the middle class to join forces in the Constitutionalist Revolution of 1932.[16] In response Vargas agreed to convoke a constituent assembly to draft a new constitution, which was ratified in 1934. Legal order, however, would prove to be short-lived: in 1935, following a failed "communist conspiracy," the state suspended all civil liberties, and in 1937 Vargas declared the Estado Novo, a corporatist dictatorship that lasted until shortly after World War II.[17]

More than five decades after his second stint in office ended with his suicide in the face of a military coup, Vargas is still an object of collective ambivalence and even affection. Although he appealed primarily to the middle class and emerging sectors of business and industry, he also granted women the right to vote and instituted the first workplace protections as well as social security and retirement pensions; on a less progressive note, he subordinated trade unions to the authority of the state, restricted the employment of nonnative Brazilians, and sponsored the torture of political opponents by the secret police. During a few key years in the mid-1930s his government was cordial with Mussolini and Hitler and notably chummy with the Ação Integralista Brasileira, the fascist party founded by the modernista poet Plínio Salgado in 1932, though it eventually curtailed the actions of the Integralists and the numerous fascist immigrant organizations, and the need to remain on good terms with the United States eventually led Brazil to support the Allies in World War II. Nothing like the sweeping cultural reforms in Mexico was ever on the table, and the state's investment in education remained limited; yet in other areas, as the historian Daryle Williams has shown, it "made cultural management its official business" by creating an extensive network of patronage and crafting new regulatory legislation.[18] In 1933 the federal government became the official sponsor of Rio's annual Carnaval parade, and it regularly paid popular musicians to act as its unofficial publicists. Meanwhile modernista artists of all political stripes were given positions in the new Ministry of Education, while government agencies generated outwardly apolitical, cultural journals that drew in writers who had long lamented the dearth of forums for their work.[19] In a speech delivered in 1951, Vargas aptly summed up the avant-garde myth his government had helped create, claiming that "the collective forces that provoked the revolutionary modernist movement in Brazilian literature . . . were the same ones that precipitated the victorious Revolution of 1930 in the social and political field."[20] The state recast modernismo's experimental ethic as an authentic expression of the popular and prescient precursor to political change while also circumscribing the movement to the literary realm so as to harness its iconoclastic edge.

Oswald de Andrade belonged to the landowning elite of São Paulo, but like a number of other dissident members of his class, he responded to the decline of the coffee economy and the growing political polarization by veering to the left. In 1931 he joined the Brazilian Communist Party, and along with his new wife Patrícia Galvão (Pagu), he launched a journal called *O Homem do Povo* (Man of the People), which lasted for eight issues before being censored by the police. Two years later the erstwhile dandy bid a public adieu to his past in the preface to his experimental novel *Serafim Ponte Grande*, completed in 1928 but left unpublished until 1933. In the brief text, he lambastes modernista bohemians for masquerading as agents of social revolution, recalling that in the heady environment of the 1920s, "the modernist movement, culminating in the anthropophagic plague, seemed to indicate an advanced phenomenon. . . . It even looked like the coffee boom might set the semicolony's nouveau riche literature on a level with costly imperialistic surrealisms."[21] Those illusions crumbled in the face of the economic crisis, "just as almost all Brazilian 'vanguardist' literature crumbled, being provincial and suspect if not extremely impoverished and reactionary" (5).

The writer would later qualify this harsh judgment. Yet it would be a mistake to interpret it as a rejection of stylistic experimentation as such, or to dismiss it, as Fernando J. Rosenberg does, as a "theatrical self-accusatory gesture" that "paradoxically seems to save Oswald from any real subjective involvement."[22] This choice of words hints at the fact that Rosenberg's own advocacy of a specifically literary "cosmopolitanism" is in part a disciplinary defense against what Loren Kruger calls the "impure autonomy" of theater.[23] As an art that requires the presence of a collective audience, as well as a social and material space in which to perform, theater presents greater obstacles to modes of interpretation that attribute a progressive function to works of art on the sole basis of their symbolic *representation* of social relations. In fact, the true aim of Oswald's critique is what Herbert Marcuse would refer to only a few years later as the "affirmative" nature of bourgeois culture, which often entertains the possibility of an alternative to the existing order but ultimately legitimates the status quo by offering "spiritual" progress and "ethical" freedom as consolation for oppression and material lack.[24] The author derides his own novel for proposing the facile solution of "transnational nudism" to the structural inequalities produced by economic imperialism and announces that, having tired of being an "upper-class clown," he will henceforth aspire to be, "if nothing else, a circus roustabout in the Proletarian Revolution"[25]—a kind of stagehand, in other words, who would rearrange the set and fashion props to facilitate the working class in performing its own creative feats in the political ring.

As was true of other Latin American avant-gardists during the 1930s, Oswald's political radicalization did in fact prompt a turn to theater. In an article published in 1935, the author explains that O *homem e o cavalo*, his first full-length play in Portuguese, "is a piece of high fantasy in which I place man in the transition—between the war horse and turf horse (bourgeois society) and horsepower (socialist society)." For this reason, it was "a book of interest to the masses."[26] Yet the limited print run and low literacy rates in Brazil at this time most likely circumscribed its audience to a small group of intellectuals. His plays O *rei da vela* (The Candle King, 1934) and *A morta* (The Dead Woman, 1937) met a similar fate.[27] It was not until 1967 that Teatro Oficina's landmark staging of O *rei da vela* became a flashpoint in the birth of Tropicália, whose unofficial spokesman Caetano Veloso adopted Oswald's notion of anthropophagy as a paradigm for the movement's cannibalizations of Brazilian popular culture, avant-garde stylistics, and mass media pop. According to the director Zé Celso, O *rei da vela* had been written under one "modernizing dictatorship" and was being staged under another more than thirty years later; his task, then, was to create a "revolution in form and content to express a non-revolution," jumbling the styles and icons of past and present in a cynical pageant of the "non-history" of Brazil. The military coup of 1964 had unmasked the impotence of the populist politics pedaled by the institutionalized Left, so Celso would change the rules of the game by psychically obliterating those who seemed to be blocking theater's access to the masses: its middle-class audiences. In his words, "If we take this public as a whole, the only way of enacting an efficacious political process upon it lies in the destruction of all its defense mechanisms, all its Manichean and historicist justifications—even when they are based on Gramsci, Lukács, and others. It is about putting it [the audience] in its place, reducing it to zero."[28] A few critics were more circumspect, pointing out that in pursuing this scorched-earth approach Oficina was also being drawn into the belly of the beast; after all, the production was the first in the company's nine-year history to be subsidized by the state.[29]

Celso and others insisted such concessions were necessary to make innovative theater under the current conditions. Furthermore, hidden strings were irrelevant since the political impact of the play's performative transgressions derived directly from what they characterized as Oswald's own aesthetic: a "supertheatricality, the overcoming of even Brechtian rationalism by means of a theatrical art that is a synthesis of all the arts and non-arts, the circus, show, revue theater, etc."[30] Teatro Oficina brought the kitsch of Carmen Miranda and tacky TV personality Chacrinha onto the stage and sent the play's outlandish characters spilling over into the audience in a calculated attack on the spectators' senses inspired by the "cruelty" of Artaud. Following acclaimed tours of Brazil the show played at international festivals in Florence and Nancy, and it opened in Paris on May 10, 1968—the very evening of the legendary Night of the Barricades, the violent battle between student strikers and police that mobilized the Parisian public and led to a real, would-be revolution. Celebrated as the moment when Brazil's theatrical vanguard finally came into its own, *O rei da vela*'s deferred debut established Oswald's reputation as a playwright who, as one of the principal actors wrote, "opens a path toward a national theater, a total theater, that is only now properly understood."[31]

But on what grounds is Oswald's theater identified as the missing piece of a national avant-garde? There are surprisingly few detailed analyses of the texts or the events surrounding their nonperformance—though perhaps this is not so surprising, given that total theater aims to render both text and stage obsolete. Instead, the most common touchstone for such claims is a fictional dialogue by Oswald published in a daily newspaper in 1943.[32] "Do teatro, que é bom" begins with an unnamed speaker's defense of an amateur group engaged in what his partner derisively refers to as "chamber theater." Speaker number one insists that such efforts should be applauded, if for no other reason than that "they give us a break from the cinema, that growing stupidification by means of the screen with which the United States flooded the world in order to take it over without resistance." Voicing an Adorno-esque critique of the culture industry, he scoffs that "when they spoke against the opium of the people, they should have made it plural and added cinema and soccer" (85). His interlocutor, however, takes issue with this extrapolation from Marx and contends that what is needed is a "theater of shock," a "stadium theater" that, along with radio, the sports arena, and the silver screen, will educate and entertain the growing masses. Tracing the history of theater from its inception in ancient Greece, he claims that in the nineteenth century, with the rise of bourgeois individualism, what was lost was "the religious character of the theater, the collective festival, festival of the masses, festival of the people" (90). His list of exemplary figures includes Ibsen, Jarry, Cocteau, and in particular Meyerhold, whose "ethic of spectacle" is lauded as the pinnacle of modern theater. This leads into a discussion of "the war-like image of fascism" cultivated by the acolytes of Stalin and "the petty-bourgeoisie of Mussolini, nursed by bureaucracy and the confessional, wanting to live dangerously in a sensational release of inhibitions" (91–92). His proposed antidote to this attack on the "Hegelian progression of the spirit" is not primarily a playwright (though Oswald may have in mind his famous Pageant of the Paterson Strike): it is the journalist and globetrotting radical John Reed. The text concludes with the first speaker, who has long since tempered his enthusiastic embrace of chamber theater, declaring that "John Reed's soldier fulfilled his mission on the living stage of contemporary history" (92). Art and history merge, onstage and offstage become one, and thesis and antithesis are resolved in the total transformation of reality.

Or are they? The dialogue's self-mocking tone calls into question the ease with which the final synthesis is achieved, while the references to contemporary political realities hint at a more serious subtext: Oswald, always unorthodox, had distanced himself from the Communist Party by this time and would break away two years later, in 1945; Stalin, denounced in the dialogue as a "villain," had executed Meyerhold three years earlier for his refusal to toe the social realist line; and in Brazil, meanwhile, the Vargas regime was paying samba musicians to sing its praises.[33] The use of the dialogue form is significant, then, because it enacts an unresolved debate in leftist circles and indicates that the outcome is not a done deal. At one point, for instance, the speaker who sings the praises of "chamber theater" points to advances in stage design and cites the work of the French director Louis Jouvet, who spent the early 1940s in exile in Brazil; calling it an "admirable reaction against the corruption brought about by the cinema," he explains that "sensing itself under attack, the theater improved," producing intimate theaters that provided a refuge for "the spirit of that fabulous Paris, which that forest ranger Hitler's filthy boot is unsuccessfully trying to crush." Rather than refuting this implicit equation of mass culture with fascism, his partner brings up Meyerhold and a long list of earlier playwrights-of-the-people, ending with the comment that "one day, perhaps soon, we may be able to add, in an honest sense, Wagner and Oberammergau" (87). The argument for the revolutionary nature of mass theater thus leads to two disturbing counterexamples that signal its potential as a vehicle for reaction: a composer celebrated by the Nazis as an icon of German nationalism, and a Bavarian village famous for its centuries-long tradition of a massive, day-long Passion Play—famous, too, for the anti-Semitic nature of the pageant and Hitler's ringing endorsement of it.[34]

Only by turning a blind eye to these apparent impasses that trail off into ellipses is it possible to read this pseudo-Platonic dialogue as a programmatic manifesto for total theater; its relation to O homem e o cavalo becomes even more complex when one realizes that "O teatro" was written nearly a decade later, at a time when, after several frustrated attempts to stage his own plays, Oswald was no longer writing theater at all. Even if we take the advocate of stadium theater to be the unequivocal mouthpiece for the author, his pedagogical injunction to "educate the world" is light-years away from the contumacious circus laborer of the Serafim preface. The two speakers define their framework as international, but the specter of the nation is inescapable because a stumbling block stands in the way of the dialectic's progression: not just the historic wax and wane of fascism, but the concurrent rise and reification of Brazil's corporatist state.

A Club of "Modern Artists"?

In drawing parallels between their own situation and the conditions under which Oswald wrote his plays, Zé Celso and others tended to paint the 1930s with a broad brush, equating the entire decade with the Vargas dictatorship.

There is a grain of truth to this, but it obscures the complexities of Oswald's would-be spectacle and the story of the "Club of Modern Artists" where it was to have been performed. After taking power in 1930, Vargas seemed to have every intention of ruling by decree indefinitely, but as part of his peace with the paulistas who rose up in arms in 1932 he agreed to return the country to constitutional rule. In hindsight, the interval between the end of the Constitutionalist Revolution and the inauguration of the new magna carta in July 1934 looks like a paradox—a phase in which the foundational fictions of democracy flowered even as the groundwork for authoritarian rule was laid.[35] On the one hand, the democratic election of delegates to the constituent assembly in May spurred the creation of a number of new regional parties and an increase in popular participation (with literate women allowed to vote for the first time), and the lengthy lead-up to the assembly's inauguration in November saw a flurry of activity on both the Left and the Right; at the same time, the federal government made inroads into the state bureaucracies and expanded the repressive apparatus, turning the Ilha dos Porcos penal colony into a notorious political prison for leftists. During the assembly's eight months of deliberations questions were raised about the nature of democracy and capitalism, yet the final draft of the constitution enshrined most of Vargas's corporatist and centralist tenets—along with certain protections for workers—and he successfully used it to retrospectively legalize his actions as provisional president. Indeed, as historians note, in 1933 and 1934 his regime reached a tacit accord with industrialists and the landed elites.[36]

Toward the end of November 1932, just a month after the Constitutionalists of São Paulo agreed to lay down their arms, two new centers of artistic activity appeared on the scene. The Sociedade de Pró-Arte Moderna (SPAM) was sponsored by society matrons and took its cues from Mário de Andrade and the Lithuanian-Brazilian painter Lasar Segall. The Clube dos Artistas Modernos (CAM), billed as a less "elitist" alternative, was run by an eclectic group of founding fathers. Emiliano Di Cavalcanti, a visual artist, was the only veteran of the Semana de Arte Moderna among them. The Cubist painter Antônio Gomide had only recently returned from several years in Paris, and Carlos da Silva Prado belonged to a younger generation, though he was a relative of Paulo Prado, the eminent (and eminently wealthy) intellectual who had brought Blaise Cendrars to Brazil and was often regarded as modernismo's elder statesman. The main mover and shaker behind CAM's creation was Flávio de Carvalho, an architect, painter, and performance artist of sorts who had already made a name for himself as a wayward scion of the local aristocracy: in 1931, he had nearly been lynched while conducting an "experiment" in which he tested Freud's ideas on mass psychology by joining a Corpus Christi procession while wearing a hat (a strict taboo) and shouting profanities.[37]

Gomide was a socialist, Di Cavalcanti had been a member of the Communist Party since 1926, and Carvalho professed no political creed, though his distaste for bourgeois morality was coupled with an interest in the collective impulse and mechanical feats of Soviet society. Both Carvalho and Gomide had thrown in their lot with the paulista forces in the recent civil war, while Di Cavalcanti (who was from Rio) had been accused of supporting Vargas and spent most of the conflict in jail. They shared neither an articulated ideology nor a particular style but something vague called "modern art." When the four men finally went public on December 24, 1932, it was not with a manifesto but a brief announcement in the *Diário da Noite* that described their intentions in innocuous terms: the club, housed in a vacant building on Rua Pedro Lessa where three of the four already shared studio space, would serve as a meeting place and also hire artistic models for collective sessions, maintain a small bar, host lectures and exhibitions, form an art library, and defend "the interests of the class." Members paid dues, but nonmembers could participate in individual events for a small fee.[38] In many respects its operating principles were similar to those of the mutual aid societies that immigrants and working-class organizations had been forming in São Paulo since the late nineteenth century. But who belonged to this so-called class, and what were its "interests"?

Most of CAM's initial eighty members were familiar faces, and several were also associates of the more upscale SPAM. If CAM differed, it was due to its greater degree of overlap with the commercial milieu—a consequence, perhaps, of the fact that whereas SPAM focused its efforts on exhibitions of visual art, CAM often served as a performance venue. One evening in January, for example, the entertainment began with the renowned carioca baritone Adacto Filho singing Mussorgsky, Yoshinori Matsuyama, and Villa-Lobos, and concluded with a rendition of the hit samba "Favela" by Paul Roulien, who had just filmed *Flying Down to Rio* with Ginger Rogers, Fred Astaire, and the Mexican star Dolores del Río. A series of concerts paired German folk songs, sung by CAM's very own German vocal quartet, with native Brazilian tunes by an ensemble under the direction of Marcelo Tupinambá, the middlebrow composer whose maxixes and *tanguinhos* could be heard in popular theatrical revues as well as in Darius Milhaud's ballets. The violinist Frank Smith performed pieces by Stravinsky, Hindemith, and Camargo Guarnieri; the former Brazilian consul in Shanghai gave a lecture on his forthcoming travelogue; a ten-person troupe presented Japanese dances and demonstrations of jujitsu and kendo; and at the beginning of May, the club held a dinner to celebrate its new accord with Pro-Arte, an artists' association in Rio led by Theodor Heuberger, a German known for his role in popularizing the Bauhaus style in Brazil.[39]

The face CAM presented to the public during this phase was far from polemical. Quite the contrary, if one can believe a gushing newspaper chronicle of a recital by the "mulatta" vocalist Elsie Houston (with piano accompaniment by Camargo Gaurnieri) on February 10, 1933. Houston was a classically trained soprano who had studied in Berlin, found minor fame in Paris, and would soon do the same in New York, where her cabaret act would feature bizarre nonverbal vocalizations billed as "voodoo songs." The program she performed at CAM was typically eclectic: selections ranged from Satie, Debussy, and Manuel de Falla to arrangements of "Incan and Brazilian songs." The anonymous reviewer professed his preference for the more autochthonous numbers, imagining the chanteuse (a native of Rio) as a mythic "Mother of the Waters who left the backlands [*sertões*], turned into a woman, and came to enchant the city people." Among these enchanted urbanites were Mário de Andrade, the rising samba star Mário Reis, the "poetess" Colombina (whose real name was Yde Schlönbach Blumenschein), and someone called Iokanaan pegged as a talent "all of São Paulo will soon know." The crowd behaved "like a group of children," demanding three encores before starting up a dance while the journalist Jayme Adour da Câmara read palms and André Dreyfus, a prominent scientist, tried to sweet-talk a young lady with technical explanations of why a straight line could at times be curved. The scene reads like an attempt to reconfigure Schiller's aesthetic state, that "middle disposition" of "semblance" and "play"—linked here to biological and cultural miscegenation—in which sense and reason are reconciled and social divisions overcome.[40] Sure enough, the desire underlying this fantasy is revealed at the article's end, when the author sheepishly confesses his wish to be an *interventor*, one of the federally appointed officials who replaced state governors after the Revolution of 1930. The reason, he explains, was that he had discovered the elusive secret that could "reunite" all of São Paulo: it was the incomparable Elsie, who "possesses the marvelous ability to make people love Brazil all the more."[41]

In his haste to gather the nation's fractious siblings around the mulatta Mother, the writer fails to mention that Houston's husband, the French surrealist Benjamin Péret, had recently been expelled from the country for his role in cofounding a Trotskyist organization. As the year wore on, however, it would become more difficult to exclude such signs of conflict from the artistic frame. On April 1—the same day the German government launched a nationwide boycott of all Jewish businesses—Plínio Salgado led the fascist Integralists down the streets of São Paulo in their first mass demonstration.[42] In June, the club collaborated with Pro-Arte's Theodor Heuberger on an exhibition of over eighty drawings and lithographs by the German artist Käthe Kollwitz, who would soon be blacklisted by the Nazi regime. This show was one of CAM's most high-profile events up to that point and drew praise from a broad spectrum of critics: Mário de Andrade extolled Kollwitz's humanistic vision in the daily *Diário de São Paulo*, while the leftist journal *O Homem Livre* published the entirety of a talk on the artist given by Mário Pedrosa, another cofounder (along with Péret) of the Trotskyist Liga Comunista Internacional and a veteran of early street battles against the Nazis from his days as a student in Berlin.[43]

But the not-so-subtle shift in the club's orientation also drew some less desirable attention. The Delegacia Estadual de Ordem Política e Social

A ARTE PROLETARIA

Brilhante conferencia da pintora sra. Tarsila do Amaral, no *Guarany* Clube dos Artistas Modernos

A SRA. TARCILA DO AMARAL QUANDO PRONUNCIAVA A SUA CONFERENCIA

Realizou-se hontem, ás 22 horas, no lube dos Artistas Modernos, a anunciada conferencia da pintora sra. arcila do Amaral, sob o thema: Arte Proletaria". A conferencista, que idou longo tempo pela Russia, aus-

deixando todos os ouvintes gratamente impressionados com as curiosas revelações da artista moderna,

INICIO DA CONFERENCIA

Antes da sra. Tarcila do Amaral iniciar a sua conferencia, o sr. Fla-

plicação, ao fim a que se destinam, em um e outro regime.

FLORAÇAO DA ARTE NOVA

Analysando os factores que actuam na formação da sociedade nova, a conferencista affirma que, dessa so-

Figure 6.1. A newspaper article on Tarsila do Amaral's lecture at CAM. The clipping was attached to a report on the event filed by the undercover agent "Guarany." Acervo do DEOPS-SP, Prontuário 2241, Arquivo Público do Estado de São Paulo.

(DEOPS) was a quasi-secret political police force created at the end of 1924, following years of intense labor unrest and shortly after the outbreak of the second Tenentes' Revolt, an insurgency of dissident army officers based in São Paulo. During the Vargas regime it intensified its activities, acquiring a reputation for repression not surpassed until the military dictatorship of 1964–1985.[44] The archive of the DEOPS (now public) contains files on almost all of the regulars at CAM, and what appears to be the earliest document in the file on the club itself is an unsigned, typewritten note denouncing the association as a "disguised nucleus of the most active communist propaganda in São Paulo."[45] As evidence it refers to an attached newspaper article from July 12 on CAM's upcoming events: on the docket for the rest of July were an exhibition of Soviet posters; a lecture by Jayme Adour da Câmara on his impressions from a trip to the Soviet Union; and a discussion of "proletarian art" by the painter Tarsila do Amaral, who had brought the aforementioned posters from the USSR. August, meanwhile, had been designated the "Month of the Insane and Children" and would feature an exhibit of drawings by mental patients and children. The file contains a second unsigned note much

like the first, and from then on, the case is taken over by a mole who is identified in reports as "Guarany."[46]

Whether or not the infiltrator knew it, his moniker was all too apt. The
Guaraní are an indigenous people who live in the southern regions of Brazil
and other neighboring countries, but the code name was probably also a nod
to the canonical novel by José Alencar (a pillar of Romantic nationalism),
and possibly even to Carlos Gomes's *Il Guarany*—the very opera modernistas had often derided for its attempt to dress the noble savage up in high art,
and the ironic inspiration for Oswald's uncouth anthropophagist. By hap-
penstance, the featured guest at the July 17 meeting (the first one for which
Guarany filed a report) was a man named Pedro Faber Halembeck, a *ser-
tanista* or inland explorer who had lived on and off for twenty years among
the Ingay people of the Amazon. Halembeck, like others in the room, might
have suspected he had an unwelcome observer in the audience. Perhaps he
even made a point of putting on a show: according to the report, Flávio
de Carvalho concluded his introductory remarks by announcing that "if an
authority of the Social Order [*Ordem Social*, a division of DEOPS] were
present," the speaker "would certainly land in jail" for what he was about to
say.[47] This apparently included making reference to the Soviet posters hang-
ing in the hall and drawing comparisons between Russia and the indigenous
societies of Brazil, both of which led the DEOPS agent to conclude that he
was at the very least a "sympathizer" of the Soviet regime. And how could
he not be in such an environment, where "one has the impression of living
among the Russians"? Even the bartenders, Guarany wrote, wore Russian-
style shirts. (In fact, a Russian named Pasha Abranova did run the bar.)[48] The
agent observed that the "physiognomic traits" of the woman beside him were
not those of a "national," so he struck up a conversation with her only to find
out that *she too* was Russian-born! This "most modern of communist propaganda" had little to do with art, he warned, but it was dangerously crafty:
"The means employed by the 'artists' are silent, subtle, they do not inspire
curiosity, but whoever enters there comes out thinking [*pensativo*]."

The authorities might have taken a different attitude if all this talk about
Indians and revolution had been confined to a marginal group of "modern
artists" with no immediate means of intervening in the productive order.
But if Guarany did go unnoticed, it was because his was not the only new
face. In a report on Tarsila do Amaral's July 29 discussion of proletarian
art, he refers to her "disguised agitation of praise for militant communism"
and sums up her speech with a phrase that is repeated like a litany in all of
the reports on the club: "It has nothing to do with art."[49] Yet the newspaper article appended to his statement suggests otherwise (figure 6.1). There
was no difference between bourgeois and proletarian art, said Tarsila, but
only "variations in the mode of their application and the ends to which
they are put"; the concept of beauty had changed over time, and the "future
socialist society" would surely bring with it a new notion, though the artist

acknowledged she did not know exactly what it would be.[50] For Guarany, that unwitting emblem of autonomous art, the most troubling part was the public to whom this implicit question was posed. "The audience," he asserts, "was almost entirely composed of individuals wearing collarless shirts and red ties, with the air of terrorists and undesirables, the majority made up of foreigners."[51] This concern with the intermingling of intellectuals and "foreign workers" is a constant throughout the file on CAM. One document specifies that the audience included large numbers of people from Belém and Bom Retiro—two of São Paulo's largest working-class neighborhoods, where Italian immigrants had recently been joined by Eastern European Jews.[52] The club also turned out to be a new haunt of Oreste Ristori, an old-timer from the heyday of anarcho-syndicalism who had acquired quasi-mythic stature on the Left (figure 6.2). In a defiantly detailed declaration Ristori gave to the police in December 1935 before being deported back to Italy, where he would be shot by the German army during World War II for his role in the antifascist resistance, he explained his decision to begin frequenting CAM as the result of his desire to "meet diverse [*diversos*] intellectuals."[53]

Ristori disliked being pigeonholed into any of the Left's proliferating factions, and so it is difficult to know exactly what he said on the numerous occasions he took the floor at CAM, just as it is difficult to know what the Trotskyists, anarchists, Communist Party faithfuls, and others argued in response. The DEOPS reports offer limited evidence of these unscripted debates, because just as Guarany locates the club's activities outside the realm of art, he exiles all leftist discourses from the "legitimate" political sphere by refusing to ascribe any value to their differences. Even so, there are moments when it becomes clear these did in fact exist. On August 3, for instance, when the featured speaker failed to show up due to trouble with the police, the shoemaker Pedro Catallo spoke in the absent man's place, outlining "divergences" between anarchists and communists.[54] Whatever he said prompted Jayme Adour da Câmara to stand up and defend the "Bolshevik regime," leading to a heated discussion in which the psychiatrist Osorio Cesar tried to discredit Catallo by calling him a police agent.[55] Such moments hint at the strain of police surveillance, mutual suspicion, and factional disputes and suggest the club was a place where alliances could be broken as well as made. At the same time, perhaps because its organizing principle was *not* explicitly political but something nebulous called "modern art," it was a site where adherents of diverse ideologies converged, both to articulate disagreements and to form contingent coalitions.

It was out of such encounters that a theatrical "experience" emerged. The desire to create an alternative to "commercial" theater had been in the air for some time, and several CAM regulars still had vivid memories of their involvement in Teatro do Brinquedo, a short-lived Rio-based project.[56] An opportunity arose in June when the club had to decide how to utilize its spacious ground floor. Two of CAM's founding fathers, Di Cavalcanti and Carlos

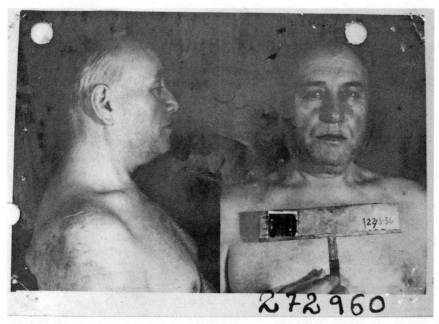

Figure 6.2. Oreste Ristori, an Italian labor agitator who regularly attended CAM, in an arrest photo from 1935 (shortly before he was deported). Acervo do DEOPS-SP, Prontuário 364, Arquivo Público do Estado de São Paulo.

Prado, were in favor of subletting the space to a commercial vendor in order to finance the club's increasingly active agenda, and it took some convincing to overcome their opposition to what was perceived as a risky financial venture.[57] One vocal proponent of what was to become the ephemeral Teatro da Experiência was Tarsila do Amaral, who in a newspaper interview hinted she would end her upcoming talk on proletarian art—the same talk where she ended up speaking about beauty before an audience of "terrorists" and "foreigners"—with a few remarks on the value of theater. The Brazilian people needed their intellectuals to be a little more "audacious," she insisted, and the most fitting medium for such audacity was the "theatrical apparatus [or "gear"; *engrenagem*]."[58] Needless to say, Carvalho studiously avoided any references to audacity in his application for a theater permit, in which he described the project as a "laboratory" that would "function with the impartial spirit of laboratory research." Its purpose would be to explore "the world of ideas" by experimenting with "settings, modes of diction, mimesis, the dramatization of new elements of expression, problems of lighting and sound, conjugated to the movement of abstract forms," all in order "to form a practical base for the psychology of entertainment."[59] Who could possibly object?

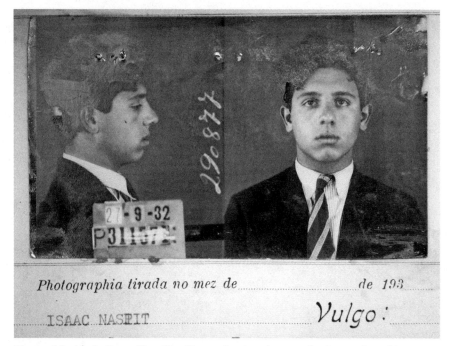

Photographia tirada no mez de .... de 193 ......

ISAAC NASPIT ....   *Vulgo :* ....

Figure 6.3. Abrão Isaac Naspit, a Romanian immigrant who is mentioned in
DEOPS reports as having attended a meeting at CAM. The file identifies him as
a communist, lists his occupation as "clothes ironer," and states that he belonged
to the Centro de Cultura e Progresso, a Jewish organization that was under
surveillance. Acervo do DEOPS-SP, Prontuário 2049, Arquivo Público do Estado
de São Paulo.

Later on Tarsila would help design the set for *O bailado do deus morto*,
along with Nonê de Andrade (the nineteen-year-old son of her ex-husband
Oswald), the engraver Lívio Abramo, and the lithographer and stage designer
Osvaldo Sampaio. Oswald de Andrade agreed to contribute a play for the
grand opening; Procópio Ferreira, a soon-to-be-legendary actor on the
commercial stage, made vague promises to collaborate at some later date;
Geraldo Ferraz, editor of the militant journal *O Homem Livre*, wrote to
Jacques Cocteau and the Belgian dramatist Fernand Crommelynck (whose
Le cocu magnifique had been staged by Meyerhold) requesting permission
to translate some of their plays, and he also requested rights to *Ubu roi* from
Alfred Jarry's descendants. Among the long list of writers who pledged to
contribute texts were the novelist Jorge Amado and Caio Prado Junior, who
had just published his seminal Marxist study *Evolução política do Brasil*
(1933) and was on his way to becoming a major influence in the Brazilian
Communist Party.[60]

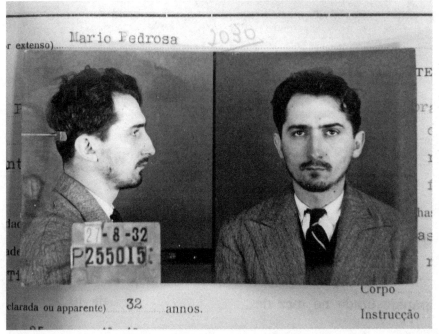

Figure 6.4. Mário Pedrosa, a prominent Trotskyist and later one of the country's best-known art critics, in an arrest photo from 1932. Acervo do DEOPS-SP, Prontuário 2030, Arquivo Público do Estado de São Paulo.

Of course, this flurry of activity would all be for naught unless the organizers could assemble an audience. Yet the club's expanding network made it reasonable to expect the small auditorium could be filled. On September 9, Caio Prado Junior's presentation on his recent trip to Russia drew six hundred people to CAM; loudspeakers were placed outside so that the long line of people unable to squeeze into the hall could hear his favorable account of the new Soviet society as well as the ensuing debate.[61] A repeat performance one week later generated two detailed accounts by DEOPS agents, one of whom indicated that the event was also used as an opportunity to fundraise for the club's upcoming venture: before Prado Junior spoke, Flávio took contributions from the nearly five hundred people in attendance for a project referred to as the "Teatro de Vanguarda."[62] A few days later, Guarany reported that the theater, likely to open that same week, would be a "theater of propaganda" where "Russian customs, etc." would be displayed.[63] But the big "spectacle" was postponed, reportedly because Oswald de Andrade was dealing with personal and financial difficulties and finally had to tell his friend Flávio he would be unable to finish the script of O homem e o cavalo in time.[64]

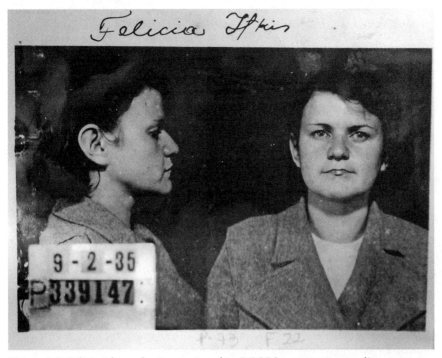

Figure 6.5. Felicia Itkis, who is mentioned in DEOPS reports as attending events at CAM, in an arrest photo from 1935. According to her file she was born in Russia in 1910 but immigrated to Brazil with her family at the age of five. Acervo do DEOPS-SP, Prontuário 0073, Arquivo Público do Estado de São Paulo.

Not until November 15 did the Teatro make its long-awaited debut with *O bailado do deus morto*, a performance thrown together over the previous few weeks by Carvalho and Henrique Costa (Henricão), a black samba composer and chauffeur who orchestrated the music in collaboration with Nonê de Andrade. The piece had little dialogue (most of it consisted of short, incantatory phrases), and were it not for the brief explanatory note included in the program the audience might have had trouble recognizing the strange spectacle as a ritualistic commemoration of a dead god—a hairy, hippopotamus-like deity who betrayed his fellow animals when he allowed himself to be seduced by an Inferior (human) Woman and the "fury of his fiery penis" was subdued.[65] Hugo Adami, a painter who played the chief Lamenter, appears to have been the only white person onstage, though like the faces of the four female performers his too was obscured by a metal mask; the five musicians played instruments of African origin (*cuíca*, *gongô*, *reco-reco*, etc.), with the drumming growing ever more frenetic as the actors evoked the disintegration of the god's body in the face of increasing mechanization, until a

Figure 6.6. The debut of *O bailado do deus morto* (Dance of the Dead God). *Diário da Noite*, November 15, 1933.

gauze curtain fell and the voice of the Lamenter delivered the final mournful line: "Psychoanalysis killed god" (92). An allegory of secularization, the play dramatizes the nostalgia for plenitude and presence à la Wagner, but it clearly also spoofs this desire. Its humorous absurdity must have lightened the atmosphere of tension at its debut: less than twenty-four hours earlier, a rally of over one thousand antifascists led by several regulars at CAM had ended in an exchange of gunfire with police after a group of Integralists had provoked an altercation.[66] Even so, Teatro da Experiência's grand opening received less scrutiny than it might have on another occasion because—whether by coincidence or design—it fell on the same day as the inauguration of the national assembly charged with drafting a new constitution.

None of the artists or spectators could know that just four years later, citing trumped up evidence of a communist uprising, Vargas would suspend the law—a right ascribed to him by this very constitution—in order to assume dictatorial powers and write a new constitution that eliminated any pretense of regional autonomy. But since Hitler (among others) had already pulled a similar move, they might have recognized as an ominous augur the events that transpired at the third performance of *O bailado do deus morto*. Around 9 p.m. on November 16, as a packed audience waited for the show to start, an inspector arrived bearing orders from the chief of the vice squad to cancel

Figure 6.7. A scene from *O bailado do deus morto* from a front-page article on the theater's closure. *Folha da Noite*, November 17, 1933.

the show on the grounds that it had yet to be duly censored and approved. According to one sensationalist tabloid, Flávio de Carvalho rebuffed the officer by yelling, "We didn't achieve the meeting of the constituent assembly just so you could curtail [*cercear*] freedom of thought!" An unnamed person seconded him: "The revolution wasn't fought so that you could imprison [*enclausurar*] the cultural manifestation of the people!"[67] Other accounts dispense with the dialogue, but all agree the officer left only to return a short while later with an imposing number of police officers, civil guards, and the chief, who entered the theater with his men and allowed the performance to proceed. Carvalho later recalled that the audience sat through the entire show in silence. Nonetheless, the strange event appeared to have a felicitous result: as articles from several newspapers tell it, the chief intimated on leaving that he had found the play's off-color humor amusing, and that although the theater would have to close temporarily, the director had only to bring in the text the next day to receive official approval.[68] It would be several days before it became known that somewhere, a different decision had been made.

When the dead god danced, what did the armed enforcers of the law see? Strangely, for all the warnings about CAM's new theater in the weeks leading up to its debut, there are no reports on any of the performances in the archive of the political police. A number of reviews appeared in the papers, but like most reviews during this era all are very brief, and by the time the next issue of magazines and journals came out, the theater's closure and the subsequent legal wrangling were what garnered attention. Reception and critique unfold over time, and the police proved successful in cutting short any discussion about what actually took place onstage. The few critics and aficionados who have since recounted the tale of Teatro da Experiência tend to rely on Flávio de Carvalho's later account of the club's activities—a text written two years after the declaration of the Estado Novo dictatorship, in an atmosphere of repression and in the wake of the Left's defeat. Published as part of the catalogue for an exhibition intended to reunite the entire modernista clan in a single retrospective, it is an exercise in revisionist history that has Carvalho echoing the language of the mole Guarany, taking pains to state his disapproval of the "extreme leftist elements, some having nothing to do with art" that "infiltrated" the club and allowed political passions to overwhelm the pursuit of rational beauty.[69] As for the authorities' response to his play, Carvalho chalks it up to the influence of the Catholic Church and outrage at what he improbably claims was the first utterance of an obscenity on a Brazilian stage.

This explanation is less than compelling because it ignores the elephant in the room. In a column published the morning after the show's debut, the critic Francisco de Sá scoffed that "'O bailado do deus morto' is nothing if not an authentic *macumba*"—black witchcraft, or a ritual practiced as part of Afro-Brazilian religions such as umbanda, which enjoyed a growth in popularity during this era but also faced increasing persecution by the police.[70] The handful of extant police reports about the theater's closure are more circumspect: there are no references to race or anything at all about the audience, which Flávio later referred to as "diverse" and far in excess of the theater's 275 seats. And yet this silence is hardly surprising. The state's emerging ideology hinged on disavowing blackness as a political factor, even as it celebrated racial mixture as an axis of national culture. (This same year also saw the publication of Gilberto Freyre's *Casa grande e senzala*, which helped advance the notion that Brazil was what the author later dubbed a "racial democracy," free from discrimination based on color.) This maneuver was quite delicate, and while there is no evidence CAM had any connections to groups such as the Frente Negra Brasileira (a black political organization founded in 1931), it is easy to imagine that the mix of people in the audience and the presence of black actors on an experimental stage where generic conventions were less fixed would have raised a red flag.[71]

A few days after the long arm of the law put an end to the fun, Oswald gave a reading of scenes from O *homem e o cavalo* upstairs in the club. In an article announcing the event he expressed confidence in the artists' ability to prevail over their opponents and spoke of plans to stage his own play: "The Teatro da Experiência's task is going to be enormous," Oswald said, because it would be "attempting to reduce, for a stage four meters in size (doubled in the auditorium, it's true), a play for a stadium or the cinema, with forty-five characters, a dog, and a horse."[72] Meanwhile, as the fate of the dead god hung in limbo, the chief of Vice asked Carvalho for scripts of the theater's upcoming productions and was given O *homem e o cavalo* along with a translation of a Russian play. He delivered the texts to the director of the DEOPS,[73] only to receive them back just three days later with a terse response: "From a rapid reading of both plays, without dwelling on minute analyses, it can be verified that this is a case of extremist literature." The memo makes no mention of talking horses, Madame Jesus, or prophesies of the death of 6 million Jews; about Oswald's play it says only that "beneath a supposed theatrical plot its true end, that is, communist propaganda, is clearly visible" (sob um supposto entrecho teatral, deixa transparecer claramente sua verdadeira finalidade).[74] On December 6, several newspapers published the final word of the chief of Vice: Teatro da Experiência was prohibited from reopening its doors on the grounds that the plays it presented were antireligious and/or communist and the space did not conform to the standards of a "proper" theater because it had no box office or dressing rooms.[75]

Men, Horses, and Missing Pieces

"A play for a stadium or the cinema." Those who link *O homem e o cavalo* to total theater, then, are not entirely off base. The play does share many formal features with projects that explicitly aspired to this ideal: it incorporates elements of mass culture genres such as *teatro de revista*, or musical revues; the theatrical action occasionally spills off the stage and into the audience; and although there is no indication that film projectors were to be used (as in the case of Piscator's theater), the principle of mediation is foregrounded through the use of loudspeakers, which transmit the voices of offstage characters. The title—"Man and the Horse"—also calls to mind the "abstract man" who is the quintessential hero of all total theater projects, while the narrative, derived from the medieval mystery, evokes a messianic sense of time that will presumably culminate in the fusion of the spiritual and the material on Judgment Day.

The moment of sublimation never occurs, however, because *O homem e o cavalo* insists on placing itself in the uncomfortable crux between the nationalization of mass politics and the emergence of a global mass culture. As a theatrical performance, Oswald's quote makes clear, the play's work is to reduce the all-encompassing spectacle of mass society, to cut it down to human size in order to magnify the political, cultural, and material processes that are at stake in representing "the whole." The play attempts to redraw the connections between art, mass culture, and anti-imperialism by harking back to a moment when the Left and the artistic vanguards appeared to be in step: its structure of nine, loosely connected tableaux featuring an international cast of characters who fight vile capitalists all across the globe seems to be modeled on Mayakovsky's *Mystery-Bouffe*, a reinvention of the medieval mystery genre first produced by Meyerhold shortly after the triumph of the Russian Revolution. The Russian play, however, is an unambiguous celebration of an unprecedented revolution, and it employs the conventions of medieval mystery plays as a way of inserting itself into a tradition familiar to its popular audiences. *O homem* presents a more troubling picture, one that is structured by the historical and ideological contradictions that had emerged in the fifteen years since the Mayakovsky play was written. By 1933, these kinds of cultural appropriations had become more questionable in light of the newly forged links between "popular" or "folk" cultures and repressive states, and in Brazil they were doubly vexed due not only to the Church's close ties to Vargas and the Integralists but also the historic role of religious drama in the process of colonization. The extent to which these two plays diverge is evident in their treatment of the holy hero himself: whereas *Mystery-Bouffe* turns Christ into a secular Redeemer who champions the cause of the proletarians, Oswald's play exposes the troubling role of popular culture in mass society by portraying Hitler as a perverse, modern-day incarnation of the Son of God.

But *O homem* does not simply discard market-driven forms of art and entertainment. In fact, many of the innovations that can be interpreted as adaptations of the medieval mystery also coincide with the conventions of teatro de revista, a genre that was quintessentially "Brazilian" in its depictions of topical events and social customs but also, as a local variant of revue theater, heir to a geographically expansive genealogy of urban mass culture. Introduced to Brazil in the 1870s, the revista had long been derided by the elite as a symptom of the country's inability to produce a "legitimate" national theater, and in the first few decades of the twentieth century many revista musicians and actors also worked in radio and film. Revista shows aimed to attract spectators of all classes, and while the plots often reinforced social hierarchies, the industry was more open than most to employing light-skinned mulattos (less often blacks) and was an important vehicle for the popularization of genres such as samba.[76] Getúlio Vargas's ties to revista, radio, and film went back to 1928 when, as a federal congressman, he sponsored a bill establishing the first legal oversight of commercial entertainment that was widely perceived as favoring the interests of authors and performers.[77] As president, he not only frequented the theater but was also known to steal the show. A Brazilian director writing in 1945 recalled that

> never was a head of government so prominent on theater stages as the victor of the Revolution of 1930. The figure of Getúlio Vargas was always the main attraction in all the revues, and he was depicted in the most sympathetic manner, incarnated in the most popular types of the masses, once dressed as a gaúcho, another time as a worker, a hunter, a revolutionary, a farmworker, a teacher, a macho, and even a tramcar driver! His figure, cause for the heartiest laughter, lingered in every spectator's heart after the laughter, touching and conquering all in the most intelligent campaign a governor could merit.

> nunca um chefe de governo foi tão focalizado em palcos teatrais, como o triunfador da Revolução de mil novecentos e trinta. A figura

de Getúlio Vargas apareceu, sempre, como atração principal de todas as revistas que se representaram, e da maneira mais simpática, incarnada nos tipos mais populares da massa, uma vez vestido de gaúcho, outra vez vestido de operário, de caçador, do revolucionário, de lavrador, de professor, de galo, e até, de motorneiro de bonde! Responsável pelas mais gostosas gargalhadas, sua figura ficava no coração de cada espectador, após a gargalhada, enternecendo a todos e a todos conquistando na mais inteligente campanha que um governador pode merecer.[78]

The very multiplicity of these onstage incarnations contributed to Vargas's construction as the ideal populist subject; his serialized image (farmworker, teacher, revolutionary) confirms what Michael Warner has said of public figures in mass-mediated societies, which "take on the function of concretizing that phantasmatic body image, or, in other words, of actualizing the otherwise indeterminate image of the people."[79] In its opening tableau, *O homem e o cavalo* plugs in to this "popular" tradition by adopting its stylistic conventions while turning its representational logic on its head in order to foreground the affinities between fascism and capitalist mass culture. The scene takes place in the "universal" sphere of heaven, where the far-from-angelic denizens include St. Peter, who claims that his celestial domain is Einstein's fourth dimension; the Four "Graças" (Graces), who are transposed into singing "Garças" (Hussies) and are immediately recognizable as the obligatory chorus line of scantily clad girls from a revue; and the Divo, a flamboyant opera singer accused by the others of having lost his "moral sense" onstage. St. Peter warns his squabbling followers, "If we destroy this stronghold of eternal change, the world will plunge into historical materialism!"[80] The venerable patriarch's very words, of course, run counter to his intention. The play reverses the usual terms of reference by placing the "ideal" directly onstage. What we see is a distinctly bourgeois afterlife in which the Garças practice phrases in English, titter over off-color jokes, and embroider handkerchiefs.

Into this mind-numbingly insipid bliss marches the Poet-Soldier, proclaiming the need to "regenerate humanity" and chastising the Garças for being "damned pacifists! Society of Nations!" (24). Although the text gives no cues as to costuming, the Poet-Soldier quotes Marinetti's mantra ("War is the world's only hygiene!"), and his strident, exclamatory style is a dead giveaway. This is not Italy, however, but the no-man's-land of nationalist ideology. The Poet-Soldier is surely a stand-in for the Italian futurist, but he is just as surely Plínio Salgado, leader of the Brazilian Integralist Party, whose slogan "God-Country-Family" is parodied in the legend that adorns the set of this tableau: "God-Country-Brothel-Hymen." Here, as throughout the play, Oswald exploits the capacity of a single theatrical image to signify multiple referents in order to draw connections between belief systems and national imaginaries that have been safely ensconced from one another by political and epistemological borders. Rather than multiple manifestations of a single president/people, we see a puppet-like Poet-Soldier raging about the need to "resolve the unemployment crisis of the furies and lightning bolts," a figure who could easily be Brazilian, Italian, German, Portuguese, or Argentine (24). The parallels are not just formal, and the scene is not just about fascism as style. Marinetti, after all, had visited Brazil in 1926; Nazi organizations funded by the German embassy flourished in southern Brazil; and while Mussolini invoked the sacred homeland, Italian immigrants were struggling to build new lives in São Paulo. By staging the rise of fascism in the realm of the "spiritual," the scene undercuts the territorialization of nationalist representation, revealing it to be a phenomenon shaped by historical and material forces whose scope is in fact global.

The ribaldry is cut short by the tableau's surprise ending, the arrival of a giant "aluminum balloon" bearing a black man who proclaims, "What a lovely little people!" (*Que povo bonitinho!*) (29). Professor Icar, it would appear, is a mutation of Auguste Piccard, the Swiss physicist who in 1932 had become the first person to ascend into the upper stratosphere, reaching some 55,800 feet in a pressurized gondola of his own invention. If *O bailado do deus morto* played on—and in some ways reinforced—a primitivist perspective on blackness, what this scene presents is a futuristic reversal of the conquest scenario. But colonial domination is predicated on the impossibility of its own reversal—a black man cannot step in to the conqueror's role and remain unscathed. So it is that in the following tableau, which takes place inside the spaceship, the Poet-Soldier proudly proclaims that he has "disembodied" its inventor (*O desencarnei!*). When the Garças protest that Icar was just a harmless "chocolate Aryan" who naturally got burned by flying too close to the sun (a wink to his Greek predecessor Icarus), the Poet accuses them of having illicit desires that are liable to "damage the race"; he goes on to explain that "if you'd talked to him before the disembodiment about the need white people have to subdue, exploit, and humiliate people of color, maybe he wouldn't have understood. Now he understands. Now we can converse about Civilization, Culture, Imperialism, Capital, Race, and other white subjects" (33).

Both mass culture and fascist idealism purport to offer this brilliant black bourgeois the "rhetorics of disincorporation" that Michael Warner identifies as necessary to gain access to mass subjecthood.[81] But for the black man, rhetoric is either purely false or all too real, so the learned Professor is now nothing but speech: he is the invisible pilot guiding the vessel through the ether, present only as the Voice of Icar, which interrupts the action on occasion to alert the passengers to planets, stars (Greta Garbo is the name of one), and other landmarks along their route. Icar hasn't been disembodied so much as turned inside out: the tableau is titled "The Interior of the Ícaro," and even the Poet-Soldier grudgingly acknowledges that without the black man's novel invention and navigational skills they would all disperse into the nothingness of the stratosphere. Although Ícar(o) is both the protective vessel and the labor keeping the operation afloat, he is unable to take his place as an individual subject onstage because, having been deprived of flesh, he can only play the role of the purely symbolic or the anonymous mass. His Voice is an aural signifier of race around which the others members of this minisociety converge—not unlike the voices of samba stars transported over the Brazilian airwaves, where they were often recast as the expression of an "authentic" popular identity that was at once racialized and yet available to all. Indeed, if radio (and mass media more generally) is the invisible "outside" of the first part of this tableau, it becomes the explicit focal point of the final scene. When the device around which they are gathered begins to emit inchoate noises, the Poet Soldier and the Garças are alarmed—something seems to be afoot "down there," in South America: "THE RADIO: Ooooooooooo! The people are invading, they respect nothing!" The Radio goes on to speak of "police," "disorder," and the firing of "shots." Could it be Revolution? the characters wonder. As it turns out, it is only a Brazilian soccer game. "We can rest easy," the Poet-Soldier announces. "The deluded masses are still amusing themselves with that business." But when he turns on the radio again, he picks up a "Bolshevik station" whose announcer is rousing listeners to take up arms in the struggle against capital (39). Rather than reifying radio, or the mass public it hails, as a transparent medium of identity, the scene acknowledges it as an apparatus and as both the means and the object of struggle.

In the following tableau, the spaceship descends to earth and we are presented with a "fascist incarnation" (45): a rapturous apocalypse at the Epsom Derby that involves every power-driven leader and his equestrian sidekick of the past several millennia, both real and fictional. Among the multitudes are Dom Sebastião and Alfonsito V, who expanded Portugal's territories in Africa; Incitatus and Bucephalus (the steeds of Caligula and Alexander the Great); the fourteenth-century Tartar conqueror Tamerlane (known for his love of the arts); Nietzsche and the Wagnerian hero Parsifal, who have decided to mend fences ("Nietzsche converted in the struggle!" [49]); and even Rocinante and Sancho Panza's burro. The Divo has attempted to penetrate the body of one of the jockeys but missed his mark and ended up as a horse talking out of its ass; the real power behind the operation is the Poet-Soldier, the "hero of all homelands" and self-proclaimed embodiment of "Spirit" who rouses the global masses to a feverish passion with bellicose demagoguery, conjuring up a host of mythic symbols that culminates in the car of Juggernaut—"the steamroller of capital" (50)—and a nude Valkyrie wearing a gas mask who runs across the stage and through the audience to the music of Wagner's *Lohengrin*.

This is a nightmarish version of total theater—described as a "thrilling spectacle," it is the moment when art and reality become one (46). Or, rather, it would be, if the mayhem were actually seen. Instead, the audience is not allowed to witness the horrific sight; the desire for immediacy is denied because all of the action, up until the Valkyrie's mad dash, takes place behind a wall at the back of the stage. The audience hears the shouts and stampedes, the roar of thunder and cannons and cacophonous speech, including an anonymous voice of resistance crying out that the idealization of war leads the young to "mutilation and death" (51). Meanwhile St. Peter and Icar peer over the wall and narrate the action for the audience. A black bourgeois and a saint born a Jew, they have no place in the paradigm of identity underlying this fascist, imperialist fantasy; unable to perform the feat of self-abstraction, they possess an inassimilable "positivity" (in Warner's terms) conveyed in this scene through the use of scenic space. The Voice of the Divo proclaims, "I am the pathos of destruction! For the white race! For the rich class! For cretinous morality! . . . Heil! Duce! Heil! Duce!" and Icar ironically notes, "Luckily I'm no longer black" (*Felizmente eu deixei de ser preto*) (51). The ontological status of St. Peter's body is also in doubt, given that in the previous tableau the Poet-Soldier explained to the Garças that he was secretly leading the saint to his death on earth, where "two days ago in Hitler's Germany the death campaign against the Jews began" (38).

But how can disembodiment be performed? The text provides no clues, and there is nothing to suggest the use of high-tech resources to conjure up a convincing illusion. What is clear is that the actor is onstage, because the character is no longer described as a Voice. Icar's dematerialization is not a demonstration of technological power, nor does it show the ability of thought to sublimate the material; the point of the performance is that it fails. The quest for the missing black body becomes a recurring theme that functions as a counterpoint to the overarching narrative of revolutionary triumph—Icar's "widow" eventually shows up with a femur that has been identified as her husband's, though by the end it is no longer certain whether it belongs to Icar or to St. Peter, the converted Jew. As the only characters that reappear throughout the play, Icar, his wife, and St. Peter fulfill the role of onstage spectators through whom the audience's view of the epic struggle between fascism and Red revolution is refracted. Any attempt to identify with them, however, can only be incomplete and discontinuous, because they are not coherent characters but rather multiplex prisms whose changing nature is defined more by its liminal status in relation to the dominant discourse of the moment than by any inherent qualities. Although they are sympathetic figures and are given some of the play's wittiest lines, they are hardly exemplary. Icar, for example, is often subject to the nostalgia of the petit bourgeoisie, but at other times he is the voice of lucidity. His name is the Portuguese acronym for the Igreja Católica Apostólica Romana, or Roman Catholic Church, yet during the fascist incarnation, he objects to the injunctions delivered by the Voice of Job and points out, "But it's propaganda for temerity and servility" (49). During the Revolution, when an international crowd of insurrectionary sailors takes over St. Peter's Ship (represented as the Vatican on a raft, which serves as a dance floor presided over by Cleopatra), St. Peter the Jew tries to reassert his role as benevolent patriarch of the Christian faith and convince the masses that they are not prepared to take power. The Red Soldier replies, "All men are prepared to eat and *trepar* ["to climb," but also a colloquial term for sex]" (64). Icar and St. Peter always seem to be on the cusp of this recognition, but none of the play's contending discourses are capable of incorporating them.

This poses interpretive challenges, particularly when it comes to the treatment of the Soviet Union. Even some sympathetic critics have felt it necessary to concede that *O homem* is marred by a naively optimistic view of communist society and several seemingly propagandistic tableaux, including one called "Industrialization," which features the Voices of Stalin and Eisenstein proclaiming the glories of the utopic society they have created. Sábato Magaldi, for instance, finds it "almost unbelievable" that a humorist of Oswald's nature "let himself be led by political passion" to commit such a lamentable "literary slide."[82] In response, he simply omits any analysis of these tableaux. This refusal to consider that the scenes might indeed have something to do with "art" has its political corollary in the myth of a monolithic Left, a distortion of history belied by the debates that were taking place at the Clube dos Artistas Modernos when *O homem* was written. Magaldi's judgment is hardly equivalent to the repressive power that shut down the stage where these tableaux were to have been performed, but it does rely on and reinforce distinctions that this earlier police action helped create. It reinscribes a mirror-like opposition between politics and aesthetics that leaves the limits of literary-critical discourse safely intact by erasing the mediating factor of theatrical representation.

In fact, what is most notable about "Industrialization" is that the "ideal" world the Soviet leader and the filmmaker claim to have created can only exist outside the space of scenic representation; their disembodied voices boom out across a stage that represents "the monumental entrance to the biggest factory in the socialist world" (71). Standing at the door, watching the happy workers entering and exiting, are representatives of the past ("we are the end of a world"): Icar, St. Peter, now playing a *sanfona* (a type of accordion from rural northeastern Brazil), and Madame Icar, who wears her husband's femur around her neck (looking, perhaps, like the stereotype of an indigenous savage). Once again, they are slapstick figures whose rhetorical inversions draw attention to the bodies we continue to see, though they no longer exist:

> ST. PETER: I was the eyes of the blind . . . Now I'm a blind man with
>   no eyes.
> ICAR: I was the legs of the legless. Now I have no legs.
> MADAME ICAR: I used to have a husband and a home.
> ICAR AND ST. PETER: Now you have two husbands and no home!

SÃO PEDRO: Eu era os olhos do cego . . . Agora sou um cego sem olhos.
ICAR: Eu era a perna do manco. Agora não tenho pernas.
MADAME ICAR: Eu tinha um marido e um lar.
ICAR E SÃO PEDRO: Agora tem dois maridos e nenhum lar! (73)

As they listen to the invisible Voice of Stalin speak of the new world that is emerging out of the "pathos of construction" (75), the three characters scoff at his hubris. "Can man, even when he possesses a consummate science, possibly compare himself to God?" asks the pious Madame Icar. The fact that they invoke a religious creed that is also an object of critique does not necessarily mean that the audience is intended to discount their words. St. Peter once again takes on the role of prophet: "They'll be forced to condemn their own madness. Their confidence is like a spiderweb in the hands of the Lord! They'll rest upon their work and it won't have consistency. They'll want to maintain it and it won't hold up!" (74). One has to wonder: if the purpose of the scene is nothing more than propaganda, what are these naysayers doing here?

Standing in stark contrast to their humorous dialogue is the Voice of Eisenstein, which comes at the end of the tableau and is followed by nothing but "Silence." His lengthy speech is a laundry list of the gains won by the agricultural revolution, phrases that could have been pulled straight from the Soviet posters that adorned CAM's walls (figure 6.8):

> Fertilizing manure, herds, agricultural machines, all recorded and raising the statistics. Neither the fire of revolt nor the great revolutionary struggle. But, after the struggle and victory, the daily life of those who work and build a better world . . . the herds that are organized, the seed selection maps, the diagrams of progress . . . Model farms. Laboratories, schools. The worker-student, the peasant-student. The conscious, selected reproduction of animal species. The end of magic. The tractor . . .

> O esterco fertilizante, os rebanhos, as máquinas agrícolas, tudo escriturado aumentando as estatísticas. Nem o incêndio da revolta nem a grande luta revolucionária. Mas, depois da luta e da vitória, a vida quotidiana dos que trabalham e constroem um mundo melhor . . . os rebanhos que se organizam, os mapas da seleção de sementes, os diagramas do progresso . . . Fazendas-modelos. Laboratórios, escolas. O operário-estudante, o camponês-estudante. A reprodução consciente e selecionada das espécies animais. O fim da magia. O trator . . . (77)

What the audience hears is a representation, not of the style of Eisenstein's avant-garde films but of their social function. This is art that has been instrumentalized and placed in the service of the state, art that is no longer

Figure 6.8. One of the Soviet propaganda posters that hung on the walls of the Clube dos Artistas Modernos. *Folha da Noite*, July 18, 1933.

distinguishable from political power. Without necessarily undermining the theoretical validity of the ideal to which Eisenstein gives voice (such a judgment must remain contingent on the play's performance), the tableau very conspicuously refuses to realize it onstage. The happy, productive workers go through the door and out of sight; the people they leave behind are those who, as Oswald said of himself, stand "outside the revolutionary axis of the world."[83] But imperialism is the axis on which this play's world turns, and it is fitting that this tableau is at its center given that Stalin's declaration of the need to build "socialism in one state" formalized a historic split between the struggle for socialism and the struggle against imperialism. Over the loudspeakers and through the giant factory door we get a glimpse of what lies on the outside of the play—the marginalization of the avant-garde and the move to enforce an aesthetic of socialist realism, a term introduced by the Union of Soviet Writers and adopted as its official doctrine the year prior to the would-be staging of Oswald's play.[84] In contrast, what takes place within this scene is not a reflection but, in Trotsky's words, a "deflection, a changing and a transformation of reality in accordance with the peculiar laws of art."[85]

O *homem* doesn't offer up politics as a total work of art, or total theatricality, but a theatrical vision of totality—rather than "dematerializing" the stage, as was Piscator's aim, Oswald materializes it, juxtaposing and superimposing historical and cultural references from around the world and across two thousand years. What we get is not Wagner, despite his characters' frequent appearances; rather, O *homem* takes Benjamin's analysis of the Trauerspiel, with its dialectical images, fragments, and ruins, and transposes it back onto the stage. O *homem* makes a mock-heroic effort to gather together Christianity, capitalism, imperialism, art, mass culture, and fascism, to overcome the contradictions of history by embodying them onstage and in the colloquial language of 1930s Brazil. The Marxist theory that several of the characters cite serves a didactic function, and the teleological impulse is by no means abandoned. But the play's raucous humor, as well as its critical insight, is a result of the tension between its own aspirations and what is actually achieved onstage.

This becomes evident in the second instance of "total theater," which occurs after the socialist revolution, on Judgment Day, when Christ himself is brought to trial for a series of heinous crimes that include colluding with Roman imperialism, serving as an agent of the reformist Second International, and, in the guise of the Emperor Constantine, coining the favored motto of all "historic fascisms"—"Let's make the revolution before the people do it" (*Façamos a revolução antes que o povo a faça*)—a quote whose actual author was a Brazilian ally of Vargas (98).[86] The tribunal is held in the former hall of the Nobel Prize, though the backdrop depicts two crosses at Golgotha. Here, at the moment when history itself is to be transcended, the stage and the audience are joined together and numerous characters are seated in the audience, among them biblical figures, artists, fictional characters, and anonymous spectators who weigh in on the trial while shouting the slogans of political parties in Brazil. For the theatrical audience, the effect would surely be one of immediacy and excitement; what is immediately experienced, however, is how capitalism divides the world in the very process of making it whole.

What drives this sprawling tableau is the attempt to capture and arrest the process through which what was once revolutionary comes to serve the cause of reaction. In the first scene, we see the biblical character Veronica (the "true image"), now a photographer and proponent of state cinema, who holds up a large ID photo of Christ that shows Hitler crucified on a swastika—"the final incarnation of anti-Semitism" (91). O *homem* thus takes the core of the medieval mystery, its most troubling aspect and the one that led Hitler to celebrate the production at Oberammergau as an expression of the Aryan spirit, and turns it on its head. Instead of the Jews killing Jesus, Jesus is the killer of Jews. Yet there is also Barabbas, the sidekick of Mary Magdalene (now a cubist) and leader of the Jewish "nationalist" resistance against the Roman Empire, whom the people chose over Jesus when given the chance to save one prisoner from death. Once a revolutionary, he is now "Baron Barabbas Rothschild," a reference to the French capitalist who sponsored Jewish settlement in Palestine in order to establish large plantations reliant on cheap Arab labor.

In another instance Fu Manchu, the pulp fiction and film character known as the Yellow Peril, rises up out of a hole in the floor from among the spectators and shouts that he had started life as a Taoist, wanting to transform the world without bloodshed; instead, imperialism has transformed him into a "cagey beast." He gets into a scuffle with D'Artagnan (protagonist of Alexandre Dumas's *The Three Musketeers*), whom he calls a "Lackey! Product of the domestication of the masses!" In response D'Artagnan hurls racist epithets at him while bragging, "Today I'm a mass phenomenon! Hitler! Mussolini! Gustavo Garapa!" (This last name is a derisive allusion to Gustavo Barroso, president of the Brazilian Academy of Letters and one of the most fiercely anti-Semitic Integralists.)[87] D'Artagnan pursues the Chinese man backstage, though the English Novelist assures the audience, "Oh! They'll end up reconciling backstage" (101). Rather than a move to transcend politics theatrically, readers get a reminder of what is not seen or transformed onstage and in the presence of the audience. The aim is not to create a "totality of effect" within the theater's four walls but to uncover the totality of social relations that defines the spectators' position in a global system that cannot be revolutionized by "art" alone.

O homem e o cavalo doesn't end with the grand apotheosis that typically capped off revistas, or with the merging of actors and audience that comes at the end of *Mystery-Bouffe*. Like the German plays Benjamin describes, it keeps the faith and fails in the quest for redemption, leaving its hollow characters to confront their (extra)terrestrial fate under the shadow of a death's head. The final tableau brings us back to the strange ménage-à-trois of St. Peter, Icar, and his wife, who are in a waiting room of the Interplanetary Railway, which connects the Socialist Earth (now the Red Planet) to Mars (home of reactionaries and boy scouts) by means of the spaceship invented by Icar. These marginal figures have been reduced to begging for coins under the watchful eyes of the GPU, the secret police of the Soviet state. "We are Marx's impoverished proletariat," Icar sighs (109). In one of the play's oddly prophetic moments, they mention that a radio announcer has just broken the news of Hitler's suicide—a path that Getúlio Vargas, too, would take in August 1954 when faced with a military coup. Icar plunges into space, dangling from a cord attached to an Ícaro as it departs the station while shouting that in death he can be the "hero of Wagner, of Jules Verne." St. Peter offers, "I'll play our funeral. The funeral of a world," then cranks out Siegfried's funeral march on his accordion. His last words, arms raised toward the heavens: "We have been judged!" (119).

Lost in the Stratosphere

St. Peter and his fellow travelers would indeed be judged—and condemned for a second time. After the head of the political police delivered his secret verdict on the play and the chief of Vice prohibited Teatro da Experiência from resuming operations, CAM requested an injunction to block the order from going into effect. In the meantime, as the case made its way to court, the theater continued to push the envelope with "Coisas de negro" (Black Things), a display of "forgotten" dances "from the era of slavery" directed by Henricão and Francisco Pires, another black musician who had been involved in *O bailado do deus morto* (figure 6.9). Performed twice each evening (at 8:30 and 10 P.M.) on several consecutive nights, the show reportedly drew large crowds, among which were many "women and young ladies of the best society" who fervently applauded the *tambu, dança das enxadas*, and what was unabashedly billed as "an authentic *macumba*."[88] Such a scenario does of course raise questions about the dubious desires, primitivist fantasies, and unequal power dynamics that might have shaped black artists' involvement in the activities of CAM; yet it would be a mistake to let the desire for a perfect purity of political intention obscure just how unusual such a show and social space were, or what radical potential they might have held for forging new alliances.

These "black things" seem to have been the last performances held at the theater before the legal decision was handed down on December 14. Judge Armando Fairbanks (a member of the Integralist Party, according to Flávio's account)[89] was clearly intent on establishing a broad precedent, and so in his verdict he refrains from saying much about the particulars of the case, noting only that "the simple reading of the two plays that accompany these reports [*O homem e o cavalo* and the Russian play] fully justifies the attitude of the police." In confirming the right of the police to censor or prohibit performances of plays, he cites a long list of laws beginning with an 1824 decree and ending with a 1928 regulation that purportedly outlawed "depressing or aggressive allusions" to religion or figures of authority—along with works that "seek to create violent antagonism between races or different classes of society or, finally, propagate ideas subversive of the order and actual organization of society." Fairbanks goes on to cite similar laws from Argentina, Italy, Belgium, France, and the United States, and then, in a bold display of Legal Order as pure performance, he substantiates a claim made by the police, who had argued that the International Geneva Convention forbid the circulation of such "subversive" materials. What this all boils down to is that it is not the role of the courts to second-guess those who enforce the law: "The power of the police cannot be imprisoned in formulas, given that police action is by its very nature indefinite and discretionary."[90] In other words, the law is a function of its own performance, and the performative act is the prerogative of those who have a monopoly on the use of physical force, ergo the state of exception is the rule. The court's decision provoked an outcry from prominent intellectuals as far away as Buenos Aires (including those associated with the journal *Sur*)[91] and a fiery speech in the national constituent assembly by an opposition delegate who decried the suppression of a valiant

FRANCISCO PIRES que dirigirá o
Tambú hoje à noite no Theatro
da Experiencia

Figure 6.9. Francisco Pires, one of the directors of "Coisas de negro" (Black Things) at the Teatro da Experiência. *Folha da Noite*, December 5, 1933.

attempt to form a "completely independent theater."[92] The club labored on for a few more weeks, hosting a fiery, four-hour talk about Mexican muralism by David Alfaro Siqueiros, who had just been expelled from Argentina while on a visit and was headed to the United States.[93] Yet within weeks the Clube dos Artistas Modernos, beset by financial difficulties and declining membership, had closed its doors.[94]

And what about *O homem e o cavalo*? Sometime the following year Oswald received a letter from his wife Pagu, who was traveling around the world as a foreign correspondent (she wished him a "good day from the land of Hitler"), informing him that while in the Soviet Union she had met the "organizer of revolutionary theater" and was certain it would be possible to stage *O homem e o cavalo* there;[95] not long after that, Oswald claimed the play had been translated into Russian, though there is no evidence a performance ever came to pass.[96] Samuel Putnam, a literary critic and communist who would become an important advocate of Brazilian literature in the United States, was also interested in staging the play and perhaps even turning it into a film. This project, too, was abandoned, though a rough translation/adaptation of the script still lies in Putnam's personal archive in Carbondale, Illinois.[97]

The critic Sábato Magaldi was correct when he stated that this sprawling spectacle "doesn't even seem to belong to the reality of Brazilian theater." The wanderings of St. Peter, Icar, and the Missus confirm the necessity of considering the avant-garde as part of a global totality; indeed, the play insists that from the very beginning the avant-garde was a "global" phenomenon. Yet the play also reveals that being integrated into a single system was what sowed the deepest divisions within the vanguard. If O homem e o cavalo is difficult to understand within the contours of Brazilian theater, and if the few critics who discuss the play struggle to contain it within the limits of literary discourse, that is because it lies in the middle of a critical split—a "transition" between "the war horse and the turf horse (bourgeois society) and horsepower (socialist society)"—that was never realized on the world stage.

Postscript

✦

Loose Ends

How should a book about an unfinished art end?

A number of years ago, when I first began research on the project that would become *The Unfinished Art of Theater*, it was hard not to feel overwhelmed by a sense of historical déjà vu. The financial crisis of 2007 was percolating and then came to pass, and even before the pundits started announcing that it was 1929 all over again, I could palpably feel the connections to a past I was just starting to piece together as the result of my readings, time spent in archives in Mexico and Brazil, and a growing intuition about certain things that were missing or never explicitly said. Over the subsequent years the parallel has been borne out in certain regards: echoes of the 1920s and 1930s are evident in the messy structural realignments of state power and global capital occurring today, the growing recognition of the limits of liberalism and the electoral system, political polarization, and (in many places, with undoubtedly more to come) physical face-offs between fascists and antifascists. Some of the questions people are now asking about art and education and their relationship to labor, capital, and the state resonate quite clearly with the ones avant-garde intellectuals were asking nearly a century ago. Without a doubt, my experiences of and perspective on the present have had a role in shaping the stories I tell in this book, which seeks to pull back on the sense of futurity so often associated with the avant-garde and insist that it is equally tied to the experience of backwardness, dependency, and uneven development.

It is important to remember, though, that history only happens once: even if (as Marx argued) history repeats itself, the first time as tragedy and the second as farce, the difference in genre is hardly inconsequential.

When I sent the full manuscript of this book to the press for review I was in Brazil, where the president, Dilma Rousseff, was facing the threat of impeachment under the pretense of a violation of budgetary rules; a little less than a year later, when I sent in my final revisions (once again from Brazil), Rousseff had long since been ousted, and the right-wing agenda of the new government was increasingly clear, as were the limitations of a Workers' Party program that had been predicated on a global commodity boom destined to go bust. The government of Getúlio Vargas, the eventual dictator who casts a shadow over the final chapter of this book, had censored artists and imprisoned intellectuals, but it had also built up the cultural bureaucracy; in contrast, one of the first acts of the new president, Michel Temer, was to shut down the Ministry of Culture, which under Lula (Rousseff's predecessor) had been led by the musician Gil Gilberto, one of the leaders of the Tropicália counterculture movement of the 1960s and 1970s who had claimed the mantle of the modernista avant-garde. Although the ministry was subsequently reinstated, defunding of universities and attacks on affirmative action have followed, and now intellectuals and artists who only recently enjoyed unprecedented prerogatives from the state (coupled with corporate funding incentivized by tax breaks) are faced with the question: Where to from here?

The situation is a little different in Mexico, where avant-garde artists of the 1920s and 1930s were more fully integrated into the creation of the postrevolutionary cultural infrastructure. There the sense of uncertainty and urgency has been building for some time, as the government has made moves to rescind the right to a public education (among other guarantees made in the Constitution of 1917) while simultaneously waging a "war on drugs" in which well over one hundred thousand have died. The first chapter of this book focuses on the theater projects of José Vasconcelos, who as the founding director of the Secretariat of Public Education created schools, sent teachers into the countryside on educational "missions," and helped foster the formation of the *vanguardias*. Decades later, the name of the town of Ayotzinapa has served as a rallying cry for opposition to the state ever since the night of September 26, 2014, when forty-three student protestors from a rural teachers' college were abducted by local police and handed over to a cartel to be killed; more recently, in Nochixtlán, Oaxaca, federal police killed six supporters of a teachers' union during a demonstration against the government's educational "reforms."

It felt wrong to end without acknowledging all of this, especially since it is plain to me that some of what is taking place today has roots in what did and didn't happen during the era of the avant-gardes. At the same time, I am wary of turning a book about the past into a pat lesson for today. I can only hope this book will prompt readers to reflect on how institutions work, what kinds of choices have to be made, and what art can and can't do. Brecht insisted that theater should bring contradictions to a head yet never allow the resolution (or revolution) to be enacted onstage—and although a book is *not* a staged play, I also prefer to leave the ends loose in recognition of the fact that the future isn't on this page.

Introduction

1. Mário de Andrade, *O banquete* (São Paulo: Livraria Duas Cidades, 1977), 61–62.

2. Décio de Almeida Prado, "O teatro e o modernismo," in *Peças, pessoas, personagens: O teatro brasileiro de Procópio Ferreira a Cacilda Becker* (São Paulo: Companhia das Letras, 1993), 15.

3. Victor Turner, *From Ritual to Theatre: The Human Seriousness of Play* (New York: Performing Arts Journal Publications, 1982), 13.

4. Leon Trotsky, "Peculiarities of Russia's Development," in *History of the Russian Revolution*, trans. Max Eastman (New York: Pathfinder, 1980), 31.

5. Hal Foster, *The Return of the Real: The Avant-Garde at the End of the Century* (Cambridge, Mass.: MIT Press, 1996), 8.

6. Mauricio Tenorio, "A Tropical Cuauhtemoc: Celebrating the Cosmic Race at the Guanabara Bay," *Anales del Instituto de Investigaciones Estéticas* 65 (1994): 93–137.

7. Tenorio mentions these details, but see also José Vasconcelos, *La raza cósmica: Misión de la raza iberoamericana* (Barcelona: Agencia Mundial de Librería, 1925), 58–66, for his visit to São Paulo.

8. For the prologue (the only part still commonly read), see José Vasconcelos, *The Cosmic Race: A Bilingual Edition*, trans. Didier T. Jaén (Baltimore: Johns Hopkins University Press, 1997).

9. Tenorio, "A Tropical Cuauhtemoc," 93.

10. Toward the end of the 1920s Brazilian modernistas associated with the Verde-Amarelista group, some of whom later founded the fascist Integralist Party, would approvingly cite Vasconcelos's notion of the cosmic race (see, for instance, Plínio Salgado's "Revolução da Anta"), but there is no indication of earlier contact.

11. In the past decade or so there has been a growing number of comparative studies on Mexico and Brazil that deal with topics ranging from literature, film, and urban protest to environmentalism, judicial reform, and multinational corporations. For the most relevant, see Esther Gabara, *Errant Modernism: The Ethos of Photography in Mexico and Brazil* (Durham, N.C.: Duke University Press, 2008); Rielle Navitski, *Public Spectacles of Violence: Sensational Cinema and Journalism in Early Twentieth-Century Mexico and Brazil* (Durham, N.C.: Duke University Press, 2017); Sergio Delgado Moya, *Delirious Consumption: Aesthetics and Consumer Capitalism in Mexico and Brazil* (Austin: University of Texas Press, 2017); and Paulo Moreira, *Literary and Cultural Relations between Mexico and Brazil: Deep Undercurrents* (New York: Palgrave Macmillan, 2013).

12. Immanuel Wallerstein, *The Capitalist World-Economy* (Cambridge: Cambridge University Press, 1979).

13. Roberto Schwarz, "As idéias fora do lugar," *Estudos CEBRAP* 3 (1973): 151–161. For a translation see "Misplaced Ideas: Literature and Society in Late-Nineteenth-Century Brazil," in *Misplaced Ideas*, trans. John Gledson (London: Verso, 1992), 19–32.

14. For a broad look at the Export Age and restructuring after 1929, see Victor Bulmer-Thomas, *The Economic History of Latin America since Independence* (Cambridge: Cambridge University Press, 2014), 50–254; and Tulio Halperín Donghi, *The Contemporary History of Latin America*, trans. John Charles Chasteen (Durham, N.C.: Duke University Press, 1993), 158–246.

15. Giovanni Arrighi, *The Long Twentieth Century: Money, Power, and the Origins of Our Times* (New York: Verso, 2010), 64.

16. Although there is no room to explore this topic here, it is worth noting that the appearance of "avant-garde" movements in the United States in the 1960s and 1970s coincides with the Vietnam War and a perceived decline in U.S. world power, exacerbated by the economic recession of the early 1970s.

17. Peter Bürger, *Theory of the Avant-Garde*, trans. Michael Shaw (Minneapolis: University of Minnesota Press, 1984).

18. Foster, *The Return of the Real*, 8.

19. Ericka Beckman, *Capital Fictions: The Literature of the Export Age* (Minneapolis: University of Minnesota Press, 2012), 42–79.

20. Julio Ramos, *Divergent Modernities: Culture and Politics in Nineteenth-Century Latin America*, trans. John D. Blanco (Durham, N.C.: Duke University Press, 2001).

21. George Yúdice points to this problem in his argument for a "conjunctural" understanding of the avant-garde that would take into account the struggle for local autonomy and the "logic of community building" in explaining the pro-modernization and statist tendencies of many peripheral avant-gardes (56). From my perspective, however, Yúdice is too willing to overlook the contradictions of these "community-building" projects, and we need to guard against taking the state (or the local) as the only means of resistance to imperialism. "Rethinking the Theory of the Avant-Garde from the Periphery," in *Modernism and Its Margins: Reinscribing Cultural Modernity from Spain and Latin America*, ed. Anthony L. Geist and José Monleón (New York: Garland, 1999), 52–80.

22. Fernando J. Rosenberg, *The Avant-Garde and Geopolitics in Latin America* (Pittsburgh: University of Pittsburgh Press, 2006), 3.

23. Trotsky, "Futurism," in *Literature and Revolution*, trans. Rose Strunsky (New York: Haymarket Books, 2005), 112–113.

24. Trotsky, "Peculiarities of Russia's Development," 31.

25. Marx makes a similar point in his "Introduction to a Critique of Hegel's Philosophy of Right," where he rails against the backwardness of Germany but also notes that in the sphere of political theory it offers a much clearer view of developments in England than that country's own philosophers do.

26. Trotsky, "Futurism," 121, 137.

27. Trotsky, "Futurism," 115.

28. Leon Trotsky, "The Formalist School of Poetry and Marxism," in *Literature and Revolution*, trans. Rose Strunsky (New York: Haymarket Books, 2005), 150.

29. One example of this move to subsume the idea of uneven development *into* the literary field as a way of bolstering the claim of literary autonomy is Pascale

Casanova, *The World Republic of Letters*, trans. M. B. DeBevoise (Cambridge, Mass.: Harvard University Press, 2004). I find it puzzling that Casanova can use the language of uneven development—even when referring to the early twentieth century—without making any reference to Trotsky and other political figures who debated this issue and explicitly addressed literary issues. (The same could also be said of Franco Moretti, despite his Marxist affiliations, and of Fredric Jameson, who is strangely silent about how Trotsky's idea might relate to his own framework of "uneven modernization.") One exception to the tendency to dehistoricize the concept and detach it from its radical political links is the Warwick Research Collective's recent *Combined and Uneven Development: Towards a New Theory of World-Literature* (Liverpool: Liverpool University Press, 2015). For work in modernist/avant-garde studies that addresses Trotsky's concept, see Ruth Jennison, *The Zukofsky Era: Modernity, Margins, and the Avant-Garde* (Baltimore: Johns Hopkins University Press, 2012); Harsha Ram, "Futurist Geographies: Uneven Modernities and the Struggle for Aesthetic Autonomy: Paris, Italy, Russia, 1909–1914," in *The Oxford Handbook of Global Modernisms*, ed. Mark Wollaeger and Matt Eatough (Oxford: Oxford University Press, 2012), 313–340; and Martin Puchner, *Poetry of the Revolution: Marx, Manifestos, and the Avant-Gardes* (Princeton, N.J.: Princeton University Press, 2005).

30. Walter Benjamin, *The Origin of German Tragic Drama*, trans. John Osborne (New York: Verso, 1998).

31. Friedrich Schiller, "On the Stage as a Moral Institution," in *Aesthetic and Philosophical Essays* (Boston: S. E. Cassino, 1884), 339.

32. David Lloyd and Paul Thomas, *Culture and the State* (New York: Routledge, 1997), 5.

33. Nicholas Ridout, *Passionate Amateurs: Theatre, Communism, and Love* (Ann Arbor: University of Michigan Press, 2013), 6.

34. Loren Kruger, *The National Stage: Theatre and Cultural Legitimation in England, France, and America* (Chicago: University of Chicago Press, 1992), 187.

35. Antonin Artaud, *The Theater and Its Double*, trans. Mary Caroline Richards (New York: Grove, 1994), 140.

36. Martin Puchner, *Stage Fright: Modernism, Anti-Theatricality, and Drama* (Baltimore: Johns Hopkins University Press, 2002).

37. Vicky Unruh, *Latin American Vanguards: The Art of Contentious Encounters* (Berkeley: University of California Press, 2004). Unruh uses the term "aesthetic activism" throughout the book.

38. On early theater history in Brazil, see Severino João Albuquerque, "The Brazilian Theater up to 1900," in *The Cambridge History of Latin American Literature*, vol. 3, ed. Roberto González Echevarría and Enrique Pupo-Walker (Cambridge: Cambridge University Press, 1996), 105–125. Also useful is the encyclopedic *História do teatro brasileiro*, vol. 1: *Das origens ao teatro professional da primeira metade do século XX* (São Paulo: Perspectiva, 2012). There is very little on Mexican theater in the nineteenth century, but see Patricia Ybarra, "Theatricality and the Public Enactment of the Mexican Colonial," in *A History of Mexican Literature*, ed. Ignacio Sánchez Prado, Anna M. Nogar, and José Ramón Ruisánchez Serra (Cambridge: Cambridge University Press, 2016), 53–65.

39. I develop these ideas in more detail elsewhere. See "*De sobremesa*, 'crónicas revestidas de galas' y el escenario ausente del modernismo hispano-

americano," *Revista Iberoamericana* 232–233 (July–December 2010): 939–956; and "Modernism's Unfinished Stage: Theatre in Latin America," in *The Modernist World*, ed. Stephen Ross and Allana Lindgren (New York: Routledge, 2015), 417–425.

40. Diana Taylor, *The Archive and the Repertoire: Performing Cultural Memory in the Americas* (Durham, N.C.: Duke University Press, 2003).

41. Fred Moten, *In the Break: The Aesthetics of the Black Radical Tradition* (Minneapolis: University of Minnesota Press, 2003), 192–210; Rebecca Schneider, *Performing Remains: Art and War in Times of Theatrical Reenactment* (New York: Routledge, 2011), 7.

42. For good overviews, see Alejandro Ortiz Bullé Goyri, *Teatro y vanguardia en el México posrevolucionario (1920–1940)* (Azcapotzalco: Universidad Autónoma Metropolitana, 2005); and "O teatro e o modernismo de 1922," in *História do teatro brasileiro*, vol. 2: *Do modernismo às tendências contemporâneas*, ed. João Roberto Faria (São Paulo: Perspectiva, 2013), 21–56.

Chapter 1

1. Enrique Krauze uses this term in his influential *Caudillos culturales en la Revolución Mexicana* (Mexico City: Siglo Veintiuno, 1976), as does Joaquín Cárdenas in *José Vasconcelos: Caudillo cultural* (Oaxaca: Universidad José Vasconcelos de Oaxaca, 2002). The scare quotes register my skepticism of the phrase, which conflates symbolic and political power and overestimates the force that "culture" had at the time.

2. "Más de cien niñas que iban a morir insoladas ayer en el Estadio Nacional," *Excélsior*, April 28, 1924. It is clear from later reports that none of the children were in serious condition.

3. Vasconcelos's communiqué was reprinted under the headline "Circular que giró el Secretario de Educación Pública," *Excélsior*, April 29, 1924. According to the paper, Vasconcelos had fifty thousand copies printed and sent out; he later repented and revoked his order, but they had already been distributed to many schools.

4. Antonio Cornejo Polar, "*Mestizaje,* Transculturation, Heterogeneity," in *The Latin American Cultural Studies Reader*, ed. Ana del Sarto, Alicia Ríos, and Abril Trigo, trans. Christopher Dennis (Durham, N.C.: Duke University Press, 2004), 116.

5. For a few months in 1940, Vasconcelos was the editor of the pro-Nazi journal *Timón*, published in Mexico by the German embassy. Much of his motivation seems to have been his anti-U.S. sentiment. See Itzhak Bar-Lewaw, *La revista "Timón" y José Vasconcelos* (Mexico City: Casa Edimex, 1971).

6. Theodor Adorno, "The Essay as Form," in *Notes to Literature*, vol. 1, trans. Shierry Weber Nicholson (New York: Columbia University Press, 1991), 11.

7. Réda Bensmäia makes a similar point when he describes the essay as a cinematic montage, a mise-en-scène or "theatricalization" that "renders language limitless in multiplying perspectives and points of view, and in highlighting the 'limits' (rhetorical, formal, and above all ideological) of other languages." "L'art de l'essai chez Montaigne," *Continuum* 3 (1991): 19.

8. Alfonso Reyes, "Las nuevas artes," in *Obras completes*, vol. 9 (Mexico City: Fondo de Cultura Económica, 1959), 400–403.

9. Jacques Derrida, "The Law of Genre," trans. Avital Ronell, *Critical Inquiry* 7 (Autumn 1980): 55.

10. For a useful critique of the discourse of hybridity in Latin America that takes Derrida's Law of Genre as its point of departure, see Joshua Lund, *The Impure Imagination: Toward a Critical Hybridity in Latin American Writing* (Minneapolis: University of Minnesota Press, 2006). See also Lund, *Mestizo State: Reading Race in Modern Mexico* (Minneapolis: University of Minnesota Press, 2012).

11. The journal was *Cuadernos*, which Arciniegas edited from 1963 to 1965. Four decades earlier, when Vasconcelos was the director of Mexico's Secretariat of Public Education, Arciniegas led a group of Colombian university students in proclaiming him "Maestro de las Américas."

12. Germán Arciniegas, "Nuestra América es un ensayo," *Cuadernos* 73 (June 1963): 356.

13. The tautological nature of this statement is underscored by the reference to José Martí's "Our America," which is now usually read as an essay. Strangely, Arciniegas does not mention this canonical text.

14. Claudio Lomnitz, "Introduction: The Project and the Labyrinth," in *Exits from the Labyrinth: Culture and Ideology in the Mexican National Space* (Berkeley: University of California Press, 1992).

15. Horacio Legrás, "El Ateneo y los orígenes del estado ético en México," *Latin American Research Review* 38, no. 2 (June 2003): 39.

16. Julio Ramos, *Divergent Modernities: Culture and Politics in Nineteenth-Century Latin America*, trans. John D. Blanco (Durham, N.C.: Duke University Press, 2001), 233. See also 238–246.

17. On Reyes (an important interlocutor for Vasconcelos), see Robert T. Conn, *The Politics of Philology: Alfonso Reyes and the Invention of the Latin American Literary Tradition* (Lewisburg, Pa.: Bucknell University Press, 2002), and Ignacio Sánchez Prado, "The Age of Utopia: Alfonso Reyes, Deep Time and the Critique of Colonial Modernity," *Romance Notes* 53, no. 1 (2013): 93–104.

18. José Vasconcelos, *The Cosmic Race: A Bilingual Edition*, trans. Didier T. Jaén (Baltimore: Johns Hopkins University Press, 1997), 29.

19. Ignacio Sánchez Prado, "El mestizaje en el corazón de la utopia: *La raza cósmica* entre Aztlán y América Latina," *Revista Canadiense de Estudios Hispánicos* 33, no. 2 (Winter 2009): 386–389.

20. Ramos, *Divergent Modernities*, 240–241.

21. As Thomas O. Beebee argues, "What makes genre ideological is our practice of speaking of it as a 'thing' rather than as the expression of a relationship between user and text." Beebee, *The Ideology of Genre: A Comparative Study of Generic Instability* (University Park: Pennsylvania State University Press, 1994), 18.

22. Fredric Jameson, *The Political Unconscious: Narrative as a Socially Symbolic Act* (Ithaca, N.Y.: Cornell University Press, 1981), 95.

23. Carlos Monsiváis, "José Vasconcelos: La búsqueda del paraíso perdido," *Comunidad* 3, no. 8 (August 1968): 353–354.

24. On Vasconcelos's activities during the revolution, see Luis A. Marentes, *José Vasconcelos and the Writing of the Mexican Revolution* (New York: Twayne, 2000), xi–31. Although he was born in the southern state of Oaxaca in 1882, Vasconcelos spent his childhood in the northern state of Coahuila, where

his father was a customs official. He attended primary school across the border in Texas and did stints in secondary schools in central Mexico and Campeche before ending up in Mexico City, where he completed a law degree. Prior to the revolution he worked for a New York firm that legalized the purchase of land and mines in Mexico.

25. José Vasconcelos, "The Military Convention of Aguascalientes Is Sovereign," in *The Sovereign Revolutionary Convention of Mexico and the Attitude of the General Francisco Villa* (Washington, D.C.: Confidential Agency of the Provisional Government of Mexico, 1915), 1. For the Spanish version (which closely corresponds to the translation), see "La convención militar de Aguascalientes es soberana," in *La tormenta* (Mexico City: Ediciones Botas, 1937), 168–193.

26. Joshua Lund and Alejandro Sánchez Lopera, "Revolutionary Mexico, the Sovereign People, and the Problem of Men with Guns," *Política Común* 7 (2015), accessed March 12, 2017, http://quod.lib.umich.edu/p/pc/12322227.0007.003?view=text;rgn=main.

27. Vasconcelos, "The Military Convention of Aguascalientes," 8.

28. For his analogy between the state of exception and the miracle, see Carl Schmitt, *Political Theology: Four Chapters on the Concept of Sovereignty*, trans. George Schwab (Chicago: University of Chicago Press, 2006), 36–52.

29. For a consideration of this moment, see Gareth Williams, *The Mexican Exception: Sovereignty, Police, and Democracy* (New York: Palgrave Macmillan, 2011), 41–63.

30. On Vasconcelos's interest in Indian philosophy, see Laura J. Torres-Rodríguez, "Orientalizing Mexico: *Estudios indostánicos* and the Place of India in José Vasconcelos's *La raza cósmica*," *Revista Hispánica Moderna* 68, no. 1 (June 2015). The Theosophical Society was founded in 1875 in New York by a group that included the U.S. Buddhist Henry Steel Olcott and Helena Blavatsky, a Russian occultist. It sought to form a Universal Brotherhood of Humanity with no distinctions based on race, creed, sex, caste, or color. On its influence among Latin American intellectuals, including Vasconcelos, see Eduardo Devés Valdés and Ricardo Melgar Bao, "Redes teosóficas y pensadores (políticos) latinoamericanos 1910–1930," *Cuadernos Americanos* 78 (1999): 137–152.

31. A second edition was published in Mexico in 1921.

32. See Raymond Skyrme, *Rubén Darío and the Pythagorean Tradition* (Gainesville: University Presses of Florida, 1975).

33. From an article in *El Universal*, March 10, 1923, cited in Tatiana Flores, *Mexico's Revolutionary Avant-Gardes: From Estridentismo to ¡30–30!* (New Haven, Conn.: Yale University Press, 2013), 71. I discuss estridentismo in chapters 2 and 3.

34. José Vasconcelos, *Pitágoras: Una teoría del ritmo* (La Habana: Siglo XX, 1916), 6.

35. Veit Erlmann, *Reason and Resonance: A History of Modern Aurality* (Cambridge, Mass.: MIT Press, 2010), 24–25.

36. Michael Golston, *Rhythm and Race in Modernist Poetry and Science* (New York: Columbia University Press, 2008).

37. Georg Simmel, "The Rhythm or Symmetry of the Contents of Life," in *The Philosophy of Money*, trans. David Frisby (New York: Routledge, 2004), 491–497.

38. One well-known example of the latter was Karl Bücher, whose *Arbeit und Rhythmus* (Labor and Rhythm, 1896) is discussed in Erlmann, *Reason and Resonance*, 289–291, and in Golston, *Rhythm and Race*, 21–24.

39. Friedrich Nietzsche, *Beyond Good and Evil: Prelude to a Philosophy of the Future*, trans. Walter Kaufmann (New York: Vintage Books, 1966), 230.

40. Emile Jacques-Dalcroze, *Rhythm, Music, and Education*, trans. Harold F. Rubinstein (New York: G. P. Putnam's Sons, 1921), xiii.

41. See Richard C. Beacham, *Adolphe Appia, Theater Artist* (Cambridge: Cambridge University Press, 1987), 42–85. Appia and Dalcroze collaborated on a celebrated production of Gluck's opera *Orfeo* at Hellerau in 1912–1913.

42. See Samuel Chávez, "Lo que es la gimnasia llamada especialmente gimnasia rítmica en sus relaciones con el baile y la gimnasia común," *El Maestro* (January–February 1922): 468–483. In 1910 Chávez had designed the Anfiteatro del Antiguo Colegio de San Idelfonso, site of Rivera's mural *La creación*.

43. For how Vasconcelos builds on Bergson, see Patrick Romanell, "Bergson in Mexico: A Tribute to José Vasconcelos," *Philosophy and Phenomenological Research* 21, no. 4 (June 1961): 501–513.

44. Jane Bennett, *Vibrant Matter: A Political Ecology of Things* (Durham, N.C.: Duke University Press, 2010). Bennett also links her ideas to a long history of philosophical monism (Lucretius, Spinoza, Bergson, Deleuze) and draws on Nietzsche, Wagner, and the figure of Prometheus as well as the language of cellular biology.

45. Golston, *Rhythm and Race*, 7.

46. José Vasconcelos, *El monismo estético: Ensayos* (Mexico City: Tipografía Murguía, 1918), 4.

47. Ibsen originally wrote the verse drama *Peer Gynt* without any intention of seeing it staged, and although the drama was published in 1867, it was not staged until 1876.

48. Louis Althusser, "Ideology and Ideological State Apparatuses (Notes toward an Investigation)," in *Lenin and Philosophy*, trans. Ben Brewster (New York: Monthly Review, 2001), 112.

49. I insist here on this "almost" in opposition to those who simply replace ideology with an emphasis on affect and habit as the sole mediums of social contestation and control. Jon Beasley-Murray, for instance, states that "the politics of habit is not the clash of ideologies within a theater of representation. It is a politics that is immanent and corporeal, that works directly through the body." But theater itself belies such a simplistic (and ultimately idealist) opposition between ideas and affect. It is inseparable from the issue of embodiment, yet as a number of scholars have pointed out, it is also derived from the same Greek root as "theory." See Beasley-Murray, *Posthegemony: Political Theory and Latin America* (Minneapolis: University of Minnesota Press, 2010), 181.

50. Martin Harries, "Theater after Film, or Dismediation," *ELH* 83, no. 2 (Summer 2016): 358. For the quotes in their original context, see Althusser, "Ideology and Ideological State Apparatuses," 120, 118.

51. Althusser, "Ideology and Ideological State Apparatuses," 108.

52. Harries, "Theater after Film," 358.

53. José Vasconcelos, *Prometeo vencedor: Tragedia moderna en un prólogo y tres actos* (Mexico City: Lectura Selecta, 1920), 5.

54. Claude Fell refers to Vasconcelos's "unfortunate incursions into the theater" in "El ideario literario de José Vasconcelos (1916–1930)," *Nueva Revista de Filología Hispánica* 42, no. 2 (1994): 550. Felipe Garrido calls *Prometeo vencedor* "an improbable work of theater that lacks dramatic interest" in his "Ulises y Prometeo: Vasconcelos y las prensas universitarias," in *José Vasconcelos: De su vida y su obra*, ed. Álvaro Matute and Martha Donís (Mexico City: UNAM, 1982), 180. For a discussion of the play that is in dialogue with an earlier iteration of my own, see David S. Dalton, "Science and the Metaphysical Body: A Critique of Positivism in the Vasconcelian Utopia," *Revista Canadiense de Estudios Hispánicos* 40, no. 3 (Spring 2016): 535–559.

55. Vasconcelos, *Prometeo vencedor*, 9.

56. Nietzsche, *The Birth of Tragedy from the Spirit of Music and the Case of Wagner*, trans. Walter Kaufmann (New York: Vintage Books, 1967), 69.

57. Andrea Wilson Nightingale, *Genres in Dialogue: Plato and the Construct of Philosophy* (Cambridge: Cambridge University Press, 2000), 194.

58. Martin Puchner, *Stage Fright: Modernism, Anti-Theatricality, and Drama* (Baltimore: Johns Hopkins University Press, 2002), 18.

59. There is also a "racial" dimension to Nietzsche's celebration of Prometheus. Nietzsche sees the myth of Prometheus as exemplifying a specifically Aryan notion of active sin, as opposed to the "passive" Semitic myth of the Fall.

60. Martin Puchner, "The Theater in Modernist Thought," *New Literary History* 33, no. 3 (Summer 2002): 528.

61. Vasconcelos, *El monismo estético*, 8.

62. Adorno, "The Essay as Form," 17.

63. See Jeffrey Sconce, *Haunted Media: Electronic Presence from Telegraphy to Television* (Durham, N.C.: Duke University Press, 2000).

64. Jorge Mañach's "Indagación del choteo" (1928) draws on Bergson's essay "On Laughter" (a point of connection with Vasconcelos). In Mexico, *relajo* was associated with the working-class *pelado* character and the actor Cantinflas, who started off performing in *carpa* (tent) theaters in the 1920s and later transitioned to cinema. Two classic texts—both regarded as essays of Mexican identity—are Samuel Ramos's *El perfil del hombre y la cultura en México* (1934) and Jorge Portilla's *Fenomenología del relajo* (1966).

65. José Vasconcelos, "El teatro al aire libre de la Universidad Nacional," *El Universal Ilustrado*, February 16, 1922, 23.

66. The verb *querer,* used here as a noun, is difficult to translate, since it can mean "wanting" (in a sexual or nonsexual sense), "wishing," or "loving."

67. José Vasconcelos, *Ulises criollo: Edición crítica* (Madrid: ALLCA XX, 2000), 408–409.

68. The *sainete* is a one-act farce, usually involving music, and was originally performed between longer plays. It originated in Spain but became popular in Latin America in the nineteenth century, where it took on regional characteristics. The *entremés* is a similar genre that was popular in Spain in the sixteenth and seventeenth centuries.

69. See John Ochoa, *The Uses of Failure in Mexican Literature and Identity* (Austin: University of Texas Press, 2004), for a very helpful and relevant discussion of the role of failure in Vasconcelos's work.

70. Letter cited in Claude Fell, *José Vasconcelos: Los años del águila (1920–1925)* (Mexico City: UNAM, 1989), 464.

71. Fell, *José Vasconcelos*, 55–58.

72. Fell, *José Vasconcelos*, 20–21.

73. Lunacharsky's play *Vasilisa the Wise* (one of several he wrote) was published in 1919. There are many striking similarities between Vasconcelos and Lunacharsky that warrant more attention from a scholar with knowledge of Russian.

74. On Vasconcelos's ideas about theater and the activities of the SEP, see Fell, *José Vasconcelos*, 463–479. For a broader view of theater in this period, see Alejandro Ortiz Bullé Goyri, *Teatro y vanguardia en el México posrevolucionario (1920–1940)* (Mexico City: Universidad Metropolitana Autónoma, 2005).

75. Vasconcelos, "El teatro al aire libre."

76. Cited in Júbilo, "Las últimas opiniones acerca del teatro nacional," *El Universal Ilustrado*, March 2, 1922, 16.

77. Vasconcelos, "El teatro al aire libre."

78. Puchner, *Stage Fright*, 7–8.

79. Vasconcelos, *El desastre* (Mexico City: Ediciones Botas, 1938), 340.

80. See Diana Briuolo Destéfano, "El Estadio Nacional: Escenario de la raza cósmica," *Crónicas* 2 (1999): 19n28.

81. "La falta de unidad se debe a la intervención de hombres sin conocimientos arquitectónicos," *Excélsior*, April 20, 1924.

82. "Diego Rivera arremete contra los 'Galindos' de las Bellas Artes a propósito del Estadio," *El Demócrata*, April 28, 1924.

83. "Los pintores y la arquitectura," *El Universal*, May 3, 1924.

84. José Vasconcelos, "Inauguración del Estadio," in *Discursos: 1920–1950* (Mexico City: Botas, 1950), 115. The speech was also published in *Excélsior*, May 4, 1924.

85. "Con un grandioso festival se inauguró ayer el Estadio Nacional," *El Universal* (May 6, 1924); "Setenta mil personas asistieron ayer al acto solemne de la inauguración del Estadio Nacional," *El Demócrata*, May 6, 1924; and the *Excélsior* article cited in note 65.

86. "Un poema de sol, de color, de ritmo y de entusiasmo, fue la inauguración del gran Estadio Nacional," *Excélsior*, May 6, 1924.

87. "Cosas de artistas," *Excélsior*, April 29, 1924. Chapters 2 and 3 discuss the estridentista movement.

88. See, for example, Salvador Pioncelly, *José Villagrán García: Protagonista de la arquitectura mexicana del siglo XX* (Mexico City: Consejo Nacional para la Cultura y las Artes, Dirección General de Publicaciones, 2004), which omits any mention of the Estadio Nacional, and Ramón Vargas, *José Villagrán García: Vida y obra* (Mexico City: Universidad Autónoma Nacional de México, 2005), which includes a photo of the stadium but never mentions it.

89. Salvador Novo, "Imágenes de México," *Artes de México* 58/59 (1964): 8.

90. Rubén Gallo, *Mexican Modernity* (Cambridge, Mass.: MIT Press, 2005), 210.

91. Vasconcelos, "Inauguración del Estadio."

Chapter 2

1. Luis Quintanilla and Carlos González, *Teatro Mexicano del Murciélago* (Mexico City: Taller Gráfico de la Nación, 1924), 2. Eyewitness accounts suggest that the director Luis Quintanilla's comments were a direct translation of the text in this souvenir program. The most complete critical narrative of the Teatro Murciélago is Alejandro Ortiz Bullé Goyri, *Teatro y vanguardia en el México posrevolucionario (1920–1940)* (Azcapotzalco: Universidad Autónoma Metropolitana, 2005), 174–187. Ortiz stresses the influence of the Italian futurists' synthetic theater on the Murciélago, despite little evidence of a direct connection.

2. Jacobo Dalevuelta, *El Universal*, September 18, 1924.

3. Until recently, the standard references on estridentismo were those of Luis Mario Schneider, including his *El estridentismo, o una literatura de estrategia* (Mexico City: Instituto Nacional de Bellas Artes, 1970). More recent studies that emphasize their work in other media include Rubén Gallo, *Mexican Modernity: The Avant-Garde and the Technological Revolution* (Cambridge, Mass.: MIT Press, 2005); Tatiana Flores, *Mexico's Revolutionary Avant-Gardes: From Estridentismo to ¡30–30!* (New Haven, Conn.: Yale University Press, 2013); and Elissa J. Rashkin, *The Stridentist Movement: The Avant-Garde and Cultural Change in the 1920s* (Lanham, Md.: Lexington Books, 2009). See also *Vanguardia estridentista: Soporte de la estética revolucionaria* (Mexico City: Consejo Nacional para la Cultura y las Artes, 2010), the catalogue for a 2010 exhibition; and *Vanguardia en México, 1915–1940* (Mexico City: Museo Nacional de Arte, 2013), an essay collection published in conjunction with a 2013 exhibition.

4. Sara Ahmed, *The Cultural Politics of Emotion* (New York: Routledge, 2004), 45.

5. See Maurizio Lazzarato, "Immaterial Labor," in *Radical Thought in Italy: A Potential Politics*, ed. Paolo Virno and Michael Hardt (Minneapolis: University of Minnesota Press, 1996), 133–147; and Paolo Virno, *A Grammar of the Multitude* (Los Angeles: Semiotext(e), 2004). For a theater perspective, see Shannon Jackson, "Just-in-Time: Performance and the Aesthetics of Precarity," *TDR: The Drama Review* 56, no. 4 (Winter 2012): 10–31.

6. Karl Marx, *Capital: A Critique of Political Economy*, trans. Ben Fewkes, vol. 1 (New York: Penguin, 1976), 899, 929.

7. In addition to the sources cited in the chapter (i.e., Rosa Luxemburg and Silvia Federici), two sources that have helped shape my thinking are Massimo De Angelis, "Separating the Doing and the Deed," *Historical Materialism* 12, no. 2 (2004): 57–88; and Tony C. Brown, "The Time of Globalization: Rethinking Primitive Accumulation," *Rethinking Marxism* 21, no. 4 (2009): 571–584.

8. F. T. Marinetti, Emilio Settimelli, and Bruno Corra, "A Futurist Theater of Essential Brevity," in F. T. Marinetti, *Critical Writings*, ed. Günter Berghaus and trans. Doug Thompson (New York: Farrar, Straus and Giroux, 2006), 200.

9. John Muse, "The Dimensions of the Moment: Modernist Shorts," *Modern Drama* 53, no. 1 (Spring 2010): 78.

10. Karl Marx, *Grundrisse: Foundations of the Critique of Political Economy*, trans. Martin Nicolaus (London: Penguin, 1973), 539.

11. David Harvey, "Between Space and Time: Reflections on the Geographical Imagination," *Annals of the Association of American Geographers* 80, no. 3 (September 1990): 426.

12. Aleksandr Tairov, *Notes of a Director*, trans. William Kuhlke (Coral Gables, Fla.: University of Miami Press, 1969), 99.

13. On the cabbage parties see Konstantin Stanislavski, *My Life in Art*, trans. Jean Benedetti (London: Routledge, 2008), 309–313. Named for the cabbage pies eaten during Lent, the parties involved actors, musicians such as Sergei Rachmaninoff, and the directors Nemirovich-Danchenko and Stanislavsky himself.

14. See Anthony G. Pearson, "The Cabaret Comes to Russia: 'Theatre of Small Forms' as Cultural Catalyst," *Theatre Quarterly* 9, no. 36 (Winter 1980): 31–44. On cabaret culture in Europe, see Harold B. Segel, *Turn-of-the-Century Cabaret* (New York: Columbia University Press, 1987), including its account of Letuchaya Mysh (255–269).

15. In his questionable "confessions," which date from 1929, Baliev stated that Trotsky even attended a show and claimed he had been imprisoned before leaving the Soviet Union. Nikita Balieff, "My Cabaret Confessions," *New Yorker*, June 22, 1929, 29.

16. Oliver M. Sayler, "The Strange Story of the Chauve-Souris," in *F. Ray Comstock and Morris Gest Have the Honor to Present Balieff's Chauve-Souris* (New York, 1923), 13.

17. Prior to this, however, Théâtre Fémina had also hosted Lugné-Poe's Théâtre de l'Oeuvre, known for its symbolist productions of August Strindberg and Henrik Ibsen. Lugné-Poe was an admirer of the Chauve-Souris and wrote at least two reviews of the show. For excerpts see Lawrence Sullivan, "Nikita Baliev's Le Théâtre de la Chauve-Souris: An Avant-Garde Theater," *Dance Research Journal* 18, no. 2 (Winter 1986–1987): 17–29.

18. According to Richard Taruskin, Stravinsky attended a performance of the Chauve-Souris with Diaghilev and Sudeikin and became infatuated with Zhenya Nikitina, the ballerina who played Katinka. Stravinsky orchestrated four short pieces for the show (including the polka for the Katinka number), and these eventually became his Suite No. 2 for Small Orchestra. Shortly afterward Stravinsky started an affair with Sudeikin's wife Vera, whom he eventually married. Taruskin, *Stravinsky and the Russian Traditions: A Biography of the Works through Mavra* (Berkeley: University of California Press, 1996), 1546–1549.

19. A.N., "Avant-Première—'La Chauve-Souris' au Théâtre Femina," *Bonsoir*, December 20, 1920, 3. My translation of the original French cited in Sullivan, "Nikita Baliev's Le Théâtre de la Chauve-Souris," 21.

20. Régis Gignoux, "Les Premières," *Figaro*, March 23, 1921, 4. My translation of the original French cited in Sullivan, "Nikita Baliev's Le Théâtre de la Chauve-Souris," 22.

21. Marx, *Capital*, 128.

22. Susan Stewart, "Miniature," in *On Longing: Narratives of the Miniature, the Gigantic, the Souvenir, the Collection* (Durham, N.C.: Duke University Press, 1993), 65.

23. Olga Hadley, *Mamontov's Private Opera: The Search for Modernism in Russian Theater* (Bloomington: Indiana University Press, 2010).

24. Quotes from reviews that compared the production to film are cited in Sullivan, "Nikita Baliev's Le Théâtre de la Chauve-Souris." Sullivan also cites Robert de Beauplan, who referred to the Chauve-Souris as an "avant-garde school" (*école d'avant-garde*) in "Le Théâtre," *La Liberté*, December 28, 1920, 3.

25. Nozière, "Femme de Luxe—La Chauve-Souris," *L'Avenir*, February 5, 1921, 2. Cited in Sullivan, "Nikita Baliev's Le Théâtre de la Chauve-Souris," 25. The Chauve-Souris's fascination with Asian and Muslim countries evokes a long history of Russian orientalism, which was linked to empire-building and continued during the Soviet period. Yet orientalism could also act as a destabilizing form of otherness, and in this case it was complicated by the fact that Baliev was from Armenia, the status of which was in question between the end of the Russian Revolution and the founding of the Soviet Union in 1922.

26. Peggy Phelan, *Unmarked: The Politics of Performance* (New York: Routledge, 1993), 146.

27. Marx, *Capital*, 1039. Says Marx: "A singer who sings like a bird is an unproductive worker. If she sells her song for money, she is to that extent a wage-labourer or merchant. But if the same singer is engaged by an entrepreneur who makes her sing to make money, then she becomes a productive worker, since she *produces* capital directly" (1044).

28. Nicholas Ridout, *Passionate Amateurs: Theatre, Communism, and Love* (Ann Arbor: University of Michigan Press, 2013), 50.

29. On June 5, the Chauve-Souris moved to the Century Roof Theater for its summer run; in preparation for this Nikolai Remisov, one of the Chauve-Souris set designers, painted and decorated the theater with Russian and orientalist iconography. The group gave its final performance on May 5, 1923, after which it returned to Paris, but it had a reprisal on Broadway in late 1923–1924 and returned several other times, also traveling to other cities across the United States. It continued to tour until 1934.

30. The performance of *No Siree!* took place at the Forty-Ninth Street Theatre for an invitation-only audience. See Billy Altman, *Laughter's Gentle Soul: The Life of Robert Benchley* (New York: W. W. Norton, 1997), 198–209.

31. The music was adapted from a song by the German composer Leon Jessel. The Chauve-Souris turned it into a runaway hit, and in 1933 the Rockettes choreographed a version for their Radio City Christmas Spectacular, which is still performed today.

32. In 1934 the writer Nathanael West submitted a proposal to the Leland Hayward agency for an "American Chauve-Souris" that included sketches of Nantucket during the days of the whaling industry, French patois songs from Louisiana, and a Harlem rent party with scat music. Jay Martin, *Nathanael West: The Art of His Life* (New York: Farrar, Straus and Giroux, 1970), 248–249.

33. Brad Evans, *Before Cultures: The Ethnographic Imagination in American Literature, 1865–1920* (Chicago: University of Chicago Press, 2005), 114.

34. In 1913 Sudeikin (sometimes spelled Soudeikine) drew inspiration from Beardsley's drawings in designing the costumes and set for the Ballets Russes's production of *La Tragedie de Salomé*, based on Oscar Wilde's play. He would later design sets for the original 1935 production of *Porgy and Bess*.

35. On Japonisme in Mexico (including Tablada's role), see Mauricio Tenorio-Trillo, *I Speak of the City: Mexico City at the Turn of the Twentieth Century* (Chicago: University of Chicago Press, 2013), 211–247.

36. José Juan Tablada, *Un día . . . poemas sintéticos* (Caracas: Imprenta Bolívar, 1919), 75.

37. José Juan Tablada, "El 'Murciélago de Moscú," *Revista de Revistas*, June 11, 1922, 39.

38. Gaston Sorbets, "Los espectáculos de la 'Chauve-Souris," *El Universal Ilustrado*, March 24, 1921, 6, is a translation of an article from *L'Illustration*. The journal also later published a translation of an article on synthetic theater by H. I. Brock, who hyped this concept in several *New York Times* articles about the Moscow Art Theater (MAT) Musical Studio, a subset of MAT directed by its cofounder Vladimir Nemirovich-Danchenko that performed in New York at the end of the 1925 in conjunction with the Chauve-Souris's second visit to Broadway. See Brock, "Lo que es el teatro sintético ruso," *El Universal Ilustrado*, December 24, 1925, 20–21, 51.

39. José Vasconcelos, *El monismo estético* (Mexico City: Tipografía Murguía, 1918), 5.

40. José Vasconcelos, *The Cosmic Race: A Bilingual Edition*, trans. Didier T. Jaén (Baltimore: Johns Hopkins University Press, 1997), 59.

41. On the early development of anthropology in Mexico, including the Museo Nacional and the role of Boas, see Mechthild Rutsch, *Entre el campo y el gabinete: Nacionales y extranjeros en la profesionalización de la antropología mexicana (1877–1920)* (Mexico City: Instituto Nacional de Antropología e Historia, 2007).

42. Manuel Gamio, *Forjando patria*, trans. Fernando Armstrong-Fumero (Boulder: University Press of Colorado, 2010), 156. Note the duality implicit in the title: like the English "to forge," *forjar* can also mean "to fabricate" and can carry the connotation of deception.

43. In *Forjando patria*, Gamio acknowledges that the followers of Emiliano Zapata have legitimate grievances but attributes their leader's appeal to "banditry" (the solution for which is "extermination without mercy") and manipulation by "reactionary elements" of previous regimes (158). He later condemned the "exotic *bolsheviks* who approve and preach destruction of foreign capital invested in Mexico, a move that would immediately bring not only foreign intervention, but the dismemberment of the Republic." *Introduction, Synthesis and Conclusions of the Work "The Population of the Valley of Teotihuacán"* (Mexico City: Dirección de Antropología, 1922), lxxxi.

44. Marx, *Capital*, 874.

45. Silvia Federici, *Caliban and the Witch* (New York: Automedia, 2004), 63–64.

46. Daniel Nemser, "Primitive Accumulation, Geometric Space, and the Construction of the 'Indian,'" *Journal of Latin American Cultural Studies* 24, no. 3 (2015): 335–352.

47. As Rosa Luxemburg wrote in 1913, "Capitalism is the first mode of economy with the weapon of propaganda, a mode which tends to engulf the entire globe and to stamp out all other economies, tolerating no rival at its side. Yet at the same time it is also the first mode of economy which is unable to exist by itself, which needs other economic systems as a medium and soil." Rosa Luxemburg, *The Accumulation of Capital*, trans. Agnes Schwarzschild (London: Routledge, 2003), 447.

48. On handicraft production and exhibitions, see Rick López, *Crafting Mexico: Intellectuals, Artisans, and the State after the Revolution* (Durham, N.C.: Duke University Press, 2010).

49. Manuel Gamio, *The Present State of Anthropological Research in Mexico* (Washington, D.C.: Government Printing Office, 1925), 22.

50. Manuel Gamio, *La población del Valle de Teotihuacán* (Mexico City: Dirección de Talleres Gráficos, 1922), xciv. For Gamio's own translation of this passage, which is less poetic than the Spanish, see his *Introduction, Synthesis and Conclusions*, xcii–xciii. Francisco Goitia is a fascinating figure who had traveled with Pancho Villa's army as its official painter, an experience that generated works such as his haunting series *Los ahorcados* (The Hanged Men).

51. Renato González Mello, "Manuel Gamio, Diego Rivera, and the Politics of Mexican Anthropology," *RES: Anthropology and Aesthetics* 45 (Spring 2004): 161–185. See chapter 1 on Vasconcelo's notion of Pythagoreanism.

52. Manuel Gamio, "El nacionalismo y las danzas regionales," in *Hacia un México Nuevo* (Mexico City, 1935), 166.

53. Evans, *Before Cultures*.

54. Gamio, *Forjando patria*, 164.

55. On both theater and ethnographic and educational film at Teotihuacán see Aurelio de los Reyes, *Manuel Gamio y el cine* (Mexico City: Universidad Nacional Autonóma de México, 1991). In 1923 Gamio also built a second open-air theater called the Teatro de la Naturaleza, where the theatrical pageant *Tlahuicole*, based on his own outline for a never-made film about an Aztec warrior, was performed (Reyes, *Manuel Gamio y el cine*, 11–30).

56. Velásquez Bringas was director of the SEP's Department of Libraries from 1924 to 1928 and later became director of the National Library. In addition to her radio show and journalistic work, she was a prominent lawyer and public defender.

57. "Inauguración del teatro mexicano regional teotihuacano," *El Universal*, May 17, 1922.

58. For a brief description of the methodology and objectives of the project, see Gamio's introduction to Roque Ceballos Novelo's *ensayo de comedia regional* "La tejedora," *Ethnos* (February–April 1923): 49–50.

59. Mauricio Tenorio-Trillo, *Mexico at the World's Fairs: Crafting a Modern Nation* (Berkeley: University of California Press, 1996), 87.

60. Rafael M. Saavedra, "La cruza," *México moderno* (June 1923): 97–109.

61. Rafael M. Saavedra, "La tejedora," *Ethnos* 1, no. 2 (February–April 1923): 49–65.

62. Ruth Hellier-Tinoco, *Embodying Mexico: Tourism, Nationalism, and Performance* (Oxford: Oxford University Press, 2011), 89–99. Hellier-Tinoco offers a detailed account of the transformation of the Dance of the Little Old Men and Night of the Dead ceremony into national icons. She discusses Carlos González and Francisco Domínguez and briefly touches on the Teatro Murciélago (79–80), though without noting its connection to the Chauve-Souris or the American Industrial Mission.

63. "En un humilde pueblo de Michoacán, en San Pedro Paracho, se inauguró el domingo próximo pasado el teatro regional," *El Heraldo*, June 12, 1923.

64. Mario Montes, "Nuevos senderos para llegar a la creación del verdadero teatro nacional y el ballet mexicano," *El Mundo*, January 24, 1923. This also mentions that Saavedra had previously staged his piece *La Cruza* at a theater in Mexico City using indigenous actors from Teotihuacán, though the performance evidently garnered little attention from the press.

65. Don Juan Manuel, "Cosas nuestras: El nuevo espectáculo nacional," *El Universal Ilustrado*, January 11, 1923, 38.

66. Patricia Aulestia, *La danza premoderna en México* (Caracas: Centro Venezolano, Instituto Nacional de Teatro-UNESCO, 1995), 28.

67. On the *moros y cristianos* tradition, see Max Harris, *Aztecs, Moors, and Christians* (Austin: University of Texas Press, 2010); and Diana Taylor, *The Archive and the Repertoire: Performing Cultural Memory in the Americas* (Durham, N.C.: Duke University Press, 2003), 30–31.

68. Especially pertinent is Vasconcelos's *Estudios indostánicos* (1920). See Laura J. Torres-Rodríguez, "Orientalizing Mexico: *Estudios indostánicos* and the Place of India in José Vasconcelos's *La raza cósmica*," *Revista Hispánica Moderna* 68, no. 1 (June 2015): 77–91.

69. Rafael Saavedra later claimed to have first heard of the Russian group from members of the visiting Ukrainian National Choir in December 1922. "El teatro sintético mexicano: 'Tiene la culpa el cilindro,' obra de Rafael Saavedra. Una acusación de plagio," *El Mundo*, September 1, 1923.

70. Rafael M. Saavedra, "El teatro mínimo mexicano: La Chinita," *El Universal Ilustrado*, March 15, 1923, 21. For a translation, see "La Chinita: A Panorama of Uruapan in Two Scenes," trans. Lilian Saunders, *Poet Lore* 37 (January 1926): 107–119.

71. According to an announcement in *Excélsior* that same day, "Tiene la culpa el cilindro" (described as a "panorama in a snapshot") was to be performed at the Teatro Arbeu in Mexico City on August 30, 1923. It is unclear whether this took place. The following day González publicly accused Saavedra of plagiarizing his idea—to which Saavedra responded by acknowledging that the literary value of the piece was negligible while still insisting that as a "PAINTER, but not a WRITER," González could not be the author. "Obra de teatro que se dice ha sido plagiado," *Excélsior*, August 31, 1921, and "El teatro sintético mexicano" (for full reference see note 69 just above).

72. El Caballero Puck, "El 'Chauve-Souris' Mexicano," *El Universal Ilustrado*, June 5, 1924, 33, 44.

73. Alejandro Ortiz Bullé Goyri and Tania Barberán, "Del café de nadie al espacio teatral" (unpublished interview with Germán List Arzubide, 1992). Cited in Ortiz Bullé Goyri, *Teatro y vanguardia*, 180.

74. Numerous newspaper articles in Mexico reported these details, and memorabilia including telegrams, letters, and speeches can be found in the scrapbook assembled by William Wallace Nichols and catalogued as American Industrial Mission to Mexico Records, 1924–1948, Manuscript and Archives Division, New York Public Library. In his communications with Nichols, the mayor offered suggestions for invitees, including Henry Ford (who did not come). The mission included prominent bankers and the presidents or vice presidents of the U.S. Steel Corporation, Westinghouse Electric & Manufacturing, International General Electric, Royal Typewriter, H. J. Heinz, Eastman Kodak, Mack Trucks, and Nestlé Food (among others).

75. See the itinerary "Programa de festejos organizados por el H. Ayuntamiento de la Ciudad de México en honor de la distinguida Misión Industrial Americana," in American Industrial Mission to Mexico Records, 1924–1948, Manuscript and Archives Division, New York Public Library.

76. According to an untitled piece of piece of paper that includes the lunch menu, the group visited the Fábrica Nacional de Vestuario y Equipo (a clothing factory). American Industrial Mission to Mexico Records, 1924–1948, Manuscript and Archives Division, New York Public Library.

77. "San Juan Teotihuacán reveló a los industriales," *Demócrata*, September 18, 1924.

78. Quoted in "La Misión Americana visitó ayer Teotihuacán," *El Universal*, September 18, 1924.

79. Quintanilla and González, *Teatro Mexicano del Murciélago*, 3.

80. For more on Bartolo Juárez, see Hellier-Tinoco, *Embodying Mexico*, 83–88.

81. Quintanilla and González, *Teatro Mexicano del Murciélago*, 5.

82. Quintanilla and González, *Teatro Mexicano del Murciélago*, 6. *Fifí* usually refers to a young man from a wealthy family who enjoys the good life without working, and as the language of the Murciélago's scene suggests, it is an emasculating term that carries connotations of homosexuality.

83. Quintanilla and González, *Teatro Mexicano del Murciélago*, 8.

84. Claudio Lomnitz, *Death and the Idea of Mexico* (New York: Zone Books, 2005), 114–116.

85. "Crónica de Jacobo Dalevuelta," *El Universal*, September 18, 1924.

86. Evans, *Before Cultures*, 115.

87. Quintanilla and González, *Teatro Mexicano del Murciélago*, 7.

88. A brief review of the September 27 performance was negative, remarking on its "visible disorientation" and "harangue" to the public while admitting the music was more pleasing. See Elizondo, "Notas teatrales," *Excélsior*, September 29, 1924. Antonio Magaña Esquivel later claimed there were two performances at the Teatro Principal, though I have not found evidence of a second. "Teatro experimental en Mexico City: 'El Murciélago,'" *El Nacional* (Mexico City), May 11, 1938.

89. On Gamio's conflict with Calles see Ángeles González Gamio, *Manuel Gamio: Una lucha sin final* (Mexico City: Universidad Nacional Autonóma de México, 1987), 79–82.

90. American Manufacturers' Export Association, "The American Industrial Mission to Mexico, 1924" (unpublished report, New York Public Library), 3.

91. For the play, see José Gorostiza, "Ventana a la calle," *El Universal Ilustrado*, November 27, 1924, 20. For his jabs at teatro sintético, see his "Glosas al momento teatral," *El Universal Ilustrado*, December 10, 1925, 63. Gorostiza was affiliated with the Contemporáneos, a group of writers often at odds with the estridentistas. On the theatrical activities of the Contemporáneos, including their Teatro de Ulises and Teatro de Orientación, see Luis Mario Schneider, *Fragua y gesta del teatro experimental en México* (Mexico City: Ediciones del Equilibrista, 1995).

92. "Fiesta en honor de los parlamentarios brasileños," *Boletín de la Secretaría de Educación Pública*, December 1, 1925, 151–155.

93. "El primer festival del teatro sintético regional mexicano," *El Universal*, November 30, 1925. The other scene incorporated from the Teatro del Murciélago was "El Cántaro Roto."

94. José Manuel Puig Casauranc, "Cuáles son los altos propósitos que se persiguen con la fundación del Teatro Sintético Nacional," *El Universal*, November

29, 1925. For a debate on the topic, see "Algunas opiniones acerca del Teatro Sintético," *El Universal Ilustrado*, October 29, 1925, 52–53.

95. Magaña Esquivel lists several pieces performed at the Casa del Estudiante Indígena, all of which were indigenous-themed. None of the pieces performed by the Murciélago at its debut seem to have been included. See his "Teatro experimental en México." In 1927 the estridentista sculptor Germán Cueto published a work of teatro sintético called "Comedia sin solución" in the group's journal *Horizonte*, though it is more in line with Italian futurist *sintesi*.

96. Carlos Mérida, "La danza y el teatro," in *Escritos de Carlos Mérida sobre el arte: La danza* (Mexico City: CENIDIAP, 1990), 143. Domínguez was also involved in the National Dance School, which I discuss in chapter 3.

97. Gamio, "El nacionalismo y las danzas regionales," 167.

98. Hellier-Tinoco stresses that this dissemination began at least as early as the 1930s with accounts of both rituals in the journal *Mexican Folkways*. On the role of traveling folkloric troupes and immigration, see her *Embodying Mexico*, 100–119.

99. Luis Quintanilla, "El murciélago mexicano," in *La pajarita de papel: P.E.N. Club de México 1924/1925* (Mexico City: Instituto Nacional de Bellas Artes, 1965), 30.

100. Starting with the Sindicato de Actores in 1922, several theater workers' unions formed during the early 1920s, and this allusion seems to suggest that the Teatro del Murciélago ran into issues (and extra expenses) with these groups.

Chapter 3

1. Leopoldo Méndez, "Proyecto elaborado con el objeto de estimular y articular la producción del dibujo a las actividades de la enseñanza en las escuelas de toda la República," August 2, 1932, Serie Subsecretaría, Caja 6/Exp. 60, Archivo Histórico de la Secretaría de Educación Pública (hereafter referred to as AHSEP). All AHSEP files were recently incorporated into the Archivo General de la Nación, and it is possible the numbering of documents has changed.

2. Carolyn Marvin, *When Old Technologies Were New: Thinking about Electric Communication in the Late Nineteenth Century* (Oxford: Oxford University Press, 1988), 8.

3. Lisa Gitelman, *Always Already New: Media, History, and the Data of Culture* (Cambridge, Mass.: MIT Press, 2006), 13.

4. Jonathan Sterne, *MP3: The Meaning of a Format* (Durham, N.C.: Duke University Press, 2012).

5. Mladen Dolar, *A Voice and Nothing More* (Cambridge, Mass.: MIT Press, 2006), 4.

6. Louis Rossetto, "In a Letter to His Kids, *Wired*'s Founding Editor Recalls the Dawn of the Digital Revolution," *Wired*, May 19, 2008, https://www.wired.com/2008/05/ff-15th-rossetto/.

7. Gitelman, *Always Already New*, 9.

8. Paul Duguid, "Material Matters: The Past and Futurology of the Book," in *The Future of the Book*, ed. Geoffrey Nunberg (Berkeley: University of California Press, 1996), 65.

9. Germán List Arzubide, *Troka el poderoso* (Mexico City: El Nacional, 1939), 19.

10. Marshall McLuhan, *Understanding Media: The Extensions of Man* (Cambridge, Mass.: MIT Press, 1994), 8.

11. J. David Bolter and Richard Grusin, *Remediation: Understanding New Media* (Cambridge, Mass.: MIT Press, 1999).

12. "On Radio Stage: Behind the Scenes at a Station Broadcasting to Thousands of Listeners," *New York Times*, March 26, 1922.

13. Rudolf Arnheim, *Radio: An Art of Sound*, trans. Margaret Ludwig and Herbert Read (New York: Da Capo, 1936), 15. See also Neil Verma, *Theater of the Mind: Imagination, Aesthetics, and American Radio Drama* (Chicago: University of Chicago Press, 2012).

14. Early on the Secretariat of Public Education made requests to purchase equipment and establish a radio station, but permission was not granted until July 15, 1924, thirteen days after Vasconcelos left office. *Una historia hecha de sonidos: Radio Educación* (Mexico City: Secretaría de Educación Pública, 2004), 37.

15. Walter Benjamin, "Theater and Radio: On the Mutual Supervision of Their Educational Roles," in *Radio Benjamin*, ed. Lecia Rosenthal, trans. Jonathan Lutes (London: Verso, 2014), 366.

16. See *Radio Benjamin* for a selection of his radio broadcasts in translation.

17. Bertolt Brecht, "The Radio as an Apparatus of Communication," in *Brecht on Theatre: The Development of an Aesthetic*, ed. and trans. John Willett (New York: Hill and Wang, 1957), 52.

18. Francisco Miranda Silva and William H. Beezley, "The Rosete Aranda Puppets: A Century and a Half of an Entertainment Enterprise," *The Americas* 67, no. 3 (January 2011): 331–354; Yolanda Jurado Rojas, *El teatro de títeres durante el porfiriato: Un estudio histórico y literario* (Puebla: Benemérita Universidad Autónoma de Puebla, 2004). Miranda Silva and Beezley emphasize the puppets' rivalry with the new media of the early twentieth century and the remediation of their key characters in film and radio.

19. José Manuel Ramos, "Al pie de la antena," *Antena*, July 7, 1924, 18.

20. Michel Chion, *The Voice in Cinema*, trans. Claudia Gorbman (New York: Columbia University Press, 1999), 19. See also the excellent discussion in Dolar, *A Voice and Nothing More*, 61–71.

21. Fernando Mejía Barquera, *La industria de la radio y la televisión y la política del estado mexicano* (Mexico City: Fundación Manuel Buendía, 1989), 39. El Buen Tono cigar company (which owned CYB) was founded in 1894 by Ernesto Pugibet, a Frenchman who resided in Mexico, and it maintained close ties to business interests in France.

22. Rubén Gallo, *Mexican Modernity: The Avant-Garde and the Technological Revolution* (Cambridge, Mass.: MIT Press, 2005), 1.

23. On the Porfirian period and the revolution, see J. Justin Castro, *Radio in Revolution: Wireless Technology and State Power in Mexico, 1897–1938* (Lincoln: University of Nebraska Press, 2016), 1–57.

24. Álvaro Obregón's regime studied potential models and entertained proposals from various parties before opting for a "mixed" (public/private) system of radio. Its primary concern was to avoid the foreign monopolies that had controlled telegraphy and telephony under Porfirio Díaz, and to place radio in the hands of "national" interests—though these were ultimately dependent on

foreign capital and manufacturers of the technology. Mejía Barquera, *La industria de la radio*, 19; Castro, *Radio in Revolution*, 59–89.

25. Manuel Maples Arce, "TSH," *El Universal Ilustrado*, April 5, 1923, 19.

26. "Un gran triunfo de 'El Universal Ilustrado' y de la 'Casa del Radio,'" *El Universal Ilustrado*, May 10, 1923, 13.

27. Carlos Noriega Hope, "Notas del director," *El Universal Ilustrado*, April 5, 1923, 11. *Hermanos de leche* (literally "milk brothers") usually referred to children who shared a wet nurse.

28. On Villa's assassination see Friedrich Katz, *The Life and Times of Pancho Villa* (Stanford: Stanford University Press, 1998), 761–782.

29. Castro, *Radio in Revolution*, 114–124.

30. The first official effort to regulate the content of broadcasting was the Ley de Comunicaciones Eléctricas of 1926, which prohibited the transmission of any information contrary to "the security of the State, harmony, peace, public order, good customs, the laws of the country and the decency of language, or that cause any scandal or attack on the constituted government or private life" (cited in Mejía Barquera, *La industria de la radio,* 43).

31. See "Fue un éxito clamoroso el estreno del teatro nacional del murciélago," *Excélsior*, September 18, 1924, which mentions radio as one of several topics the members of the Murciélago were studying for possible future sketches.

32. "Irradiación inaugural," *Irradiador*, no. 1 (1923).

33. Leon Trotsky, "Futurism," in *Literature and Revolution*, trans. Rose Strunsky (New York: Haymarket Books, 2005), 112. According to Harsha Ram, the translation of the first part of this sentence is incorrect: the translation reads, "the backward countries that were without any special degree of spiritual culture," whereas the original refers to "countries that were backward but which possessed a certain degree of spiritual culture." "Futurist Geographies: Uneven Modernities and the Struggle for Aesthetic Autonomy: Paris, Italy, Russia, 1909–1914," in Mark Wollaeger and Matt Eatough, *The Oxford Handbook of Global Modernisms* (Oxford: Oxford University Press, 2012), 4.

34. Trotsky, "Radio, Science, Technology and Society," in *Radiotext(e)*, ed. Neil Strauss (New York: Semiotext(e), 1993), 241.

35. Trotsky, "Revolutionary and Socialist Art," in *Literature and Revolution*, 200.

36. For more on Estridentópolis see Germán List Arzubide's quixotic "history" of the group, *El movimiento estridentista* (Jalapa: Ediciones de Horizonte, 1927).

37. On the Macuiltepec Radio Station, see Lynda Klich, "Estridentópolis: Achieving a Post-Revolutionary Utopia in Jalapa," *Journal of Decorative and Propaganda Arts* 26 (2010): 126–128. A fascinating radio-related work from this period that reveals more skepticism toward the technology is Xavier Icaza's *Magnavox* (1926).

38. For details on Jara's ouster and the political situation in Veracruz, see Elissa J. Rashkin, *The Stridentist Movement in Mexico* (Lanham, Md.: Lexington Books, 2009), 167–186.

39. Manuel Maples Arce, *Soberana juventud* (Madrid: Plenitud, 1967), 226–254.

40. On the Cuetos' involvement with Cercle et Carré, see Serge Fachereau, "Germán Cueto," in *Germán Cueto* (Madrid: Museo Nacional Centro de Arte Reina Sofía, 2004), 38–54.

41. Rashkin, *The Stridentist Movement in Mexico*, 226–227. On *¡30–30!*, see Flores, *Mexico's Revolutionary Avant-Gardes*, 265–302.

42. Interview with List Arzubide quoted in Deborah Caplow, *Leopoldo Méndez: Revolutionary Art and the Mexican Print* (Austin: University of Texas Press, 2007), 71.

43. On the League of Revolutionary Writers and Artists and the Taller de Gráfica Popular (Popular Graphics Workshop), see Caplow, *Leopoldo Méndez*.

44. This period of political polarization from about 1929 to 1933 coincided with the so-called left turn of the Comintern. See Barry Carr, *Marxism and Communism in Twentieth-Century Mexico* (Lincoln: University of Nebraska Press, 1992); Luis F. Ruiz, "Where Have All the Marxists Gone? Marxism and the Historiography of the Mexican Revolution," in *Militantes, intelectuales y revolucionarios: Ensayos sobre marxismo e izquierda en América Latina*, ed. Carlos Aguirre (Raleigh: A Contracorriente, 2013), 387–410; and José Revueltas, *Ensayo de un proletariado sin cabeza* (Mexico City: Logos, 1962), the classic critique of the party by a brother of Silvestre Revueltas (composer of Troka's theme song).

45. "Conoce la policía a los comunistas del discurso por radio," *Excélsior,* November 13, 1931. While all official reports confirm the involvement of Campa and List Arzubide, some name Hernán Laborde, the head of the Mexican Communist Party, as the second accomplice rather than Siqueiros.

46. "La voz del Partido Comunista de México desde la 'X.E.W.,' " *El Machete,* November 10 and 20, 1931. The article also insists that neither Siqueiros nor List Arzubide were party members. Siqueiros had been expelled not long before (though he would later rejoin), and List Arzubide went in and out of the party. Mejía Barquera (61n25) claims the takeover of XEW was carried out by Rosendo Gómez Lorenzo, the editor of *El Machete*, and Evelio Vadillo, whose experience in the Soviet Union inspired José Revueltas's novel *Los errores*.

47. "Juventud, estridentismo y el comunismo (entrevista con James Wallace Wilkie 25 marzo 1964)," *Frente a la Revolución Mexicana: 17 protagonistas de la etapa constructiva. Entrevistas de historia oral*, ed. James Wallace Wilkie and Edna Monzón de Wilkie, vol. 2 (Mexico City: Universidad Autónoma Metropolitana, 1995), 252.

48. Dolar, *A Voice and Nothing More*, 10.

49. For an "official" history of the SEP's radio activities going up to the 1990s, see *Historia hecha de sonidos*. The SEP station was first launched in 1924 with the call letters CYE (later changed to CZE, and then XFX).

50. Maples Arce served as a federal congressman from 1932 to 1934. Mentioned in Rashkin, *The Stridentist Movement*, 224.

51. Teatro Orientación was funded by the SEP from 1932 to 1934 and again from 1936 to 1938; it performed works by Mexican writers (including Villaurrutia) and European and U.S. modernists including Eugene O'Neill and Jean Cocteau. See Luis Mario Schneider, *Fragua y gesta del teatro experimental en México* (Mexico City: Ediciones del Equilibrista, 1995).

52. For an account and some highlights from the reports, see *Una historia hecha de sonidos*, 59–69.

53. Maples Arce in the first page of an untitled document from 1932 or 1933 included among documents related to reorganization of XFX, Serie Radioeducación, Caja 9474/Exp. 37, AHSEP.

54. "Al C. Subsecretario de la Secretaría de Educación Presente," February 11, 1933, Serie Radioeducación, Caja 9474/Exp. 37, AHSEP. Throughout the 1930s the SEP greatly expanded the number of radio listeners by distributing receivers in the rural schools it built. See Elena Jackson Albarrán, *Seen and Heard in Mexico: Children and Revolutionary Cultural Nationalism* (Lincoln: University of Nebraska Press, 2014), 129–174.

55. "Al C. Subsecretario de la Secretaría de Educación Presente," February 11, 1933, Serie Radioeducación, Caja 9474/Exp. 37, AHSEP.

56. List Arzubide, *Troka el poderoso: Cuentos infantiles* (Mexico City: El Nacional, 1939). Only one partial Troka script remains in the archive (from the initial proposal submitted by Leopoldo Méndez, discussed in the following paragraph and cited in note 1), and it corresponds almost word-for-word with the text identified as Troka's First Appearance in the 1939 collection.

57. See citation in note 1.

58. In most of the correspondence sent to Troka via the station schoolchildren and teachers spelled his name with a *c* ("Troca"). The word *troca* is still used in northern Mexico to refer to a truck.

59. List Arzubide wrote up a report on the topic, which is in the Acervo de Leopoldo Méndez, CENIDIAP, Mexico City. It was published as "Una visita al Teatro de los Niños de Leningrado," in Germán List Arzubide, *Tres comedias para el teatro infantil* (Mexico City: Secretaría de Educación Pública, 1936), iii–xix. An unsigned article on puppet theater in *El Maestro Rural* (a journal published by the SEP and distributed to rural schoolteachers) states that the SEP's guiñol troupes were modeled after the Soviet troupes and cites Natalya Sats, director of the Moscow Children's Theater. See "Teatro de muñecos," *El Maestro Rural* 6, no. 7 (1935): 36–37. Although the SEP puppeteers were well aware of the Rosete Aranda company and other examples of Mexican puppetry, they rejected this tradition as trivial and devoid of educational value.

60. Critics have overlooked Méndez's role as a puppet practitioner and theorist, though his archive includes multiple manuscripts for speeches and essays he wrote on the topic. One of the few to touch on this is Caplow, *Leopoldo Méndez*, 85–89.

61. Some sources suggest a connection, but this is hard to verify. Puppetry does not appear to have been central to Cercle et Carré, but some of its artists (Enrico Prampolini, Sophie Taeuber, László Moholy-Nagy) had worked with marionettes, and the group's cofounder Joaquín Torres-García was known for his constructivist toys. In an article in the April 15, 1930, issue of the group's journal, the Russian set designer Vera Idelson draws a connection between puppetry and abstraction: citing Edward Gordon Craig and Maurice Maeterlinck's call to replace human actors with marionettes, she argues instead for counterpoising human and mechanical actors, and states that the movement of marionettes offers "pure, abstract movement, movement in itself." "Problèmes du Théatre," in *Cercle et carré: Collection complète (1930)* (Paris: J. M. Place, 1977).

62. For details on how the puppet project began see Sonia Iglesias Cabrera and Guillermo Murray Prisant, *Piel de papel, manos de palo* (Mexico City: Consejo Nacional de las Artes y Culturas, 1995).

63. List Arzubide also wrote and broadcast a cycle of historical radio dramas with his brother Armando. He created two other children's programs: El Médico

Familiar (The Family Doctor) and El Periquillo Andarín, who taught children history and geography by narrating his travels around Mexico. El Periquillo was also the name of a popular puppet used by the guiñol troupes.

64. *El teatro guiñol de Bellas Artes (Época de oro en México) / The Puppetry of the Institute of Fine Arts (Golden Age)* (Mexico City: Instituto Nacional de Bellas Artes / Editorial RM, 2010), 14. Like other sources, this book stresses the connection between the puppet movement and the progressive Cárdenas regime. See also Iglesias Cabrera and Prisant, *Piel de papel,* which mistakenly claims that the SEP's troupes were founded in 1934—the year Cárdenas became president (183).

65. See, for example, Caplow, *Leopoldo Méndez,* 87; Juan Solís, "Troka el poderoso: Disección del espíritu mecánico de una época," in *Vanguardia en México, 1915–1940,* ed. Renato González Mello, Anthony Stanton, and Evelyn Useda Miranda (Mexico City: Instituto Nacional de Bellas Artes, 2013), 127.

66. This piece has evolved over time, and recordings of several different versions are available online (some featuring Alejandro Benítez and others Pablo Cueto). My description is based on the video at https://vimeo.com/3271539, accessed December 15, 2017.

67. Rebecca Schneider, *Performing Remains: Art and War in Times of Theatrical Reenactment* (London: Routledge, 2011), 6–7.

68. The podcast is available at http://radioartnet.net/11/2015/07/07/radio-y-estridentismo-ii-troka-el-poderoso-cuentos-para-el-radio-1933/. For the Fonoteca Nacional, which was officially inaugurated in 2008, see www.fonoteca nacional.gob.mx/. Both last accessed December 15, 2017.

69. As Philip Auslander and others have argued, "liveness" is a historical construct that arose in reaction to and in dialogue with new forms of technological mediation. *Liveness: Performance in a Mediatized Culture* (New York: Routledge, 1999). The *Oxford English Dictionary* dates the first recorded use of the word "live" in this sense from 1934. The equivalent in Spanish (*en vivo*) was not yet part of the vocabulary of those involved in the SEP's station, though their frequent comparisons between radio and theater suggest they were working through this issue.

70. Scott Cutler Shershow, *Puppets and "Popular" Culture* (Ithaca, N.Y.: Cornell University Press, 1995), 22.

71. List Arzubide, *Troka el poderoso.* Although there is no clear evidence, it seems likely that Troka fell silent around 1937, when XFX was placed under the direct control of a centralized agency that managed the federal government's various radio stations.

72. On *Que viva México,* see Masha Salazkina, *In Excess: Sergei Eisenstein's Mexico* (Chicago: University of Chicago Press, 2009). For another fascinating point of comparison see Christina Kiaer, *Imagine No Possessions: The Socialist Objects of Russian Constructivism* (Cambridge, Mass.: MIT Press, 2005).

73. See Christopher Bracken, "The Language of Things: Walter Benjamin's Primitive Thought," *Semiotica* 138–140 (2002): 321–349.

74. A translation, *Much Ado about Kasper,* is included along with other broadcasts (including one on "Berlin Puppet Theater") in the volume *Radio Benjamin.*

75. Sigmund Freud, *Totem and Taboo: Resemblances between the Psychic Lives of Savages and Neurotics,* trans. A. A. Brill (New York: Vintage, 1946), 112.

76. See, for instance, Angelina Beloff, *Muñecos animados: Historia, técnica y función educativa del teatro de muñecos en México y en el mundo* (Mexico City: Secretaría de Educación Pública, 1945).

77. "Al Jefe de Bellas Artes de la Directora del Jardín de Niños Manuel Gutiérrez Nájera, Luisa Castañeda," August 31, 1933, CNAP-FR-LM-C19-E785-D2165, Acervo de Leopoldo Méndez, Centro Nacional de Investigación, Documentación e Información de Artes Plásticas (henceforth CENIDIAP).

78. For a description and discussion of the score see Eduardo Contreras Soto, *Silvestre Revueltas en escena y en pantalla: La música de Silvestre Revueltas para el cine y la escena* (Mexico City: Instituto Nacional de Bellas Artes y Literatura: Instituto Nacional de Antropología e Historia, 2012), 26–39. Contreras Soto interviewed List Arzubide in 1994, but at the ripe old age of ninety-six he did not remember whether the pantomime version of *Troka* was ever performed. I thank Contreras Soto for his emails pointing me toward key sources.

79. On *¡30–30!* (first staged November 21, 1931), see Margarita Tortajada Quiroz, *La danza escénica de la Revolución Mexicana* (Mexico City: Instituto Nacional de Estudios Históricos de la Revolución Mexicana, 2000), 16–26. The music was by Francisco Domínguez. For more on Campobello's dance-related work see Manuel Ricardo Cuellar, "Imagining a Festive Nation: Queer Embodiments and Dancing Histories of Mexico" (PhD diss., University of California, Berkeley, 2016), 56–82.

80. Carlos Mérida, "La danza y el teatro," in *Escritos de Carlos Mérida sobre el arte: La danza* (Mexico City: CENIDIAP, 1990), 127.

81. Campobello's half-sister Gloria was also a dance instructor at the school, as was Hipólito Zybine, a Russian dancer who had settled in Mexico. On the creation of the Escuela Nacional de Danza, see Margarita Tortajada Quiroz, *Danza y poder* (Mexico City: CENIDIAP, 1995), 66–78.

82. "Troka (pantomima bailable para niños)," unsigned and undated document, CNAP-FR-LM-C18-E729-D2090, Acervo Leopoldo Méndez, CENIDIAP.

83. Mérida cites *Petrushka* in his discussion of Russian dance in "La danza y el teatro" (133), and List Arzubide and Méndez were familiar with the character due to their investigations into Russian theater.

84. See Tortajada, *Danza y poder*, 72–76, on early performances, which included a ballet by Francisco Domínguez and indigenous or folk dances choreographed by the Campobellos.

85. See, for example, an unsigned memo regarding the program for an upcoming open-air festival in the Colonia Morelos zone of Mexico City in February 1935, where twenty-five hundred programs are requested. The program includes a mariachi group from the SEP's Division of Music, three short plays by one of the puppet troupes, a jarabe (traditional dance) by Gloria and Nellie Campobello, and a "farce" that seems to have involved children and perhaps puppets. "Programa para el Festival cultural al aire libre en Colonia Morelos," unsigned memo from 1935, Serie Teatro, Caja 6–34/Exp. 1/Faja 8, AHSEP. Memos and programs from the archives of XFX indicate that the station sometimes broadcast festivals.

86. Agustín Yáñez, "Ideas para la reorganización de la Dirección de Radio de la SEP," February 28, 1932, Serie Radioeducación, Caja 9474/Exp. 37, AHSEP.

87. Sterne, *The Audible Past*.

88. Readers can consult Albarrán, *Seen and Heard in Mexico*, 129–174, for details about some of the children's drawings in a chapter on the SEP's radio station. Although Albarrán also devotes a separate chapter to the guiñol movement, she does not mention the radio/puppet connection.

Chapter 4

1. Ignácio de Loyola Brandão, *Teatro Municipal de São Paulo: Grandes momentos* (São Paulo: Dórea Books and Art, 1993), 44.

2. Sábato Magaldi and Maria Thereza Vargas, *Cem anos de teatro em São Paulo (1875–1974)* (São Paulo: SENAC, 2000), 96.

3. A *passadista* is someone who is retrograde or stuck in the past. Mário de Andrade, "Prefácio interessantíssimo," in *Poesias completas* (São Paulo: Livraria Martins, 1966), 14. The above is my translation, but see also "Extremely Interesting Preface," in *Hallucinated City: Paulicéia desvairada*, trans. Jack E. Tomlins (Nashville: Vanderbilt University Press, 1968), 5–18. Tomlins translates *teorias-avós* as "granddaddy-theories," overlooking the gendering of "theories" as feminine. (It is also worth noting that both of Mário's own grandmothers were mulatta.)

4. Mladen Dolar, "If Music Be the Food of Love," in Slavoj Žižek and Mladen Dolar, *Opera's Second Death* (New York: Routledge, 2002), 3.

5. In 2015, the archive of the Fundação Casa de Rui Barbosa finally allowed access to a letter Mário wrote to his close friend Manuel Bandeira on April 7, 1928, in which he explicitly refers to his "homosexuality" and how rumors of it constrained his social life. Parts of the letter had been published in a 1966 collection of their correspondence, but this section was excised.

6. For an unusually frank speculation on Mário's sexuality by one of his former disciples, see Moacir Werneck de Castro, *Mário de Andrade: Exílio no Rio* (Rio de Janeiro: Rocco, 1989), 83–102. Mário's short story "Federico Paciência" (1924) deals with a homosexual relationship.

7. Karl Marx, *Capital: A Critique of Political Economy*, vol. 1, trans. Ben Fowkes (London: Penguin Books, 1990), 935.

8. See the introduction to this book for a brief discussion of the export age, which is dated from 1870 to 1930.

9. Roberto Schwarz, "As idéias fora do lugar," *Estudos CEBRAP* 3 (1973): 151–161. For a translation see "Misplaced Ideas: Literature and Society in Late-Nineteenth-Century Brazil," in *Misplaced Ideas*, trans. John Gledson (London: Verso, 1992), 19–32. Because the language of Schwarz's essay is key to my reading and the published translation does not always convey the original's subtleties, I translate directly from the Portuguese.

10. See Schwarz's classic study, *A Master on the Periphery of Capitalism*, trans. John Gledson (Durham, N.C.: Duke University Press, 2002). On Machado, see G. Reginald Daniel, *Machado de Assis: Multiracial Identity and the Brazilian Novelist* (University Park: Pennsylvania State University Press, 2012).

11. Brazil was not the only Latin American country where intellectuals of ambiguous racial and sexual affiliations took on symbolic roles during this period. On a case in Chile (with connections to Mexico), see Licia Fiol-Matta, *A Queer Mother of the Nation: The State and Gabriela Mistral* (Minneapolis: University of Minnesota Press, 2001).

12. Elizabeth Freeman, "Packing History, Count(er)ing Generations," *New Literary History* 31, no. 4 (Autumn 2000): 727–744.

13. Siobhan B. Somerville, *Queering the Color Line: Race and the Invention of Sexuality in American Culture* (Durham, N.C.: Duke University Press, 2000), 3.

14. Sodomy laws had not existed in Brazil since 1830, though laws against cross-dressing and vagrancy were used to restrict displays of "deviant" sexuality. See James N. Green, *Beyond Carnival: Male Homosexuality in Twentieth-Century Brazil* (Chicago: University of Chicago Press, 1999), 20–23. The first major literary work about same-sex relations, Adolfo Caminha's naturalist novel *Bom-Crioulo* (1895), portrays a loving (if ultimately violent) relationship between two sailors, one black and the other blond and blue-eyed.

15. See Green, *Beyond Carnival*, 55–59.

16. Heather Love, *Feeling Backward: Loss and the Politics of Queer History* (Cambridge, Mass.: Harvard University Press, 2007), 3.

17. Theodor Adorno, "Bourgeois Opera," in *Opera through Other Eyes*, ed. and trans. David J. Levin (Stanford: Stanford University Press, 1994), 25.

18. Edward Said, *Culture and Imperialism* (New York: Vintage Books, 1993), 114.

19. Dolar, "If Music Be the Food of Love," 91.

20. On the eighteenth century, see Rogério Budasz, *Teatro e música na América portuguesa: Convenções, repertório, raça, gênero e poder* (Curitiba: DeArtes UFPR, 2008); Vanda Bellard Freire, *Rio de Janeiro, século XIX: Cidade de ópera* (Rio de Janeiro: Garamond, 2013), 17–18.

21. On the effort to create a national opera, see André Heller-Lopes, "Brazil's Ópera Nacional (1857–1863): Music, Society, and the Birth of Brazilian Opera in Nineteenth-Century Rio de Janeiro" (PhD diss., Kings College London, 2010).

22. See Freire, *Rio de Janeiro, século XIX*; and Cristina Magaldi, *Music in Imperial Rio de Janeiro: European Culture in a Tropical Milieu* (Lanham, Md.: Scarecrow, 2004), 35–65.

23. In 2017, the Teatro Amazonas commemorated the twentieth anniversary of the Festival Amazonas de Ópera (FAO). For more on opera houses in Brazil, see Benedito Lima de Toledo and Elza B. de Oliveira Marques, "Opera Houses," *Journal of Decorative and Propaganda Arts* 21 (1995): 42–59.

24. Mário de Andrade, "O movimento modernista," in *Aspectos da literatura brasileira* (São Paulo: Livraria Martins, 1950), 236.

25. Of the more than 4 million immigrants who arrived in Brazil during the years of the First Republic (1889–1930), 2.5 million settled in São Paulo. See www.v-brazil.com/information/geography/sao-paulo/history.html, accessed May 10, 2010.

26. Census figures are from the website of the Município de São Paulo, http://sempla.prefeitura.sp.gov.br/historico/tabelas.php, accessed May 10, 2010.

27. Antônio Barreto do Amaral, *História dos velhos teatros de São Paulo (da Casa da Ópera à inauguração do Teatro Municipal)* (São Paulo: Governo do Estado de São Paulo, 1979), 391–394.

28. Brandão, *Teatro Municipal*, 19.

29. R. Severo, *Monographia do Theatro Municipal de São Paulo* (São Paulo, 1911), 39–40.

30. Brandão, *Teatro Municipal*, 21.

31. *Il Guarany* (with a libretto written in Italian by Antonio Scalvini and Carlo D'Ormeville) is based on the classic novel *O Guarani* by the Brazilian writer José Alencar. Gomes was originally from Campinas (in São Paulo State).

32. For an in-depth comparison of the Colombo and the Municipal, see Aiala Teresa Levy, "Forging an Urban Public: Theaters, Audiences, and the City in São Paulo, Brazil, 1854–1924" (PhD diss., University of Chicago, 2016), 89–152. Levy notes that nearly two hundred theaters were inaugurated in São Paulo between 1890 and 1924 (338).

33. Álvaro Lins, *Jornal de Crítica*, 1a série (Rio de Janeiro: José Olympio, 1941), 191.

34. *Paulista* refers to someone or something from São Paulo State. Residents of the city of São Paulo are referred to as *paulistanos*, but the modernistas typically used the broader term *paulista*, and their discourse of civic pride was tied not only to the city but to the entire region.

35. Abguar Bastos, "O café, pai do movimento modernista de 1922," *Diretrizes*, June 24, 1943, 17.

36. On this see Annateresa Fabris, *O futurismo paulista: Hipóteses para o estudo da chegada da vanguarda ao Brasil* (São Paulo: Perspectiva, 1994).

37. Sérgio Miceli, *Intelectuais e classe dirigente no Brasil (1920–1945)* (São Paulo: DIFEL, 1979), 24–26. The term is apropos, given Oswald and Mário's shared last name (though they were not related). Miceli stresses that Mário was the only major modernista writer who had not studied law, the usual path for well-to-do young men. See also Miceli, "Mário de Andrade: A invenção do moderno intelectual brasileiro," in *Um enigma chamado Brasil: 29 intérpretes e um país*, ed. André Botelho and Lilia Moritz Schwarz (São Paulo: Companhia das Letras, 2009), 160–172.

38. Oswald de Andrade, "O meu poeta futurista," *Jornal do Commercio* (São Paulo), May 27, 1921. Reprinted in Mário da Silva Brito, *História do modernismo brasileiro* (São Paulo: Saraiva, 1958), 199–201.

39. Curiously, Mário sent Marinetti a copy of *Paulicéia desvairada* shortly after it was published. However, when Marinetti visited Brazil on a lecture tour in 1926, Mário snubbed him. See Jeffrey T. Schnapp and João Cezar de Castro Rocha, "Brazilian Velocities: On Marinetti's 1926 Trip to South America," *South Central Review* 13, nos. 2/3 (1996): 105–156.

40. Fernando Goes makes this claim in "História da *Paulicéia desvairada*," *Revista do Arquivo Municipal* (1946): 95. Critics continue to repeat it, though surely the affair would have caused less scandal if Mário had simply not responded. I suspect this reflects the desire to see Mário as a victim, an image he himself often fostered.

41. Oswald de Andrade, "O meu poeta futurista."

42. Mário de Andrade, "Futurista?!," *Jornal do Commercio* (São Paulo), June 6, 1921. Reprinted in Brito, *História do modernismo brasileiro*, 204–208.

43. Friedrich Nietzsche, "The Case of Wagner," in *The Birth of Tragedy and The Case of Wagner*, trans. Walter Kaufmann (New York: Vintage Books, 1967), 184. See also Oskar Panizza's characterization of *Parsifal* as a "homosexual opera" in his article (from 1895) "Bayreuth and Homosexuality: A Reflection," *Opera Quarterly* 22, no. 2 (2006): 324–328; and Hanns Fuchs's 1903 text "*Parsifal*

and Eroticism in Wagner's Music," trans. John Urang, *Opera Quarterly* 22, no. 2 (2006): 334–344, which argues that although Parsifal is not a "clinical" homosexual, he does practice a Platonic form of "spiritual homosexuality" (340). Both Panizza and Fuchs also characterize Wagner's relationship with his patron Ludwig II as pseudo-homosexual in nature.

44. Richard Wagner, *Opera and Drama*, trans. William Ashton Ellis (Lincoln: University of Nebraska Press, 1995), 236.

45. Filippo Marinetti, "Down with the Tango and Parsifal!," in *Critical Writings*, ed. Günter Berghaus and trans. Doug Thompson (New York: Farrar, Straus and Giroux), 133.

46. Telê Ancona Lopez refers to the harlequin as a *traje teórico*—a theoretical garment or suit—and connects this motif to cubism and Dadaism. "Arlequim e modernidade," in *Mariodeandradiando* (São Paulo: HUCITEC, 1996), 17–83.

47. Andrade, *Hallucinated City*, 23.

48. José Miguel Wisnik, "Machado maxixe: O caso Pestana," in *Sem receita: Ensaios e canções* (São Paulo: PubliFolha, 2004), 64. This quote is particularly apt evidence of the connection among racial mixture, music, and the "secret" since it refers to a story by Machado de Assis about a musician who specializes in the popular genre known as maxixe.

49. Hélios (Menotti del Picchia), "Chronica social: Maravalhas," *Correio Paulistano*, November 16, 1921.

50. Hélios (Menotti del Picchia), "Chronica social: Semana de Arte Moderna," *Correio Paulistano*, February 11, 1922. All texts and speeches related to the Week of Modern Art that I discuss in this chapter are reprinted in Maria Eugênia Boaventura, ed., *22 por 22: A Semana de Arte Moderna vista pelos seus contemporâneos* (São Paulo: Edusp, 2000).

51. References to the bandeirantes were common among São Paulo boosters, including Oswald and Mário de Andrade (though in Mário's case they often have an ironic edge). See Saulo Gouveia, *The Triumph of Brazilian Modernism: The Metanarrative of Emancipation and Counter-Narratives* (Chapel Hill: University of North Carolina Press, 2013).

52. Menotti del Picchia, "Arte moderna: A conferência do Dr. Menotti del Picchia no Municipal . . . ," *Correio Paulistano*, February 17, 1922.

53. A *fancaria* is a factory where cotton textiles are produced (so this is probably a jab at the cheap material used in the costumes), but it can also signify anything prefabricated, of poor quality, and made purely for profit.

54. Benjamin associates the decline of the aura with film, which he opposes to theater, but Del Picchia's speech suggests the contrast may be more tenuous than Benjamin acknowledges. See Walter Benjamin, "The Work of Art in the Age of Its Technological Reproducibility," in *The Work of Art in the Age of Its Technological Reproducibility and Other Writings on Media*, ed. Michael Jennings, Brigid Doherty, and Thomas Y. Levin, trans. Edmund Jephcott and Harry Zohn (Cambridge, Mass.: Harvard University Press, 2008), 19–55.

55. The maxixe (sometimes referred to as the Brazilian tango) is a popular, urban dance that originated in Rio in the late nineteenth and early twentieth centuries and became popular for a while in the United States. It is usually said to have developed out of a mix of European dances (i.e., polka) and an Afro-Brazilian dance, the *lundu*.

56. For a cultural history of the city of São Paulo during the 1920s that also draws on operatic metaphors, see Nicolau Sevcenko, *Orfeu extático na metrópole: São Paulo, sociedade e cultura nos frementes anos 20* (São Paulo: Companhia das Letras, 1992).

57. Maria Eugênia Boaventura, "Chuva de batatas," in *22 por 22*, 21. Boaventura offers an excellent overview of the debates the Week of Modern Art provoked in the press.

58. Oswald de Andrade, "Semana de Arte Moderna," *Jornal do Commercio* (São Paulo), February 12, 1922.

59. In colonial times *entradas* were the state-sponsored correlate to the *bandeiras*: whereas the bandeiras were private enterprises that prospected for minerals and captured indigenous slaves, the entradas were excursions intended to expand the Brazilian territory in the name of the Portuguese Crown.

60. Júlio Freire, "Crônica . . . ! Futurista! . . . ," *A Vida Moderna* (São Paulo), February 23, 1922.

61. Oswald de Andrade, "O modernismo," *Revista Anhembi* 17, no. 49 (December 1954): 31.

62. See Jorge Schwartz, *Caixa modernista* (São Paulo: Edusp, Imprenta Oficial, Governo do Estado de São Paulo, 2003), for the program and exhibition catalogue. In an article published the day of the talk, Menotti del Picchia (writing as Hélios) stated that Mário would proclaim "infernal things about the amazing creations of the futurist painters, justifying the canvases that have caused so much scandal and shouting in the *hall* of the Municipal." See his "Chronica social: A segunda batalha," *Correio Paulistano*, February 15, 1922. Months afterward, in a Belgian journal, Sérgio Milliet would recall Mário "with his beautiful head like that of a beardless apostle, tall and svelte, round eyeglasses and bald head, explaining, over heckles and sarcastic comments, theories of modern art and affirming with a strong voice amidst the booing, 'the old ones will die, sirs.'" See his "Une semaine d'art moderne à São Paulo (Les arts plastiques)," *Lumière* 3, no. 7 (April 15, 1922).

63. The claim that Mário read parts of *A escrava* is repeated in countless academic articles, dissertations, and websites. It seems to have originated with Telê Ancona Lopez, the official curator of his archive at the Instituto de Estudos Brasileiros for many years and author of numerous studies about his work. In her chronology of his career, which has been reprinted in several publications, she speculates that he most likely read an initial version of *A escrava*, which had already been announced in the journal *Klaxon* under the title *A poesia moderna*. See the year 1922 in "Cronologia," in *Eu sou trezentos, sou trezentos-e-cincoenta: Uma "autobiografía" de Mário de Andrade* (São Paulo: Universidade de São Paulo, Instituto de Estudos Brasileiros, 1992).

64. Mário de Andrade, "O movimento modernista," 232.

65. Mário de Andrade, "A escrava que não é Isaura," in *Obra imatura* (São Paulo: Livraria Martins, 1960), 22.

66. See the introduction for my discussion of Trotsky's critique of the Russian futurists and his conception of relative autonomy.

67. Aracy A. Amaral, for instance, includes a reproduction of the image and describes its formal characteristics in detail without speculating on its significance in her *Artes plásticas na Semana de 22* (São Paulo: Perspectiva, 1970), 142.

68. The second Tenentes' Revolt, often seen as a precursor to the Revolution of 1930, began in São Paulo on July 5, 1924, and sparked uprisings in other cities. After briefly securing control of São Paulo, the main forces withdrew into the interior and waged a guerrilla campaign known as "The Long March" for the next three years under the leadership of Miguel Costa and Luís Carlos Prestes. Prestes later became a prominent figure in the Brazilian Communist Party.

69. Brandão, *Teatro Municipal*, 46.

70. All page numbers for quotations in both English and Portuguese are from the bilingual version of the text (with translation by Tomlins) in *Hallucinated City*, 77–99.

71. Mário de Andrade, "Notas de Arte Moderna," *A Gazeta* (São Paulo), February 7, 1922.

72. Filippo Marinetti et al., "A Futurist Theater of Essential Brevity," in Filippo Marinetti, *Critical Writings*, ed. Günter Berghaus, trans. Doug Thompson (New York: Farrar, Straus and Giroux, 2006), 203.

73. Benedito Nunes, "Mário de Andrade: As enfibraturas do modernismo," *Revista Iberoamericana* 50, no. 126 (January–March 1984): 63–75. Nunes does not mention the historical meaning of the word *sandapilário*.

74. Vicky Unruh, *Latin American Vanguards: The Art of Contentious Encounters* (Berkeley: University of California Press, 1994), 26–27.

75. Richard Wagner, *Die Meistersinger von Nürnberg: Opera in Three Acts*, trans. Susan Webb (New York: Metropolitan Opera Guild, 1992), 103.

76. Howard E. Smither, "Oratorio," *Grove Music Online*, accessed December 23, 2017, https://doi.org/10.1093/gmo/9781561592630.article.20397.

77. Richard Wagner, *The Art-work of the Future and Other Works*, trans. William Ashton Ellis (Lincoln: University of Nebraska Press, 1993). Quotes come from 131 ("sexless embryos"); 151 ("unnatural abortion"); and 184 ("each separate art").

78. Theodor Adorno, *In Search of Wagner*, trans. Rodney Livingstone (London: Verso, 2005). Adorno explains that Walther von Stolzing "wishes to re-establish the old feudal immediacy, as opposed to the bourgeois division of labor enshrined in the guilds" (83). As a result of their reconciliation, "bourgeois innovation and archaic regression meet in the phantasmagoria" (84).

79. Martin Puchner, *Stage Fright: Modernism, Anti-Theatricality, and Drama* (Baltimore: Johns Hopkins University Press, 2002), 15.

80. One possibility would be to perform *As enfibraturas* as a radio play, which was apparently done in 1942 to commemorate the twentieth anniversary of the Week of Modern Art. See Otávio de Freitas Júnior, letter to Mário de Andrade, March 11, 1942, MA-C-CPL3193, Instituto de Estudos Brasileiros, Universidade de São Paulo.

81. In particular, see Nick Salvato, *Uncloseting Drama: American Modernism and Queer Performance* (New Haven, Conn.: Yale University Press, 2010).

82. Although he does not relate it to the "split" form of the oratorio, Justin Read notes the gender ambiguity of My Madness in *Modern Poetics and Hemispheric American Cultural Studies* (New York: Palgrave Macmillan, 2009), 82.

83. "The area quickly became a meeting ground for men interested in same-sex erotic activity. . . . Propriety and impropriety, bourgeois respectability and erotic

homosociability coexisted precariously in this urban landscape." Green, *Beyond Carnival*, 94.

84. Andrade, "O movimento modernista," 231–232. Note again that Mário states that his speech was about "plastic arts," which suggests it was *not* an early version of *The Slave That Is Not Isaura*.

85. Paulo Prado, *Retrato do Brasil: Ensaio sobre a tristeza brasileira* (Rio de Janeiro: F. Briguiet, 1931), 182.

86. Love, *Feeling Backward*, 64.

87. Andrade, "O movimento modernista," 232.

Chapter 5

1. Ignácio Loyola de Brandão, *Teatro Municipal de São Paulo: Grandes momentos* (São Paulo: Dórea Books and Art, 1993), 44. Caruso performed seven operas at the Theatro Municipal de São Paulo during the 1917 season. He also performed in Rio de Janeiro, though neither he nor Sarah Bernhardt ever performed at the Teatro Amazonas.

2. Mário de Andrade, "O phonographo," *Diário Nacional*, February 24, 1928. Reprinted in Flávia Camargo Toni, ed., *A música popular na vitrola de Mário de Andrade* (São Paulo: Senac São Paulo, 2004), 263–265.

3. Roberto Schwarz, "As idéias fora do lugar," *Estudos CEBRAP* 3 (1973): 151–161.

4. Although I do not address this in the chapter, there are interesting similarities between Mário's works and the scripts/dramatic outlines for operas and ballets that Cuban writer Alejo Carpentier (also a musicologist) wrote at this very same time. His works were also not performed (though the music was). See Mareia Quintero Rivera, "Relecturas de lo popular: Ópera y ballet en la obra de Mário de Andrade y Alejo Carpentier," *Revista Iberoamericana* 217 (October–December 2006): 867–882.

5. Esther Gabara, *Errant Modernism: The Ethos of Photography in Mexico and Brazil* (Durham, N.C.: Duke University Press, 2008), 36–45. Gabara also connects Mário's "errancy" to Schwarz's notion of ideas out of place, but her embrace of Mário's "critical nationalism" overlooks some of its more troubled aspects and (in my view) makes the very move that Schwarz critiques.

6. Michael Taussig, *Mimesis and Alterity: A Particular History of the Senses* (New York: Routledge, 1992), 208.

7. Theodor Adorno, "Bourgeois Opera," in *Opera through Other Eyes*, ed. and trans. David J. Levin (Stanford: Stanford University Press, 1994), 41.

8. Thomas Edison, "The Phonograph and Its Future," *North American Review* 126, no. 262 (May–June 1878): 527.

9. Jonathan Sterne, *The Audible Past: Cultural Origins of Sound Reproduction* (Durham, N.C.: Duke University Press, 2003), 298.

10. Jesse Walter Fewkes, "A Contribution to Passamaquoddy Folk-lore," *Journal of American Folklore* 3, no. 11 (October–December 1890): 257.

11. Franz Boas, "On Alternating Sounds," *American Anthropologist* 2, no. 1 (January 1889): 47.

12. Brian Hochman, *Savage Preservation: The Ethnographic Origins of Modern Media Technology* (Minneapolis: University of Minnesota Press, 2014), 77.

See also Erika Brady, *A Spiral Way: How the Phonograph Changed Ethnography* (Jackson: University Press of Mississippi, 1999).

13. Lisa Gitelman, *Scripts, Grooves, and Writing Machines: Representing Technology in the Edison Era* (Stanford: Stanford University Press, 2000), 125.

14. Karl Hagstrom Miller, *Segregating Sound: Inventing Folk and Pop Music in the Age of Jim Crow* (Durham, N.C.: Duke University Press, 2010).

15. Patrick Feaster and Jacob Smith, "Reconfiguring the History of Early Cinema through the Phonograph," *Film History* 21, no. 4 (December 2009): 314–315.

16. *Cabbages and Kings* (1904) was inspired by O. Henry's experience as a fugitive in Honduras, and the short story is "The Phonograph and the Graft." See Sarah J. Townsend, "His Master's Voice? A Hemispheric History of Phonographic Fictions," *Revista Hispánica Moderna* 70, no. 2 (December 2017): 197–216.

17. Humberto M. Franceschi, *Registro sonoro por meios mecânicos no Brasil* (Rio de Janeiro: Studio HMF, 1984), 19.

18. Flora Süssekind, *Cinematograph of Words: Literature, Technique, and Modernization in Brazil*, trans. Paulo Henriques Britto (Stanford: Stanford University Press, 1997), 33.

19. The *lundu* and modinha were popular genres that had gained favor among the Brazilian elite. (The *lundu*, also a dance, has obvious African influences whereas the modinha evolved out of European forms.) Details about Figner's early recordings and his itinerary come from Franceschi, *A Casa Edison e seu tempo* (Rio de Janeiro: Sarapuí, 2002), 17–22, and *Registro sonoro*, 15–17. Süssekind cites a newspaper article about the anti-Republican speech in her *Cinematograph of Words*, 34.

20. Franceschi, *A Casa Edison*, 22.

21. Franceschi, *Registro sonoro*, 28.

22. Franceschi, *A Casa Edison*, 194–218.

23. The word "phonograph" originally referred to machines that played cylinders (which were eventually phased out), but in practice it was often used as a synonym for "gramophone" (a term more common in Britain).

24. Suisman, *Selling Sounds: The Commercial Revolution in American Music* (Cambridge, Mass.: Harvard University Press, 2009), 104.

25. Geoffrey Jones, "The Gramophone Company: An Anglo-American Multinational, 1898–1931," *Business History Review* 59, no. 1 (Spring 1985): 81.

26. William Howland Kenney, *Recorded Music in American Life: The Phonograph and Popular Memory, 1890–1945* (Oxford: Oxford University Press, 1999), 49.

27. Lawrence W. Levine, *Highbrow/Lowbrow: The Emergence of Cultural Hierarchy in America* (Cambridge, Mass.: Harvard University Press, 1988), 85–104.

28. Kenney, *Recorded Music in American Life*, 45, 50.

29. Kenney, *Recorded Music in American Life*, 62–63.

30. Information on Victor recordings comes from the Discography of American Historical Recordings (http://adp.library.ucsb.edu/index.php).

31. Victor ads appeared in newspapers, some of which featured an entire page on the industry by the late 1920s, and in magazines such as *O Malho* and

Fon-Fon. Until the late 1920s almost all recordings listed were of classical music or opera.

32. "A razão de ser da presente revista," *Phono-arte* 1, no. 1 (August 15, 1928): 1.

33. "A razão de ser da presente revista," 1.

34. Blackface minstrelsy was not unknown in Brazil, though it does not appear to have been a well-established genre. In his essay "Lundu do escravo" (1928), Mário tells of a white circus clown named Antoninho Correia who blacked up to perform a *lundu* about a slave. In *Música, doce música* (São Paulo: Martins, 1963), 74–80.

35. See Marc Hertzman, *Making Samba: A New History of Race and Music in Brazil* (Durham, N.C.: Duke University Press, 2013); Carlos Sandroni, *Feitiço decente: Transformações do samba no Rio de Janeiro (1917–1933)* (Rio de Janeiro: Jorge Zahar/UFRJ, 2001).

36. Marc Hertzman, "Making Music and Masculinity in Vagrancy's Shadow: Race, Wealth, and *Malandragem* in Post-Abolition Rio de Janeiro," *Hispanic American Historical Review* 90, no. 4 (November 2010): 600.

37. "Propaganda carnavalesco," an editorial in the February 28, 1931, issue of *Phono-arte*, mentions that Victor had started this practice the year before and repeated it, with Columbia following its lead.

38. Michael Denning, *Noise Uprising: The Audiopolitics of a World Musical Revolution* (London: Verso, 2015).

39. "A nova fábrica de discos de São Paulo," *Diário Nacional*, October 21, 1928.

40. "O intérprete auditor," *Phono-arte* 1, no. 14 (February 28, 1929): 2.

41. Mário de Andrade, *Macunaíma*, trans. E. A. Goodland (New York: Random House, 1984), 168.

42. Menotti del Picchia, Plínio Salgado, and Cassiano Ricardo, "O actual momento literário," *Correio Paulistano*, May 17, 1929. For their earlier texts, see Menotti del Picchia, Plínio Salgado, and Cassiano Ricardo, *O Curupira e o Carão* (São Paulo: Helios, 1927).

43. Oswald de Andrade, "Cannibalist Manifesto," trans. Leslie Bary, *Latin American Literary Review* 19, no. 38 (July–December 1991): 40.

44. Pronominare (Oswald de Andrade), "Uma adesão que não nos interessa," *Revista de Antropofagia*, June 12, 1929.

45. See "Os três sargentos" (April 14, 1929) and "Miss Macunaíma" (June 26, 1929).

46. The figure of Makunaíma appears in the second volume of Koch-Grünberg's *Vom Roraima zum Orinoco—Mythen und Legenden der Taulipang und Arekuná Indianern*, published in 1924. For details on how the novel incorporates Koch-Grünberg's work, see "Vínculos: Makunaíma/Macunaíma," in Mário de Andrade, *Macunaíma, o herói sem nenhum caráter*, ed. Telê Ancona Lopez (Paris: ALLCA XX, 1996), 397–423.

47. *O turista aprendiz* includes Mário's diary of his journey and the newspaper chronicles he wrote for the *Diário Nacional* during his second "ethnographic voyage" to northeastern Brazil. See Fernando Fonseca Pacheco, "Archive and Newspaper as Media in Mário's Ethnographic Journals," *Hispanic Review* 84, no. 2 (Spring 2016): 171–190; Gabara, *Errant Modernism*.

48. On Mário's relationship to Claude and Dina Lévi-Strauss, see Fernanda Peixoto, "Mário e os primeiros tempos da USP," *Revista do Patrimônio Histórico e Artístico Nacional—Mário de Andrade* 30 (2002): 156–169.

49. Maria Ligia Coelho Prado, *A democracia ilustrada: O Partido Democrático de São Paulo, 1926–1934* (São Paulo: Atica, 1986), 172–174.

50. Paulo Duarte, *Mário de Andrade por ele mesmo* (São Paulo: HUCITEC, 1977), 49–50. Among others Duarte cites as frequent attendees at these gatherings are the singer Elsie Houston, her husband Benjamin Péret (a French surrealist), and Paulo Ribeiro de Magalhães. Mário later recalled the initial meetings as "almost exclusively a repetition of the Week of Modern Art," though he remained silent and "immensely insulated" as others discussed politics. *O empalhador de passarinho* (São Paulo: Livraria Martins, 1948), 24.

51. Mário de Andrade, "Uma excursão ao Rio Amazonas," *Diário Nacional*, August 20, 1927.

52. Mário de Andrade, "A Ciranda," *Diário Nacional*, December 8, 1927. Reprinted in Andrade, *O turista aprendiz*, 335–336.

53. Mário de Andrade, "O phonographo," *Diário Nacional*, February 24, 1928. At this point Mário apparently had no access to a phonograph either at home or at the conservatory.

54. This was the Discoteca di Stato, now called Instituto Centrale per i Beni Sonori ed Audiovisivi.

55. Roquette-Pinto, a physician who taught courses on anthropology at the National Museum, made recordings of the Nambikwara and Parecís in 1912 while on an expedition led by the army engineer and explorer Cândido Rondon. Roquette-Pinto also founded the first radio station in Brazil in 1923.

56. Sterne, *The Audible Past*, 315.

57. Mário de Andrade, "Discos e phonógrafos," *Diário Nacional*, March 11, 1928.

58. The critic and folklorist Antônio Bento de Araújo Lima tried to help Mário acquire a sufficiently small and cheap phonograph in Rio before his trip to the Northeast. See his letters to Mário dated April 18, 1928 (MA-C-CPL4067), and May 27, 1928 (MA-C-CPL4068). The poet Jorge de Lima in Maceió (a city Mário visited on his trip) suggested that he might be able to find an *apparelho registrador* (presumably a phonograph) when he arrived. See his letter to Mário dated February 15, 1929, MA-C-CPL4150, IEB.

59. Mário's record collection is now part of his archive at the Instituto de Estudos Brasileiros (IEB). For an inventory of his "popular" discs, including his annotations and related references in his writings, see Toni, *A música popular na vitrola de Mário de Andrade*. Another useful source that includes many references to Mário is Camila Koshiba Gonçalves, *Música em 78 rotações: "Discos a todos os preços" na São Paulo dos anos 30* (São Paulo: Alameda, 2013).

60. Paulo Ribeiro de Magalhães, letter to Mário de Andrade, November 6, 1930, MA-C-CPL4414, IEB. Cornélio Pires served as a mediator between musicians and the industry and helped to establish *música caipira* (roughly equivalent to hillbilly music) as a commercial genre.

61. Paulo Ribeiro de Magalhães, letter to Mário de Andrade, August 5, 1931, MA-C-CPL4427, IEB.

62. Mário de Andrade, "Carnaval tá ahi," *Diário Nacional*, January 18, 1931.

63. Mário de Andrade, "Gravação nacional," *Diário Nacional*, August 10, 1930.

64. See, for instance, Bryan McCann's excellent *Hello, Hello Brazil: Popular Music in the Making of Modern Brazil* (Durham, N.C.: Duke University Press, 2004), 16. In stressing Mário's opposition to the industry (which was quite true in his later years), McCann points to the chronicle "Música popular," which he dates to the late 1920s, but the text (which I discuss at the end of this chapter) is actually from 1939.

65. *Phono-arte* printed the lyrics of "Canção Marinha," released on Brunswick no. 10.021, in its February 15, 1930, edition.

66. Andrade, *Música, doce música*, 118, from the text "Marcelo Tupinambá" (1924).

67. In 1931, Mário published several chronicles in the *Diário Nacional* criticizing the poor quality of the Rádio Educadora Paulista's programming, and he was averse to the Vargas government's propagandistic use of radio. At certain points he did express an interest in the democratizing potential of radio (as in his chronicle "A língua radiofônica" from 1940), and in 1936, as director of São Paulo's Department of Culture, he oversaw plans for a *Rádio-Escola* (Radio-School) that would broadcast concerts from the Theatro Municipal and play recordings from the department's archive of recordings; Mário himself, however, was opposed to the Rádio-Escola, and it never came to pass. See his letter to Paulo Duarte dated April 3, 1938, in Duarte, *Mário de Andrade por ele mesmo*, 159.

68. Mário de Andrade, "Prefácio," in Telê Ancona Lopez, *Macunaíma: A margem e o texto* (São Paulo: HUCITEC, 1974), 87–89.

69. Mário de Andrade, "Quartas musicais," *Diário Nacional*, January 15, 1930.

70. Andrade, "Carnaval tá ahi."

71. Schwarz, "As idéias fora do lugar." See my discussion of Schwarz in chapter 4.

72. Schwarz, "As idéias fora do lugar," 160.

73. Antonio Candido, "Dialectic of Malandroism," in *On Literature and Society*, trans. Howard S. Becker (Princeton, N.J.: Princeton University Press, 1995), 83.

74. Roberto Schwarz, "Objective Form: Reflections on the Dialectic of Roguery," trans. John Gledson, in *Literary Materialisms*, ed. Mathias Nilges and Emilio Sauri (New York: Palgrave Macmillan, 2013), 194.

75. Mário de Andrade, "Temporada Lírica," *Diário Nacional*, September 19, 1928.

76. Mário de Andrade, *Ensaio sobre música brasileira* (São Paulo: Chiarato & Cia., 1928), 5.

77. *Esquisito* and its English cognate "exquisite" obviously share the same etymology, and it is worth noting that the latter was used as a synonym for "foppish" or "dandyish" in the early twentieth century.

78. Schwarz, "As idéias fora do lugar," 159.

79. Oscar Lorenzo Fernández, letter to Mário de Andrade, December 4, 1927, MA-C-CPL2706, IEB.

80. Mário de Andrade, "Ópera em seis quadros," unpublished manuscript, MA-MMA-087, IEB.

81. Heitor Villa-Lobos, letter to Mário de Andrade, December 25, 1928, MA-C-CPL6994, IEB.

82. On the relationship between the two men, see Sarah Tyrell, "M. Camargo Guarnieri and the Influence of Mário de Andrade's Modernism," *Latin American Music Review* 29, no. 1 (Spring/Summer 2008): 43–63.

83. Roberto da Matta, *Carnivals, Rogues, and Heroes: An Interpretation of the Brazilian Dilemma*, trans. John Drury (Notre Dame: University of Notre Dame Press, 1991), 219.

84. Mário de Andrade, "Chronica de Malazarte I," *América Brasileira* 22 (October 1923): 289.

85. Mário de Andrade, letter to Manuel Bandeira, September 10, 1928, in Mário de Andrade and Manuel Bandeira, *Correspondência*, ed. Marcos Antonio de Moraes (São Paulo: Edusp/IEB, 2000), 404.

86. Lindolfo Gomes, "Uma das de Pedro Malasarte," in *Contos populares colhidos da tradição oral em Minas por Lindopho Gomes* (Juiz de Fora: Dias Cardoso, 1918), 109–111.

87. Luis Quintanilla, letter to Mário de Andrade, September 30, 1928, MA-C-CPL6032, IEB.

88. There are two extant manuscripts of the libretto in Mário's archive. The first is handwritten; the second is the typed version, which includes his very light edits. The most significant change is a change in the subtitle from "Opera cómica em 1 ato" to "Opera bufa em um ato / texto regional." Here I quote from the published version that is based on Mário's typewritten manuscript. Mário de Andrade, "Malazarte," *Revista do Instituto de Estudos Brasileiros* 33 (1992): 59–67.

89. Brad Evans, *Before Culture: The Ethnographic Imagination in American Literature, 1865–1920* (Chicago: University of Chicago Press, 2005), 217n4.

90. Andrade, "Chronica de Malazarte I," 288.

91. Guarnieri and Lamberto Baldi thought that limiting the action to the inside of the house was "undramatic," and when *Pedro Malazarte* was finally staged in 1952, the stage was divided, with the interior of the house on one side and on the other a *terreiro de São João*, or place where rituals for the São João festival are held. This is where the *ciranda* took place (with the actor-singers visible to the audience). See Eurico Nogueira França, "A primeira audição universal de 'Pedro Malazarte,' de Camargo Guarnieri," *Correio da Manhã* (Rio de Janeiro), May 25, 1952.

92. Marion Verhaalen, *Camargo Guarnieri, Brazilian Composer* (Bloomington: Indiana University Press, 2005), 162–165.

93. Antônio Rangel Bandeira, "'Pedro Malazarte'—Uma ópera frustrada," in *Caixa de música* (Rio de Janeiro: Serviço de Documentação do MEC, 1959), 51–56. For a more positive take on the 1952 staging, see Nogueira França, "A primeira audição." The opera was also staged in Buenos Aires in 1969, in São Paulo and Belo Horizonte in 1994, and at the Teatro Amazonas in Manaus in 2005.

94. See Miceli, "Mário de Andrade," for a succinct analysis of the role of Mário and his intellectual colleagues in the Revolução Constitucionalista.

95. In 1938, Vargas removed the mayor of São Paulo (Fábio Prado) from his post, and Mário was called on to participate in the creation of the Serviço do Patrimônio Histórico e Artístico Nacional. Accounts of his early death often link

it to his disappointment over the "failure" of the Department of Culture. See Duarte, *Mário de Andrade*, 49–58, and Roberto Barbato Junior, *Missionários de uma utopia nacional-popular: Os intelectuais e o Departamento de Cultura em São Paulo* (São Paulo: FAPESP; Annablume, 2004), 37–48.

96. Barbato, *Missionários*, 179–186.

97. See Barbato, *Missionários*, 151–163.

98. Rebecca Schneider, "Performance Remains," *Performance Research* 6, no. 2 (2001): 105.

99. Andrade, "Música popular," 278.

Chapter 6

1. José Celso Martinez Corrêa, "First Untimely Considerations on the Creation of the Anhangabaú da Feliz Cidade," *Anhangabaudafelizcidade: A Máquina do Desejo em Movimento* (blog), http://anhangabaudafelizcidade.blogspot.com /2012/09/first-untimely-considerations-on.html, accessed June 15, 2017.

2. "Situação atual do projeto" (transcript from interview of Zé Celso Martinez Corrêa by Marilú Cabañas for Rádio Cultural AM, January 24, 2005), http://teatroficina.com.br/en/radio-cultura-am-situacao-atual-do-projeto/, accessed December 23, 2017.

3. Sábato Magaldi, "A mola propulsora da utopia," in Oswald de Andrade, *O homem e o cavalo* (São Paulo: Globo, 1990), 6.

4. Walter Benjamin, *The Origin of German Tragic Drama*, trans. John Osborne (London: Verso, 1998), 176.

5. See Paul Ryder, "The Living Theater in Brazil," *TDR* 15, no. 3 (Summer 1971): 20–29, for photos and statements by the directors Julian Beck and Judith Malina.

6. Richard Schechner, *Between Theater and Anthropology* (Philadelphia: University of Pennsylvania Press, 1985), 221.

7. See Praise Zenenga, "The Total Theater Aesthetic Paradigm in African Theater," in *The Oxford Handbook of Dance and Theater*, ed. Nadine George-Graves (New York: Oxford University Press, 2015); and Izabella Labedzka, "In Search of the Total Theatre," in *Gao Xingjian's Idea of Theatre from the Word to the Image* (Boston: Brill, 2008), 179–218.

8. George Mosse, *The Nationalization of the Masses: Political Symbolism and Mass Movements in Germany from the Napoleonic Wars through the Third Reich* (New York: Howard Fertig, 1975), 2.

9. Richard Wagner, "The Artwork of the Future," trans. William Ashton Ellis, in *The Artwork of the Future and Other Works* (Lincoln: University of Nebraska Press, 1993), 185.

10. On modernism's complex relationship to Wagner, see Juliet Koss, *Modernism after Wagner* (Minneapolis: University of Minnesota Press, 2010); Martin Puchner, *Stage Fright: Modernism, Anti-Theatricality and Drama* (Baltimore: Johns Hopkins University Press, 2002).

11. Max Horkheimer and Theodor W. Adorno, *Dialectic of Enlightenment*, trans. John Cumming (New York: Continuum, 1993), 124. For a genealogy that traces the Gesamtkunstwerk through the Bauhaus, Brecht, Leni Riefenstahl's film *Triumph of the Will*, Disney theme parks, Andy Warhol, and the "total immersion" of cyberspace, see Matthew Wilson Smith, *The Total Work of Art: From*

Bayreuth to Cyberspace (New York: Routledge, 2007). See also Randall Packer and Ken Jordan, eds., *Multimedia: From Wagner to Virtual Reality* (New York: Norton, 2001), for an anthology of primary texts ending with a coda by the multimedia performance artist Laurie Anderson.

12. Sergei Eisenstein, "Through Theater to Cinema," in *Film Form: Essays in Film Theory and the Film Sense* (New York: Meridian Books, 1957), 8.

13. Antonin Artaud, "The Theater of Cruelty (First Manifesto)," in *Selected Writings*, ed. Susan Sontag (Berkeley: University of California Press, 1976), 250.

14. Erwin Piscator, "Theatre of Totality and Total Theatre," in *Erwin Piscator: Political Theatre 1920–1966*, ed. Ludwig Hoffman, trans. Margaret Vallance (London: Arts Council of Great Britain, 1971), 66.

15. Jeffrey T. Schnapp, "Border Crossings: Italian/German Peregrinations of the *Theater of Totality*," *Critical Inquiry* 21, no. 1 (Autumn 1994): 96.

16. Oswald de Andrade would later depict the aftermath of this event in his 1943 novel *A Revolução Melancólica*, which was intended to be the first of five novels imagined as murals like those of the Mexican muralists, particularly David Alfaro Siqueiros.

17. Vargas surrendered power in 1945 while facing a military coup. He was elected to the presidency in 1951 and served until August 24, 1954, when he committed suicide in the face of opposition from army officers.   ˈ

18. Daryle Williams, *Culture Wars in Brazil: The First Vargas Regime, 1930–1945* (Durham, N.C.: Duke University Press, 2001), 51.

19. In addition to Williams, *Culture Wars in Brazil*, see Randal Johnson, "The Dynamics of the Brazilian Literary Field, 1930–1945," *Luso-Brazilian Review* 31, no. 2 (Winter 1994): 5–22.

20. Quoted in Lúcia Lippi Oliveira, "As raízes da ordem: Os intelectuais, a cultura e o estado," in *A Revolução de 30: Seminário internacional* (Brasília: Editora Universidade de Brasília, 1982), 508.

21. Oswald de Andrade, "Preface," in *Seraphim Grosse Pointe*, trans. Kenneth D. Jackson and Albert Bork (Austin: New Latin Quarter, 1979), 4.

22. Fernando J. Rosenberg, *The Avant-Garde and Geopolitics in Latin America* (Pittsburgh: Pittsburgh University Press, 2006), 147.

23. Loren Kruger, *The National Stage: Theatre and Cultural Legitimation in England, France, and America* (Chicago: University of Chicago Press, 1992).

24. Herbert Marcuse, "The Affirmative Character of Culture," in *Negations: Essays in Critical Theory*, trans. Jeremy J. Shapiro (Boston: Beacon, 1968).

25. This is my translation from the Portuguese ("ser pelo menos, casaca de ferro na Revolução Proletária") from the preface to *Serafim Ponte Grande* (São Paulo, 1933), 9. "Casaca de ferro" can also refer to a naval soldier, and the published translation by Jackson and Bork renders it as "Knight in Armor," but this overlooks the circus metaphors in the text, which quite clearly suggest it signifies a roustabout.

26. Oswald de Andrade, "Bilhetino a Paulo Emílio," in *Estética e Política*, ed. Maria Eugênia da Gama Alves (São Paulo: Globo, 1991), 51–52.

27. Only *O rei da vela* is available in translation. See "The Candle King," trans. Ana Bernstein and Sarah J. Townsend, in *Stages of Conflict: A Critical Anthology of Latin American Theater and Performance*, ed. Diana Taylor and Sarah J. Townsend (Ann Arbor: University of Michigan Press, 2008), 145–172.

28. Quoted in Roberto Schwarz, "Culture and Politics in Brazil," 158n10. For the original quotation (in French), see José Celso Martinez Corrêa, "Anthropophage," *Partisans* 47 (1969): 70.

29. See, for instance, João Apolinário, "'O Rei da Vela' é uma encenação-manifesto," *Folha de São Paulo*, October 2, 1967.

30. José Celso Martinez Corrêa, "O Rei da Vela: Manifesto do Oficina (September 4, 1967)," in *Tropicália: Uma revolução na cultura brasileira (1967–1972)*, ed. Carlos Basualdo (São Paulo: Cosac Naify, 2007), 233. For more on the staging see Christopher Dunn, *Brutality Garden: Tropicalia and the Emergence of a Brazilian Counterculture* (Chapel Hill: University of North Carolina Press, 2001), 77–82.

31. Fernando Peixoto, "Uma dramaturgia lúcida e radical," in Oswald de Andrade, *O rei da vela* (São Paulo: Difusão Européia do Livro, 1967), 29.

32. Oswald de Andrade, "Do teatro, que é bom," in *Ponta de Lança* (Rio de Janeiro: Civilização Brasileira, 1972).

33. See Jairo Severiano, *Getúlio Vargas e a música popular* (Rio de Janeiro: Editora da Fundação Getúlio Vargas, 1983). This is not to say, however, that the Vargas regime was able to control samba; for an account that emphasizes its subversive elements, see Bryan McCann, *Hello, Hello Brazil: Popular Music in the Making of Modern Brazil* (Durham, N.C.: Duke University Press, 2004).

34. Hitler attended Oberammergau in 1930 and 1934. For an account of the tradition see James Shapiro, *Oberammergau: The Troubled History of the World's Most Famous Passion Play* (New York: Pantheon, 2000).

35. This parallels the processes occurring in Germany and Italy, but also (as Giorgio Agamben argues) in liberal democratic regimes, where the right of the sovereign to declare a state of exception became normalized as a paradigm of government during this era. Agamben, *State of Exception*, trans. Kevin Attell (Chicago: University of Chicago Press, 2005).

36. Robert Levine, *The Vargas Regime: The Critical Years, 1934–1938* (New York: Columbia University Press, 1970), 8–15.

37. For the artist's own account and analysis of the event, see Flávio de Carvalho, *Experiência No. 2* (São Paulo: Irmãos, 1931).

38. "Clube de Artistas Modernos—Gomide, Di Cavalcanti, Carlos Prado, Flávio de Carvalho formam o grupo organizador," *Diário da Noite*, December 24, 1932.

39. The details in this paragraph come from the chronology of CAM's activities in J. Toledo, *Flávio de Carvalho: O comedor de emoções* (São Paulo: Brasiliense, 1994), and are confirmed by articles in newspapers including the *Correio de São Paulo*, *Folha da Noite*, and *Diário da Noite*.

40. Friedrich Schiller, "Twentieth Letter," in *On the Aesthetic Education of Man*, trans. Elizabeth M. Wilkinson and L. A. Willoughby (Oxford: Clarendon, 1992).

41. "Elsie Houston," *Folha da Noite*, February 11, 1933.

42. On Integralismo see Rosa Maria Feiteiro Cavalari, *Integralismo: Ideologia e organização de um partido de massa no Brasil (1932–1937)* (Bauru: Editora da Universidade do Sagrado Coração, 1999).

43. See Mário de Andrade, "Kaethe Kollwitz," *Diário de São Paulo*, June 9, 1933; and Mário Pedrosa, "As tendencias sociais da arte e Käthe Kollwitz," *O Homem Livre*, July 2, 1933; July 8, 1933; July 17, 1933; and July 24, 1933.

44. On this history and the archive see *No coração das trevas: O DEOPS/SP visto por dentro* (São Paulo: Arquivo do Estado/Imprensa Oficial, 2001).

45. Unsigned and undated memo to Dr. A Caiuby, Delegado da Ordem Social, Prontuário DEOPS-SP 2241 (Clube dos Artistas Modernos), Arquivo do Estado de São Paulo, São Paulo. The accompanying article is from the *Diário da Noite*. Note: At the time I consulted the DOEPS files the numbering of the individual documents within folders was irregular or nonexistent. All DEOPS documents cited below are at the Arquivo do Estado de São Paulo.

46. It is possible the mole was Rolando Henrique Guarany, who is cited in many DEOPS reports as an antifascist leader, but one assumes (perhaps mistakenly) that an undercover agent would be more discreet.

47. Document titled "Relatório reservado: Club dos Artistas Modernos, rua Pedro lessa, n. 2," July 18, 1933, Prontuário DEOPS-SP 2241.

48. Toledo, *Flávio de Carvalho*, 134.

49. Unsigned and undated report to Dr. A. Caiuby, D. D. Delegado da Ordem Social, Prontuário DEOPS-SP 2241.

50. "A arte proletária, brilhante conferencia da pintora sra. Tarsila do Amaral no Clube dos Artistas Modernos" (clipping from unidentified newspaper attached to document cited in note 57 above), Prontuário DEOPS-SP 2241.

51. See note 49 just above.

52. Report by Reservado J. de Moraes, November 29, 1933, Prontuário DEOPS-SP 2241.

53. Statement of Orestes Ristori to police, December 13, 1935, Prontuário DEOPS-SP 364.

54. Report by Guarany, August 4, 1933, Prontuário DEOPS-SP 2241.

55. Unsigned report to Exmo. Snr. Doutor Chefe do Gabinete de Investigações, August 23, 1933, Prontuário DEOPS-SP 2241.

56. Teatro de Brinquedo was founded by Álvaro and Eugénia Moreyra in 1927. It lasted for only a few months, but the following year the group also performed at the Theatro Municipal in São Paulo with Flávio de Carvalho as one of its participants.

57. Toledo, *Flávio de Carvalho*, 177.

58. "Tarsila do Amaral fará uma conferencia sobre 'Arte proletaria,'" *Folha da Noite*, July 26, 1933.

59. Excerpts from the license application are reprinted in Carvalho, "A epopéa do Teatro da Experiência," *RASM–Revista Anual do Salão de Maio* 1 (May 1939). Carvalho doesn't mention the TotalTheater, or any other artistic influences, but he was probably familiar with Piscator and Gropius: the Bauhaus artists were a significant influence on modernista architects in Brazil, and CAM had a close affiliation with Theodor Heuberger, a German known for his role in popularizing the Bauhaus style in Brazil.

60. These details come from Toledo, *Flávio de Carvalho*, 179–180.

61. Flávio de Carvalho later claimed the line of attendees stretched for more than 150 meters down the street. See his "Recordação do Clube dos Artistas Modernos," *RASM–Revista Anual do Salão do Maio* 1 (May 1939): 38.

62. Report by Mário de Souza, September 18, 1933, Prontuário DEOPS-SP 2241.

63. Report ("Informe Reservado") by Guarany, September 19, 1933, Prontuário DEOPS-SP 2241.

64. Toledo, *Flávio de Carvalho*, 180.

65. Flávio de Carvalho, *A origem animal de Deus e O bailado do deus morto* (São Paulo: Difusão Européia do Livro, 1973), 88.

66. Reports identify the anarchist Aristides Lobo as the main ringleader of the antifascists and also cite the anarchist shoemaker Pedro Catallo; both also appear in reports on CAM. See also "A manifestação anti-integralista do dia 14 de novembro," *O Homem Livre*, November 20, 1933.

67. "O Theatro da Experiencia às voltas com a polícia!" *O Dia* (São Paulo), November 17, 1933.

68. See "O Theatro da Experiencia às voltas com a polícia!"; "Após o ensaio de hontem o 'Diário da Noite' ouve tres opiniões sobre o discutido 'Bailado do Deus morto' no Theatro da Experiencia," *Diário da Noite* (São Paulo), November 17, 1933.

69. Carvalho, "Recordação do Clube dos Artistas Modernos," 39.

70. Francisco de Sá, "O 'Theatro da Experiencia' é um caso de polícia!" *Platéa*, November 16, 1933.

71. The Frente Negra Brasileira (Brazilian Black Front) started in São Paulo, with chapters later forming in several other cities. The political orientation of its members was far from uniform, as evidenced by the split between its two most prominent leaders: Arlindo Veiga dos Santos was a conservative nativist who expressed support for Hitler and the Brazilian Integralists, whereas José Correia Leite moved increasingly toward international socialism and pan-Africanism. See Paulina L. Alberto, *Terms of Inclusion: Black Intellectuals in Twentieth-Century Brazil* (Chapel Hill: University of North Carolina Press, 2011), 110–150.

72. "A leitura de algumas scenas de 'O Homem e o Cavallo' será feita hoje à noite, pelo sr. Oswald de Andrade," *Diário da Noite* (São Paulo), November 21, 1933.

73. Report from Delegado de Costumes Costa Netto to Ignacio da Costa Ferreira (D. D. Delegado de Ordem Social), November 28, 1933, Prontuário DEOPS-SP 2241. The Russian play is identified as *Esperança* (Hope) and its author as Nicolaieff.

74. Mimeograph of letter from Delegado de Ordem Social to Exmo. snr. Dr. Costa Netto (D. D. Delegado de Costumes), December 1, 1933, Prontuário DEOPS-SP 2241.

75. See "O Theatro da Experiência condemnado de morte pela polícia de costumes," *O Dia*, December 6, 1933; and "A policia impediu a realização do espetáculo do Theatro de Experiência," in *Folha da Manhã*, December 10, 1933.

76. There were even some short-lived "all-mulatto" and "all-black" revista companies. On teatro de revista and the "massification" of social identity in Rio, see Tiago de Melo Gomes, *Um espelho no palco: Identidades sociais e massificaçao da cultura no teatro de revista dos anos 1920* (Campinas: Editora da Universidade Estadual de Campinas, 2004).

77. The "Lei Getúlio Vargas" granted copyright protection to composers and playwrights, regulated the use of recorded music, and required owners of theater establishments to cover medical expenses for actors injured on the job. For an analysis of Vargas's relationship to musicians and theater artists, see Marc Hertzman, *Making Samba: A New History of Race and Music in Brazil* (Durham, N.C.: Duke University Press, 2013), 170–193.

78. Luiz Iglézias, *O teatro da minha vida* (Rio de Janeiro: Livraria Editora Zelio Valverde, 1945), 139.

79. Michael Warner, "The Mass Public and the Mass Subject," in *Publics and Counterpublics* (New York: Zone Books, 2002), 172.

80. Andrade, *O homem e o cavalo*, 26.

81. Warner, "The Mass Public," 165.

82. Magaldi, "A mola propulsora da utopia," 9–10.

83. Andrade, *Seraphim Grosse Point*, 3.

84. See Boris Groys, *The Total Art of Stalinism: Avant-Garde, Aesthetic Dictatorship, and Beyond* (Princeton, N.J.: Princeton University Press, 1992), for the provocative (and to my mind simplistic) claim that "under Stalin the dream of the avant-garde was in fact fulfilled and the life of society was organized in monolithic artistic forms, though of course not those that the avant-garde itself had favored." In other words, socialist realism was the result of the "internal logic" of the avant-garde itself (9).

85. Leon Trotsky, "The Formalist School of Poetry and Marxism," in *Literature and Revolution*, ed. William Keach, trans. Rose Strunksy (Chicago: Haymarket Books, 2005), 175.

86. The line is from a 1929 speech by Antônio Carlos Ribeiro de Andrada, president of the state of Minas Gerais and a future leader of the Revolution of 1930.

87. The leftist journal *O Homem Livre* frequently referred to Barroso as "Gustavinho da Garapa." *Garapa* is sugarcane juice, and the epithet is probably a comment on his syrupy, sentimental writing style.

88. "'Coisas de negro' no Theatro da Experiencia," *Diário da Noite*, December 7, 1933.

89. Carvalho, "A epopéa do Teatro da Experência," 46.

90. "A Sentença do Juiz Fairbanks," *Diário da Noite*, December 14, 1933.

91. J. Toledo notes that those who protested CAM's closure included Victoria Ocampo (the Argentine founder of *Sur*) as well as international collaborators such as Waldo Frank, Alfonso Reyes, and José Ortega y Gasset. He also cites an article criticizing CAM's closure in the Buenos Aires newspaper *Crítica*. See Toledo, *Flávio de Carvalho*, 210.

92. Speech by Zoroastro Gouvêia quoted in Wilson Martins, *História da inteligência brasileira*, vol. 7 (São Paulo: Cultrix-EDUSP, 1979), 11–12.

93. Toledo, *Flávio de Carvalho*, 169–170.

94. Toledo, *Flávio de Carvalho*, 211. The last DEOPS report on CAM is about a meeting held on January 9, 1934, at which two members of the directorate expressed their resolution to stand strong and keep the club open. Report by Guarany, January 11, 1934, DEOPS-SP Prontuário 2241.

95. Patrícia Galvão (Pagu), letter to Oswald de Andrade, OA-02-2-00257, Acervo Oswald de Andrade, Centro de Documentação IEL-UNICAMP, Universidade de Campinas.

96. Andrade, "Bilhetinho a Paulo Emílio," 52.

97. Oswald mentions Putnam's plans in "Bilhetinho a Paulo Emílio." The translation/loose adaptation, titled "Horse and the Man: A Mythological-Historical Extravaganza, with a Meaning for These Times," is in Special Collections, Morris Library, Southern Illinois University, Carbondale.

INDEX

Page numbers in **boldface** refer to illustrations.

Houston, Elsie, 223–224, 283n50
Huerta Muzquiz, Elena, 121

Ibsen, Henrik, 44, 67, 220, 257n47
ideology, 44–45, 257n49. *See also*
  Schwarz, Roberto
Ihering, Hermann von, 168
Independence Centenary International
  Exposition, 6–7
Institutional Revolutionary Party (PRI),
  21, 23, 33, 111, 116, 121
Integralist Party, 24, 190, 217, 224, 236,
  237, 251n10
Iokanaan, 224
Irradiador, 86–87, 113
Itkis, Felicia, **231**

Jameson, Fredric, 36
Jara Corona, Heriberto, 87, 114–115
jarabe tapatío, 4, 27, 60, 92
Jarry, Alfred, 220, 229
Jewett, Sarah Orne, 73
Jolson, Al, 73
Jouvet, Louis, 221
Juárez, Benito, 39

Kahlo, Frida, 13
Kandinsky, Wassily, 115, 214
Koch-Grünberg, Theodor, 190, 198
Kollwitz, Käthe, 224
Kruger, Loren, 16–17, 218

labor (artistic), 16, 23, 34, 42, 66, 68,
  72, 97
Laborde, Hernán, 270n46
Lacan, Jacques, 118, 124
Lago, Roberto, 121
Le Corbusier, 61, 115
Leduc, Renato, 46
Legrás, Horacio, 34
Lessing, Gotthold Ephraim, 32
Letuchaya Mysh. See Chauve-Souris
Levine, Lawrence W., 183
Lévi-Strauss, Claude, 190–191
Liebknecht, Karl, 56
List Arzubide, Germán, 86–87, 100,
  115–121, 124–130, 270nn45–46,
  271n63, 273n78
Living Theater troupe, 213

Lloyd, David, 16
Lomnitz, Claudio, 33, 34, 92
Love, Heather, 144–145, 173
Lugné-Poe (Aurélien-Marie Lugné), 200,
  261n17
Luís, Washington, 158, 217
Lula da Silva, Luiz Inácio, 210, 250
Lunacharsky, Anatoly, 56–57, 259n73
Lund, Joshua, 37
Luxemburg, Rosa, 56, 263n47

Mabou Mimes, 213
Machado de Assis, Joaquim, 143
Madero, Francisco, 37, 38, 39
"Maese Pedro" (pseudonym), 108–111
Magaldi, Sábato, 138, 211, 241, 248
Magalhães, Paulo Ribeiro de, 193, 205,
  283n50
Magaña Esquivel, Antonio, 266n88,
  267n95
malandro figure, 178, 185–186, 196,
  199–200, 203
Malfatti, Anita, 137, 150, 150, 155
Mallarmé, Stéphane, 17, 48–49, 52, 171,
  214
Maples Arce, Manuel, 39–40, 86, 112–
  115, 119; Urbe, 87, 113–114, 122
Marconi, Guglielmo, 104
Marcuse, Herbert, 218
Marinetti, Filippo Tommaso, 18, 67,
  151, 153, 162, 166, 216, 237–238,
  276n39
Martí, José, 255n13
Marvin, Carolyn, 101
Marx, Karl, 65–66, 67–68, 69, 72,
  77–78, 79, 139, 140–141, 154, 220,
  249, 252n25, 262n27. *See also* capital
Matta, Roberto da, 200
Mayakovsky, Vladimir, 116, 161, 211,
  214–15, 235–236, 245
McCann, Bryan, 64
McCormack, John, 184
McLuhan, Marshall, 103
media theory, 101–105, 110, 111–112
Mella, Julio Antonio, 116
Méndez, Leopoldo, 115–116, 120, 127–
  129, 271n60
Mérida, Carlos, 96–97, 127–129
mestizaje, 29–30, 33, 53–54